THERE ARE THOUSANDS of worlds, all different from ours. Chrestomanci's world is the one next door to us, and the difference here is that magic is as common as music is with us. It is full of people working magic—warlocks, witches, thaumaturges, sorcerers, fakirs, conjurors, hexers, magicians, mages, shamans, diviners and many more—from the lowest Certified witch right up to the most powerful of enchanters. Enchanters are strange as well as powerful. Their magic is different and stronger and many of them have more than one life.

Now, if someone did not control all these busy magic-users, ordinary people would have a horrible time and probably end up as slaves. So the government appoints the very strongest enchanter there is to make sure no one misuses magic. This enchanter has nine lives and is known as "the Chrestomanci." You pronounce it KREST-OH-MAN-SEE. He has to have a strong personality as well as strong magic.

DIANA WYNNE JONES

The Chronicles of
CHRESTOMANCI

✦ VOLUME II ✦

Books by
DIANA WYNNE JONES

Diana Wynne Jones

The Chronicles of CHRESTOMANCI

✦ VOLUME II ✦

THE MAGICIANS OF CAPRONA

WITCH WEEK

A GREENWILLOW BOOK

An Imprint of HarperCollinsPublishers

Eos is an imprint of HarperCollins Publishers.

The Chronicles of Chrestomanci, Volume II
Copyright © 2001 by Diana Wynne Jones
The Magicians of Caprona copyright © 1980 by Diana Wynne Jones
Witch Week copyright © 1982 by Diana Wynne Jones

Library of Congress Cataloging-in-Publication Data
Jones, Diana Wynne.
  Chronicles of Chrestomanci / Diana Wynne Jones.
    p.   cm.
"Greenwillow Books."
  Contents: v. 1. Charmed life. The lives of Christopher Chant—v. 2. Witch Week. The magi-
cians of Caprona.
  Summary: Adventures of the Chrestomanci, an enchanter with nine lives, whose job is to
control the practice of magic in the infinite parallel universes of the Twelve Related Worlds.
  ISBN-13: 978-0-06-447268-5 (v.1 : pbk.) ISBN-10: 0-06-447268-X (v.1 : pbk.)
  ISBN-13: 978-0-06-447269-2 (v.2 : pbk.) ISBN-10: 0-06-447269-8 (v.2 : pbk.)
  [1. Fantasy. 2. Magic—Fiction. 3. Witchcraft—Fiction.] I. Title.
PZ7.J684 Cj 2001   00-39614
[Fic]—dc21

First Eos paperback edition, 2007

THE MAGICIANS OF
CAPRONA

AUTHOR'S NOTE

The World of Chrestomanci is not the same as this one. It is a world parallel to ours, where magic is as normal as mathematics, and things are generally more old-fashioned. In Chrestomanci's world, Italy is still divided into numbers of small States, each with its Duke and capital city. In our world, Italy became one united country long ago.

Though the two worlds are not connected in any way, this story somehow got through. But it came with some gaps, and I had to get help filling them. Clare Davis, Gaynor Harvey, Elizabeth Carter and Graham Belsten discovered for me what happened in the magicians' single combat. And my husband, J. A. Burrow, with some advice from Basil Cottle, actually found the true words of the *Angel of Caprona*. I would like to thank them all very much indeed.

For John

1

SPELLS ARE THE HARDEST THING in the world to get right. This was one of the first things the Montana children learned. Anyone can hang up a charm, but when it comes to making that charm, whether it is written or spoken or sung, everything has to be just right, or the most impossible things happen.

An example of this is young Angelica Petrocchi, who turned her father bright green by singing a wrong note. It was the talk of all Caprona—indeed of all Italy—for weeks.

The best spells still come from Caprona, in spite of the recent troubles, from the Casa Montana or the Casa Petrocchi. If you are using words that really work, to improve reception on your radio or to grow tomatoes, then the chances are that someone in your family has been on a holiday to Caprona and brought the spell back. The Old Bridge in Caprona is lined with little stone booths, where long colored envelopes, scrips and scrolls hang from strings like bunting. You can get spells there from every spellhouse in Italy. Each spell is labeled as to its use and stamped with the sign of the house which made it. If you want to find out who made your spell, look among your family papers. If you find a long cherry-colored scrip stamped with a black leopard, then it came from the Casa Petrocchi. If you find a leaf-green envelope bearing a winged horse, then the House of Montana made it. The spells of both houses are so good that ignorant people think that even the envelopes can work magic. This, of course, is nonsense. For, as Paolo and Tonino Montana were told over and over again, a spell is the right words delivered in the right way.

The great houses of Petrocchi and Montana go back to the first founding of the State of Caprona, seven hundred years or more ago. And they are bitter rivals. They are not even on speaking terms. If a Petrocchi and a Montana meet in one of Caprona's narrow golden-stone streets, they turn their eyes aside and edge past as if they were both walking past a pig-sty. Their children are sent to different schools and warned never, ever to exchange a word with a child from the other house.

Sometimes, however, parties of young men and women of the Montanas and the Petrocchis happen to meet when they are strolling on the wide street called the Corso in the evenings. When that happens, other citizens take shelter at once. If they fight with fists and stones, that is bad enough, but if they fight with spells, it can be appalling.

An example of this is when the dashing Rinaldo Montana caused the sky to rain cowpats on the

Corso for three days. It created great distress among the tourists.

"A Petrocchi insulted me," Rinaldo explained, with his most flashing smile. "And I happened to have a new spell in my pocket."

The Petrocchis unkindly claimed that Rinaldo had misquoted his spell in the heat of the battle. Everyone knew that all Rinaldo's spells were love-charms.

The grown-ups of both houses never explained to the children just what had made the Montanas and the Petrocchis hate one another so. That was a task traditionally left to the older brothers, sisters and cousins. Paolo and Tonino were told the story repeatedly, by their sisters Rosa, Corinna and Lucia, by their cousins Luigi, Carlo, Domenico and Anna, and again by their second-cousins Piero, Luca, Giovanni, Paula, Teresa, Bella, Angelo and Francesco. They told it themselves to six smaller cousins as they grew up. The Montanas were a large family.

Two hundred years ago, the story went, old Ricardo Petrocchi took it into his head that the Duke of Caprona was ordering more spells from the Montanas than from the Petrocchis, and he wrote old Francesco Montana a very insulting letter about it. Old Francesco was so angry that he promptly invited all the Petrocchis to a feast. He had, he said, a new dish he wanted them to try. Then he rolled Ricardo Petrocchi's letter up into long spills and cast one of his strongest spells over it. And it turned into spaghetti. The Petrocchis ate it greedily and were all taken ill, particularly old Ricardo—for nothing disagrees with a person so much as having to eat his own words. He never forgave Francesco Montana, and the two families had been enemies ever since.

"And that," said Lucia, who told the story oftenest, being only a year older than Paolo, "was the origin of spaghetti."

It was Lucia who whispered to them all the terrible heathen customs the Petrocchis had: how they never went to Mass or confessed; how they never had baths or changed their clothes; how none of them ever got married but just—in an even lower whisper—had babies like kittens; how they were apt to drown their unwanted babies, again like kittens, and had even been known to eat unwanted uncles and aunts; and how they were so dirty that you could smell the Casa Petrocchi and hear the flies buzzing right down the Via Sant' Angelo.

There were many other things besides, some of them far worse than these, for Lucia had a vivid imagination. Paolo and Tonino believed every one, and they hated the Petrocchis heartily, though it was years before either of them set eyes on a Petrocchi. When they were both quite small, they did sneak off one morning, down the Via Sant' Angelo almost as far as the New Bridge, to look at the Casa Petrocchi. But there was no smell and no flies buzzing to guide them, and their sister Rosa found them before they found it. Rosa, who was eight years older than Paolo and quite grown-up even then, laughed when they explained their difficulty, and good-naturedly took them to the Casa Petrocchi. It was in the Via Cantello, not the Via Sant' Angelo at all.

Paolo and Tonino were most disappointed in it. It was just like the Casa Montana. It was large, like the Casa Montana, and built of the same golden stone of Caprona, and probably just as old. The great front gate was old knotty wood, just like their own, and there was even the same golden figure of the Angel on the wall above the gate. Rosa told them that both Angels were in memory of the Angel who had come to the first Duke of Caprona bringing a scroll of music from Heaven—but the boys knew that. When Paolo pointed out that the Casa Petrocchi did not seem to smell much, Rosa bit her lip and said gravely that there were not many windows in the outside walls, and they were all shut.

"I expect everything happens around the yard inside, just like it does in our Casa," she said. "Probably all the smelling goes on in there."

They agreed that it probably did, and wanted to wait to see a Petrocchi come out. But Rosa said she thought that would be most unwise, and pulled them away. The boys looked over their shoulders as she dragged them off and saw that the Casa Petrocchi had four golden-stone towers, one at each corner, where the Casa Montana only had one, over the gate.

"It's because the Petrocchis are show-offs," Rosa said, dragging. "Come on."

Since the towers were each roofed with a little

hat of red pan-tiles, just like their own roofs or the roofs of all the houses in Caprona, Paolo and Tonino did not think they were particularly grand, but they did not like to argue with Rosa. Feeling very let down, they let her drag them back to the Casa Montana and pull them through their own large knotty gate into the bustling yard beyond. There Rosa left them and ran up the steps to the gallery, shouting, "Lucia! Lucia, where are you? I want to *talk* to you!"

Doors and windows opened into the yard all around, and the gallery, with its wooden railings and pan-tiled roof, ran around three sides of the yard and led to the rooms on the top floor. Uncles, aunts, cousins large and small, and cats were busy everywhere, laughing, cooking, discussing spells, washing, sunning themselves or playing. Paolo gave a sigh of contentment and picked up the nearest cat.

"I don't think the Casa Petrocchi *can* be anything like this inside."

Before Tonino could agree, they were swooped on lovingly by Aunt Maria, who was fatter than Aunt Gina, but not as fat as Aunt Anna. "Where have you been, my loves? I've been ready for your lessons for half an hour or more!"

Everyone in the Casa Montana worked very hard. Paolo and Tonino were already being taught the first rules for making spells. When Aunt Maria was busy, they were taught by their father, Antonio. Antonio was the eldest son of Old Niccolo, and would be head of the Casa Montana when Old

Niccolo died. Paolo thought this weighed on his father. Antonio was a thin, worried person who laughed less often than the other Montanas. He was different. One of the differences was that, instead of letting Old Niccolo carefully choose a wife for him from a spell-house in Italy, Antonio had gone on a visit to England and come back married to Elizabeth. Elizabeth taught the boys music.

"If I'd been teaching that Angelica Petrocchi," she was fond of saying, "she'd never have turned anything green."

Old Niccolo said Elizabeth was the best musician in Caprona. And that, Lucia told the boys, was why Antonio got away with marrying her. But Rosa told them to take no notice. Rosa was proud of being half English.

Paolo and Tonino were probably prouder to be Montanas. It was a grand thing to know you were born into a family that was known worldwide as the greatest spell-house in Europe—if you did not count the Petrocchis. There were times when Paolo could hardly wait to grow up and be like his cousin, dashing Rinaldo. Everything came easily to Rinaldo. Girls fell in love with him, spells dripped from his pen. He had composed seven new charms before he left school. And these days, as Old Niccolo said, making a new spell was not easy. There were so many already. Paolo admired Rinaldo desperately. He told Tonino that Rinaldo was a true Montana.

Tonino agreed, because he was more than a

year younger than Paolo and valued Paolo's opinions, but it always seemed to him that it was Paolo
who was the true Montana. Paolo was as quick as
Rinaldo. He could learn without trying spells which
took Tonino days to acquire. Tonino was slow. He
could only remember things if he went over them
again and again. It seemed to him that Paolo had
been born with an instinct for magic which he just
did not have himself.

Tonino was sometimes quite depressed about
his slowness. Nobody else minded in the least. All
his sisters, even the studious Corinna, spent hours
helping him. Elizabeth assured him he never sang
out of tune. His father scolded him for working too
hard, and Paolo assured him that he would be
streets ahead of the other children when he went to
school. Paolo had just started school. He was as
quick at ordinary lessons as he was at spells.

But when Tonino started school, he was just as
slow there as he was at home. School bewildered
him. He did not understand what the teachers
wanted him to do. By the first Saturday he was so
miserable that he had to slip away from the Casa
and wander around Caprona in tears. He was missing for hours.

"I can't help being quicker than he is!" Paolo
said, almost in tears too.

Aunt Maria rushed at Paolo and hugged him.
"Now, now, don't you start too! You're as clever as
my Rinaldo, and we're all proud of you."

"Lucia, go and look for Tonino," said

Elizabeth. "Paolo, you mustn't worry so. Tonino's soaking up spells without knowing he is. I did the same when I came here. Should I tell Tonino?" she asked Antonio. Antonio had hurried in from the gallery. In the Casa Montana, if anyone was in distress, it always fetched the rest of the family.

Antonio rubbed his forehead. "Perhaps. Let's go and ask Old Niccolo. Come on, Paolo."

Paolo followed his thin, brisk father through the patterns of sunlight in the gallery and into the blue coolness of the Scriptorium. Here his other two sisters, Rinaldo and five other cousins, and two of his uncles, were all standing at tall desks copying spells out of big leather-bound books. Each book had a brass lock on it so that the family secrets could not be stolen. Antonio and Paolo tiptoed through. Rinaldo smiled at them without pausing in his copying. Where other pens scratched and paused, Rinaldo's raced.

In the room beyond the Scriptorium, Uncle Lorenzo and Cousin Domenico were stamping winged horses on leaf-green envelopes. Uncle Lorenzo looked keenly at their faces as they passed and decided that the trouble was not too much for Old Niccolo alone. He winked at Paolo and threatened to stamp a winged horse on him.

Old Niccolo was in the warm mildewy library beyond, consulting over a book on a stand with Aunt Francesca. She was Old Niccolo's sister, and therefore really a great-aunt. She was a barrel of a lady, twice as fat as Aunt Anna and even more passionate than Aunt Gina. She was saying passionately, "But the spells of the Casa Montana always have a certain elegance. This is graceless! This is—"

Both round old faces turned towards Antonio and Paolo. Old Niccolo's face, and his eyes in it, were round and wondering as the latest baby's. Aunt Francesca's face was too small for her huge body, and her eyes were small and shrewd. "I was just coming," said Old Niccolo. "I thought it was Tonino in trouble, but you bring me Paolo."

"Paolo's not in trouble," said Aunt Francesca.

Old Niccolo's round eyes blinked at Paolo. "Paolo," he said, "what your brother feels is not your fault."

"No," said Paolo. "I think it's school really."

"We thought that perhaps Elizabeth could explain to Tonino that he can't avoid learning spells in this Casa," Antonio suggested.

"But Tonino has ambition!" cried Aunt Francesca.

"I don't think he does," said Paolo.

"No, but he is unhappy," said his grandfather. "And we must think how best to comfort him. I know." His baby face beamed. "Benvenuto."

Though Old Niccolo did not say this loudly, someone in the gallery immediately shouted, "Old Niccolo wants Benvenuto!" There was running and calling down in the yard. Somebody beat on a waterbutt with a stick. "Benvenuto! Where's that cat got to? Benvenuto!"

Naturally, Benvenuto took his time coming.

He was boss cat at the Casa Montana. It was five minutes before Paolo heard his firm pads trotting along the tiles of the gallery roof. This was followed by a heavy thump as Benvenuto made the difficult leap down, across the gallery railing onto the floor of the gallery. Shortly, he appeared on the library windowsill.

"So there you are," said Old Niccolo. "I was just going to get impatient."

Benvenuto at once shot forward a shaggy black hind leg and settled down to wash it, as if that was what he had come there to do.

"Ah no, please," said Old Niccolo. "I need your help."

Benvenuto's wide yellow eyes turned to Old Niccolo. He was not a handsome cat. His head was unusually wide and blunt, with gray gnarled patches on it left over from many, many fights. Those fights had pulled his ears down over his eyes, so that Benvenuto always looked as if he were wearing a ragged brown cap. A hundred bites had left those ears notched like holly leaves. Just over his nose, giving his face a leering, lopsided look, were three white patches. Those had nothing to do with Benvenuto's position as boss cat in a spell-house. They were the result of his partiality for steak. He had got under Aunt Gina's feet when she was cooking, and Aunt Gina had spilled hot fat on his head. For this reason, Benvenuto and Aunt Gina always pointedly ignored one another.

"Tonino is unhappy," said Old Niccolo.

Benvenuto seemed to feel this worthy of his attention. He withdrew his projecting leg, dropped to the library floor and arrived on top of the book-stand, all in one movement, without seeming to flex a muscle. There he stood, politely waving the one beautiful thing about him—his bushy black tail. The rest of his coat had worn to a ragged brown. Apart from the tail, the only thing which showed Benvenuto had once been a magnificent black Persian was the fluffy fur on his hind legs. And, as every other cat in Caprona knew to its cost, those fluffy breeches concealed muscles like a bulldog's.

Paolo stared at his grandfather talking face to face with Benvenuto. He had always treated Benvenuto with respect himself, of course. It was well known that Benvenuto would not sit on your knee, and scratched you if you tried to pick him up. He knew all cats helped spells on wonderfully. But he had not realized before that cats understood so much. And he was sure Benvenuto was answering Old Niccolo, from the listening sort of pauses his grandfather made. Paolo looked at his father to see if this was true. Antonio was very ill at ease. And Paolo understood from his father's worried face that it was very important to be able to understand what cats said, and that Antonio never could. I shall have to start learning to understand Benvenuto, Paolo thought, very troubled.

"Which of you would you suggest?" asked Old Niccolo. Benvenuto raised his right front paw and gave it a casual lick. Old Niccolo's face curved into his beaming baby's smile. "Look at that!" he said. "He'll do it himself!" Benvenuto flicked the tip of his tail sideways. Then he was gone, leaping back to the window so fluidly and quickly that he might have been a paintbrush painting a dark line in the air. He left Aunt Francesca and Old Niccolo beaming, and Antonio still looking unhappy. "Tonino is taken care of," Old Niccolo announced. "We shall not worry again unless he worries us."

2

❧❧

TONINO WAS ALREADY FEELING soothed by the bustle in the golden streets of Caprona. In the narrower streets, he walked down the crack of sunlight in the middle, with washing flapping overhead, playing that it was sudden death to tread on the shadows. In fact, he died a number of times before he got as far as the Corso. A crowd of tourists pushed him off the sun once. So did two carts and a carriage. And once, a long, gleaming car came slowly growling along, hooting hard to clear the way.

When he was near the Corso, Tonino heard a tourist say in English, "Oh look! Punch and Judy!" Very smug at being able to understand, Tonino dived and pushed and tunneled until he was at the front of the crowd and able to watch Punch beat Judy to death at the top of his little painted sentry-box. He clapped and cheered, and when someone puffed and panted into the crowd too, and pushed him aside, Tonino was as indignant as the rest. He had quite forgotten he was miserable. "Don't shove!" he shouted.

"Have a heart!" protested the man. "I must see Mr. Punch cheat the Hangman."

"Then be quiet!" roared everyone, Tonino included.

"I only said—" began the man. He was a large damp-faced person, with an odd excitable manner.

"Shut up!" shouted everyone.

The man panted and grinned and watched with his mouth open Punch attack the policeman. He might have been the smallest boy there. Tonino looked irritably sideways at him and decided the man was probably an amiable lunatic. He let out such bellows of laughter at the smallest jokes, and he was so oddly dressed. He was wearing a shiny red silk suit with flashing gold buttons and glittering medals. Instead of the usual tie, he had white cloth folded at his neck, held in place by a brooch which winked like a teardrop. There were glistening buckles on his shoes, and golden rosettes at his knees. What with his sweaty face and his white shiny teeth showing as he laughed, the man glistened all over.

Mr. Punch noticed him too. "Oh what a clever fellow!" he crowed, bouncing about on his little wooden shelf. "I see gold buttons. Can it be the Pope?"

"Oh no it isn't!" bellowed Mr. Glister, highly delighted.

"Can it be the Duke?" cawed Mr. Punch.

"Oh no it isn't!" roared Mr. Glister, and everyone else.

"Oh yes it is," crowed Mr. Punch.

While everyone was howling *"Oh no it isn't!"* two worried-looking men pushed their way through the people to Mr. Glister.

"Your Grace," said one, "the Bishop reached the Cathedral half an hour ago."

"Oh bother!" said Mr. Glister. "Why are you lot always bullying me? Can't I just—until this ends? I love Punch and Judy."

The two men looked at him reproachfully.

"Oh—very well," said Mr. Glister. "You two pay the showman. Give everyone here something." He turned and went bounding away into the Corso, puffing and panting.

For a moment, Tonino wondered if Mr. Glister was actually the Duke of Caprona. But the two men made no attempt to pay the showman, or anyone else. They simply went trotting demurely after Mr. Glister, as if they were afraid of losing him. From this, Tonino gathered that Mr. Glister was indeed a lunatic—a rich one—and they were humoring him.

"Mean things!" crowed Mr. Punch, and set about tricking the Hangman into being hanged instead of him. Tonino watched until Mr. Punch bowed and retired in triumph into the little painted villa at the back of his stage. Then he turned away, remembering his unhappiness.

He did not feel like going back to the Casa Montana. He did not feel like doing anything particularly. He wandered on, the way he had been going, until he found himself in the Piazza Nuova, up on the hill at the western end of the city. Here he sat gloomily on the parapet, gazing across the River Voltava at the rich villas and the Ducal Palace, and at the long arches of the New Bridge, and wondering if he was going to spend the rest of his life in a fog of stupidity.

The Piazza Nuova had been made at the same time as the New Bridge, about seventy years ago, to give everyone the grand view of Caprona Tonino was looking at now. It was breathtaking. But the trouble was, everything Tonino looked at had something to do with the Casa Montana.

Take the Ducal Palace, whose golden-stone towers cut clear lines into the clean blue of the sky opposite. Each golden tower swept outwards at the top, so that the soldiers on the battlements, beneath the snapping red and gold flags, could not be reached by anyone climbing up from below. Tonino could see the shields built into the battlements, two a side, one cherry, one leaf-green, showing that the Montanas and the Petrocchis had added a spell to defend each tower. And the great white marble front below was inlaid with other marbles, all colors of the rainbow. And among those colors were cherry-red and leaf-green.

The long golden villas on the hillside below the

Palace each had a leaf-green or cherry-red disc on their walls. Some were half hidden by the dark spires of the elegant little trees planted in front of them, but Tonino knew they were there. And the stone and metal arches of the New Bridge, sweeping away from him towards the villas and the Palace, each bore an enamel plaque, green and red alternately. The New Bridge had been sustained by the strongest spells the Casa Montana and the Casa Petrocchi could produce. At the moment, when the river was just a shingly trickle, they did not seem necessary. But in winter, when the rain fell in the Apennines, the Voltava became a furious torrent. The arches of the New Bridge barely cleared it. The Old Bridge—which Tonino could see by craning out and sideways—was often under water, and the funny little houses along it could not be used. Only Montana and Petrocchi spells deep in its foundations stopped the Old Bridge being swept away.

Tonino had heard Old Niccolo say that the New Bridge spells had taken the entire efforts of the entire Montana family. Old Niccolo had helped make them when he was the same age as Tonino. Tonino could not have done. Miserable, he looked down at the golden walls and red pan-tiles of Caprona below. He was quite certain that every single one hid at least a leaf-green scrip. And the most Tonino had ever done was help stamp the winged horse on the outside. He was fairly sure that was all he ever would do.

He had a feeling somebody was calling him. Tonino looked round at the Piazza Nuova. Nobody. Despite the view, the Piazza was too far for the tourists to come. All Tonino could see were the mighty iron griffins which reared up at intervals all around the parapet, reaching iron paws to the sky. More griffins tangled into a fighting heap in the center of the square to make a fountain. And even here, Tonino could not get away from his family. A little metal plate was set into the stone beneath the huge iron claws of the nearest griffin. It was leaf-green. Tonino found he had burst into tears.

Among his tears, he thought for a moment that one of the more distant griffins had left its stone perch and come trotting round the parapet towards him. It had left its wings behind, or else had them tightly folded.

He was told, a little smugly, that cats do not need wings. Benvenuto sat down on the parapet beside him, staring accusingly.

Tonino had always been thoroughly in awe of Benvenuto. He stretched out a hand to him timidly. "Hallo, Benvenuto."

Benvenuto ignored the hand. It was covered with water from Tonino's eyes, he said, and it made a cat wonder why Tonino was being so silly.

"There are our spells everywhere," Tonino explained. "And I'll never be able—Do you think it's because I'm half English?"

Benvenuto was not sure quite what difference

that made. All it meant, as far as he could see, was that Paolo had blue eyes like a Siamese and Rosa had white fur—

"Fair hair," said Tonino.

—and Tonino himself had tabby hair, like the pale stripes in a tabby, Benvenuto continued, unperturbed. And those were all cats, weren't they?

"But I'm so stupid—" Tonino began.

Benvenuto interrupted that he had heard Tonino chattering with those kittens yesterday, and he had thought Tonino was a good deal cleverer than they were. And before Tonino went and objected that those were only kittens, wasn't Tonino only a kitten himself?

At this, Tonino laughed and dried his hand on his trousers. When he held the hand out to Benvenuto again, Benvenuto rose up, very high on all four paws, and advanced to it, purring. Tonino ventured to stroke him. Benvenuto walked around and around, arched and purring, like the smallest and friendliest kitten in the Casa. Tonino found himself grinning with pride and pleasure. He could tell from the waving of Benvenuto's brush of a tail, in majestic, angry twitches, that Benvenuto did not altogether like being stroked—which made it all the more of an honor.

That was better, Benvenuto said. He minced up to Tonino's bare legs and installed himself across them, like a brown muscular mat. Tonino went on stroking him. Prickles came out of one end of the mat and treadled painfully at Tonino's thighs. Benvenuto continued to purr. Would Tonino look at it this way, he wondered, that they were both, boy and cat, a part of the most famous Casa in Caprona, which in turn was part of the most special of all the Italian States?

"I know that," said Tonino. "It's because I think it's wonderful too that I—Are we really so special?"

Of course, purred Benvenuto. And if Tonino were to lean out and look across at the Cathedral, he would see why.

Obediently, Tonino leaned and looked. The huge marble bubbles of the Cathedral domes leaped up from among the houses at the end of the Corso. He knew there never was such a building as that. It floated, high and white and gold and green. And on the top of the highest dome the sun flashed on the great golden figure of the Angel, poised there with spread wings, holding in one hand a golden scroll. It seemed to bless all Caprona.

That Angel, Benvenuto informed him, was there as a sign that Caprona would be safe as long as everyone sang the tune of the Angel of Caprona. The Angel had brought that song in a scroll straight from Heaven to the First Duke of Caprona, and its power had banished the White Devil and made Caprona great. The White Devil had been prowling around Caprona ever since, trying to get back into the city, but as long as the Angel's song was sung, it would never succeed.

"I know that," said Tonino. "We sing the *Angel* every day at school." That brought back the main part of his misery. "They keep making me learn the story—and all sorts of things—and I can't, because I know them already, so I can't learn properly."

Benvenuto stopped purring. He quivered, because Tonino's fingers had caught in one of the many lumps of matted fur in his coat. Still quivering, he demanded rather sourly why it hadn't occurred to Tonino to tell them at school that he knew these things.

"Sorry!" Tonino hurriedly moved his fingers. "But," he explained, "they keep saying you have to do them this way, or you'll never learn properly."

Well, it was up to Tonino of course, Benvenuto said, still irritable, but there seemed no point in learning things twice. A cat wouldn't stand for it. And it was about time they were getting back to the Casa.

Tonino sighed. "I suppose so. They'll be worried." He gathered Benvenuto into his arms and stood up.

Benvenuto liked that. He purred. And it had nothing to do with the Montanas being worried. The aunts would be cooking lunch, and Tonino would find it easier than Benvenuto to nick a nice piece of veal.

That made Tonino laugh. As he started down the steps to the New Bridge, he said, "You know,

26

Benvenuto, you'd be a lot more comfortable if you let me get those lumps out of your coat and comb you a bit."

Benvenuto stated that anyone trying to comb him would get raked with every claw he possessed.

"A brush then?"

Benvenuto said he would consider that.

It was here that Lucia encountered them. She had looked for Tonino all over Caprona by then and she was prepared to be extremely angry. But the sight of Benvenuto's evil lopsided countenance staring at her out of Tonino's arms left her with almost nothing to say. "We'll be late for lunch," she said.

"No we won't," said Tonino. "We'll be in time for you to stand guard while I steal Benvenuto some veal."

"Trust Benvenuto to have it all worked out," said Lucia. "What is this? The start of a profitable relationship?"

You could put it that way, Benvenuto told Tonino. "You could put it that way," Tonino said to Lucia.

At all events, Lucia was sufficiently impressed to engage Aunt Gina in conversation while Tonino got Benvenuto his veal. And everyone was too pleased to see Tonino safely back to mind too much. Corinna and Rosa minded, however, that afternoon, when Corinna lost her scissors and Rosa her hairbrush. Both of them stormed out onto the gallery.

Paolo was there, watching Tonino gently and carefully snip the mats out of Benvenuto's coat. The hairbrush lay beside Tonino, full of brown fur.

"And you can really understand everything he says?" Paolo was saying.

"I can understand all the cats," said Tonino. "Don't move, Benvenuto. This one's right on your skin."

It says volumes for Benvenuto's status—and therefore for Tonino's—that neither Rosa nor Corinna dared say a word to him. They turned on Paolo instead. "What do you mean, Paolo, standing there letting him mess that brush up? Why couldn't you make him use the kitchen scissors?"

Paolo did not mind. He was too relieved that he was not going to have to learn to understand cats himself. He would not have known how to begin.

From that time forward, Benvenuto regarded himself as Tonino's special cat. It made a difference to both of them. Benvenuto, what with constant brushing—for Rosa bought Tonino a special hairbrush for him—and almost as constant supplies filched from under Aunt Gina's nose, soon began to look younger and sleeker. Tonino forgot he had ever been unhappy. He was now a proud and special person. When Old Niccolo needed Benvenuto, he had to ask Tonino first. Benvenuto flatly refused to do anything for anyone without Tonino's permission. Paolo was very amused at how angry Old Niccolo got.

"That cat has just taken advantage of me!" he stormed. "I ask him to do me a kindness and what do I get? Ingratitude!"

In the end, Tonino had to tell Benvenuto that he was to consider himself at Old Niccolo's service while Tonino was at school. Otherwise Benvenuto simply disappeared for the day. But he always, unfailingly, reappeared around half past three, and sat on the waterbutt nearest the gate, waiting for Tonino. And as soon as Tonino came through the gate, Benvenuto would jump into his arms.

This was true even at the times when Benvenuto was not available to anyone. That was mostly at full moon, when the lady cats wauled enticingly from the roofs of Caprona.

Tonino went to school on Monday, having considered Benvenuto's advice. And, when the time came when they gave him a picture of a cat and said the shapes under it went: Ker-a-ter, Tonino gathered up his courage and whispered, "Yes. It's a C and an A and a T. I know how to read."

His teacher, who was new to Caprona, did not know what to make of him, and called the Headmistress. "Oh," she was told. "It's another Montana. I should have warned you. They all know how to read. Most of them know Latin too—they use it a lot in their spells—and some of them know English as well. You'll find they're about average with sums, though."

So Tonino was given a proper book while the

other children learned their letters. It was too easy for him. He finished it in ten minutes and had to be given another. And that was how he discovered about books. To Tonino, reading a book soon became an enchantment above any spell. He could never get enough of it. He ransacked the Casa Montana and the Public Library, and he spent all his pocket money on books. It soon became well known that the best present you could give Tonino was a book—and the best book would be about the unimaginable situation where there were no spells. For Tonino preferred fantasy. In his favorite books, people had wild adventures with no magic to help or hinder them.

Benvenuto thoroughly approved. While Tonino read, he kept still, and a cat could be comfortable sitting on him. Paolo teased Tonino a little about being such a bookworm, but he did not really mind. He knew he could always persuade Tonino to leave his book if he really wanted him. Antonio was worried. He worried about everything. He was afraid Tonino was not getting enough exercise. But everyone else in the Casa said this was nonsense. They were proud of Tonino. He was as studious as Corinna, they said, and, no doubt, both of them would end up at Caprona University, like Great-Uncle Umberto. The Montanas always had someone at the University. It meant they were not selfishly keeping the Theory of Magic to the family, and it was also very useful to have access to the spells in the University Library.

Despite these hopes for him, Tonino continued to be slow at learning spells and not particularly quick at school. Paolo was twice as quick at both. But as the years went by, both of them accepted it. It did not worry them. What worried them far more was their gradual discovery that things were not altogether well in the Casa Montana, nor in Caprona either.

3

IT WAS BENVENUTO who first worried Tonino. Despite all the care Tonino gave him, he became steadily thinner and more ragged again. Now Benvenuto was roughly the same age as Tonino. Tonino knew that was old for a cat, and at first he assumed that Benvenuto was just feeling his years. Then he noticed that Old Niccolo had taken to looking almost as worried as Antonio, and that Uncle Umberto called on him from the University almost every day. Each time he did, Old Niccolo or Aunt Francesca would ask for Benvenuto and Benvenuto would come back tired out. So he asked Benvenuto what was wrong.

Benvenuto's reply was that they might let a cat have some peace, even if the Duke was a booby. And he was not going to be pestered by Tonino into the bargain.

Tonino consulted Paolo, and found Paolo worried too. Paolo had been noticing his mother. Her fair hair had lately become several shades paler with all the white in it, and she looked nervous all the time. When Paolo asked Elizabeth what was the matter, she said, "Oh nothing, Paolo—only all this makes it *so* difficult to find a husband for Rosa."

Rosa was now eighteen. The entire Casa was busy discussing a husband for her, and there did, now Paolo noticed, seem much more fuss and anxiety about the matter than there had been over Cousin Claudia, three years before. Montanas had to be careful who they married. It stood to reason. They had to marry someone who had some talent at least for spells or music; and it had to be someone the rest of the family liked; and, above all, it had to be someone with no kind of connection with the Petrocchis. But Cousin Claudia had found and married Arturo without all the discussion and worry that was going on over Rosa. Paolo could only suppose the reason was "all this," whatever Elizabeth had meant by that.

Whatever the reason, argument raged. Anxious Antonio talked of going to England and consulting someone called Chrestomanci about it. "We want a really strong spell-maker for her," he said. To which Elizabeth replied that Rosa was Italian and should marry an Italian. The rest of the family agreed, except that they said the Italian must be from Caprona. So the question was who.

Paolo, Lucia and Tonino had no doubt. They wanted Rosa to marry their cousin Rinaldo. It seemed to them entirely fitting. Rosa was lovely, Rinaldo handsome, and none of the usual objections could possibly be made. There were two snags, however. The first was that Rinaldo showed no interest in Rosa. He was at present desperately in love with a real English girl—her name was Jane Smith, and Rinaldo had some difficulty pronouncing it—and she had come to copy some of the pictures in the Art Gallery down on the Corso. She was a romantic girl. To please her, Rinaldo had taken to wearing black, with a red scarf at his neck, like a bandit. He was said to be considering growing a bandit moustache too. All of which left him with no time for a cousin he had known all his life.

The other snag was Rosa herself. She had never cared for Rinaldo. And she seemed to be the only person in the Casa who was entirely unconcerned about who she would marry. When the argument raged loudest, she would shake the blond hair on her shoulders and smile. "To listen to you all," she said, "anyone would think I have no say in the matter at all. It's really funny."

All that autumn, the worry in the Casa Montana grew. Paolo and Tonino asked Aunt Maria what it was all about. Aunt Maria at first said that they were too young to understand. Then, since she had moments when she was as passionate as Aunt Gina or even Aunt Francesca, she told them suddenly and fervently that Caprona was going to the dogs. "Everything's going wrong for us," she said. "Money's short, tourists don't come here, and we get weaker every year. Here are Florence, Pisa and Siena all gathering round like vultures, and each year one of them gets a few more square miles of Caprona. If this goes on we shan't be a State any more. And on top of it all, the harvest failed this year. It's all the fault of those degenerate Petrocchis, I tell you! Their spells don't work any more. We Montanas can't hold Caprona up on our own! And the Petrocchis don't even try! They just keep turning things out in the same old way, and going from bad to worse. You can see they are, or that child wouldn't have been able to turn her father green!"

This was disturbing enough. And it seemed to be plain fact. All the years Paolo and Tonino had been at school, they had grown used to hearing that there had been this concession to Florence; that Pisa had demanded that agreement over fishing rights; or that Siena had raised taxes on imports to Caprona. They had grown too used to it to notice. But now it all seemed ominous. And worse shortly followed. News came that the Old Bridge had been seriously cracked by the winter floods.

This news caused the Casa Montana real dismay. For that bridge should have held. If it gave, it meant that the Montana charms in the foundations had given too. Aunt Francesca ran shrieking into the yard. "Those degenerate Petrocchis! They can't even sustain an old spell now! We've been betrayed!"

Though no one else put it quite that way, Aunt Francesca probably spoke for the whole family.

As if that was not enough, Rinaldo set off that evening to visit his English girl, and was led back to the Casa streaming with blood, supported by his

35

cousins Carlo and Giovanni. Rinaldo, using curse words Paolo and Tonino had never heard before, was understood to say he had met some Petrocchis. He had called them degenerate. And it was Aunt Maria's turn to rush shrieking through the yard, shouting dire things about the Petrocchis. Rinaldo was the apple of Aunt Maria's eye.

Rinaldo had been bandaged and put to bed, when Antonio and Uncle Lorenzo came back from viewing the damage to the Old Bridge. Both looked very serious. Old Guido Petrocchi himself had been there, with the Duke's contractor, Mr. Andretti. Some very deep charms had given. It was going to take the whole of both families, working in shifts, at least three weeks to mend them.

"We could have used Rinaldo's help," Antonio said.

Rinaldo swore that he was well enough to get out of bed and help the next day, but Aunt Maria would not hear of it. Nor would the doctor. So the rest of the family was divided into shifts, and work went on day and night. Paolo, Lucia and Corinna went to the bridge straight from school every day. Tonino did not. He was still too slow to be much use. But from what Paolo told him, he did not think he was missing much. Paolo simply could not keep up with the furious pace of the spells. He was put to running errands, like poor Cousin Domenico. Tonino felt very sympathetic towards Domenico. He was the opposite of his dashing brother Rinaldo in every way, and he could not keep up with the pace of things either.

Work had been going on, often in pouring rain, for nearly a week, when the Duke of Caprona summoned Old Niccolo to speak to him.

Old Niccolo stood in the yard and tore what was left of his hair. Tonino laid down his book (it was called *Machines of Death* and quite fascinating) and went to see if he could help.

"Ah, Tonino," said Old Niccolo, looking at him with the face of a grieving baby, "I have gigantic problems. Everyone is needed on the Old Bridge, and that ass Rinaldo is lying in bed, and I have to go before the Duke with *some* of my family. The Petrocchis have been summoned too. We cannot appear less than they are, after all. Oh *why* did Rinaldo choose such a time to shout stupid insults?"

Tonino had no idea what to say, so he said, "Shall I get Benvenuto?"

"No, no," said Old Niccolo, more upset than ever. "The Duchess cannot abide cats. Benvenuto is no use here. I shall have to take those who are no use on the bridge. You shall go, Tonino, and Paolo and Domenico, and I shall take your Uncle Umberto to look wise and weighty. Perhaps that way we shan't look so very thin."

This was perhaps not the most flattering of invitations, but Tonino and Paolo were delighted nevertheless. They were delighted even though it rained hard the next day, the drilling white rain of winter. The dawn shift came in from the Old Bridge under shiny umbrellas, damp and disgruntled. Instead of resting, they had to turn to and get the party ready for the Palace.

The Montana family coach was dragged from the coach-house to a spot under the gallery, where it was carefully dusted. It was a great black thing with glass windows and monster black wheels. The Montana winged horse was emblazoned in a green shield on its heavy doors. The rain continued to pour down. Paolo, who hated rain as much as the cats did, was glad the coach was real. The horses were not. They were four white cardboard cutouts of horses, which were kept leaning against the wall of the coach-house. They were an economical idea of Old Niccolo's father's. As he said, real horses ate and needed exercise and took up space the family could live in. The coachman was another cardboard cut-out—for much the same reasons—but he was kept inside the coach.

The boys were longing to watch the cardboard figures being brought to life, but they were snatched indoors by their mother. Elizabeth's hair was soaking from her shift on the bridge and she was yawning until her jaw creaked, but this did not prevent her doing a very thorough scrubbing, combing and dressing job on Paolo and Tonino. By the time they came down into the yard again, each with his hair scraped wet to his head and wearing uncomfortable broad white collars above their stiff Eton jackets, the spell was done. The spell-streamers had been carefully wound into the harness, and the coachman clothed in a paper coat covered with spells on the inside. Four glossy white horses were stamping as they were backed into their traces. The coachman was sitting on the box adjusting his leaf-green hat.

"Splendid!" said Old Niccolo, bustling out. He looked approvingly from the boys to the coach. "Get in, boys. Get in, Domenico. We have to pick up Umberto from the University."

Tonino said good-bye to Benvenuto and climbed into the coach. It smelt of mold, in spite of the dusting. He was glad his grandfather was so cheerful. In fact everyone seemed to be. The family cheered as the coach rumbled to the gateway, and Old Niccolo smiled and waved back. Perhaps, Tonino thought, something good was going to come from this visit to the Duke, and no one would be so worried after this.

The journey in the coach was splendid. Tonino had never felt so grand before. The coach rumbled and swayed. The hooves of the horses clattered over the cobbles just as if they were real, and people hurried respectfully out of their way. The coachman was as good as spells could make him. Though puddles dimpled along every street, the coach was hardly splashed when they drew up at the University, with loud shouts of "Whoa there!"

Uncle Umberto climbed in, wearing his red and gold Master's gown, as cheerful as Old Niccolo. "Morning, Tonino," he said to Paolo. "How's your cat? Morning," he said to Domenico. "I hear the

Petrocchis beat you up." Domenico, who would have died sooner than insult even a Petrocchi, went redder than Uncle Umberto's gown and swallowed noisily. But Uncle Umberto never could remember which younger Montana was which. He was too learned. He looked at Tonino as if he was wondering who he was, and turned to Old Niccolo. "The Petrocchis are sure to help," he said. "I had word from Chrestomanci."

"So did I," said Old Niccolo, but he sounded dubious.

The coach rumbled down the rainswept Corso and turned out across the New Bridge, where it rumbled even more loudly. Paolo and Tonino stared out of the rainy windows, too excited to speak. Beyond the swollen river, they clopped uphill, where cypresses bent and lashed in front of rich villas, and then among blurred old walls. Finally they rumbled under a great archway and made a crisp turn around the gigantic forecourt of the Palace. In front of their own coach, another coach, looking like a toy under the huge marble front of the Palace, was just drawing up by the enormous marble porch. This carriage was black too, with crimson shields on its doors, in which ramped black leopards. They were too late to see the people getting out of it, but they gazed with irritated envy at the coach itself and the horses. The horses were black, beautiful slender creatures with arched necks.

"I think they're *real* horses," Paolo whispered to Tonino.

Tonino had no time to answer, because two footmen and a soldier sprang to open the carriage door and usher them down, and Paolo jumped down first. But after him, Old Niccolo and Uncle Umberto were rather slow getting down. Tonino had time to look out of the further window at the Petrocchi carriage moving away. As it turned, he distinctly saw the small crimson flutter of a spell-streamer under the harness of the nearest black horse. So there! Tonino thought triumphantly. But he rather thought the Petrocchi coachman was real. He was a pale young man with reddish hair which did not match his cherry-colored livery, and he had an intent, concentrating look, as if it was not easy driving those unreal horses. That look was too human for a cardboard man.

When Tonino finally climbed down on Domenico's nervous heels, he glanced up at their own coachman for comparison. He was efficient and jaunty. He touched a stiff hand to his green hat and stared straight ahead. No, the Petrocchi coachman was real all right, Tonino thought enviously.

Tonino forgot both coachmen as he and Paolo followed the others into the Palace. It was so grand, and so huge. They were taken through vast halls with shiny floors and gilded ceilings, which seemed to go on for miles. On either side of the long walls there were statues, or soldiers, or footmen, adding to the magnificence in rows. They felt so battered by all the grandeur that it was quite a relief when they were shown into a room only about the size of the Casa Montana yard. True, the floor was shiny and the ceiling painted to look like a sky full of wrestling angels, but the walls were hung with quite comfortable red cloth and there was a row of almost plain gilt chairs along each side.

Another party of people was shown into the room at the same time. Domenico took one look at them and turned his eyes instantly on the painted angels of the ceiling. Old Niccolo and Uncle Umberto behaved as if the people were not there at all. Paolo and Tonino tried to do the same, but they found it impossible.

So these were the Petrocchis, they thought, sneaking glances. There were only four of them, to their five. One up to the Montanas. And two of those were children. Clearly the Petrocchis had been as hard-pressed as the Montanas to come before the Duke with a decent party, and they had, in Paolo and Tonino's opinion, made a bad mistake in leaving one of their family outside with the coach. They were not impressive. Their University representative was a frail old man, far older than Uncle Umberto, who seemed almost lost in his red and gold gown. The most impressive one was the leader of the party, who must be Old Guido himself. But he was not particularly old, like Old Niccolo, and though he wore the same sort of black frock-coat as Old Niccolo and carried the same sort of shiny hat, it looked odd on Old Guido because he had a bright red beard. His hair was rather long, crinkly and black. And though he stared ahead in a bleak, important way, it was hard to forget that his daughter had once accidentally turned him green. Paolo and Tonino both sneaked fascinated glances, wondering what that red beard would look like as bright green.

The two children were both girls. Both had reddish hair. Both had prim, pointed faces. Both wore bright white stockings and severe black dresses and were clearly odious. The main difference between them was that the younger—who seemed about Tonino's age—had a large bulging forehead, which made her face even primmer than her sister's. It was possible that one of them was the famous Angelica, who had turned Old Guido green. The boys stared at them, trying to decide which it might be, until they encountered the prim, derisive stare of the elder girl. It was clear she thought they looked ridiculous. But Paolo and Tonino knew they still looked smart—they felt so uncomfortable—so they took no notice.

After they had waited a while, both parties began to talk quietly among themselves, as if the others were not there. Tonino murmured to Paolo, "Which one is Angelica?"

"I don't know," Paolo whispered.

"Didn't you see them at the Old Bridge then?"

"I didn't see any of them. They were all down the other—"

Part of the red hanging swung aside and a lady hurried in. "I'm so sorry," she said. "My husband has been delayed."

Everyone in the room bent their heads and

murmured "Your Grace" because this was the Duchess. But Paolo and Tonino kept their eyes on her while they bent their heads, wanting to know what she was like. She had a stiff grayish dress on, which put them in mind of a statue of a saint, and her face might almost have been part of the same statue. It was a statue-pale face, almost waxy, as if the Duchess were carved out of slightly soapy marble. But Tonino was not sure the Duchess was really like a saint. Her eyebrows were set in a strong sarcastic arch, and her mouth was tight with what looked like impatience. For a second, Tonino thought he felt that impatience—and a number of other unsaintly feelings—pouring into the room from behind the Duchess's waxy mask like a strong rank smell.

The Duchess smiled at Old Niccolo. "Signor Niccolo Montana?" There was no scrap of impatience, only stateliness. Tonino thought to himself, I've been reading too many books. Rather ashamed, he watched Old Niccolo bow and introduce them all. The Duchess nodded graciously and turned to the Petrocchis. "Signor Guido Petrocchi?"

The red-bearded man bowed in a rough, brusque way. He was nothing like as courtly as Old Niccolo. "Your Grace. With me are my great-uncle Dr. Luigi Petrocchi, my elder daughter, Renata, and my younger daughter, Angelica."

Paolo and Tonino stared at the younger girl, from her bulge of forehead to her thin white legs. So *this* was Angelica. She did not look capable of doing anything wrong, or interesting.

The Duchess said, "I believe you understand why—"

The red curtains were once more swept aside. A bulky excited-looking man raced in with his head down, and took the Duchess by one arm. "Lucrezia, you must come! The scenery looks a treat!"

The Duchess turned as a statue might turn, all one piece. Her eyebrows were very high and her mouth pinched. "My lord Duke!" she said freezingly.

Tonino stared at the bulky man. He was now wearing slightly shabby green velvet with big brass buttons. Otherwise, he was exactly the same as the big damp Mr. Glister who had interrupted the Punch and Judy show that time. So he had been the Duke of Caprona after all! And he was not in the least put off by the Duchess's frigid look. "You must come and look!" he said, tugging at her arm, as excited as ever. He turned to the Montanas and the Petrocchis as if he expected them to help him pull the Duchess out of the room—and then seemed to realize that they were not courtiers. "Who are you?"

"These," said the Duchess—her eyebrows were still higher and her voice was strong with patience— "these are the Petrocchis and the Montanas awaiting your pleasure, my lord."

The Duke slapped a large, damp-looking hand to his shiny forehead. "Well I'm blessed! The people who make spells! I was thinking of sending for you.

45

Have you come about this enchanter-fellow who's got his knife into Caprona?" he asked Old Niccolo.

"My lord!" said the Duchess, her face rigid.

But the Duke broke away from her, beaming and gleaming, and dived on the Petrocchis. He shook Old Guido's hand hugely, and then the girl Renata's. After that, he dived around and did the same to Old Niccolo and Paolo. Paolo had to rub his hand secretly on his trousers after he let go. He was wet. "And they say the young ones are as clever as the old ones," the Duke said happily. "Amazing families! Just the people I need for my play—my pantomime, you know. We're putting it on here for Christmas and I could do with some special effects."

The Duchess gave a sigh. Paolo looked at her rigid face and thought that it must be hard, dealing with someone like the Duke.

The Duke dived on Domenico. "Can you arrange for a flight of cupids blowing trumpets?" he asked him eagerly. Domenico swallowed and managed to whisper the word "illusion." "Oh good!" said the Duke, and dived at Angelica Petrocchi. "And you'll love my collection of Punch and Judys," he said. "I've got hundreds!"

"How nice," Angelica answered primly.

"My lord," said the Duchess, "these good people did not come here to discuss the theater."

"Maybe, maybe," the Duke said, with an impatient, eager wave of his large hand. "But while they're here, I might as well ask them about that too.

Mightn't I?" he said, diving at Old Niccolo.

Old Niccolo showed great presence of mind. He smiled. "Of course, Your Grace. No trouble at all. After we've discussed the State business we came for, we shall be happy to take orders for any stage-effects you want."

"So will we," said Guido Petrocchi, with a sour glance at the air over Old Niccolo.

The Duchess smiled graciously at Old Niccolo for backing her up, which made Old Guido look sourer than ever, and fixed the Duke with a meaning look.

It seemed to get through to the Duke at last. "Yes, yes," he said. "Better get down to business. It's like this, you see—"

The Duchess interrupted, with a gentle fixed smile. "Refreshments are laid out in the small Conference Room. If you and the adults like to hold your discussion there, I will arrange something for the children here."

Guido Petrocchi saw a chance to get even with Old Niccolo. "Your Grace," he barked stiffly, "my daughters are as loyal to Caprona as the rest of my house. I have no secrets from them."

The Duke flashed him a glistening smile. "Quite right! But they won't be half as bored if they stay here, will they?"

Quite suddenly, everyone except Paolo and Tonino and the two Petrocchi girls was crowding away through another door behind the red hangings. The Duke leaned back, beaming. "I tell you

47

what," he said. "You must come to my pantomime, all of you. You'll love it! I'll send you tickets. Coming, Lucrezia."

The four children were left standing under the ceiling full of wrestling angels.

After a moment, the Petrocchi girls walked to the chairs against the wall and sat down. Paolo and Tonino looked at one another. They marched to the chairs on the opposite side of the room and sat down there. It seemed a safe distance. From there, the Petrocchi girls were dark blurs with thin white legs and foxy blobs for heads.

"I wish I'd brought my book," said Tonino.

They sat with their heels hooked into the rungs of their chairs, trying to feel patient. "I think the Duchess must be a saint," said Paolo, "to be so patient with the Duke."

Tonino was surprised Paolo should think that. He knew the Duke did not behave much like a duke should, while the Duchess was every inch a duchess. But he was not sure it was right, the way she let them know how patient she was being. "Mother dashes about like that," he said, "and Father doesn't mind. It stops him looking worried."

"Father's not a Duchess," said Paolo.

Tonino did not argue because, at that moment, two footmen appeared, pushing a most interesting trolley. Tonino's mouth fell open. He had never seen so many cakes together in his life before. Across the room, there were black gaps in the faces of the Petrocchi girls. Evidently they had never seen so many cakes either. Tonino shut his mouth quickly and tried to look as if he saw such sights every day.

The footmen served the Petrocchi girls first. They were very cool and seemed to take hours choosing. When the trolley was finally wheeled across to Paolo and Tonino, they found it hard to seem as composed. There were twenty different kinds of cake. They took ten each, with greedy speed, so that they had one of every kind between them and could swap if necessary. When the trolley was wheeled away, Tonino just managed to spare a glance from his plate to see how the Petrocchis were doing. Each girl had her white knees hooked up to carry a plate big enough to hold ten cakes.

They were rich cakes. By the time Paolo reached the tenth, he was going slowly, wondering if he really cared for meringue as much as he had thought, and Tonino was only on his sixth. By the time Paolo had put his plate neatly under his chair and cleaned himself with his handkerchief, Tonino, sticky with jam, smeared with chocolate and cream and infested with crumbs, was still doggedly ploughing through his eighth. And this was the moment the Duchess chose to sit smiling down beside Paolo.

"I won't interrupt your brother," she said, laughing. "Tell me about yourself, Paolo." Paolo did not know what to answer. All he could think of was the mess Tonino looked. "For instance," the Duchess asked helpfully, "does spell-making come easily to you? Do you find it hard to learn?"

"Oh no, Your Grace," Paolo said proudly. "I learn very easily." Then he was afraid this might upset Tonino. He looked quickly at Tonino's pastry-plastered face and found Tonino staring gravely at the Duchess. Paolo felt ashamed and responsible. He wanted the Duchess to know that Tonino was not just a messy staring little boy. "Tonino learns slowly," he said, "but he reads all the time. He's read all the books in the Library. He's almost as learned as Uncle Umberto."

"How remarkable," smiled the Duchess.

There was just a trace of disbelief in the arch of her eyebrows. Tonino was so embarrassed that he took a big bite out of his ninth cake. It was a great pastry puff. The instant his mouth closed round it, Tonino knew that, if he opened his mouth again, even to breathe, pastry would blow out of it like a hailstorm, all over Paolo and the Duchess. He clamped his lips together and chewed valiantly. And, to Paolo's embarrassment, he went on staring at the Duchess. He was wishing Benvenuto was there to tell him about the Duchess. She muddled him. As she bent smiling over Paolo, she did not look like the haughty, rigid lady who had been so patient with the Duke. And yet, perhaps because she was not being patient, Tonino felt the rank strength of the unsaintly thoughts behind her waxy smile, stronger than ever.

Paolo willed Tonino to stop chewing and goggling. But Tonino went on, and the disbelief in the Duchess's eyebrows was so obvious, that he blurted out, "And Tonino's the only one who can talk to Benvenuto. He's our boss cat, Your—" He remembered the Duchess did not like cats. "Er—you don't like cats, Your Grace."

The Duchess laughed. "But I don't mind hearing about them. What about Benvenuto?"

To Paolo's relief, Tonino turned his goggle eyes from the Duchess to him. So Paolo talked on. "You see, Your Grace, spells work much better and stronger if a cat's around, and particularly if Benvenuto is. Besides Benvenuto knows all sorts of things—"

He was interrupted by a thick noise from Tonino. Tonino was trying to speak without opening his mouth. It was clear there was going to be a pastry-storm any second. Paolo snatched out his jammy, creamy handkerchief and held it ready.

The Duchess stood up, rather hastily. "I think I'd better see how my other guests are getting on," she said, and went swiftly gliding across to the Petrocchi girls.

The Petrocchi girls, Paolo noticed resentfully, were ready to receive her. Their handkerchiefs had been busy while the Duchess talked to Paolo, and now their plates were neatly pushed under their chairs too. Each had left at least three cakes. This much encouraged Tonino. He was feeling rather unwell. He put the rest of the ninth cake back beside the tenth and laid the plate carefully on the next chair. By this time, he had managed to swallow his mouthful.

"You shouldn't have told her about Benvenuto," he said, hauling out his handkerchief. "He's a family secret."

"Then you should have said something yourself instead of staring like a dummy," Paolo retorted. To his mortification both Petrocchi girls were talking merrily to the Duchess. The bulge-headed Angelica was laughing. It so annoyed Paolo that he said, "Look at the way those girls are sucking up to the Duchess!"

"I didn't do that," Tonino pointed out.

As Paolo wanted to say he wished Tonino had, he found himself unable to say anything at all. He sat sourly watching the Duchess talking to the girls across the room, until she got up and went gliding away. She remembered to smile and wave at Paolo and Tonino as she went. Paolo thought that was good of her, considering the asses they had made of themselves.

Very soon after that, the curtains swung aside and Old Niccolo came back, walking slowly beside Guido Petrocchi. After them came the two gowned great-uncles, and Domenico came after that. It was like a procession. Everyone looked straight ahead, and it was plain they had a lot on their minds. All four children stood up, brushed crumbs off, and followed the procession. Paolo found he was walking beside the elder girl, but he was careful not to look at her. In utter silence, they marched to the great Palace door, where the carriages were moving along to receive them.

The Petrocchi carriage came first, with its black horses patched and beaded with rain. Tonino took another look at its coachman, rather hoping he had made a mistake. It was still raining and the man's clothes were soaked. His red Petrocchi hair was brown with wet under his wet hat. He was shivering as he leaned down, and there was a questioning look on his pale face, as if he was anxious to be told what the Duke had said. No, he was real all right. The Montana coachman behind stared into space, ignoring the rain and his passengers equally. Tonino felt that the Petrocchis had definitely come out best.

4

❧❦

WHEN THE COACH WAS moving, Old Niccolo
leaned back and said, "Well, the Duke is very good-
natured, I'll say that. Perhaps he's not such a fool as
he seems."

Uncle Umberto answered, with deepest gloom,
"When my father was a boy, *his* father went to the
Palace once a week. He was received as a friend."

Domenico said timidly, "At least we sold some
stage-effects."

"That," said Uncle Umberto crushingly, "is just
what I'm complaining of."

Tonino and Paolo looked from one to the other,
wondering what had depressed them so.

Old Niccolo noticed them looking. "Guido
Petrocchi wished those disgusting daughters of his
to be present while we conferred with the Duke," he
said. "I shall not—"

"Oh good Lord!" muttered Uncle Umberto.
"One doesn't listen to a Petrocchi."

"No, but one trusts one's grandsons," said Old
Niccolo. "Boys, old Caprona's in a bad way, it seems.

The States of Florence, Pisa and Siena have now united against her. The Duke suspects they are paying an enchanter to—"

"Huh!" said Uncle Umberto. "Paying the Petrocchis."

Domenico, who had been rendered surprisingly bold by something, said, "Uncle, I could *see* the Petrocchis were no more traitors than we are!"

Both old men turned to look at him. He crumpled.

"The fact is," Old Niccolo continued, "Caprona is not the great State she once was. There are many reasons, no doubt. But we know, and the Duke knows—even Domenico knows—that each year we set the usual charms for the defense of Caprona, and each year we set them stronger, and each year they have less effect. Something—or someone—is definitely sapping our strength. So the Duke asks what else we can do. And—"

Domenico interrupted with a squawk of laughter. "And we said we'd find the words to the *Angel of Caprona*!"

Paolo and Tonino expected Domenico to be crushed again, but the two old men simply looked gloomy. Their heads nodded mournfully. "But I don't understand," said Tonino. "The *Angel of Caprona*'s got words. We sing them at school."

"Hasn't your mother taught you—?" Old Niccolo began angrily. "Ah, no. I forgot. Your mother is English."

"One more reason for careful marriages,"

Uncle Umberto said dismally.

By this time, what with the rain ceaselessly pattering down as well, both boys were thoroughly depressed and alarmed. Domenico seemed to find them funny. He gave another squawk of laughter.

"Be quiet," said Old Niccolo. "This is the last time I take you where brandy is served. No, boys, the *Angel* has not got the right words. The words you sing are a makeshift. Some people say that the glorious Angel took the words back to Heaven after the White Devil was vanquished, leaving only the tune. Or the words have been lost since. But everyone knows that Caprona cannot be truly great until the words are found."

"In other words," Uncle Umberto said irritably, "the *Angel of Caprona* is a spell like any other spell. And without the proper words, any spell is only at half force, even if it is of divine origin." He gathered up his gown as the coach jerked to a stop outside the University. "And we—like idiots—have pledged ourselves to complete what God left unfinished," he said. "The presumption of man!" He climbed out of the coach, calling to Old Niccolo, "I'll look in every manuscript I can think of. There must be a clue somewhere. Oh this confounded rain!"

The door slammed and the coach jerked on again.

Paolo asked, "Have the Petrocchis said they'll find the words too?"

Old Niccolo's mouth bunched angrily. "They have. And I should die of shame if they did it before we did. I—" He stopped as the coach lurched around the corner into the Corso. It lurched again, and jerked. Sprays of water flew past the windows.

Domenico leaned forward. "Not driving so well, is he?"

"Quiet!" said Old Niccolo, and Paolo bit his tongue in a whole succession of jerks. Something was wrong. The coach was not making the right noise.

"I can't hear the horses' hooves," Tonino said, puzzled.

"I thought that was it!" Old Niccolo snapped. "It's the rain." He let down the window with a bang, bringing in a gust of watery wind, and, regardless of faces staring up at him from under wet umbrellas, he leaned out and bellowed the words of a spell. "And drive quickly, coachman! There," he said, as he pulled the window up again, "that should get us home before the horses turn to pulp. What a blessing this didn't happen before Umberto got out!"

The noise of the horses' hooves sounded again, clopping over the cobbles of the Corso. It seemed that the new spell was working. But, as they turned into the Via Cardinale, the noise changed to a spongy *thump-thump*, and when they came to the Via Magica the hooves made hardly a sound. And the lurching and jerking began again, worse than ever. As they turned to enter the gate of the Casa Montana, there came the most brutal jerk of all. The coach tipped forward, and there was a crash as the pole hit the cobbles. Paolo got his window open in time to see the limp paper figure of the coachman flop off the box into a puddle. Beyond him, two wet cardboard horses were draped over their traces.

"That spell," said Old Niccolo, "lasted for days in my grandfather's time."

"Do you mean it's that enchanter?" Paolo asked. "Is he spoiling all our spells?"

Old Niccolo stared at him, full-eyed, like a baby about to burst into tears. "No, lad. I fancy not. The truth is, the Casa Montana is in as bad a way as Caprona. The old virtue is fading. It has faded generation by generation, and now it is almost gone. I am ashamed that you should learn it like this. Let's get out, boys, and start dragging."

It was a wretched humiliation. Since the rest of the family were all either asleep or at work on the Old Bridge, there was no one to help them pull the coach through the gate. And Domenico was no use. He confessed afterwards that he could not remember getting home. They left him asleep in the coach and dragged it in, just the three of them. Even Benvenuto dashing through the rain did not cheer Tonino much.

"One consolation," panted their grandfather. "The rain. There is no one about to see Old Niccolo dragging his own coach."

Paolo and Tonino did not find much consolation in that. Now they understood the growing unease in the Casa, and it was not pleasant. They understood why everyone was so anxious about the Old Bridge, and so delighted when, just before Christmas, it was mended at last. They understood, too, the worry about a husband for Rosa. As soon as the bridge was repaired, everyone went back to discussing that. And Paolo and Tonino knew why everyone agreed that the young man Rosa must choose, must have, if he had nothing else, a strong talent for spells.

"To improve the breed, you mean?" said Rosa. She was very sarcastic and independent about it. "Very well, dear Uncle Lorenzo, I shall only fall in love with men who can make paper horses waterproof."

Uncle Lorenzo blushed angrily. The whole family felt humiliated by those horses. But Elizabeth was trying not to laugh. Elizabeth certainly encouraged Rosa in her independent attitude. Benvenuto informed Tonino it was the English way. Cats liked English people, he added.

"Have we really lost our virtue?" Tonino asked Benvenuto anxiously. He thought it was probably the explanation for his slowness.

Benvenuto said that he did not know what it was like in the old days, but he knew there was enough magic about now to make his coat spark. It seemed like a lot. But he sometimes wondered if it was being applied properly.

Around this time, twice as many newspapers found their way into the Casa. There were journals from Rome and magazines from Genoa and Milan, as well as the usual Caprona papers. Everyone read them eagerly and talked in mutters about the attitude of Florence, movements in Pisa and opinion hardening in Siena. Out of the worried murmurs, the word *War* began to sound, more and more frequently. And, instead of the usual Christmas songs, the only tune heard in the Casa Montana, night and day, was the *Angel of Caprona*.

The tune was sung, in bass, tenor and soprano. It was played slowly on flutes, picked out on guitars and lilted on violins. Every one of the Montanas lived in hope that he or she would be the person to find the true words. Rinaldo had a new idea. He procured a drum and sat on the edge of his bed beating out the rhythm, until Aunt Francesca implored him to stop. And even that did not help. Not one of the Montanas could begin to set the right words to the tune. Antonio looked so worried that Paolo could scarcely bear to look at him.

With so much worry about, it was hardly surprising that Paolo and Tonino looked forward daily to being invited to the Duke's pantomime. It was the one bright spot. But Antonio and Rinaldo went to the Palace—on foot—to deliver the special effects, and came back without a word of invitation. Christmas came. The entire Montana family went to church, in the beautiful marble-fronted Church of Sant' Angelo, and behaved with great devotion. Usually it was only Aunt Anna and Aunt Maria who were notably religious, but now everyone felt they had something to pray for. It was only when the time came to sing the *Angel of Caprona* that the Montana devotion slackened. An absent-minded look came over their faces, from Old Niccolo to the smallest cousin. They sang:

> "Merrily his music ringing,
> See an Angel cometh singing,
> Words of peace and comfort bringing
> To Caprona's city fair.

> "Victory that faileth never,
> Friendship that no strife can sever,
> Lasting strength and peace for ever,
> For Caprona's city fair.

> "See the Devil flee astounded!
> In Caprona now is founded
> Virtue strong and peace unbounded—
> In Caprona's city fair."

Every one of them was wondering what the real words were.

They came home for the family celebrations, and there was still no word from the Duke. Then Christmas was over. New Year drew on and passed too, and the boys were forced to realize that there would be no invitation after all. Each told himself he had known the Duke was like that. They did not speak of it to one another. But they were both bitterly disappointed.

They were roused from their gloom by Lucia racing along the gallery, screaming, "Come and look at Rosa's young man!"

"What?" said Antonio, raising his worried face from a book about the Angel of Caprona. "What? Nothing's decided yet."

Lucia leaped from foot to foot. She was pink with excitement. "Rosa's decided for herself! I knew she would. Come and see!"

Led by Lucia, Antonio, Paolo, Tonino and Benvenuto raced along the gallery and down the stone stairs at the end. People and cats were streaming through the courtyard from all directions, hurrying to the room called the Saloon, beyond the dining room.

Rosa was standing near the windows, looking happy but defiant, with both hands clasped around the arm of an embarrassed-looking young man with ginger hair. A bright ring winked on Rosa's finger. Elizabeth was with them, looking as happy as Rosa and almost as defiant. When the young man saw the family streaming through the door and crowding towards him, his face became bright pink and his hand went up to loosen his smart tie. But, in spite of that, it was plain to everyone that, underneath, the young man was as happy as Rosa. And Rosa was so happy that she seemed to shine, like the Angel over the gate. This made everyone stare, marveling. Which, of course, made the young man more embarrassed than ever.

Old Niccolo cleared his throat. "Now look here," he said. Then he stopped. This was Antonio's business. He looked at Antonio.

Paolo and Tonino noticed that their father looked at their mother first. Elizabeth's happy look seemed to reassure him a little. "Now, just who are you?" he said to the young man. "How did you meet my Rosa?"

"He was one of the contractors on the Old Bridge, Father," said Rosa.

"And he has enormous natural talent, Antonio," said Elizabeth, "and a beautiful singing voice."

"All right, all right," said Antonio. "Let the boy speak for himself, women."

The young man swallowed, and helped the swallow down with a shake of his tie. His face was now very pale. "My name is Marco Andretti," he said in a pleasant, if husky, voice. "I—I think you met my brother at the bridge, sir. I was on the other shift. That's how I came to meet Rosa." The way he smiled down at Rosa left everybody hoping that he would be fit to become a Montana.

"It'll break their hearts if Father says no," Lucia whispered to Paolo. Paolo nodded. He could see that.

Antonio was pulling his lip, which was a thing he did when his face could hold no more worry than it did already. "Yes," he said. "I've met Mario Andretti, of course. A very respectable family." He made that sound not altogether a good thing. "But I'm sure you're aware, Signor Andretti,

63

that ours is a special family. We have to be careful who we marry. First, what do you think of the Petrocchis?"

Marco's pale face went fiery red. He answered with a violence which surprised the Montanas, "I hate their guts, Signor Montana!" He seemed so upset that Rosa pulled his arm down and patted it soothingly.

"Marco has personal family reasons, Father," she said.

"Which I'd prefer not to go into," Marco said.

"We—well, I'll not press you for them," Antonio said, and continued to pull his lip. "But, you see, our family must marry someone with at least some talent for magic. Have you any ability there, Signor Andretti?"

Marco Andretti seemed to relax at this. He smiled, and gently took Rosa's hands off his sleeve. Then he sang. Elizabeth had been right about his voice. It was a golden tenor. Uncle Lorenzo was heard to rumble that he could not think what a voice like that was doing outside the Milan Opera.

> "A golden tree there grows, a tree
> Whose golden branches bud with green. . . ."

sang Marco. As he sang, the tree came into being, rooted in the carpet between Rosa and Antonio, first as a faint gold shadow, then as a rattling metal shape, dazzling gold in the shafts of sunlight from

the windows. The Montanas nodded their appreciation. The trunk and each branch, even the smallest
twig, was indeed pure gold. But Marco sang on, and
as he sang, the gold twigs put out buds, pale and fist-
shaped at first, then bright and pointed. Instants
later, the tree was in leaf. It was moving and rattling
constantly to Marco's singing. It put out pink and
white flowers in clusters, which budded, expanded
and dropped, as quickly as flames in a firework.
The room was full of scent, then of petals fluttering
like confetti. Marco still sang, and the tree still
moved. Before the last petal had fallen, pointed
green fruit was swelling where the flowers had
been. The fruit grew brownish and swelled, and
swelled and turned bulging and yellow, until the
tree drooped under the weight of a heavy crop of big
yellow pears.

> "... *With golden fruit for everyone,*"

Marco concluded. He put up a hand, picked one
of the pears and held it, rather diffidently, out to
Antonio.

There were murmurs of appreciation from the
rest of the family. Antonio took the pear and sniffed
it. And he smiled, to Marco's evident relief. "Good
fruit," he said. "That was very elegantly done,
Signor Andretti. But there is one more thing I must
ask you. Would you agree to change your name to
Montana? That is our custom, you see."

"Yes, Rosa told me," said Marco. "And—and this is a difficulty. My brother needs me in his firm, and he too wants to keep his family name. Would it be all right if I'm known as Montana when I'm here, and as—as Andretti when I'm at home with my brother?"

"You mean you and Rosa wouldn't live here?" Antonio asked, astonished.

"Not all the time. No," said Marco. From the way he said it, it was clear he was not going to change his mind.

This was serious. Antonio looked at Old Niccolo. And there were grave faces all round at the thought of the family being broken up.

"I don't see why they shouldn't," said Elizabeth.

"Well—my great-uncle did it," Old Niccolo said. "But it was not a success. His wife ran off to Sicily with a greasy little warlock."

"That doesn't mean *I'm* going to!" Rosa said.

The family wavered, with the tree gently rattling in their midst. Everyone loved Rosa. Marco was clearly nice. Nobody wanted to break their hearts. But this idea of living away from the Casa—!

Aunt Francesca heaved herself forward, saying, "I side with Elizabeth. Our Rosa has found herself a nice boy with more talent and a better voice than I've seen outside our family for years. Let them get married."

Antonio looked dreadfully worried at this, but he did not pull his lip. He seemed to be relaxing, ready to agree, when Rinaldo set the tree rattling furiously by pushing his way underneath it.

"Just a moment. Aren't we all being a bit trustful? Who is this fellow, after all? Why haven't we come across him and his talents before?"

Paolo hung his head and watched Rinaldo under his hair. This was Rinaldo in the mood he least admired. Rinaldo loud and aggressive, with an unpleasant twist to his mouth. Rinaldo was still a little pale from the cut on his head, but this went rather well with the black clothes and the red brigand's scarf. Rinaldo knew it did. He flung up his head with an air, and contemptuously brushed off a petal that had fallen on his black sleeve. And he looked at Marco, challenging him to answer.

The way Marco looked back showed that he was quite ready to stand up to Rinaldo. "I've been at college in Rome until recently," he said. "If that's what you mean."

Rinaldo swung round to face the family. "So he says," he said. "He's done a pretty trick for us, and said all the right things—but so would anyone in his place." He swung round on Marco. It was so dramatic that Tonino winced and even Paolo felt a little unhappy. "I don't trust you," said Rinaldo. "I've seen your face before somewhere."

"At the Old Bridge," said Marco.

"No, not there. It was somewhere else," said Rinaldo.

And this must be true, Tonino realized. Marco

did have a familiar look. And Tonino could not have seen him at the Old Bridge, because Tonino had never been there.

"Do you want me to fetch my brother, or my priest, to vouch for me?" asked Marco.

"No," said Rinaldo rudely. "I want the truth."

Marco took a deep breath. "I don't want to be unfriendly," he said. The arm Rosa was not holding bent, and so did the fist on the end of it. Rinaldo gave it a look as if he welcomed it, and swaggered a step nearer.

"Please!" Rosa said uselessly.

Benvenuto moved in Tonino's arms. Into Tonino's head came a picture of a large stripy tomcat swaggering on the Casa roof—Benvenuto's roof. Tonino nearly laughed. Benvenuto's muscular back legs pushed him backwards into Paolo as Benvenuto took off. Benvenuto landed between Rinaldo and Marco. There was a gentle "Ah!" from the rest of the family. They knew Benvenuto would settle it.

Benvenuto deliberately ignored Rinaldo. Arching himself tall, with his tail straight up like a cypress tree, he minced to Marco's legs and rubbed himself around them. Marco undoubled his fist and bent to hold his hand out to Benvenuto. "Hallo," he said. "What's your name?" He paused, for Benvenuto to tell him. "I'm pleased to meet you, Benvenuto," he said.

The "Ah!" from the family was loud and long

this time. It was followed by cries of, "Get out of it, Rinaldo! Don't make a fool of yourself! Leave Marco alone!"

Though Rinaldo was nothing like as easily crushed as Domenico, even he could not stand up to the whole family. When he looked at Old Niccolo and saw Old Niccolo waving him angrily aside, he gave up and shoved his way out of the room.

"Rosa and Marco," said Antonio, "I give my provisional consent to your marriage."

Upon that, everyone hugged everyone else, shook hands with Marco and kissed Rosa. Very flushed and happy, Marco plucked pear after pear from the golden tree and gave them to everyone, even the newest baby. They were delicious pears, ripe to perfection. They melted in mouths and dribbled down chins.

"I don't want to be a spoilsport," Aunt Maria said, slurping juice in Paolo's ear, "but a tree in the Saloon is going to be a nuisance."

But Marco had thought of that. As soon as the last pear was picked, the tree began to fade. Soon it was a clattering golden glitter, a vanishing shadow-tree, and then it was not there at all. Everyone applauded. Aunt Gina and Aunt Anna fetched bottles of wine and glasses, and the Casa drank to the health of Rosa and Marco.

"Thank goodness!" Tonino heard Elizabeth say. "I was so nervous for her!"

On the other side of Elizabeth, Old Niccolo was

telling Uncle Lorenzo that Marco was a real acqui-
sition, because he could understand cats. Tonino felt
a little wistful at this. He went outside into the chilly
yard. As he had expected, Benvenuto was now
curled up in the sunny patch on the gallery steps. He
undulated his tail in annoyance at Tonino. He had
just settled down for a sleep.

But Marco could *not* understand cats, Benvenuto
said irritably. He knew Benvenuto's name, because
Rosa had told him, but he had no idea what
Benvenuto had actually said to him. Benvenuto had
told him that he and Rinaldo would get thoroughly
scratched if they started a fight in the Casa—neither
of them was boss cat here. Now, if Tonino would go
away, a cat could get some sleep.

This was a great relief to Tonino. He now felt
free to like Marco as much as Paolo did. Marco was
fun. He was never in the Casa for very long, because
he and his brother were building a villa out beyond
the New Bridge, but he was one of the few people
Tonino laid down his book to talk to. And that,
Lucia told Rosa, was a compliment indeed.

Rosa and Marco were to be married in the
spring. They laughed about it constantly as they
swept in and out of the Casa together. Antonio and
Uncle Lorenzo walked out to the villa where Mario
Andretti lived, and arranged it all. Mario Andretti
came to the Casa to settle the details. He was a large
fat man—who drove a shrewd bargain, Aunt
Francesca said—and quite different from Marco.

The most notable thing about him was the long white motor car he came in.

Old Niccolo looked at that car reflectively. "It smells," he said. "But it looks more reliable than a cardboard horse." He sighed. He still felt deeply humiliated. All the same, after Mario Andretti had driven away, Tonino was very interested to be sent out to the post with two letters. One was addressed to Ferrari, the other to Rolls-Royce in England.

In the normal way, the talk in the Casa would have been all about that car and those two letters. But they passed unnoticed in the anxious murmurs about Florence, Siena and Pisa. The only topic able to drown out the talk of war was Rosa's wedding dress. Should it be long or short? With a train, or not? And what kind of veil? Rosa was quite as independent about that as she had been over Marco.

"I suppose I have no say in it at all," she said. "I shall have it knee-length one side and a train ten feet long on the other, I think. And no veil. Just a black mask."

This thoroughly offended Aunt Maria and Aunt Gina, who were the chief arguers. What with the noise they made, and the twanging the other side of the room, where Antonio had roped Marco in to help find the words to the *Angel*, Tonino was unable to concentrate on his book. He took it along the gallery to the library, hoping for peace there.

But Rinaldo was leaning on the gallery rail outside the library, looking remarkably sinister, and he stopped Tonino. "That Marco," he said. "I *wish* I could remember where I saw him. I've seen him in the Art Gallery with Rosa, but it wasn't there. I know it was somewhere much more damaging than that."

Tonino had no doubt that Rinaldo knew all sorts of damaging places. He took his book into the library, hoping that Rinaldo would not remember the place, and settled down in the chilly mustiness to read.

The next moment, Benvenuto landed on his book with a thump.

"Oh get off!" said Tonino. "I start school tomorrow, and I want to finish this first."

No, said Benvenuto. Tonino was to go to Old Niccolo *at once*. A flurry of scrips, spells, yellow parchment rolls and then a row of huge red books passed behind Tonino's eyes. It was followed by a storm of enormous images. Giants were running, banging, smoking and burning, and they all wore red and gold. But not yet. They were preparing to fight, marching in great huge boots. Benvenuto was so urgent that it took all Tonino's skill to sort out what he meant.

"All right," said Tonino. "I'll tell him." He got up and pelted round the gallery, past Rinaldo, who said, "What's the hurry?" to Old Niccolo's quarters. Old Niccolo was just coming out.

"Please," said Tonino, "Benvenuto says to get out the war-spells. The Duke is calling up the Reserves."

Old Niccolo stood so very quiet and wide-eyed that Tonino thought he did not believe it. Old Niccolo was feeling for the door-frame. He seemed to think it was missing.

"You did hear me, did you?" Tonino asked.

"Yes," said Old Niccolo. "Yes, I heard. It's just so soon—so sudden. I wish the Duke had warned us. So war is coming. Pray God our strength is still enough."

5

✦⟐✦

BENVENUTO'S NEWS caused a stampede in the Casa
Montana. The older cousins raced to the Scriptorium and began packing away all the usual spells,
inks and pens. The aunts fetched out the special
inks for use in war-spells. The uncles staggered
under reams of fresh paper and parchment.
Antonio, Old Niccolo and Rinaldo went to the
library and fetched the giant red volumes, with
WAR stamped on their spines, while Elizabeth
raced to the music room with all the children to put
away the ordinary music and set out the tunes and
instruments of war.

Meanwhile, Rosa, Marco and Domenico raced
out into the Via Magica and came back with newspapers. Everyone at once left what they were doing
and crowded into the dining room to see what the
papers said.

They made a pile of people, all craning over the
table. Rinaldo was standing on a chair, leaning over
three aunts. Marco was underneath, craning anxiously sideways, head to head with Old Niccolo, as

Rosa flipped over the pages. There were so many other people packed in and leaning over that Lucia, Paolo and Tonino were forced to squat with their chins on the table, in order to see at all.

"No, nothing," Rosa said, flipping over the second paper.

"Wait," said Marco. "Look at the Stop Press."

Everyone swayed towards it, pushing Marco further sideways. Then Tonino almost knew where he had seen Marco before.

"There it is," said Antonio.

All the bodies came upright, with their faces very serious.

"Reserve mobilized, right enough," said Rosa. "Oh, Marco!"

"What's the matter?" Rinaldo asked jeeringly from his chair. "Is Marco a Reservist?"

"No," said Marco. "My—my brother got me out of it."

Rinaldo laughed. "What a patriot!"

Marco looked up at him. "I'm a Final Reservist," he said, "and I hope you are too. If you aren't, it will be a pleasure to take you around to the Army Office in the Arsenal this moment."

The two glared at one another. Once again there were shouts to Rinaldo to stop making a fool of himself. Sulkily, Rinaldo climbed down and stalked out.

"Rinaldo is a Final Reservist," Paolo assured Marco.

"I thought he must be," Marco said. "Look, I

must go. I—I must tell my brother. Rosa, I'll see you tomorrow if I can."

When Tonino fell asleep that night, the room next door to him was full of people talking of war and the *Angel of Caprona*, with occasional digressions about Rosa's wedding dress. Tonino's head was so full of these things that he was quite surprised, when he went to school, not to hear them talked of there. But no one seemed to have noticed there might be a war. True, some of the teachers looked grave, but that might have been just their natural feelings at the start of a new term.

Consequently, Tonino came home that afternoon thinking that maybe things were not so bad after all. As usual, Benvenuto leaped off the waterbutt and sprang into his arms. Tonino was rubbing his face against Benvenuto's nearest ragged ear, when he heard a carriage draw up behind him. Benvenuto promptly squirmed out of Tonino's arms. Tonino, very surprised, looked around to find him trotting, gently and politely, with his tail well up, towards a tall man who was just coming in through the Casa gate.

Benvenuto stood, his brush of tail waving slightly at the tip, his hind legs canted slightly apart under his fluffy drawers, staring gravely at the tall man. Tonino thought peevishly that, from behind, Benvenuto often looked pretty silly. The man looked almost as bad. He was wearing an exceedingly expensive coat with a fur collar and a tweed traveling cap with daft earflaps. And he bowed to Benvenuto.

"Good afternoon, Benvenuto," he said, as grave as Benvenuto himself. "I'm glad to see you so well. Yes, I'm very well thank you."

Benvenuto advanced to rub himself around the stranger's legs.

"No," said the man. "I beg you. Your hairs come off."

And Benvenuto stopped, without abating an ounce of his uncommon politeness.

By this time, Tonino was extremely resentful. This was the first time for years that Benvenuto had behaved as if anyone mattered more than Tonino. He raised his eyes accusingly to the stranger's. He met eyes even darker than his own, which seemed to spill brilliance over the rest of the man's smooth dark face. They gave Tonino a jolt, worse than the time the horses turned back to cardboard. He knew, beyond a shadow of doubt, that he was looking at a powerful enchanter.

"How do you do?" said the man. "No, despite your accusing glare, young man, I have never been able to understand cats—or not more than in the most general way. I wonder if you would be kind enough to translate for me what Benvenuto is saying."

Tonino listened to Benvenuto. "He says he's very pleased to see you again and welcome to the Casa Montana, sir." The sir was from Benvenuto, not Tonino. Tonino was not sure he cared for strange enchanters who walked into the Casa and took up Benvenuto's attention.

"Thank you, Benvenuto," said the enchanter. "I'm very pleased to be back. Though, frankly, I've seldom had such a difficult journey. Did you know your borders with Florence and Pisa were closed?" he asked Tonino. "I had to come in by sea from Genoa in the end."

"Did you?" Tonino said, wondering if the man thought it was his fault. "Where did you come from then?"

"Oh, England," said the man.

Tonino warmed to that. This then could not be the enchanter the Duke had talked about. Or could he? Tonino was not sure how far away enchanters could work from.

"Makes you feel better?" asked the man.

"Mother's English," Tonino admitted, feeling he was giving altogether too much away,

"Ah!" said the enchanter. "Now I know who you are. You're Antonio the Younger, aren't you? You were a baby when I saw you last, Tonino."

Since there is no reply to that kind of remark, Tonino was glad to see Old Niccolo hastening across the yard, followed by Aunt Francesca and Uncle Lorenzo, with Antonio and several more of the family hurrying behind them. They closed round the enchanter, leaving Tonino and Benvenuto beyond, by the gate.

"Yes, I've just come from the Casa Petrocchi," Tonino heard the stranger say. To his surprise, everyone accepted it, as if it were the most natural thing for the stranger to have done—as natural as the way he took off his ridiculous English hat to Aunt Francesca.

"But you'll stay the night with us," said Aunt Francesca.

"If it's not too much trouble," the stranger said.

In the distance, as if they already knew—as they unquestionably did in a place like the Casa Montana—Aunt Maria and Aunt Anna went clambering up the gallery steps to prepare the guest-room above. Aunt Gina emerged from the kitchen, held her hands up to Heaven, and dashed indoors again. Thoughtfully, Tonino gathered up Benvenuto and asked exactly who this stranger was.

Chrestomanci, of course, he was told. The most powerful enchanter in the world.

"Is he the one who's spoiling our spells?" Tonino asked suspiciously.

Chrestomanci, he was told—impatiently, because Benvenuto evidently thought Tonino was being very stupid—is always on our side.

Tonino looked at the stranger again—or rather, at his smooth dark head sticking out from among the shorter Montanas—and understood that Chrestomanci's coming meant there was a crisis indeed.

The stranger must have said something about him. Tonino found them all looking at him, his family smiling lovingly. He smiled back shyly.

"Oh, he's a good boy," said Aunt Francesca.

Then they all surged, talking, across the yard. "What makes it particularly difficult," Tonino heard Chrestomanci saying, "is that I am, first and foremost, an employee of the British Government. And Britain is keeping out of Italian affairs. But luckily I have a fairly wide brief."

Almost at once, Aunt Gina shot out of the kitchen again. She had canceled the ordinary supper and started on a new one in honor of Chrestomanci. Six people were sent out at once for cakes and fruit, and two more for lettuce and cheese. Paolo, Corinna and Lucia were caught as they came in chatting from school and told to go at once to the butcher's. But, at this point, Rinaldo erupted furiously from the Scriptorium.

"What do you mean, sending all the kids off like this!" he bawled from the gallery. "We're up to our ears in war-spells here. I need copiers!"

Aunt Gina put her hands on her hips and bawled back at him. "And I need steak! Don't you stand up there cheeking me, Rinaldo Montana! English people always eat steak, so steak I must have!"

"Then cut pieces off the cats!" screamed Rinaldo. "I need Corinna and Lucia up here!"

"I tell you they are going to run after *me* for once!" yelled Aunt Gina.

"Dear me," said Chrestomanci, wandering into the yard. "What a very Italian scene! Can I help in any way?" He nodded and smiled from Aunt Gina to Rinaldo. Both of them smiled back, Rinaldo at his most charming.

"You would agree I need copiers, sir, wouldn't you?" he said.

"Bah!" said Aunt Gina. "Rinaldo turns on the

charm and I get left to struggle alone! As usual! All right. Because it's war-spells, Paolo and Tonino can go for the steak. But wait while I write you a note, or you'll come back with something no one can chew."

"So glad to be of service," Chrestomanci murmured, and turned away to greet Elizabeth, who came racing down from the gallery waving a sheaf of music and fell into his arms. The heads of the five little cousins Elizabeth had been teaching stared wonderingly over the gallery rail. "Elizabeth!" said Chrestomanci. "Looking younger than ever!" Tonino stared as wonderingly as his cousins. His mother was laughing and crying at once. He could not follow the torrent of English speech. "Virtue," he heard, and "war" and, before long, the inevitable "*Angel of Caprona*." He was still staring when Aunt Gina stuck her note into his hand and told him to make haste.

As they hurried to the butcher's, Tonino said to Paolo, "I didn't know Mother knew anyone like Chrestomanci."

"Neither did I," Paolo confessed. He was only a year older than Tonino, after all, and it seemed that Chrestomanci had last been in Caprona a very long time ago. "Perhaps he's come to find the words to the *Angel*," Paolo suggested. "I hope so. I don't want Rinaldo to have to go away and fight."

"Or Marco," Tonino agreed. "Or Carlo or Luigi or even Domenico."

Because of Aunt Gina's note, the butcher

treated them with great respect, "Tell her this is the last good steak she'll see, if war is declared," he said, and he passed them each a heavy, squashy pink arm-load.

They arrived back with their armfuls just as a cab set down Uncle Umberto, puffing and panting, outside the Casa gate. "I am right, Chrestomanci *is* here? Eh, Paolo?" Uncle Umberto asked Tonino.

Both boys nodded. It seemed easier than explaining that Paolo was Tonino.

"Good, good!" exclaimed Uncle Umberto and surged into the Casa, where he found Chrestomanci just crossing the yard. "The *Angel of Caprona*," Uncle Umberto said to him eagerly. "Could you—?"

"My dear Umberto," said Chrestomanci, shaking his hand warmly, "everyone here is asking me that. For that matter, so was everyone in the Casa Petrocchi too. And I'm afraid I know no more than you do. But I shall think about it, don't worry."

"If you could find just a line, to get us started," Uncle Umberto said pleadingly.

"I *will* do my best—" Chrestomanci was saying, when, with a great clattering of heels, Rosa shot past. From the look on her face, she had seen Marco arriving. "I promise you that," Chrestomanci said, as his head turned to see what Rosa was running for.

Marco came through the gate and stopped so dead, staring at Chrestomanci, that Rosa charged into him and nearly knocked him over. Marco staggered a bit, put his arms round Rosa, and went on staring at Chrestomanci. Tonino found himself holding his breath. Rinaldo was right. There *was* something about Marco. Chrestomanci knew it, and Marco knew he knew. From the look on Marco's face, he expected Chrestomanci to say what it was.

Chrestomanci indeed opened his mouth to say something, but he shut it again and pursed his lips in a sort of whistle instead. Marco looked at him uncertainly.

"Oh," said Uncle Umberto, "may I introduce—" He stopped and thought. Rosa he usually remembered, because of her fair hair, but he could not place Marco. "Corinna's fiancé," he suggested.

"I'm Rosa," said Rosa. "This is Marco Andretti."

"How do you do?" Chrestomanci said politely. Marco seemed to relax. Chrestomanci's eyes turned to Paolo and Tonino, standing staring. "Good heavens!" he said. "Everyone here seems to live such exciting lives. What have you boys killed?"

Paolo and Tonino looked down in consternation, to find that the steak was leaking on to their shoes. Two or three cats were approaching meaningly.

Aunt Gina appeared in the kitchen doorway. *"Where's my steak?"*

Paolo and Tonino sped towards her, leaving a pattering trail. "What was all that about?" Paolo panted to Tonino.

"I don't know," said Tonino, because he didn't, and because he liked Marco.

Aunt Gina shortly became very sharp and passionate about the steak. The leaking trail attracted every cat in the Casa. They were underfoot in the kitchen all evening, mewing pitifully. Benvenuto was also present, at a wary distance from Aunt Gina, and he made good use of his time. Aunt Gina erupted into the yard again, trumpeting.

"Tonino! *Ton-in-ooh!*"

Tonino laid down his book and hurried outside. "Yes, Aunt Gina?"

"That cat of yours has stolen a whole pound of steak!" Aunt Gina trumpeted, flinging a dramatic arm skyward.

Tonino looked, and there, sure enough, Benvenuto was, crouched on the pan-tiles of the roof, with one paw holding down quite a large lump of meat. "Oh dear," he said. "I don't think I can make him give it back, Aunt Gina."

"I don't want it back. Look where it's been!" screamed Aunt Gina. "Tell him from me that I shall wring his evil neck if he comes near me again!"

"My goodness, you do seem to be at the center of everything," Chrestomanci remarked, appearing beside Tonino in the yard. "Are you always in such demand?"

"I shall have hysterics," declared Aunt Gina. "And no one will get any supper." Elizabeth and Aunt Maria and Cousins Claudia and Teresa immediately came to her assistance and led her tenderly back indoors.

"Thank the Lord!" said Chrestomanci. "I'm not sure I could stand hysterics and starvation at once. How did you know I was an enchanter, Tonino? From Benvenuto?"

"No. I just knew when I looked at you," said Tonino.

"I see," said Chrestomanci. "This is interesting. Most people find it impossible to tell. It makes me wonder if Old Niccolo is right, when he talks of the virtue leaving your house. Would you be able to tell another enchanter when you looked at him, do you think?"

Tonino screwed up his face and wondered. "I might. It's the eyes. You mean, would I know the enchanter who's spoiling our spells?"

"I think I mean that," said Chrestomanci. "I'm beginning to believe there is someone. I'm sure, at least, that the spells on the Old Bridge were deliberately broken. Would it interfere with your plans too much, if I asked your grandfather to take you with him whenever he has to meet strangers?"

"I haven't got any plans," said Tonino. Then he thought, and he laughed. "I think you make jokes all the time."

"I aim to please," Chrestomanci said.

However, when Tonino next saw Chrestomanci, it was at supper—which was magnificent, despite Benvenuto and the hysterics—and Chrestomanci was very serious indeed. "My dear Niccolo," he said, "my mission *has* to concern the misuse of magic, not the balance of power in Italy. There would be no end of trouble if I was caught trying to stop a war."

Old Niccolo had his look of a baby about to cry. Aunt Francesca said, "We're not asking this personally—"

"But, my dear," said Chrestomanci, "don't you see that I can only do something like this as a personal matter? Please ask me personally. I shan't let the strict terms of my mission interfere with what I owe my friends." He smiled then, and his eyes swept around everyone gathered at the great table, very affectionately. He did not seem to exclude Marco. "So," he said, "I think my best plan for the moment is to go on to Rome. I know certain quarters there, where I can get impartial information, which should enable me to pin down this enchanter. At the moment, all we know is that he exists. If I'm lucky, I can prove whether Florence, or Siena, or Pisa is paying him—in which case, they and he can be indicted at the Court of Europe. And if, while I'm at it, I can get Rome, or Naples, to move on Caprona's behalf, be very sure I shall do it."

"Thank you," said Old Niccolo.

For the rest of supper, they discussed how Chrestomanci could best get to Rome. He would have to go by sea. It seemed that the last stretch of border, between Caprona and Siena, was now closed.

Much later that night, when Paolo and Tonino were on their way to bed, they saw lights in the Scriptorium. They tiptoed along to investigate. Chrestomanci was there with Antonio, Rinaldo and Aunt Francesca, going through spells in the big red books. Everyone was speaking in mutters, but they heard Chrestomanci say, "This is a sound combination, but it'll need new words." And on another page, "Get Elizabeth to put this in English, as a surprise factor." And again, "Ignore the tune. The only tune which is going to be any use to you at the moment is the *Angel*. He can't block that."

"Why just those three?" Tonino whispered.

"They're best at making new spells," Paolo whispered back. "We need new war-spells. It sounds as if the other enchanter knows the old ones."

They crept to bed with an excited, urgent feeling, and neither of them found it easy to sleep.

Chrestomanci left the next morning before the children went to school. Benvenuto and Old Niccolo escorted him to the gate, one on either side, and the entire Casa gathered to wave him off. Things felt both flat and worrying once he was gone. That day, there was a great deal of talk of war at school. The teachers whispered together. Two had left, to join the Reserves. Rumors went around the classes. Someone told Tonino that war would be declared next Sunday, so that it would be a Holy War. Someone else told Paolo that all the Reserves had been issued with two left boots, so that they would not be able to fight. There was no truth in these things. It was just that everyone now knew that war was coming.

The boys hurried home, anxious for some real news. As usual, Benvenuto leaped off his waterbutt. While Tonino was enjoying Benvenuto's undivided attention again, Elizabeth called from the gallery, "Tonino! Someone's sent you a parcel."

Tonino and Benvenuto sprang for the gallery stairs, highly excited. Tonino had never had a parcel before. But before he got anywhere near it, he was seized on by Aunt Maria, Rosa and Uncle Lorenzo. They seized on all the children who could write and hurried them to the dining room. This had been set up as another Scriptorium. By each chair was a special pen, a bottle of red war-ink and a pile of strips of paper. There the children were kept busy fully two hours, copying the same war-charm, again and again. Tonino had never been so frustrated in his life. He did not even know what shape his parcel was. He was not the only one to feel frustrated.

"Oh, why?" complained Lucia, Paolo and young Cousin Lena.

"I know," said Aunt Maria. "Like school again. Start writing."

"It's exploiting children, that's what we're doing," Rosa said cheerfully. "There are probably laws against it, so do complain."

"Don't worry, I will," said Lucia. "I am doing."

"As long as you write while you grumble," said Rosa.

"It's a new spell-scrip for the Army," Uncle Lorenzo explained. "It's very urgent."

"It's hard. It's all new words," Paolo grumbled.

"Your father made it last night," said Aunt Maria. "Get writing. We'll be watching for mistakes."

When finally, stiff-necked and with red

splodges on their fingers, they were let out into the yard, Tonino discovered that he had barely time to unwrap the parcel before supper. Supper was early that night, so that the elder Montanas could put in another shift on the army-spells before bedtime.

"It's worse than working on the Old Bridge," said Lucia. "What's that, Tonino? Who sent it?"

The parcel was promisingly book-shaped. It bore the stamp and the arms of the University of Caprona. This was the only indication Tonino had that Uncle Umberto had sent it, for, when he wrenched off the thick brown paper, there was no letter, not even a card. There was only a new shiny book. Tonino's face beamed. At least Uncle Umberto knew this much about him. He turned the book lovingly over. It was called *The Boy Who Saved His Country*, and the cover was the same shiny, pimpled red leather as the great volumes of war-spells.

"Is Uncle Umberto trying to give you a hint, or something?" Paolo asked, amused. He and Lucia and Corinna leaned over Tonino while he flipped through the pages. There were pictures, to Tonino's delight. Soldiers rode horses, soldiers rode machines; a boy hung from a rope and scrambled up the frowning wall of a fortress; and, most exciting of all, a boy stood on a rock with a flag, confronting a whole troop of ferocious-looking dragoons. Sighing with anticipation, Tonino turned to Chapter One: *How Giorgio uncovered an Enemy Plot*.

"*Supper!*" howled Aunt Gina from the yard.

"Oh I shall go mad! Nobody attends to me!"

Tonino was forced to shut the lovely book again and hurry down to the dining room. He watched Aunt Gina anxiously as she doled out minestrone. She looked so hectic that he was convinced Benvenuto must have been at work in the kitchen again.

"It's all right," Rosa said. "It's just she thought she'd got a line from the *Angel of Caprona*. Then the soup boiled over and she forgot it again."

Aunt Gina was distinctly tearful. "With so much to do, my memory is like a sieve," she kept saying. "Now I've let you all down."

"Of course you haven't, Gina my dear," said Old Niccolo. "This is nothing to worry about. It will come back to you."

"But I can't even remember what language it was in!" wailed Aunt Gina.

Everyone tried to console her. They sprinkled grated cheese on their soup and slurped it with special relish, to show Aunt Gina how much they appreciated her, but Aunt Gina continued to sniff and accuse herself. Then Rinaldo thought of pointing out that she had got further than anyone else in the Casa Montana. "None of the rest of us has any of the *Angel of Caprona* to forget," he said, giving Aunt Gina his best smile.

"Bah!" said Aunt Gina. "Turning on the charm, Rinaldo Montana!" But she seemed a good deal more cheerful after that.

Tonino was glad Benvenuto had nothing to do

with it this time. He looked around for Benvenuto. Benvenuto usually took up a good position for stealing scraps, near the serving table. But tonight he was nowhere to be seen. Nor, for that matter, was Marco.

"Where's Marco?" Paolo asked Rosa.

Rosa smiled. She seemed quite cheerful about it. "He has to help his brother," she said, "with fortifications."

That brought home to Paolo and Tonino the fact that there was going to be a war. They looked at one another nervously. Neither of them was quite sure whether you behaved in the usual way in wartime, or not. Tonino's mind shot to his beautiful new book. *The Boy Who Saved His Country*. He slurped the title through his mind, just as he was slurping his soup. Had Uncle Umberto meant to say to him, find the words to the *Angel of Caprona*, and save your country, Tonino? It would indeed be the most marvelous thing if he, Tonino Montana, could find the words and save his country. He could hardly wait to see how the boy in the book had done it.

As soon as supper was over, he sprang up, ready to dash off and start reading. And once again he was prevented. This time it was because the children were told to wash up supper. Tonino groaned. And, again, he was not the only one.

"It isn't fair!" Corinna said passionately. "We slave all afternoon at spells, and we slave all evening at washing-up! I know there's going to be a war, but

I still have to do my exams. How am I ever going to do my homework?" The way she flung out an impassioned arm made Paolo and Tonino think that Aunt Gina's manner must be catching.

Rather unexpectedly, Lucia sympathized with Corinna. "I think you're too old to be one of us children," she said. "Why don't you go away and do your homework and let me organize the kids?"

Corinna looked at her uncertainly. "What about your homework?"

"I've not got much. I'm not aiming for the University like you," Lucia said kindly. "Run along." And she pushed Corinna out of the dining room. As soon as the door was shut, she turned briskly to the other children. "Come on. What are you lot standing gooping for? Everyone take a pile of plates to the kitchen. Quick march, Tonino. Move, Lena and Bernardo. Paolo, you take the big bowls."

With Lucia standing over them like a sergeant major, Tonino had no chance to slip away. He trudged to the kitchen with everyone else, where, to his surprise, Lucia ordered everyone to lay the plates and cutlery out in rows on the floor. Then she made them stand in a row themselves, facing the rows of greasy dishes.

Lucia was very pleased with herself. "Now," she said, "this is something I've always wanted to try. This is washing-up-made-easy, by Lucia Montana's patent method. I'll tell you the words. They go to the *Angel of Caprona*. And you're all to sing after me—"

"Are you sure we should?" asked Lena, who was a very law-abiding cousin.

Lucia gave her a look of scalding contempt. "If some people," she remarked to the whitewashed beams of the ceiling, "don't know true intelligence when they see it, they are quite at liberty to go and live with the Petrocchis."

"I only asked," Lena said, crushed.

"Well, don't," said Lucia. "This is the spell. . . ."

Shortly, they were all singing lustily:

> *"Angel, clean our knives and dishes,*
> *Clean our spoons and salad bowls,*
> *Wash our saucepans, hear our wishes,*
> *Angel, make our forks quite clean."*

At first, nothing much seemed to happen. Then it became clear that the orange grease was certainly slowly clearing from the plates. Then the lengths of spaghetti stuck to the bottom of the largest saucepan started unwinding and wriggling like worms. Up over the edge of the saucepan they wriggled, and over the stone floor, to ooze themselves into the waste-cans. The orange grease and the salad-oil traveled after them, in rivulets. And the singing faltered a little, as people broke off to laugh.

"Sing, *sing*!" shouted Lucia. So they sang.

Unfortunately for Lucia, the noise penetrated to the Scriptorium. The plates were still pale pink and rather greasy, and the last of the spaghetti was still wriggling across the floor, when Elizabeth and Aunt Maria burst into the kitchen.

"Lucia!" said Elizabeth.

"You irreligious brats!" said Aunt Maria.

"I don't see what's so wrong," said Lucia.

"She doesn't see—Elizabeth, words fail!" said Aunt Maria. "How can I have taught her so little and so badly? Lucia, a spell is not *instead* of a thing. It is only to *help* that thing. And on top of that, you go and use the *Angel of Caprona*, as if it was any old tune, and not the most powerful song in all Italy! I—I could box your ears, Lucia!"

"So could I," said Elizabeth. "Don't you understand we need all our virtue—the whole combined strength of the Casa Montana—to put into the warcharms? And here you go frittering it away in the kitchen!"

"Put those plates in the sink, Paolo," ordered Aunt Maria. "Tonino, pick up those saucepans. The rest of you pick up the cutlery. And now you'll wash them properly."

Very chastened, everyone obeyed. Lucia was angry as well as chastened. When Lena whispered, "I *told* you so!" Lucia broke a plate and jumped on the pieces.

"Lucia!" snapped Aunt Maria, glaring at her. It was the first time any of the children had seen her look likely to slap someone.

"Well, how was I to know?" Lucia stormed. "Nobody ever explained—nobody *told* me spells were like that!"

"Yes, but you knew perfectly well you were doing something you shouldn't," Elizabeth told her, "even if you didn't know why. The rest of you, stop sniggering. Lena, you can learn from this too."

All through doing the washing-up properly—which took nearly an hour—Tonino was saying to himself, "And *then* I can read my book at last." When it was finally done, he sped out into the yard. And there was Old Niccolo hurrying down the steps to meet him in the dark.

"Tonino, may I have Benvenuto for a while, please?"

But Benvenuto was still not to be found. Tonino began to think he would die of book-frustration. All the children joined in hunting and calling, but there was still no Benvenuto. Soon, most of the grown-ups were looking for him too, and still Benvenuto did not appear. Antonio was so exasperated that he seized Tonino's arm and shook him.

"It's too bad, Tonino! You must have known we'd need Benvenuto. Why did you let him go?"

"I didn't! You *know* what Benvenuto's like!" Tonino protested, equally exasperated.

"Now, now, now," said Old Niccolo, taking each of them by a shoulder. "It is quite plain by now that Benvenuto is on the other side of town, making vile noises on a roof somewhere. All we can do is hope someone empties a jug of water on him soon. It's not Tonino's fault, Antonio."

Antonio let go Tonino's arm and rubbed both hands on his face. He looked very tired. "I'm sorry,

Tonino," he said. "Forgive me. Let us know as soon as Benvenuto comes back, won't you?"

He and Old Niccolo hurried back to the Scriptorium. As they passed under the light, their faces were stiff with worry.

"I don't think I like war, Tonino," Paolo said. "Let's go and play table-tennis in the dining room."

"I'm going to read my book," Tonino said firmly. He thought he would get like Aunt Gina if anything else happened to stop him.

6

❧◆❧

TONINO READ HALF THE NIGHT. With all the grown-ups hard at work in the Scriptorium, there was no one to tell him to go to bed. Corinna tried, when she had finished her homework, but Tonino was too deep in the book even to hear her. And Corinna went respectfully away, thinking that, as the book had come from Uncle Umberto, it was probably very learned.

It was not in the least learned. It was the most gripping story Tonino had ever read. It started with the boy, Giorgio, going along a mysterious alleyway near the docks on his way home from school. There was a peeling blue house at the end of the alley and, just as Giorgio passed it, a scrap of paper fluttered from one of its windows. It contained a mysterious message, which led Giorgio at once into a set of adventures with the enemies of his country. Each one was more exciting than the last.

Well after midnight, when Giorgio was holding a pass single-handed against the enemy, Tonino happened to hear his father and mother coming to bed. He was forced to leave Giorgio lying wounded and dive into bed himself. All night he dreamed of notes fluttering from the windows of peeling blue houses, of Giorgio—who was sometimes Tonino himself and sometimes Paolo—and of villainous enemies—most of whom seemed to have red beards and black hair, like Guido Petrocchi—and, as the sun rose, he was too excited to stay asleep. He woke up and went on reading.

When the rest of the Casa Montana began to stir, Tonino had finished the book. Giorgio had saved his country. Tonino was quivering with excitement and exhaustion. He wished the book was twice as long. If it had not been time to get up, he would have gone straight back to the beginning and started reading the book again.

And the beauty of it, he thought, eating breakfast without noticing, was that Giorgio had saved his country, not only single-handed, but without a spell coming into it anywhere. If Tonino was going to save Caprona, that was the way he would like to do it.

Around Tonino, everyone else was complaining and Lucia was sulking. The washing-up spell was still about in the kitchen. Every cup and plate was covered with a thin layer of orange spaghetti grease, and the butter tasted of soap.

"What did she *use*, in Heaven's name?" groaned Uncle Lorenzo. "This coffee tastes of tomato."

"Her own words to the *Angel of Caprona*," Aunt Maria said, and shuddered as she picked up her greasy cup.

"Lucia, you fool!" said Rinaldo. "That's the strongest tune there is."

"All right, all right. Stop going on at me. I'm sorry!" Lucia said angrily.

"So are the rest of us, unfortunately," sighed Uncle Lorenzo.

If only I could be like Giorgio, Tonino thought, as he got up from the table. I suppose what I should have to do is to find the words to the *Angel*. He went to school without seeing anything on the way, wondering how he could manage to do that, when the rest of his family had failed. He was realistic enough to know that he was simply not good enough at spells to make up the words in the ordinary way. It made him sigh heavily.

"Cheer up," said Paolo, as they went into school.

"I'm all right," Tonino said. He was surprised Paolo should think he was miserable. He was not miserable at all. He was wrapped in delightful dreams. Maybe I can do it by accident, he thought.

He sat in class composing strings of gibberish to the tune of the *Angel*, in hopes that some of it might be right. But that did not seem satisfactory, somehow. Then, in a lesson that was probably History—for he did not hear a word of it—it struck him, like a blinding light, what he had to do. He had to *find* the words, of course. The First Duke must have had them written down somewhere and lost the paper. Tonino was the boy whose mission it was to discover that lost paper. No nonsense about making up words, just straight detective work. And Tonino was positive that the book had been a clue. He must find a peeling blue house, and the paper with the words on would be somewhere near.

"Tonino," asked the teacher, for the fourth time, "where did Marco Polo journey to?"

Tonino did not hear the question, but he realized he was being asked something. "*The Angel of Caprona*," he said.

Nobody at school got much sense out of Tonino that day. He was full of the wonder of his discovery. It did not occur to him that Uncle Umberto had looked in every piece of writing in the University Library, and not found the words to the *Angel*. Tonino knew.

After school, he avoided Paolo and his cousins. As soon as they were safely headed for the Casa Montana, Tonino set off in the opposite direction, towards the docks and quays by the New Bridge.

An hour later, Rosa said to Paolo, "What's the matter with Benvenuto? Look at him."

Paolo leaned over the gallery rail beside her. Benvenuto, looking surprisingly small and piteous, was running backwards and forwards just inside the gate, mewing frantically. Every so often, as if he was too distracted to know what he was doing, he sat down, shot out a hind leg, and licked it madly. Then he leaped up and ran about again.

Paolo had never seen Benvenuto behave like this. He called out, "Benvenuto, what's the matter?"

Benvenuto swung around, crouching low on the ground, and stared urgently up at him. His eyes were like two yellow beacons of distress. He gave a string of mews, so penetrating and so demanding that Paolo felt his stomach turn uneasily.

"What is it, Benvenuto?" called Rosa.

Benvenuto's tail flapped in exasperation. He gave a great leap and vanished somewhere out of sight. Rosa and Paolo hung by their midriffs over the rail and craned after him. Benvenuto was now standing on the waterbutt, with his tail slashing. As soon as he knew they could see him, he stared fixedly at them again and uttered a truly appalling noise.

Wong wong wong wong-wong-wong!

Paolo and Rosa, without more ado, swung towards the stairs and clattered down them. Benvenuto's wails had already attracted all the other cats in the Casa. They were running across the yard and dropping from roofs before Paolo and Rosa were halfway down the stairs. They were forced to step carefully to the waterbutt among smooth furry bodies and staring, anxious green or yellow eyes.

"Mee-ow-ow!" Benvenuto said peremptorily, when they reached him.

He was thinner and browner than Paolo had

ever seen him. There was a new rent in his left ear, and his coat was in ragged spikes. He looked truly wretched. *"Mee-ow-ow!"* he reiterated, from a wide pink mouth.

"Something's wrong," Paolo said uneasily. "He's trying to say something." Guiltily, he wished he had kept his resolution to learn to understand Benvenuto. But when Tonino could do it so easily, it had never been worth the bother. Now here was Benvenuto with an urgent message—perhaps word from Chrestomanci—and he could not understand it. "We'd better get Tonino," he said.

Benvenuto's tail slashed again. *"Mee-ow-ow!"* he said, with tremendous force and meaning. Around Paolo and Rosa, the pink mouths of all the other cats opened too. *"MEE-OW-OW!"* It was deafening. Paolo stared helplessly.

It was Rosa who tumbled to their meaning. "Tonino!" she exclaimed. "They're saying *Tonino*! Paolo, where's Tonino?"

With a jolt of worry, Paolo realized he had not seen Tonino since breakfast. And as soon as he realized that, Rosa knew it too. And, such was the nature of the Casa Montana, that the alarm was given then and there. Aunt Gina shot out of the kitchen, holding a pair of kitchen tongs in one hand and a ladle in the other. Domenico and Aunt Maria came out of the Saloon, and Elizabeth appeared in the gallery outside the Music Room with the five little cousins. The door of the Scriptorium opened, filled with anxious faces.

Benvenuto gave a whisk of his tail and leaped for the gallery steps. He bounded up them, followed by the other cats; and Paolo and Rosa hurried up too, in a sort of shoal of leaping black and white bodies. Everyone converged on Antonio's rooms. People poured out of the Scriptorium, Elizabeth raced around the gallery, and Aunt Maria and Aunt Gina clambered up the steps by the kitchen quicker than either had ever climbed in her life. The Casa filled with the sound of hollow running feet.

The whole family jammed themselves after Rosa and Paolo into the room where Tonino was usually to be found reading. There was no Tonino, only the red book lying on the windowsill. It was no longer shiny. The pages were thick at the edges and the red cover was curling upwards, as if the book was wet.

Benvenuto, with his jagged brown coat up in a ridge along his back and his tail fluffed like a fox's brush, landed on the sill beside the book and rashly put his nose forward to sniff at it. He leaped back again, shaking his head, crouching, and growling like a dog. Smoke poured up from the book. People coughed and cats sneezed. The book curled and writhed on the sill, amid clouds of smoke, exactly as if it were on fire. But instead of turning black, it turned pale gray-blue where it smoked, and looked slimy. The room filled with a smell of rotting.

"Ugh!" said everybody.

Old Niccolo barged members of his family right and left to get near it. He stood over it and sang, in a strong tenor voice almost as good as Marco's, three strange words. He sang them twice before he had to break off coughing. "Sing!" he croaked, with tears pouring down his face. "All of you."

All the Montanas obediently broke into song, three long notes in unison. And again. And again. After that, quite a number of them had to cough, though the smoke was distinctly less. Old Niccolo recovered and waved his arms, like the conductor of a choir. All who could, sang once more. It took ten repetitions to halt the decay of the book. By that time, it was a shriveled triangle, about half the size it had been. Gingerly, Antonio leaned over and opened the window beyond it, to let out the last of the smoke.

"What was it?" he asked Old Niccolo. "Someone trying to suffocate us all?"

"I thought it came from Umberto," Elizabeth faltered. "I never would have—"

Old Niccolo shook his head. "This thing never came from Umberto. And I don't think it was meant to kill. Let's see what kind of spell it is." He snapped his fingers and held out a hand, rather like a surgeon performing an operation. Without needing to be told, Aunt Gina put her kitchen tongs into his hand. Carefully, gently, Old Niccolo used the tongs to open the cover of the book.

"A good pair of tongs ruined," Aunt Gina said.

"Ssh!" said Old Niccolo. The shriveled pages of the book had stuck into a gummy block. He snapped his fingers and held out his hand again. This time, Rinaldo put the pen he was carrying in it.

"And a good pen," he said, with a grimace at Aunt Gina.

With the pen as well as the tongs, Old Niccolo was able to pry the pages of the book apart without touching them and peel them over, one by one. Chins rested on both Paolo's shoulders as everyone craned to see, and there were chins on the shoulders of those with the chins. There was no sound but the sound of breathing.

On nearly every page, the printing had melted away, leaving a slimy, leathery surface quite unlike paper, with only a mark or so left in the middle. Old Niccolo looked closely at each mark and grunted. He grunted again at the first picture, which had faded like the print, but left a clearer mark. After that, though there was no print on any of the pages, the remaining mark was steadily clearer, up to the center of the book, when it began to become more faded again, until the mark was barely visible on the back page.

Old Niccolo laid down the pen and the tongs in terrible silence. "Right through," he said at length. People shifted and someone coughed, but nobody said anything. "I do not know," said Old Niccolo, "the substance this object is made of, but I know a calling-charm when I see one. Tonino must have been like one hypnotized, if he had read all this."

"He was a bit strange at breakfast," Paolo whispered.

"I am sure he was," said his grandfather. He looked reflectively at the shriveled stump of the book and then around at the crowded faces of his family. "Now who," he asked softly, "would want to set a strong calling-charm on Tonino Montana? Who would be mean enough to pick on a child? Who would—?" He turned suddenly on Benvenuto, crouched beside the book, and Benvenuto cowered right down, quivering, with his ragged ears flat against his flat head. "Where were you last night, Benvenuto?" he asked, more softly still.

No one understood the reply Benvenuto gave as he cowered, but everyone knew the answer. It was in Antonio and Elizabeth's harrowed faces, in the set of Rinaldo's chin, in Aunt Francesca's narrowed eyes, narrowed almost out of existence, and in the way Aunt Maria looked at Uncle Lorenzo; but most of all, it was in the way Benvenuto threw himself down on his side, with his back to the room, the picture of a cat in despair.

Old Niccolo looked up. "Now isn't that odd?" he said gently. "Benvenuto spent last night chasing a white she-cat—over the roofs of the Casa Petrocchi." He paused to let that sink in. "So Benvenuto," he said, "who knows a bad spell when he sees one, was not around to warn Tonino."

"But *why*?" Elizabeth asked despairingly.

Old Niccolo went, if possible, quieter still. "I

can only conclude, my dear, that the Petrocchis are being paid by Florence, Siena, or Pisa."

There was another silence, thick and meaningful. Antonio broke it. "Well," he said, in such a subdued, grim way that Paolo stared at him. "Well? Are we going?"

"Of course," said Old Niccolo. "Domenico, fetch me my small black spell-book."

Everyone left the room, so suddenly, quietly and purposefully that Paolo was left behind, not clear what was going on. He turned uncertainly to go to the door, and realized that Rosa had been left behind too. She was sitting on Tonino's bed, with one hand to her head, white as Tonino's sheets.

"Paolo," she said, "tell Claudia I'll have the baby, if she wants to go. I'll have all the little ones."

She looked up at Paolo as she said it, and she looked so strange that Paolo was suddenly frightened. He ran gladly out into the gallery. The family was gathering, still quiet and grim, in the yard. Paolo ran down there and gave his message. Protesting little ones were pushed up the steps to Rosa, but Paolo did not help. He found Elizabeth and Lucia and pushed close to them. Elizabeth put an arm around him and an arm around Lucia.

"Keep close to me, loves," she said. "I'll keep you safe." Paolo looked across her at Lucia and saw that Lucia was not frightened at all. She was excited. She winked at him. Paolo winked back and felt better.

A minute later, Old Niccolo took his place at the head of the family and they all hurried to the gate. Paolo had just forced his way through, jostling his mother on one side and Domenico on the other, when a carriage drew up in the road, and Uncle Umberto scrambled out of it. He came up to Old Niccolo in that grim, quiet way everyone seemed to be moving.

"Who is kidnapped? Bernardo? Domenico?"

"Tonino," replied Old Niccolo. "A book, with the University arms on the wrapping."

Uncle Umberto answered, "Luigi Petrocchi is also a member of the University."

"I bear that in mind," said Old Niccolo.

"I shall come with you to the Casa Petrocchi," said Uncle Umberto. He waved at the cab-driver to tell him to go. The man was only too ready to. He nearly pulled his horses over on their sides, trying to turn them too quickly. The sight of the entire Casa Montana grimly streaming into the street seemed altogether too much for him.

That pleased Paolo. He looked back and forth as they swung down the Via Magica, and pride grew in him. There were such a lot of them. And they were so single-minded. The same intent look was in every face. And though children pattered and young men strode, though the ladies clattered on the cobbles in elegant shoes, though Old Niccolo's steps were short and bustling, and Antonio, because he could not wait to come at the Petrocchis, walked with long lunging steps, the common purpose gave the whole family a common rhythm. Paolo could almost believe they were marching in step.

The concourse crowded down the Via Sant' Angelo and swept around the corner into the Corso, with the Cathedral at their backs. People out shopping hastily gave them room. But Old Niccolo was too angry to use the pavement like a mere pedestrian. He led the family into the middle of the road and they marched there like a vengeful army, forcing cars and carriages to draw in to the curbs, with Old Niccolo stepping proudly at their head. It was hard to believe that a fat old man with a baby's face could look so warlike.

The Corso bends slightly beyond the Archbishop's Palace. Then it runs straight again by the shops, past the columns of the Art Gallery on one side and the great gilded doors of the Arsenal on the other. They swung around that bend. There, approaching from the opposite direction, was another similar crowd, also walking in the road. The Petrocchis were on the march too.

"Extraordinary!" muttered Uncle Umberto.

"Perfect!" spat Old Niccolo.

The two families advanced on one another. There was utter silence now, except for the cloppering of feet. Every ordinary citizen, as soon as they saw the entire Casa Montana advancing on the entire Casa Petrocchi, made haste to get off the street. People knocked on the doors of perfect strangers and were let in without question. The manager of Grossi's, the biggest shop in Caprona, threw open his plateglass doors and sent his assistants out to fetch in everyone nearby. After which he clapped the doors shut and locked a steel grille down in front of them. From between the bars, white faces stared out at the oncoming spell-makers. And a troop of Reservists, newly called up and sloppily marching in crumpled new uniforms, were horrified to find themselves caught between the two parties. They broke and ran, as one crumpled Reservist, and sought frantic shelter in the Arsenal. The great gilt doors clanged shut on them just as Old Niccolo halted, face-to-face with Guido Petrocchi.

"Well?" said Old Niccolo, his baby eyes glaring.

"Well?" retorted Guido, his red beard jutting.

"Was it," asked Old Niccolo, "Florence or Pisa that paid you to kidnap my grandson Tonino?"

Guido Petrocchi gave a bark of contemptuous laughter. "You mean," he said, "was it Pisa or Siena who paid you to kidnap my daughter Angelica?"

"Do you imagine," said Old Niccolo, "that saying that makes it any less obvious that you are a baby-snatcher?"

"Do you," asked Guido, "accuse me of lying?"

"*Yes!*" roared the Casa Montana. *"Liar!"*

"And the same to you!" howled the Casa Petrocchi, crowding up behind Guido, lean and ferocious, many of them red-haired. *"Filthy liars!"*

The fighting began while they were still shouting. There was no knowing who started it. The roars on either side were mixed with singing and muttering. Scrips fluttered in many hands. And the air was suddenly full of flying eggs. Paolo received one, a very greasy fried egg, right across the mouth, and it made him so angry that he began to shout egg-spells too, at the top of his voice. Eggs splattered down, fried eggs, poached eggs, scrambled eggs, new-laid eggs, and eggs so horribly bad that they were like bombs when they burst. Everyone slithered on the eggy cobbles. Egg streamed off the ends of people's hair and spattered everyone's clothes.

Then somebody varied it with a bad tomato or so. Immediately, all manner of unpleasant things were flying about the Corso: cold spaghetti and cowpats—though these may have been Rinaldo's idea in the first place, they were very quickly coming from both sides—and cabbages; squirts of oil and showers of ice; dead rats and chicken livers. It was no wonder that the ordinary people kept out of the way. Egg and tomato ran down the grilles over Grossi's windows and splashed the white columns of the Art Gallery. There were loud clangs as rotten cabbages hit the brass doors of the Arsenal.

This was the first, disorganized phase of the battle, with everyone venting his fury separately. But, by the time everyone was filthy and sticky, their fury took shape a little. Both sides began on a more organized chant. It grew, and became two strong rhythmic choruses.

The result was that the objects flying about the Corso rose up into the air and began to rain down as much more harmful things. Paolo looked up to see a cloud of transparent, glittering, frozen-looking pieces tumbling out of the sky at him. He thought it was snow at first, until a piece hit his arm and cut it.

"Vicious beasts!" Lucia screamed beside him. "It's broken glass!"

Before the main body of the glass came down, Old Niccolo's penetrating tenor voice soared above the yells and the chanting. "Testudo!"

Antonio's full bass backed him up: "Testudo!" and so did Uncle Lorenzo's baritone. Feet tramped. Paolo knew this one. He bowed over, tramping regularly, and kept up the charm with them. The whole family did it. *Tramp, tramp, tramp.* "Testudo, testudo, testudo!" Over their bent heads, the glass splinters bounced and showered harmlessly off an invisible barrier. "Testudo." From the middle of the bowed backs, Elizabeth's voice rang up sweetly in yet another spell. She was joined by Aunt Anna, Aunt Maria and Corinna. It was like a soprano descant over a rhythmic tramping chorus.

Paolo knew without being told that he must keep up the shield-charm while Elizabeth worked her spell. So did everyone else. It was extraordinary, exciting, amazing, he thought. Each Montana picked up the slightest hint and acted on it as if it were orders. He risked glancing up and saw that the descant spell was working. Every glass splinter, as it hit the unseen shield Paolo was helping to make, turned into an angry hornet and buzzed back at the Petrocchis. But the Petrocchis simply turned them into glass splinters again and hurled them back. At the same time, Paolo could tell from the rhythm of their singing that some of them were working to destroy the shield charm. Paolo sang and tramped harder than ever.

Meanwhile, Rinaldo's voice and his father's were singing gently, deeply, at work on something yet again. More of the ladies joined in the hornet-song so that the Petrocchis would not guess. And all the while, the *tramp*, *tramp* of the shield charm was kept up by everyone else. It could have been the grandest chorus in the grandest opera ever, except that it all had a different purpose. The purpose came with a perfect roar of voices. The Petrocchis threw up their arms and staggered. The cobbles beneath them heaved and the solid Corso began to give way into a pit. Their instant reply was another huge sung chord, with discords innumerable. And the Montanas suddenly found themselves inside a wall of flame.

There was total confusion. Paolo staggered for safety, with his hair singed, over cobbles that quaked and heaved under his shoes. "Voltava!" he sang frantically. "Voltava!" Behind him, the flames hissed. Clouds of steam blotted out even the tall Art

Gallery as the river answered the charm and came swirling up the Corso. Water was knee-deep around Paolo, up to his waist, and still rising. There was too much water. Someone had sung out of tune, and Paolo rather thought it was him. He saw his cousin Lena almost up to her chin in water and grabbed her. Towing Lena, he staggered through the current, over the heaving road, trying to make for the Arsenal steps.

Someone must have had the sense to work a cancel-spell. Everything suddenly cleared, steam, water and smoke together. Paolo found himself on the steps of the Art Gallery, not by the Arsenal at all. Behind him, the Corso was a mass of loose cobbles, shiny with mud and littered with cowpats, tomatoes and fried eggs. There could hardly have been more mess if Caprona had been invaded by the armies of Florence, Pisa and Siena.

Paolo felt he had had enough. Lena was crying. She was too young. She should have been left with Rosa. He could see his mother picking Lucia out of the mud, and Rinaldo helping Aunt Gina up.

"Let's go home, Paolo," whimpered Lena.

But the battle was not really finished. Montanas and Petrocchis were up and down the Corso in little angry, muddy groups, shouting abuse at one another.

"I'll give you broken glass!"

"You started it!"

"You lying Petrocchi swine! Kidnapper!"

"Swine yourself! Spell-bungler! Traitor!"

Aunt Gina and Rinaldo slithered over to what looked like a muddy boulder in the street and heaved at it. The vast bulk of Aunt Francesca arose, covered with mud and angrier than Paolo had ever seen her.

"You filthy Petrocchis! I demand single combat!" she screamed. Her voice scraped like a great saw-blade and filled the Corso.

7

❧❧

AUNT FRANCESCA'S CHALLENGE seemed to rally both sides. A female Petrocchi voice screamed, "We agree!" and all the muddy groups hastened towards the middle of the Corso again.

Paolo reached his family to hear Old Niccolo saying, "Don't be a fool, Francesca!" He looked more like a muddy goblin than the head of a famous family. He was almost too breathless to speak.

"They have insulted us and fought us!" said Aunt Francesca. "They deserve to be disgraced and drummed out of Caprona. And I shall do it! I'm more than a match for a Petrocchi!" She looked it, vast and muddy as she was, with her huge black dress in tatters and her gray hair half undone and streaming over one shoulder.

But the other Montanas knew Aunt Francesca was an old woman. There was a chorus of protest. Uncle Lorenzo and Rinaldo both offered to take on the Petrocchi champion in her place.

"No," said Old Niccolo. "Rinaldo, you were wounded—"

He was interrupted by catcalls from the Petrocchis. "Cowards! We want single combat!"

Old Niccolo's muddy face screwed up with anger. "Very well, they shall have their single combat," he said. "Antonio, I appoint you. Step forward."

Paolo felt a gush of pride. So his father was, as he had always thought, the best spell-maker in the Casa Montana. But the pride became mixed with alarm, when Paolo saw the way his mother clutched Antonio's arm, and the worried, reluctant look on his father's mud-streaked face.

"Go on!" Old Niccolo said crossly.

Slowly, Antonio advanced into the space between the two families, stumbling a little among the loose cobbles. "I'm ready," he called to the Petrocchis. "Who's your champion?"

It was clear that there was some indecision among the Petrocchis. A dismayed voice said, "It's Antonio!" This was followed by a babble of talk. From the turning of heads and the uncertain heaving about, Paolo thought they were looking for a Petrocchi who was unaccountably missing. But the fuss died away, and Guido Petrocchi himself stepped forward. Paolo could see several Petrocchis looking as alarmed as Elizabeth.

"I'm ready too," said Guido, baring his teeth angrily. Since his face was plastered with mud, it made him look quite savage. He was also large and sturdy. He made Antonio look small, gentle and fragile. "And I demand an unlimited contest!"

snarled Guido. He seemed even angrier than Old Niccolo.

"Very well," Antonio said. There could have been the least shake in his voice. "You're aware that means a fight to the finish, are you?"

"Suits me perfectly," said Guido. He was like a giant saying "Fee-fi-fo-fum." Paolo was suddenly very frightened.

It was at this moment that the Ducal Police arrived. They had come in, quietly and cunningly, riding bicycles along the pavements. No one noticed them until the Chief of Police and his lieutenant were standing beside the two champions.

"Guido Petrocchi and Antonio Montana," said the lieutenant, "I arrest you——"

Both champions jumped, and turned to find blue braided uniforms on either side of them.

"Oh go away," said Old Niccolo, hastening forward. "What do you have to interfere for?"

"Yes, go away," said Guido. "We're busy."

The lieutenant flinched at Guido's face, but the Chief of Police was a bold and dashing man with a handsome moustache, and he had his reputation to keep up as a bold and dashing man. He bowed to Old Niccolo. "These two are under arrest," he said. "The rest of you I order to sink your differences and remember there is about to be a war."

"We're at war already," said Old Niccolo. "Go away."

"I regret," said the Chief of Police, "that that is impossible."

"Then don't say you weren't warned," said Guido.

There was a short burst of song from the adults of both families. Paolo wished he knew that spell. It sounded useful. As soon as it was over, Rinaldo and a swarthy young Petrocchi came over to the two policemen and towed them away backwards. They were as stiff as the tailor's dummies in the barred windows of Grossi's. Rinaldo and the other young man laid them against the steps of the Art Gallery and returned each to his family, without looking at one another. As for the rest of the Ducal Police, they seemed to have vanished, bicycles and all.

"Ready now?" said Guido.

"Ready," said Antonio.

And the single combat commenced.

Looking back on it afterwards, Paolo realized that it could not have lasted more than three minutes, though it seemed endless at the time. For, in that time, the strength, skill and speed of both champions was tried to the utmost. The first, and probably the longest, part was when the two were testing one another for an opening, and comparatively little seemed to happen. Both stood, leaning slightly forward, muttering, humming, occasionally flicking a hand. Paolo stared at his father's strained face and wondered just what was going on. Then, momentarily, Guido was a man-shaped red-and-white check duster. Someone gasped. But Antonio almost simultaneously became a cardboard man covered with green triangles. Then both flicked back to themselves again.

The speed of it astounded Paolo. A spell had not only been cast on both sides, but also a counter-spell, and a spell counter to that, all in the time it took someone to gasp. Both combatants were panting and looking warily at each other. It was clear they were very evenly matched.

Again there was a space when nothing seemed to happen, except a sort of flickering on both sides. Then suddenly Antonio struck, and struck so hard that it was plain he had all the time been building a strong spell, beneath the flicker of trivial spells designed to keep Guido occupied. Guido gave a shout and dissolved into dust, which swept away backwards in a spiral. But, somehow, as he dissolved, he threw *his* strong spell at Antonio. Antonio broke into a thousand little pieces, like a spilled jigsaw puzzle.

For an ageless time, the swirl of dust and the pile of broken Antonio hung in midair. Both were struggling to stay together and not to patter down on the uprooted cobbles of the Corso. In fact, they were still struggling to make spells too. When, at last, Antonio staggered forward in one piece, holding some kind of red fruit in his right hand, he had barely time to dodge. Guido was a leopard in mid-spring.

Elizabeth screamed.

Antonio threw himself to one side, heaved a breath and sang. *"Oliphans!"* His usually silky voice was rough and ragged, but he hit the right notes. A gigantic elephant, with tusks longer than Paolo was tall, cut off the low sun and shook the Corso as it advanced, ears spread, to trample the attacking leopard. It was hard to believe the great beast was indeed worried, thin Antonio Montana.

For a shadow of a second, the leopard was Guido Petrocchi, very white in the face and luridly red in the beard, gabbling a frantic song. *"Hickory-dickory-muggery mus!"* And he must have hit the right notes too. He seemed to vanish.

The Montanas were raising a cheer at Guido's cowardice, when the elephant panicked. Paolo had the merest glimpse of a little tiny mouse scampering aggressively at the great front feet of the elephant, before he was running for his life. The shrill trumpeting of Antonio seemed to tear his ears apart. Behind him, Paolo knew that the elephant was stark, staring mad, trampling this way and that among terrified Montanas. Lucia ran past him, carrying Lena clutched backwards against her front. Paolo grabbed little Bernardo by one arm and ran with him, wincing at the horrible brazen, braying squeal from his father.

Elephants are afraid of mice, horribly afraid. And there are very few people who can shift shape without taking the nature of the shape they shift to. It seemed that Guido Petrocchi had not only won, but got most of the Montanas trampled to death into the bargain.

But when Paolo next looked, Elizabeth was standing in the elephant's path, staring up at its wild little eyes. "Antonio!" she shouted. "*Antonio*, control yourself!" She looked so tiny and the elephant was coming so fast that Paolo shut his eyes.

He opened them in time to see the elephant in the act of swinging his mother up onto its back. Tears of relief so clouded Paolo's eyes that he almost failed to see Guido's next attack. He was simply aware of a shattering noise, a horrible smell, and a sort of moving tower. He saw the elephant swing around, and Elizabeth crouch down on its back. It was now being confronted by a vast iron machine, even larger than itself, throbbing with mechanical power and filling the Corso with nasty blue smoke. This thing ground slowly towards Antonio on huge moving tracks. As it came, a gun in its front swung down to aim between the elephant's eyes.

On the spur of the moment, Antonio became another machine. He was in such a hurry, and he knew so little about machines, that it was a very bizarre machine indeed. It was pale duck-egg blue, with enormous rubber wheels. In fact, it was probably made of rubber all through, because the bullet from Guido's machine bounced off it and crashed into the steps of the Arsenal. Most people threw themselves flat.

"Mother's *inside* that thing!" Lucia screamed to Paolo, above the noise.

Paolo realized she must be. Antonio had had no time to put Elizabeth down. And now he was barging recklessly at Guido, *bang*-bounce, *bang*-bounce. It must have been horrible for Elizabeth. Luckily, it only lasted a second. Elizabeth and Antonio suddenly appeared in their own shapes, almost under the mighty tracks of the Guido-machine. Elizabeth ran—Paolo had not known she could run so fast—like the wind towards the Arsenal. And it may have been Petrocchi viciousness, or perhaps simple confusion, but the great Guido-tank swung its gun down to point at Elizabeth.

Antonio called Guido a very bad name, and threw the tomato he still had in his hand. The red fruit hit, and splashed, and ran down the iron side. Paolo was just wondering what use that was, when the tank was not there any more. Nor was Guido. In his place was a giant tomato. It was about the size of a pumpkin. And it simply sat in the road and did not move.

That was the winning stroke. Paolo could tell it was from the look on Antonio's face as he walked up to the tomato. Disgusted and weary, Antonio bent down to pick up the tomato. There were scattered groans from the Petrocchis, and cheers, not quite certain and even more scattered, from the Montanas.

Then somebody cast yet another spell.

This time, it was a thick wet fog. No doubt, at the beginning, it would not have seemed so terrible, but, after all the rest, just when the fight was over, Paolo felt it was the last straw. All he could see, in front of his eyes, was thick whiteness. After he had taken a breath or so, he was coughing. He could hear coughing all around, and far off into the distance, which was the only thing which showed him he was not entirely alone. He turned his head from trying to see who else was coughing, and found he could not see Lucia. Nor could he find Bernardo, and he knew he had been holding Bernardo's arm a second before. As soon as he realized that, he found he had lost his sense of direction too. He was all alone, coughing and shivering, in cold white emptiness.

"I am not going to lose my head," Paolo told himself sternly. "My father didn't, and so I shan't. I shall find somewhere to shelter until this beastly spell is over. Then I shall go home. I don't care if Tonino is still missing—" He stopped then, because a thought came to him, like an astonishing discovery. "We're never going to find Tonino this way, anyway," he said. And he knew it was true.

With his hands stretched out in front of him and his eyes spread very wide in hopes of seeing something—which was unlikely, since they were streaming from the fog, and so was his nose— Paolo coughed and sniffed and shuffled his way forward until his toes came up against stone. Paolo looked down, but he could not see what it was. He tried lifting one foot, with his toes scraping against the obstruction. And, after a few inches, the obstruction stopped and his foot shot forward. It was a ledge, then. Probably the curb. He had been near the edge of the road when he ran away from the elephant. He got both feet on the curb and shuffled forward six inches—then he fell upstairs over what seemed to be a body.

It gave Paolo such a shock that he dared not move at first. But he soon realized that the body beneath him was shivering, as he was, and trying to cough and mutter at the same time. "Holy Mary—" Paolo heard, in a hoarse blurred voice. Very puzzled, Paolo put out a careful hand and felt the body. His fingers met cold metal buttons, uniform braid, and, a little above that, a warm face—which gave a croak as Paolo's cold hand met its mouth—and a large furry moustache beneath the nose.

Angel of Caprona! Paolo thought. It's the Chief of Police!

Paolo got himself to his knees on what must be the steps of the Art Gallery. There was no one around he could ask, but it did not seem fair to leave someone lying helpless in the fog. It was bad enough if you could move. So hoping he was doing the right thing, Paolo knelt and sang, very softly, the most general cancel-spell he could think of. It had no effect on the fog—that was evidently very strong magic—but he heard the Chief of Police roll over on his side and groan. Boots scraped as he tested his legs. *"Mamma mia!"* Paolo heard him moan.

He sounded as if he wanted to be alone. Paolo left him and crawled his way up the Gallery steps. He had no idea he had reached the top, until he hit his elbow on a pillar and drove his head into Lucia's stomach at the same moment. Both of them said some extremely unpleasant things.

"When you've quite finished swearing," Lucia said at length, "you can get between these pillars with me and keep me warm." She coughed and shivered. "Isn't this awful? Who did it?" She coughed again. The fog had made her hoarse.

"It wasn't us," said Paolo. "We'd have known. Ow, my elbow!" He took hold of her for a guide and wedged himself down beside her. He felt better like that.

"The pigs," said Lucia. "I call this a mean trick. It's funny—you spend your life being told what pigs they are, and thinking they *can't* be, really. Then you meet them, and they're worse than you were told. Was it you singing just now?"

"I fell over the Chief of Police on the steps," said Paolo.

Lucia laughed. "I fell over the other one. I sang a cancel-spell too. He was lying on all the corners of the stairs and it must have bruised him all over when I fell on him."

"It's bad enough when you can move," Paolo agreed. "Like being blind."

"Horrible," said Lucia. "That blind beggar in the Via Sant' Angelo—I shall give him some money tomorrow."

"The one with white eyes?" said Paolo. "Yes, so shall I. And I never want to see another spell."

"To tell you the truth," said Lucia, "I was wishing I dared burn the Library and the Scriptorium down. It came to me like a blinding flash—just before I fell over that policeman—that no amount of spells are going to work on those beastly kidnappers."

"That's just what I thought!" exclaimed Paolo.

"I know the only way to find Tonino—"

"Hang on," said Lucia. "I think the fog's getting thinner."

She was right. When Paolo leaned forward, he could see two dark lumps below, where the Chief of Police and his lieutenant were sitting on the steps with their heads in their hands. He could see quite a stretch of the Corso beyond them—cobbles which were dark and wet-looking, but, to his surprise, neither muddy nor out of place.

"Someone's put it all back!" said Lucia.

The fog thinned further. They could see the glimmering doors of the Arsenal now, and the entire foggy width of the Corso, with every cobblestone back where it should be. Somewhere about the middle of it, Antonio and Guido Petrocchi were standing facing one another.

"Oh, they're not going to begin again, are they?" wailed Paolo.

But, almost at once, Antonio and Guido swung round and walked away from one another.

"Thank goodness!" said Lucia. She and Paolo turned to one another, smiling with relief.

Except that it was not Lucia. Paolo found himself staring into a white pointed face, and eyes darker, larger and shrewder than Lucia's. Surrounding the face were draggled dark red curls. The smile died from the face and horror replaced it as Paolo stared. He felt his own face behaving the same way. He had been huddling up against a Petrocchi! He knew which one, too. It was the elder of the two who had been at the Palace. Renata, that was her name. And she knew him too.

"You're that blue-eyed Montana boy!" she exclaimed. She made it sound quite disgusting.

Both of them got up. Renata backed into the pillars, as if she was trying to get inside the stone, and Paolo backed away along the steps.

"I thought you were my sister Lucia," he said.

"I thought you were my cousin Claudio," Renata retorted.

Somehow, they both made it sound as if it was the other one's fault.

"It wasn't my fault!" Paolo said angrily. "Blame the person who made the fog, not me. There's an enemy enchanter."

"I know. Chrestomanci said," said Renata.

Paolo felt he hated Chrestomanci. He had no business to go and say the same things to the Petrocchis as he said to the Montanas. But he hated the enemy enchanter even more. He had been responsible for the most embarrassing thing which had ever happened to Paolo. Muttering with shame, Paolo turned to run away.

"No, stop! *Wait!*" Renata said. She said it so commandingly that Paolo stopped without thinking, and gave Renata time to snatch hold of his arm. Instead of pulling away, Paolo stood quite still and attempted to behave with the dignity becoming to a Montana. He looked at his arm, and at Renata's hand holding it, as if both had become one composite slimy toad. But Renata hung on. "Look all you like," she said. "I don't care. I'm not letting go until you tell me what your family has done with Angelica."

"Nothing," Paolo said contemptuously. "We wouldn't touch one of you with a barge-pole. What have you lot done with Tonino?"

An odd little frown wrinkled Renata's white forehead. "Is that your brother? Is he really missing?"

"He was sent a book with a calling-spell in it," said Paolo.

"A book," said Renata slowly, "got Angelica too. We only realized when it shriveled away."

She let go of Paolo's arm. They stared at one another in the blowing remains of the fog.

"It must be the enemy enchanter," said Paolo.

"Trying to take our minds off the war," said Renata. "Tell your family, won't you?"

"If you tell yours," said Paolo.

"Of course I will. What do you take me for?" said Renata.

In spite of everything, Paolo found himself laughing. "I think you're a Petrocchi!" he said.

But when Renata began to laugh too, Paolo realized it was too much. He turned to run away, and found himself facing the Chief of Police. The Chief of Police had evidently recovered his dignity. "Now then, you children. Move along," he said.

Renata fled, without more ado, red in the face with the shame of being caught talking to a Montana. Paolo hung on. It seemed to him that he ought to report that Tonino was missing.

"I said move along!" repeated the Chief of Police, and he pulled down his jacket with a most threatening jerk.

Paolo's nerve broke. After all, an ordinary policeman was not going to be much help against an enchanter. He ran.

He ran all the way to the Casa Montana. The fog and the wetness did not extend beyond the Corso. As soon as he turned into a side road, Paolo found himself in the bleak shadows and low red sun of a winter evening. It was like being shot back into another world—a world where things happened as they should, where one's father did not turn into a mad elephant, where, above all, one's sister did not turn out to be a Petrocchi. Paolo's face fired with shame as he ran. Of all the awful things to happen!

The Casa Montana came in sight, with the familiar Angel safely over the gate. Paolo shot in under it, and ran into his father. Antonio was standing under the archway, panting as if he too had run all the way home.

"Who—? Oh, Paolo," said Antonio. "Stay where you are."

"Why?" asked Paolo. He wanted to get in, where it was safe, and perhaps eat a large lump of bread and honey. He was surprised his father did not feel the same. Antonio looked tired out, and his clothes were torn and muddy rags. The arm he stretched out to keep Paolo in the gateway was half bare and covered with scratches. Paolo was going to protest, when he saw that something was indeed wrong. Most of the cats were in the gateway too, crouching around with their ears flattened. Benvenuto was patrolling the entrance to the yard, like a lean brown ferret. Paolo could hear him growling.

Antonio's scratched hand took Paolo by the shoulder and pulled him forward so that he could see into the yard. "Look."

Paolo found himself blinking at foot-high letters, which seemed to hang in the air in the middle of the yard. In the fading light, they were glowing an unpleasant, sick yellow.

STOP ALL SPELLS
OR YOUR CHILD SUFFERS.
CASA PETROCCHI

The name was in sicker and brighter letters. They were meant to make no mistake about who had sent the message.

After what Renata had said, Paolo knew it was wrong. "It *wasn't* the Petrocchis," he said. "It's that enchanter Chrestomanci told us about."

"Yes, to be sure," said Antonio.

Paolo looked up at him and saw that his father did not believe him—probably had not even attended to him. "But it's true!" he said. "He wants us to stop making war-spells."

Antonio sighed, and drew himself together to

explain to Paolo. "Paolo," he said, "nobody but Chrestomanci believes in this enchanter. In magic, as in everything else, the simplest explanation is always best. In other words, why invent an unknown enchanter, when you have a known enemy with known reasons for hating you? Why shouldn't it be the Petrocchis?"

Paolo wanted to protest, but he was still too embarrassed about Renata to say that Angelica Petrocchi was missing too. He was struggling to find something that he *could* say, which might convince his father, when a square of light sprang up in the gallery as a door there opened.

"Rosa!" shouted Antonio. His voice cracked with anxiety.

The shape of Rosa appeared in the light, carrying Cousin Claudia's baby. The light itself was so orange and so right, beside the sick glow of the letters floating in the yard, that Paolo was flooded with relief. Behind Rosa, there was Marco, carrying another little one.

"Praised be!" said Antonio. He shouted, "Are you all right, Rosa? How did those words come here?"

"We don't know," Rosa called back. "They just appeared. We've been trying to get rid of them, but we can't."

Marco leaned over the rails and called, "It's not true, Antonio. The Petrocchis wouldn't do a thing like this."

Antonio called back, "Don't go around saying that, Marco." He said it so forbiddingly that Paolo knew nothing he said was going to be believed. If he had had a chance of convincing Antonio, he had now lost it.

8

❧✦❧

WHEN TONINO CAME TO HIS SENSES—at, incidentally, the precise moment when the enchanted book began to shrivel away—he had, at first, a nightmare feeling that he was shut in a cardboard box. He rolled his head sideways on his arms. He seemed to be lying on his face on a hard but faintly furry floor. In the far distance, he could blurrily see someone else, leaning up against a wall like a doll, but he felt too queer to be very interested in that. He rolled his head around the other way and saw the panels of a wall quite near. That told him he was in a fairly long room. He rolled his head to stare down at the furry floor. It was patterned, in a pattern too big for his eyes to grasp, and he supposed it was a carpet of some kind. He shut his blurry eyes and tried to think what had happened.

He remembered going down near the New Bridge. He had been full of excitement. He had read a book which he thought was telling him how to save Caprona. He knew he had to find an alleyway with a peeling blue house at the end of it. It seemed a bit silly now. Tonino knew things never happened the way they did in books. Even then, he had been rather amazed to find that there *was* an alleyway with, really and truly, a peeling blue house at the end of it. And, to his huge excitement, there was a scrap of paper fluttering down at his feet. The book was coming true. Tonino had bent down and picked up the paper.

And, after that, he had known nothing till this moment.

That was really true. Tonino took himself through what had happened several times, but each time his memories stopped in exactly the same place—with himself picking up the scrap of paper. After that, it was all a vague sense of nightmare. By this time, he was fairly sure he had been the victim of a spell. He began to feel ashamed of himself. So he sat up.

He saw at once why he had seemed to dream he was shut up in a cardboard box. The room he was in was long and low, almost exactly the shape of a shoebox. The walls and ceiling were painted cream-color—a sort of whitish cardboard-color, in fact—but they seemed to be wood, because there were carvings picked out in gold paint on them. There was a crystal chandelier hanging from the ceiling, although the light came from four long windows in one of the longer walls; a rich carpet on the floor, and a very elegant dining table and chairs by the wall opposite the windows. There were two silver candlesticks on the table. Altogether the place was extremely elegant—and wrong, somehow.

Tonino sat trying to puzzle out just what was wrong. The room was awfully bare. But that was not quite it. There was something strange about the daylight coming through the four long windows, as if the sun was somehow further away than it should be. But that was not quite it either. Tonino's eyes went to the four bands of too-faded sunlight falling through the windows onto the carpet, and then traveled along the carpet. At the end, he came to the person leaning up against the wall. It was Angelica Petrocchi, who had been at the Palace. Her eyes were closed beneath her bulge of forehead, and she looked ill. So she had been caught too.

Tonino looked back at the carpet. That was an odd thing. It was not really a carpet. It had been painted on the slightly furry substance of the floor. Tonino could see the brush strokes in the sprawling pattern. And the reason he had thought the pattern was too big was because it *was* too big. It was the wrong size for the rest of the room.

More puzzled than ever, Tonino struggled to his feet. He felt a little wobbly, so he put a hand on the gilded panels of the wall to steady himself. That felt furry too, except where it was gold. The gold was flat, but not quite hard, like—Tonino thought, but no other likeness came to him—like paint. He ran his hand over the apparently carved panel. It was a total cheat. It was not even wood, and the carving was painted on, in lines of brown, blue and gold. Whoever had caught him was trying to seem richer than they were, but doing it very badly.

There were movements at the other end of the room. Angelica Petrocchi was wavering to her feet, and she too was running her hand over the painted carving. Very anxiously and cautiously, she turned and looked at Tonino.

"Will you let me go now, please?" she said.

There was a little wobble in her voice that showed Tonino she was very frightened. So was he, now he came to think of it. "I can't let you go," he said. "I didn't catch you. Neither of us can go. There isn't a door."

That was the wrong thing he had been trying not to notice. And as soon as he said it, he wished he had kept his mouth shut. Angelica screamed. And the sound sent Tonino into a panic too. There was no door! He was shut into a cardboard box with a Petrocchi child!

Tonino may have screamed as well—he was not sure. When he caught up with himself, he had one of the elegant chairs in his hands and was battering at the nearest window with it. That was more frightening than ever. The glass did not break. It was made of some slightly rubbery stuff, and the chair bounced off. Beyond him, the Petrocchi girl was banging away at another window with one of the silver candlesticks, screaming all the time.

Outside the window, Tonino could clearly see the smug spire-shape of a little cypress tree, lit by afternoon sun. So they were in one of those rich villas near the Palace, were they? Just let him get *out*! He lifted the chair and smashed it against the window with all his strength.

He made no impression on the window, but the chair came to pieces. Two ill-glued legs fell off it, and the rest crumpled to splintery matchwood. Tonino thought it was disgustingly badly made. He threw it to the painted carpet and fetched another chair. This time, for variety, he attacked the wall beside the window. Pieces of that chair came away and flew about, and Tonino was left with its painted seat—painted to look like embroidery, just as the floor was painted to look like carpet. He drove it into the wall, again and again. It made large brown dents. Better still, the wall shook and leaped about, sounding muffled and hollow, as if it were made of something very cheap. Tonino beat at it and yelled. Angelica beat at the wall and the window impartially with her candlestick, and went on screaming.

They were stopped by a terrible hammering. Someone seemed to be dealing hundreds of thunderous blows on the ceiling. The room was like the inside of a drum. It was too loud to bear. The Petrocchi girl dropped her candlestick and rolled on the floor. Tonino found himself crouching down, with his hands to his ears, looking up at the chandelier jiggling overhead. He thought his head would burst.

The pounding stopped. There was no sound except a whimper, which Tonino rather thought came from him.

A great huge voice spoke through the ceiling. "That's better. Now be quiet, or you won't get any food. And if you try any more tricks, you'll be punished. Understand?"

Tonino and Angelica both sat up. *"Let us out!"* they screamed.

There was no answer, only a distant shuffling. The owner of the huge voice seemed to be going away.

"A mean trick with an amplifying spell," Angelica said. She picked up the candlestick and looked at it with disgust. The branched part was bent at right angles to the base. "What *is* this place?" she said. "Everything's so shoddy."

They got up and went to the windows again, in hopes of a clue. Several little spire-shaped trees were clearly to be seen, just outside, and a sort of terrace beyond that. But, peer as they might, all they could make out further off was queer blue distance, with one or two square-shaped mountains catching the sun on a glossy corner or so. There seemed to be no sky.

"It's a spell," said Angelica. Her voice suggested she might be going to panic again. "A spell to stop us knowing where we are."

Tonino supposed it must be. There was no other way of accounting for the strange absence of view. "But I'm sure I know," he said, "by those trees. We're in one of those rich villas by the Palace."

"You're right," agreed Angelica. The panic had left her voice. "I shall never envy those people again. Their lives are all show."

They turned from the windows and discovered that the vast banging had dislodged one of the wall panels behind the dining table. It hung open like a door. They shoved one another out of the way to reach it first. But there was only a cupboard-sized bathroom, without a window.

"Good," said Angelica. "I was wondering what we'd do. And at least we'll have water." She reached out to one of the taps over the small washbasin. It came away in her hand. Under it was a blob of glue on white china. It was clear the tap had never been meant to be used. Angelica stared at it with such a ridiculous look of bewilderment that Tonino laughed. She drew herself up at that. "Don't you laugh at me, you beastly Montana!" She stalked out into the main room and threw the useless tap on to the table with a clump. Then she sat in one of the two remaining chairs and rested her elbows gloomily on the table.

After a while, Tonino did the same. The chair creaked under him. So did the table. Though its surface was painted to look like smooth mahogany, close to, it was all blobs of varnish and huge splinters. "There's nothing that's not shoddy," he said.

"Including you, Whatyoumecall Montana!" Angelica said. She was still angry.

"My name's Tonino," Tonino said.

"It's the last twist of the knife, being shut up with a Montana!" Angelica said. "Whatever your name is. I shall have to put up with all your filthy habits."

"Well, I've got to put up with yours," Tonino said irritably. It suddenly struck him that he was all alone, far from the friendly bustle of the Casa Montana. Even when he was hidden in a corner of the Casa with a book, he knew the rest of the family was all around him. And Benvenuto would be purring and pricking him, to remind him he was not alone. Dear old Benvenuto. Tonino was afraid he was going to cry—in front of a Petrocchi too. "How did they catch you?" he said, to take his mind off it.

"With a book." A slight, woeful smile appeared on Angelica's tight white face. "It was called *The Girl Who Saved Her Country*, and I thought it was from Great-Uncle Luigi. I still think it was a good story." She looked defiantly at Tonino.

Tonino was annoyed. It was not pleasant to think he had been caught by the same spell as a Petrocchi. "Me too," he said gruffly.

"And *I* haven't got any filthy habits!" snapped Angelica.

"Yes you have. All the Petrocchis have," said Tonino. "But I expect you don't realize because they're normal to you."

"I like that!" Angelica picked up the broken tap, as if she had half a mind to throw it.

"I don't care about your habits," said Tonino. Nor did he. All he wanted to do was find some way out of this nightmare room and go home. "How shall we get out of here?"

"Through the ceiling," Angelica said sarcastically.

Tonino looked upwards. There was that chandelier. If they could give it a pull, it might well rip a hole in the shoddy ceiling.

"Don't be stupid," said Angelica. "If there's a spell out in front, there's bound to be one up there to stop us getting out."

Tonino feared she was right, but it was worth a try. He climbed from his chair onto the table. He thought he could reach the chandelier from there if he stood up. There was a violent creaking. Before Tonino could begin to stand up, the table swayed away sideways, as if all four of its legs were loose.

"Get down!" said Angelica.

Tonino got down. It was clear the table would fall to pieces if he stayed on it. Gloomily he pushed the crooked legs straight again. "So that's no good," he said.

"Unless," said Angelica, suddenly bright and pert, "we steady it with a spell."

Tonino transferred his miserable look from the table legs to her sharp little face. He sighed. The subject had been bound to come up. "You'll have to do the spell," he said. Angelica stared at him. He could feel his face heating up. "I hardly know any spells," he said. "I—I'm slow."

He had expected Angelica to laugh, and she did. But he thought she need not have laughed in such a mean, exultant way, nor keep saying, "Oh that's good!" like that.

"What's so funny?" he said. "You can laugh! I know all about you turning your father green. You're no better than me!"

"Want to bet?" said Angelica, still laughing.

"No," said Tonino. "Just make the spell."

"I can't," said Angelica. It was Tonino's turn to stare, and Angelica's turn to blush. A thin bright pink spread right up the bulge of her forehead, and she put her chin up defiantly. "I'm hopeless at spells," she said. "I've never got a spell right in my life." Seeing Tonino still staring, she said, "It's a pity you didn't bet. I'm *much* worse than you are."

Tonino could not credit it. "How?" he said. "Why? Can't you learn spells either, then?"

"Oh, I can *learn* them all right." Angelica took up the broken tap again and scribbled angrily with it, great yellow scratches in the varnished top of the table. "I know hundreds of spells," she said, "but I always get them wrong. For a start, I'm tone-deaf. I can't sing a tune right to save my life. Like now." Carefully, as if she was a craftsman doing a fine carving, she peeled up a long yellow curl of varnish from the table, using the tap as a gouge. "But it's not only that," she said angrily, following her work intently. "I get words wrong too—everything wrong. And my spells always work, that's the worst of it. I've turned all my family all colors of the rainbow. I've turned the baby's bath into wine, and the wine into gravy. I turned my own head back to front once. I'm much worse than you. I *daren't* do spells. About all I'm good for is understanding cats. And I even turned my cat purple too."

Tonino watched her working away with the tap, with rather mixed feelings. If you looked at it practically, this was the worst possible news. Neither of them had a hope against the powerful spell-maker who had caught them. On the other hand, he had never met anyone who was worse at spells than he was. He thought, a little smugly, that at least he had never made a mistake in a spell, and that made him feel good. He wondered how the Casa Montana would feel if he kept turning them all colors of the rainbow. He imagined the stern Petrocchis must hate it. "Doesn't your family mind?" he asked.

"Not much," Angelica said, surprisingly. "They don't mind it half as much as I do. Everyone has a good laugh every time I make a new mistake—but they don't let anyone talk about it outside the Casa. Papa says I'm notorious enough for turning him green, and he doesn't like me to be even *seen* anywhere until I've grown out of it."

"But you went to the Palace," said Tonino. He thought Angelica must be exaggerating.

"Only because Cousin Monica was having her baby and everyone was so busy on the Old Bridge," said Angelica. "He had to take Renata off her shift and get my brother out of bed to drive the coach, in order to have enough of us."

"There were five of us," Tonino said, smugly.

"Our horses collapsed in the rain." Angelica turned from her gouging and looked at Tonino keenly. "So my brother said yours were bound to have collapsed too, because you only had a cardboard coachman."

Uncomfortably, Tonino knew Angelica had scored a point. "Our coachman collapsed too," he admitted.

"I thought so," said Angelica, "from the look on your face." She went back to scraping the table, conscious of victory.

"It wasn't our fault!" Tonino protested. "Chrestomanci says there's an enemy enchanter."

Angelica took such a slice out of the varnish that the table swooped sideways and Tonino had to push it straight. "And he's got us now," she said. "And he's taken care to get the two who are no good at spells. So how do we get out of here and spite him, Tonino Montana? Any ideas?"

Tonino sat with his chin in his hands and thought. He had read enough books, for goodness sake. People were always being kidnapped in books. And in his favorite books—this was like a bad joke—they escaped without using magic of any kind. But there was no door. That was what made it seem impossible. Wait a moment! The vast voice had promised them food. "If they think we're behaving," he said, "they'll bring us supper probably. And they've got to bring the food in somehow. If we watch where it comes in, we ought to be able to get out the same way."

"There's bound to be a spell on the entrance," Angelica said gloomily.

"Do stop bleating away about spells!" said Tonino. "Don't you Petrocchis ever talk about anything else?"

Angelica did not reply, but simply scraped away with her tap. Tonino sat wanly in his creaking chair thinking over the few spells he really knew. The most useful seemed to be a simple cancel-spell.

"A cancel-spell," Angelica said irritatingly, scratching carefully with the tap. The floor around her feet was heaped with yellow curls of varnish. "That might hold the entrance open. Or isn't a cancel-spell one of the ones you know?"

"I know a cancel-spell," said Tonino.

"So does my baby brother," said Angelica. "He'd probably be more use."

Their supper arrived. It appeared, without warning, on a tray, floating towards them from the windows. It took Tonino completely by surprise.

"*Spell!*" Angelica squawked at him. "Don't just stare!"

Tonino sang the spell. Hurried and surprised though he was, he was *sure* he got it right. But it was the tray the spell worked on. The tray, and the food on it, began to grow. Within seconds, it was bigger than the tabletop. And it still floated towards the table, growing as it came. Tonino found himself backing away from two steaming bath-sized bowls of soup and two great orange thickets of spaghetti, all of which were getting steadily vaster the nearer they came. By now, there was not much room around the edges of the tray. Tonino backed against the end wall, wondering if Angelica's trouble with spells was catching. Angelica herself was squashed against the bathroom door. Both of them were in danger of being cut in two.

"Get down on the floor!" Tonino shouted.

They slithered hurriedly down the wall, underneath the tray, which hung over them like a too low ceiling. The huge odor of spaghetti was quite oppressive.

"What have you done?" Angelica said, coming towards Tonino on hands and knees. "You didn't get it right."

"Yes, but if it gets much bigger, it might break the room open," said Tonino.

Angela sank back on her knees and looked at him with what was nearly respect. "That's almost a good idea."

But it was only almost. The tray certainly met all four walls. They heard it thump against them. There was a deal of swaying, creaking and squeezing, from the tray and from the walls, but the walls did not give. After a moment it was clear that the tray was not being allowed to get any bigger.

"There *is* a spell on this room," Angelica said. It was not meant to be I-told-you-so. She was miserable.

Tonino gave up and sang the cancel-spell, carefully and correctly. The tray shrank at once. They were left kneeling on the floor looking at a reasonable-sized supper laid neatly in the center of the table. "We might as well eat it," he said.

Angelica annoyed him thoroughly again by saying, as she picked up her spoon, "Well, I'm glad to know I'm not the only person who gets my spells wrong."

"I know I got it right," Tonino muttered into his spoon, but Angelica chose not to hear.

After a while, he was even more annoyed to find, every time he looked up, that Angelica was staring at him curiously. "What's the matter now?" he said at last, quite exasperated.

"I was waiting to see your filthy eating habits," she said. "But I think you must be on your best behavior."

"I always eat like this!" Tonino saw that he had wound far too much spaghetti on his fork. He hurriedly unwound it.

The bulge of Angelica's forehead was wavy with frown lines. "No you don't. Montanas always eat disgustingly because of the way Old Ricardo Petrocchi made them eat their words."

"Don't talk nonsense," said Tonino. "Anyway, it was Old Francesco Montana who made the Petrocchis eat *their* words."

"It was not!" Angelica said heatedly. "It was the first story I ever learned. The Petrocchis made the Montanas eat their spells disguised as spaghetti."

"No they didn't. It was the other way around!" said Tonino. "It was the first story I ever learned too."

Somehow, neither of them felt like finishing their spaghetti. They laid their forks down and went on arguing.

"And because of eating those spells," said Angelica, "the Montanas went quite disgusting and started eating their uncles and aunts when they died."

"We do not!" said Tonino. "You eat babies."

"How dare you!" said Angelica. "You eat cow-pats for pizzas, and you can smell the Casa Montana right on the Corso."

"The Casa Petrocchi smells all down the Via Sant' Angelo," said Tonino, "and you can hear the flies buzzing from the New Bridge. You have babies like kittens and—"

"That's a lie!" shrieked Angelica. "You just put that about because you don't want people to know that the Montanas never get married properly!"

"Yes we do!" bawled Tonino. "It's you who don't!"

"I like that!" yelled Angelica. "I'll have you know, my brother got married, in church, just after Christmas. So there!"

"I don't believe you," said Tonino. "And my sister's going to get married in Spring, so—"

"I was a *bridesmaid*!" screamed Angelica.

While they argued, the tray quietly floated off the table and vanished somewhere near the windows. Tonino and Angelica looked irritably around for it, extremely annoyed that they had once again missed noticing how it got in and out.

"Now look what you've done!" said Angelica.

"It's your fault for telling lies about my family," said Tonino.

9

"IF YOU'RE NOT CAREFUL," said Angelica, glowering under the bulge of her forehead, "I shall sing the first spell that comes into my head. And I hope it turns you into a slug."

That was a threat indeed. Tonino quailed a little. But the honor of the Montanas was at stake. "Take back what you said about my family," he said.

"Only if you take back what you said about mine," said Angelica. "Swear by the Angel of Caprona that none of those dreadful lies are true. Look. I've got the Angel here. Come and swear." Her pink finger jabbed down at the tabletop. She reminded Tonino of his school teacher on a bad day.

He left his creaking chair and leaned over to see what she was pointing at. Angelica fussily dusted away a shower of yellow varnish to show him that she indeed had the Angel, scratched with the useless tap into the top of the table. It was quite a good drawing, considering that the tap was not a good gouge and had shown a tendency to slip about. But Tonino was not prepared to admire it. "You've forgotten the scroll," he said.

Angelica jumped up, and her flimsy chair crashed over backwards. "That does it! You've asked for it!" She marched over to the empty space by the windows and took up a position of power. From there, with her hands raised, she looked at Tonino to see if he was going to relent. Tonino would have liked to relent. He did not want to be a slug. He sought about in his mind for some way of giving in which did not look like simple cowardice. But, as with everything, he was too slow. Angelica flounced around, so that her arms were no longer at quite the right angle.

"Right," she said. "I shall make it a cancel-spell, to cancel you out." And she began to sing.

Angelica's voice was horrible, sharp and flat by turns, and wandering from key to key. Tonino would have liked to interrupt her, or at least distract her by making noises, but he did not quite dare. That might only make things worse. He waited while Angelica squawked out a couple of verses of a spell which seemed to center around the words *turn the spell around, break the spell off*. Since he was a boy and not a spell, Tonino rather hoped it would not do anything to him.

Angelica raised her arms higher for the third verse and changed key for the sixth time. "Turn the spell off, break the spell around—"

"That's wrong," said Tonino.

"Don't you dare put me off!" snapped Angelica, and turned around to say it, which sent the angle of her arms more thoroughly wrong than ever. One hand was now pointing at a window. "I command the unbinding of that which was bound," she sang, cross and shrill.

Tonino looked quickly down at himself, but he seemed to be still there, and the usual color. He told himself that he had known all along that such a bungled spell could not possibly work.

There came a great creaking from the ceiling, just above the windows. The whole room swayed. Then, to Tonino's amazement, the entire front wall of the room, windows and all, split away from the side walls and the ceiling, and fell outwards with a soft clatter—a curiously soft sound for the whole side of a house. A draught of musty-smelling air blew in through the open space.

Angelica was quite as astonished as Tonino. But that did not prevent her turning to him with a smug and triumphant smile. "See? My spells always work."

"Let's get out," said Tonino. "Quick. Before somebody comes."

They ran out across the painted panels between the windows, across the marks Tonino had made with the chair. They stepped down off the surprisingly clean, straight edge, where the wall had joined the ceiling, onto the terrace in front of the house. It appeared to be made of wood, not of stone as Tonino had expected. And beyond that—

They stopped, just in time, at the edge of a huge cliff. Both of them swayed forward, and caught at one another. The cliff went down sheer, into murky darkness. They could not see the bottom. Nor could they see much more when they looked straight ahead. There was a blaze of red-gold sunlight there, dazzling them.

"There's still a spell on the view," said Tonino.

"In that case," said Angelica, "let's just keep walking. There must be a road or a garden that we can't see."

There certainly should have been something of the kind, but it neither felt nor looked like that. Tonino was sure he could sense vast hollow spaces below the cliff. There were no city sounds, and only a strangely musty smell.

"Coward!" said Angelica.

"You go," said Tonino.

"Only if you go too," she said.

They hovered, glaring at one another. And, as they hovered, the blaze of sunlight was cut off by an immense black shape. *"Naughty!"* said a vast voice. "Bad children shall be punished."

A force almost too strong to feel swept them away onto the fallen wall. The fallen wall rose briskly back into its place, sweeping Angelica and Tonino with it, helplessly sliding and rolling, until they thumped onto the painted carpet. By that time, Tonino was so breathless and dizzy that he hardly heard the wall snap back into place with a click.

After that, the dizziness grew worse. Tonino knew he was in the grip of another spell. He struggled against it furiously, but whoever was casting it was immensely strong. He felt surging and bumping. The light from the windows changed, and changed again. Almost he could have sworn, the room was being *carried*. It stopped with a jolt. He heard Angelica's voice gabbling a prayer to Our Lady, and he did not blame her. Then there was a mystifying gap in what Tonino knew.

He came to himself because whoever was casting the spell wanted him to. Tonino was quite sure of that. The punishment would not be so much fun, unless Tonino knew about it.

He was in a confusion of light and noise—there was a huge blur of it to one side—and he was racing up and down a narrow wooden platform, dragging (of all things!) a string of sausages. He was wearing a bright red nightgown and there was a heaviness on the front of his face. Each time he reached one end of the wooden platform, he found a white cardboard dog there, with a frill around its neck. The dog's cardboard mouth opened and shut. It was making feeble cardboard attempts to get the sausages.

The noise was terrific. Tonino seemed to be making some of it himself. "What a clever fellow! What a clever fellow!" he heard himself squawking, in a voice quite unlike his own. It was like the noise you make singing into paper over a comb. The rest of the noise was coming from the lighted space to one side. Vast voices were roaring and laughing, mixed with tinny music.

"This is a dream!" Tonino told himself. But he

knew it was not. He had a fair idea what was happening, though his head still felt muzzy and his eyes were blurred. As he raced back down the little platform, he turned his bleary eyes inwards, towards the heaviness on his face. Sure enough, blurred and doubled, he could see a great red and pink nose there. He was Mr. Punch.

Naturally, then, he tried to dig in his heels and stop racing up and down, and to lift his hand and wrench off the huge pink nose. He could not do either. More than that, whoever was making him be Mr. Punch promptly took mean pleasure in making him run faster and whirl the sausages about harder.

"Oh, very good!" yelled someone from the lighted space.

Tonino thought he knew that voice. He sped towards the cardboard Dog Toby again, whirled the sausages away from its cardboard jaws and waited for his head and eyes to stop feeling so fuzzy. He was sure they would. The mean person wanted him conscious. "What a clever fellow!" he squawked. As he raced down the stage the other way, he snatched a look across his huge nose towards the lighted space, but it was a blur. So he snatched a look towards the other side.

He saw the wall of a golden villa there, with four long windows. Beside each window stood a little dark cypress tree. Now he knew why the strange room had seemed so shoddy. It was only meant as scenery. The door on the outside wall was painted on. Between the villa and the stage was a hole. The person who was working the puppets ought to have been down there, but Tonino could only see empty blackness. It was all being done by magic.

Just then he was distracted by a cardboard person diving upwards from the hole, squawking that Mr. Punch had stolen his sausages. Tonino was forced to stand still and squawk back. He was glad of a rest by then. Meanwhile, the cardboard dog seized the sausages and dived out of sight with them. The audience clapped and shouted, "Look at Dog Toby!" The cardboard person sped past Tonino squawking that he would fetch the police.

Once again, Tonino tried to look out at the audience. This time, he could dimly see a brightly lit room and black bulky shapes sitting in chairs, but it was like trying to see something against the sun. His eyes watered. A tear ran down the pink beak on his face. And Tonino could feel that the mean person was delighted to see that. He thought Tonino was crying. Tonino was annoyed, but also rather pleased; it looked as if the person could be fooled by his own mean thoughts. He stared out, in spite of the dazzle, trying to see the mean person, but all he could clearly see was a carving up near the roof of the lighted room. It was the Angel of Caprona, one hand held out in blessing, the other holding the scroll.

Then he was jumped around to face Judy. On the other side of him, the wall had gone from the front of the villa. The scene was the room he knew only too well, with the chandelier artistically alight.

Judy was coming along the stage holding the white rolled-up shape of the baby. Judy wore a blue nightdress and a blue cap. Her face was mauve, with a nose in the middle of it nearly as large and red as Tonino's. But the eyes on either side of it were Angelica's, alternately blinking and wide with terror. She blinked beseechingly at Tonino as she squawked, "I have to go out, Mr. Punch. Mind you mind the baby!"

"Don't want to mind the baby!" he squawked.

All through the long silly conversation, he could see Angelica's eyes blinking at him, imploring him to think of a spell to stop this. But of course Tonino could not. He did not think Rinaldo, or even Antonio, could stop anything as powerful as this. Angel of Caprona! he thought. Help us! That made him feel better, although nothing stopped the spell. Angelica planted the baby in his arms and dived out of sight.

The baby started to cry. Tonino first squawked abuse at it, then took it by the end of its long white dress and beat its brains out on the platform. The baby was much more realistic than Dog Toby. It may have been only cardboard, but it wriggled and waved its arms and cried most horribly. Tonino could almost have believed it was Cousin Claudia's baby. It so horrified him that he found he was repeating the words of the *Angel of Caprona* as he swung the baby up and down. And those might not have been the right words, but he could feel they were doing something. When he finally flung the white bundle over the front of the stage, he could see the shiny floor the baby fell on, away below. And when he looked up at the clapping spectators, he could see them too, equally clearly.

The first person he saw was the Duke of Caprona. He was sitting on a gilded chair, in a glitter of buttons, laughing gigantically. Tonino wondered how he could laugh like that at something so horrible, until he remembered that he had stood himself, a score of times, and laughed himself sick, at just the same thing. But those had been only puppets. Then it dawned on Tonino that the Duke thought they *were* puppets. He was laughing at the skill of the showman.

"What a clever fellow!" squawked Tonino, and was made to dance about gleefully, without wanting to in the least. But as he danced, he looked sharply at the rest of the audience, to see who it was who knew he was not a puppet.

To his terror, a good half of them knew. Tonino met a knowing look on the faces of the three grave men surrounding the Duke, and the same on the elegantly made-up faces of the two ladies with the Duchess. And the Duchess—as soon as Tonino saw the amused arch of the Duchess's eyebrows and the little, secret smile on her mouth, he knew she was the one doing it. He looked her in the eyes. Yes, she was an enchantress. That was what had so troubled him about her when he saw her before. And the Duchess saw him look, and smiled less secretly, because Tonino could do nothing about it.

That really frightened Tonino. But Angelica came swooping upwards again, with a large stick clutched in her arms, and he had no time to think.

"What have you done with the baby?" squawked Angelica. And she belabored Tonino with the stick. It really hurt. It knocked him to his knees and went on bashing at him. Tonino could see Angelica's lips moving. Though her silly squeaky voice kept saying, "I'll teach you to kill the baby!" her mouth was forming the words of the *Angel of Caprona*. That was because she knew what came next.

Tonino said the words of the *Angel* too and tried to stay crouched on the floor. But it was no good. He was made to spring up, wrest the stick from Judy and beat Angelica with it. He could see the Duke laughing, and the courtiers smiling. The Duchess's smile was very broad now, because, of course, Tonino was going to have to beat Angelica to death.

Tonino tried to hold the stick so that it would only hit Angelica lightly. She might be a Petrocchi and a thoroughly irritating girl, but she had not deserved this. But the stick leaped up and down of its own accord, and Tonino's arms went with it. Angelica fell on her knees and then on her face. Her squawks redoubled, as Tonino smote away at her back, and then her voice stopped. She lay with her head hanging down from the front of the platform, looking just like a puppet. Tonino found himself having to kick her down the empty space between the false villa and the stage. He heard the distant *flop* as she fell. And then he was forced to skip and cackle with glee, while the Duchess threw back her head and laughed as heartily as the Duke.

Tonino hated her. He was so angry and so miserable that he did not mind at all when a cardboard policeman appeared and he chased him with the stick too. He laid into the policeman as if he was the Duchess and not a cardboard doll at all.

"Are you all right, Lucrezia?" he heard the Duke say.

Tonino looked sideways as he dealt another mighty swipe at the policeman's cardboard helmet. He saw the Duchess wince as the stick landed. He was not surprised when the policeman was immediately whisked away and he himself forced into a violent capering and even louder squawking. He let himself do it. He felt truly gleeful as he squawked, "What a clever fellow!" for what felt like the thousandth time. For he understood what had happened. The Duchess *was* the policeman, in a sort of way. She was putting some of herself into all the puppets to make them work. But he must not let her know he knew. Tonino capered and chortled, doing his best to seem terrified, and kept his eyes on that carving of the Angel, high up over the door of the room.

And now the hooded Hangman-puppet appeared, dragging a little wooden gibbet with a string noose dangling from it. Tonino capered cautiously. This was where the Duchess did for him unless he was very careful. On the other hand, if this Punch and Judy show went as it should, he might just do for the Duchess.

The silly scene began. Tonino had never worked so hard at anything in his life. He kept repeating the words of the *Angel* in his head, both as a kind of prayer and as a smoke screen, so that the Duchess would not understand what he was trying to do. At the same time, he thought, fiercely and vengefully, that the Hangman was not just a puppet—it was the Duchess herself. And, also at the same time, he attended to Mr. Punch's conversation with all his might. This had to go right.

"Come along, Mr. Punch," croaked the Hangman. "Just put your head in this noose."

"How do I do that?" asked Mr. Punch and Tonino, both pretending hard to be stupid.

"You put your head in here," croaked the Hangman, putting one hand through the noose.

Mr. Punch and Tonino, both of them quivering with cunning, put his head first one side of the noose, then the other. "Is this right? Is this?" Then, pretending even harder to be stupid, "I can't see how to do it. You'll have to show me."

Either the Duchess was wanting to play with Tonino's feelings, or she was trying the same cunning. They went through this several times. Each time, the Hangman put his hand through the noose to show Mr. Punch what to do. Tonino did not dare look at the Duchess. He looked at the Hangman and kept thinking, That's the Duchess, and reciting the *Angel* for all he was worth. At last, to his relief, the Duke became restive.

"Come on, Mr. Punch!" he shouted.

"You'll have to put your head in and show me," Mr. Punch and Tonino said, as persuasively as he knew how.

"Oh well," croaked the Hangman. "Since you're so stupid." And he put his cardboard head through the noose.

Mr. Punch and Tonino promptly pulled the rope and hanged him. But Tonino thought, This is the *Duchess*! and went as limp and heavy as he could. For just a second, his full puppet's weight swung on the end of the rope.

It only lasted that second. Tonino had a glimpse of the Duchess on her feet with her hands to her throat. He felt real triumph. Then he was thrown, flat on his face, across the stage, unable to move at all. There he was forced to lie. His head hung down from the front of the stage, so that he could see very little. But he gathered that the Duchess was being led tenderly away, with the Duke fussing around her.

I think I feel as pleased as Punch, he thought.

10

❧◆❧

PAOLO NEVER WANTED to remember that night afterwards. He was still staring at the sick yellow message in the yard, when the rest of the family arrived. He was crowded aside to let Old Niccolo and Aunt Francesca through, but Benvenuto spat at them like hot fat hitting fire and would not let them pass.

"Let be, old boy," Old Niccolo said. "You've done your best." He turned to Aunt Francesca. "I shall never forgive the Petrocchis," he said. "Never." Paolo was once again struck by how wretched and goblinlike his grandfather looked. He had thought Old Niccolo was helping vast, panting, muddy Aunt Francesca along, but he now wondered if it was not the other way around. "Well. Let's get rid of this horrible message," Old Niccolo said irritably to the rest of them.

He raised his arms to start the family on the spell and collapsed. His hands went to his chest. He slid to his knees, and his face was a strange color. Paolo

164

thought he was dead until he saw him breathing, in uneven jerks. Elizabeth, Uncle Lorenzo and Aunt Maria rushed to him.

"Heart attack," Uncle Lorenzo said, nodding over at Antonio. "Get that spell going. We've got to get him indoors."

"Paolo, run for the doctor," said Elizabeth.

As Paolo ran, he heard the burst of singing behind him. When he came back with the doctor, the message had vanished and Old Niccolo had been carried up to bed. Aunt Francesca, still muddy, with her hair hanging down one side, was roving up and down the yard like a moving mountain, crying and wringing her hands.

"Spells are forbidden," she called out to Paolo. "I've stopped everything."

"And a good thing too!" the doctor said sourly. "A man of Niccolo Montana's age has no business to be brawling in the streets. And make your great-aunt lie down," he said to Paolo. "She'll be in bed next."

Aunt Francesca would only go to the Saloon, where she refused even to sit down. She raged up and down, wailing about Old Niccolo, weeping about Tonino, declaring that the virtue had gone from the Casa Montana for good, and uttering terrible threats against the Petrocchis. Nobody else was much better. The children cried with tiredness. Elizabeth and the aunts worried about Old Niccolo, and then about Aunt Francesca. In the Scriptorium, among all the abandoned spells, Antonio and the uncles sat rigid with worry, and the rest of the Casa was full of older cousins wandering about and cursing the Petrocchis.

Paolo found Rinaldo leaning moodily on the gallery rail, in spite of it being dark now and really quite cold. "Curse those Petrocchis," he said gloomily to Paolo. "We can't even earn a living now, let alone help if there's a war."

Paolo, in spite of his misery, was very flattered that Rinaldo seemed to think him old enough to talk family business to. He said, "Yes, it's awful," and tried to lean on the rail in the same elegant attitude as Rinaldo. It was not easy, since Paolo was not nearly tall enough, but he leaned and prepared the arguments he would use to persuade Rinaldo that Tonino was in the hands of an enemy enchanter. That was not easy either. Paolo knew that Rinaldo would not listen to him if he dropped the least small hint that he had talked to a Petrocchi—and besides, he would have died rather than told his cousin. But he knew that, if he persuaded Rinaldo, Rinaldo would rescue Tonino in five dashing minutes. Rinaldo was a true Montana.

While he thought, Rinaldo said angrily, "What possessed that stupid brat Tonino to read that blessed book? I shall give him something to think about when we get him back!"

Paolo shivered in the cold. "Tonino always reads

books." Then he shifted a bit—the elegant attitude was not at all comfortable—and asked timidly, "How shall we get him back?" This was not at all what he had planned to say. He was annoyed with himself.

"What's the use?" Rinaldo said. "We know where he is—in the Casa Petrocchi. And if he's uncomfortable there, it's his own fault!"

"But he's not!" Paolo protested. As far as he could see in the light from the yard lamp, Rinaldo turned and looked at him jeeringly. The discussion seemed to be getting further from the way he had planned it every second. "An enemy enchanter's got him," he said. "The one Chrestomanci talked about."

Rinaldo laughed. "Load of old crab-apples, Paolo. Our friend had been talking to the Petrocchis. He invented his convenient enchanter because he wanted us all working for Caprona. Most of us saw through it at once."

"Then who made that mist on the Corso?" Paolo said. "It wasn't us, and it wasn't them."

But Rinaldo only said, "Who said it wasn't them?"

As Paolo could not say it was Renata Petrocchi, he could not answer. Instead, he said rather desperately, "Come with me to the Casa Petrocchi. If you used a finding-spell, you could *prove* Tonino isn't there."

"What?" Rinaldo seemed astounded. "What kind of fool do you take me for, Paolo? I'm not going to take on a whole family of spell-makers single-handed. And if I go there and use a spell, and they do something to Tonino, everyone's going to blame me, aren't they? For something we know anyway. It's not worth it, Paolo. But I tell you what—"

He was interrupted by Aunt Gina trumpeting below in the yard. "Notti's is the only chemist open by now. Tell him it's for Niccolo Montana!"

With some relief, Paolo dropped the elegant attitude entirely and leaned over the rail to watch Lucia and Corinna hurry through the yard with the doctor's prescription. The sight gave his stomach a wrench of worry. "Do you think Old Niccolo's going to die, Rinaldo?"

Rinaldo shrugged. "Could be. He's pretty old. It's about time the old idiot gave up anyway. I shall be one step closer to being head of the Casa Montana then."

A peculiar thing happened inside Paolo's head then. He had never given much thought to who might follow Antonio—for it was clear his father would follow Old Niccolo—as head of the Casa Montana. But he had never, for some reason, thought it might be Rinaldo. Now he tried to imagine Rinaldo doing the things Old Niccolo did. And as soon as he did, he saw Rinaldo was quite unsuitable. Rinaldo was vain, and selfish—and cowardly, provided he could be a coward and still keep up a good appearance. It was as if Rinaldo had said a powerful spell to clear Paolo's eyes.

It never occurred to Rinaldo, expert spell-maker

though he was, that a few ordinary words could make such a difference. He bent towards Paolo and dropped his voice to a melodious murmur. "I was going to tell you, Paolo. I'm going around enlisting all the young ones. We're going to swear to work a secret revenge on the Petrocchis. We'll do something worse than make them eat their words. Are you with me? Will you swear to join the plan?"

Maybe he was in earnest. It would suit Rinaldo to work in secret, with lots of willing helpers. But Paolo was sure that this plan was a step in Rinaldo's plans to be head of the Casa. Paolo sidled away along the rail.

"Are you game?" Rinaldo whispered, laughing a little.

Paolo sidled beyond grabbing-distance. "Tell you later." He turned and scudded away. Rinaldo laughed and did not try to catch him. He thought Paolo was scared.

Paolo went down into the yard, feeling more lonely than he had felt in his life. Tonino was not there. Tonino was not vain, or selfish, or cowardly. And nobody would help him find Tonino. Paolo had not noticed until now how much he depended on Tonino. They did everything important together. Even if Paolo was busy on his own, he knew Tonino was there somewhere, sitting reading, ready to put his book down if Paolo needed him. Now there seemed to be nothing for Paolo to do. And the whole Casa reeked of worry.

He went to the kitchen, where there seemed,

at last, to be something happening. All his small cousins were there. Rosa and Marco were trying to make soup for them.

"Come in and help, Paolo," Rosa said. "We're going to put them to bed after soup, but we're having a bit of trouble."

Both she and Marco were looking tired and flustered. Most of the little ones were grizzling, including the baby. The trouble was Lucia's spell. Paolo understood this because Marco dumped the baby in his arms. Its wrapper was covered with orange grease. "Yuk!" said Paolo.

"I know," said Rosa. "Well, Marco, better try again. Clean saucepan. Clean water. The very last packet of soup powder—don't make that face, Paolo. We've got through all the vegetables. They just sail away to the waste-bins, and they're moldy before they get there."

Paolo looked nervously at the door, wondering if the enemy enchanter was powerful enough to overhear him. "Try a cancel-spell," he whispered.

"Aunt Gina went through them all this afternoon," said Rosa. "No good. Little Lucia used the *Angel of Caprona*, you see. We're trying Marco's way now. Ready, Marco?"

Rosa opened the packet of soup and held it over the saucepan. As the dry pink powder poured into the water, Marco leaned over the saucepan and sang furiously. Paolo watched them nervously. This was just what the message told them not to do, he was sure. When all the powder was in the water, Rosa and Marco peered anxiously into the saucepan. "Have we done it?" asked Marco.

"I think—" Rosa began, and ended in a yell of exasperation. "Oh no!" The little pasta shells in the powder had turned into real sea-shells, little gray ones. "With *creatures* in!" Rosa said despairingly, dipping a spoonful out. "Where is Lucia?" she said. "Bring her here. Tell her I—No, don't. Just fetch her, Paolo."

"She's gone to the chemist," said Paolo.

There was shouting in the yard. Paolo passed the greasy baby to the nearest cousin and shot outside, dreading another sick yellow message about Tonino. Or there was just a chance the noise was Lucia.

It was neither. It was Rinaldo. The uncles must have left the Scriptorium, for Rinaldo was making a bonfire of spells in the middle of the yard. Domenico, Carlo and Luigi were busily carrying armfuls of scrips, envelopes and scrolls down from the gallery. Paolo recognized, already curling among the flames, the army-charms he and the other children had spent such a time copying. It was a shocking waste of work.

"This is what the Petrocchis have forced us to!" shouted Rinaldo, striking an attitude beside the flames. It was evidently part of his plan to enlist the young ones.

Paolo was glad to see Antonio and Uncle Lorenzo hurry out of the Saloon.

"Rinaldo!" shouted Antonio. "Rinaldo, we're

worried about Umberto. We want you to go to the University and enquire."

"Send Domenico," said Rinaldo, and turned back to the flames.

"No," said Antonio. "You go." There was something about the way he said it that caused Rinaldo to back away from him.

"I'll go," said Rinaldo. He held up one hand, laughing. "I was only joking, Uncle Antonio."

He left at once: "Take those spells back," Uncle Lorenzo said to the other three cousins. "I hate to see good work wasted." Domenico, Carlo and Luigi obeyed without a word. Antonio and Uncle Lorenzo went to the bonfire and tried to stamp out the flames, but they were burning too strongly. Paolo saw them look at one another, rather guiltily, and then lean forward and whisper a spell over the fire. It flicked out as if it had been turned off with a switch. Paolo sighed worriedly. It was plain that no one in the Casa Montana could drop the habit of using spells. He wondered how long it would be before the enemy enchanter noticed.

"Fetch a light!" Antonio shouted to Domenico. "And sort out the ones that aren't burned."

Paolo went back to the kitchen before they asked him to help. The bonfire had given him an idea.

"There is quite a bit of mince," Rosa was saying. "Dare we try with that?"

"Why don't you," said Paolo, "take the food to

the dining room? I'll light a fire there, and you can cook it on that."

"The boy's a genius!" said Marco.

They did that. Rosa cooked by relays and Marco made cocoa. The children were fed first, Paolo included. Paolo sat on one of the long benches, thinking it was almost enjoyable—except if he thought of Tonino, or Old Niccolo in bed upstairs. He was very pleased and surprised when a sudden bundle of claw and warm-iron muscle landed on his knee. Benvenuto was missing Tonino too. He rubbed against Paolo with a kind of desperation, but he would not purr.

Rosa and Marco were getting up to put the young ones to bed, when there was a sudden great clanging, outside in the night.

"Good Heavens!" said Rosa, and opened the yard door.

The noise flooded in, an uneven metal sound, hasty and huge. The nearest—*clang-clang-clang*—was so near that it could only be the bell of Sant' Angelo's. Behind it, the bell of the Cathedral tolled. And beyond that, now near, now faint and tinny, every bell in every church in Caprona beat and boomed and clashed and chimed. Corinna and Lucia came racing in, their faces bright with cold and excitement.

"We're at war! The Duke's declared war!"

Marco said he thought he had better go. "Oh no, don't!" Rosa cried out. "Not yet. By the way, Lucia—"

Lucia took a quick look at the cooking in the hearth. "I'll go and take Aunt Gina the prescription," she said, and prudently ran away.

Marco and Rosa looked at one another. "Three States against us and no spells to fight with," said Marco. "We're not likely to have a long and happy marriage, are we?"

"Mr. Notti says the Final Reserve is being called up tomorrow," Corinna said encouragingly. She caught Rosa's eye. "Come on, you kids," she said to four cousins at random. "Bed time."

While the young ones were being put to bed, Paolo sat nursing Benvenuto, feeling more dismal than ever. He wondered if there would be soldiers from Florence and Pisa and Siena in Caprona by tomorrow. Would guns fire in the streets? He thought of big marble chips shot off the Cathedral, the New Bridge broken, despite all the spells in it, and swarthy enemy soldiers dragging Rosa off screaming. And he saw that all this could really have happened by the end of the week.

Here, he became quite certain that Benvenuto was trying to tell him something. He could tell from the accusing stare of Benvenuto's yellow eyes. But he simply could not understand.

"I'll try," he said to Benvenuto. "I really will try."

He had, fleetingly, the feeling that Benvenuto was glad. Encouraged by this, Paolo bent his head and stared at Benvenuto's urgent face. But it did no good. All that Paolo could get out of it was a picture in his mind—a picture of somewhere with a colored marble front, very large and beautiful.

"The Church of Sant' Angelo?" he said doubtfully.

While Benvenuto's tail was still lashing with annoyance, Rosa and Marco came back. "Oh dear!" Rosa said to Marco. "There's Paolo taking all the troubles of the Casa on his shoulders again!"

Paolo looked up in surprise.

Marco said, "You look just like Antonio sometimes."

"I can't understand Benvenuto," Paolo said despairingly.

Marco sat on the table beside him. "Then he'll have to find some other way of telling us what he wants," he said. "He's a clever cat—the cleverest I've ever known. He'll do it." He put out a hand and Benvenuto let him stroke his head. "Your ears," said Marco, "Sir Cat, are like sea-holly without the prickles."

Rosa perched on the table too, on the other side of Paolo. "What is it, Paolo? Tonino?"

Paolo nodded. "Nobody will believe me that the enemy enchanter's got him."

"We do," said Marco.

Rosa said, "Paolo, it's just as well he's got Tonino and not you. Tonino'll take it much more calmly."

Paolo was a little bewildered. "Why do you two believe in the enchanter and no one else does?"

"What makes you think he exists?" Marco countered.

Even to Rosa and Marco, Paolo could not bring himself to tell of his embarrassing encounter with a Petrocchi. "There was a horrible fog at the end of the fight," he said.

Rosa and Marco jumped around delightedly. Their hands met with a smack over Paolo's head. "It worked! It worked!" And Marco added, "We were hoping someone would mention a certain fog! Did there seem to have been a large-scale cancel-spell with it, by any chance?"

"Yes," said Paolo.

"*We* made that fog," Rosa said. "Marco and me. We were hoping to stop the fighting, but it took us ages to make it, because all the magic in Caprona was going into the fight."

Paolo digested this. That took care of the one piece of proof that did not depend on the word of a Petrocchi. Perhaps the enchanter did not exist after all. Perhaps Tonino really was at the Casa Petrocchi. He remembered that Renata had not said Angelica was missing until the fog cleared and she knew who he was. "Look," he said. "Will you two come to the Casa Petrocchi with me and see if Tonino's there?"

He was aware that Rosa and Marco were exchanging some kind of look above his head. "Why?" said Rosa.

"Because," said Paolo. "Because." The need to persuade them cleared his wits at last. "Because Guido Petrocchi said Angelica Petrocchi was missing too."

"I'm afraid we can't," Marco said, with what sounded like real regret. "You'd understand, if you knew how pressing our reasons are, believe me!"

Paolo did not understand. He knew that, with these two, it was not cowardice, or pride, or anything like that. That only made it more maddening. "Oh, nobody will help!" he cried out.

Rosa put her arm around him. "Paolo! You're just like Father. You think you have to do everything yourself. There is one thing we can do."

"Call Chrestomanci?" said Marco.

Paolo felt Rosa nod. "But he's in Rome," he objected.

"It doesn't matter," said Marco. "He's that kind of enchanter. If he's near enough and you need him enough, he comes when you call."

"I must cook!" said Rosa, jumping off the table.

Just before the second supper was ready, Rinaldo came back, in great good spirits. Uncle Umberto and old Luigi Petrocchi had had another fight, in the dining-hall of the University. That was why Uncle Umberto had not turned up to see how Old Niccolo was. He and Luigi were both in bed, prostrated with exhaustion. Rinaldo had been drinking wine with some students who told him all about the fight. The students' supper had been ruined. Cutlets and pasta had flown about, followed by chairs, tables and benches. Umberto had tried to drown Luigi in a soup tureen, and Luigi had replied by hurling the whole of the Doctors' supper at Umberto. The students were going on strike. They did not mind the fight, but Luigi had shown them that the Doctors' food was better than theirs.

Paolo listened without truly attending. He was thinking about Tonino and wondering if he dared depend on the word of a Petrocchi.

11

❦

AFTER A WHILE, someone came and picked Tonino up. That was unpleasant. His legs and arms dragged and dangled in all directions, and he could not do anything about it. He was plunged somewhere much darker. Then he was left to lie amid a great deal of bumping and scraping, as if he were in a box which was being pushed across a floor. When it stopped, he found he could move. He sat up, trembling all over.

He was in the same room as before, but it seemed to be much smaller. He could tell that, if he stood up, his head would brush the little lighted chandelier in the ceiling. So he was larger now; where he had been three inches tall before, he must now be more like nine. The puppets must be too big for their scenery, and the false villa meant to look as if it was some distance away. And, with the Duchess suddenly taken ill, none of her helpers had bothered what size Tonino was. They had simply made sure he was shut up again.

"Tonino," whispered Angelica.

Tonino whirled around. Half the room was full of a pile of lax puppet bodies. He scanned the cardboard head of the policeman, then his enemy the Hangman, and the white sausage of the baby, and came upon Angelica's face halfway up the pile. It was her own face, though swollen and tearstained. Tonino clapped his hand to his nose. To his relief, the red beak was gone, though he still seemed to be wearing Mr. Punch's scarlet nightgown.

"I'm sorry," he said. His teeth seemed to be chattering. "I tried not to hurt you. Are your bones broken?"

"No—o," said Angelica. She did not sound too sure. "Tonino, what happened?"

"I hanged the Duchess," Tonino said, and he felt some vicious triumph as he said it. "I didn't kill her though," he added regretfully.

Angelica laughed. She laughed until the heap of puppets was shaking and sliding about. But Tonino could not find it funny. He burst into tears, even though he was crying in front of a Petrocchi.

"Oh dear," said Angelica. "Tonino, stop it! Tonino—please!" She struggled out from among the puppets and hobbled looming through the room. Her head banged the chandelier and sent it tinkling and casting mad shadows over them as she knelt down beside Tonino. "Tonino, please stop. She'll be furious as soon as she feels better." Angelica was wearing Judy's blue cap and Judy's blue dress still. She took off the blue cap and held it out to Tonino. "Here. Blow on that. I used the baby's dress. It made me feel better." She tried to smile at him, but the smile went hopelessly crooked in her swollen face. Angelica's large forehead must have hit the floor first. It was now enlarged by a huge red bump. Under it, the grin looked grotesque.

Tonino understood it was meant for a smile and smiled back, as well as he could for his chattering teeth.

"Here." Angelica loomed back through the room to the pile of puppets and heaved at the Hangman. She returned with his black felt cape. "Put this on."

Tonino wrapped himself in the cape and blew his nose on the blue cap and felt better.

Angelica heaved more puppets about. "I'm going to wear the policeman's jacket," she said. "Tonino—have you thought?"

"Not really," said Tonino. "I sort of know."

He had known from the moment he looked at the Duchess. She was the enchanter who was sapping the strength of Caprona and spoiling the spells of the Casa Montana. Tonino was not sure about the Duke—probably he was too stupid to count. But in spite of the Duchess's enchantments, the spells of the Casa Montana—and the Casa Petrocchi—must still be strong enough to be a nuisance to her. So he and Angelica had been kidnapped to blackmail both houses into stopping making spells. And if they stopped, Caprona would be defeated. The frightening part was that Tonino and Angelica were the only two people who knew, and the Duchess did not

care that they knew. It was not only that even someone as clever as Paolo would never think of looking
in the Palace, inside a Punch and Judy show: it must
mean that the two of them would be dead before
anyone found them.

"We absolutely have to get away," said Angelica.
"Before she's better from being hanged."

"She'll have thought of that," said Tonino.

"I'm not sure," said Angelica. "I could tell
everyone was startled to death. They let me see you
being put through the floor, and I think we could
get out that way. It will be easier now we're bigger."

Tonino fastened the cape around him and
struggled to his feet, though he felt almost too tired
and bruised to bother. His head hit the chandelier too. Huge flickering shadows fled around the
room and made the heap of puppets look as if they
were squirming about. "Where did they put me
through?" he said.

"Just where you're standing," said Angelica.

Tonino backed against the windows and looked
at the place. He would not have known there was
any opening. But, now Angelica had told him, he
could see, disguised by the painted swirls of the carpet and confused by the swinging light, the faintest
black line. The outline made an oblong about the
size of the shoddy dining table. The tray of supper
must have come through that way too.

"Sing an opening spell," Angelica commanded
him.

"I don't know one," Tonino was forced to confess.

He could tell by the stiff way Angelica stood that she was trying not to say a number of nasty things. "Well I don't dare," she said. "You saw what happened last time. If I do anything, they'll catch us again and punish us by making us be puppets. And I couldn't bear another time."

Tonino was not sure he could bear it either, even though, now he thought about it, he was not sure it had been a punishment. The Duchess had probably intended to make them perform anyway. She was quite mean enough. On the other hand, he was not sure he could stand another of Angelica's botched spells, either. "Well, it's only a trapdoor," he said. "It must be held up by one of those little hooks. Let's try bashing at it with the candlesticks."

"And if there's a spell on it?" said Angelica. "Oh, come on. Let's try."

They seized a candlestick each and knelt beside the windows, knocking diligently at the scarcely-seen black line. The cardboard was tough and pulpy. The candlesticks shortly looked like metal weeping willow trees. But they succeeded in making a crumbly hollow in the middle of one edge of the hidden door. Tonino thought he could see a glimmer of metal showing. He raised his bent candlestick high to deliver a mighty blow.

"*Stop!*" hissed Angelica.

There were large shuffling footsteps somewhere. Tonino lowered the candlestick by gentle fractions and scarcely dared breathe. A distant voice grumbled. . . . "Mice then" . . . "Nothing here. . . ."

It was suddenly very much darker. Someone had switched off a light, leaving them only with the bluish glimmer of the little chandelier. The footsteps shuffled. A door bumped, and there was silence.

Angelica laid her candlestick down and began trying to tear at the cardboard with her fingers. Tonino got up and wandered away. It was no good. Someone was going to hear them, whatever they did. The Palace was full of footmen and soldiers. Tonino would have given up then and waited for the Duchess to do her worst. Only now he was standing up, the cardboard room seemed so small. Half of it was filled with the puppets. There was hardly room to move. Tonino wanted to hurl himself at the walls and scream. He did make a movement, and knocked the table. Because he was so much bigger and heavier now, the table swayed and creaked.

"I know!" he said. "Finish drawing the Angel."

The bump on Angelica's forehead turned up to him. "I'm not in the mood for doodling."

"Not a doodle, a spell," Tonino explained. "And then pull the table over us while we make a hole in the trapdoor."

Angelica did not need telling that the Angel was the most potent spell in Caprona. She threw the candlestick aside and scrambled up. "That might just work," she said. "You know, for a Montana, you have very good ideas." Her head hit the chandelier again. In the confusion of swinging shadows, they could not find the tap Angelica had been drawing with. Tonino had to jam his head and arm into the tiny bathroom and pull off the other useless tap.

Even when the shadows stopped swinging, the Angel scratched on the table was hard to see. It now looked faint and small.

"He needs his scroll," said Angelica. "And I'd better put in a halo to make sure he's holy."

Angelica was now so much bigger and stronger that she kept dropping the tap. The halo, when she had scratched it in, was too big, and the scroll would not go right. The table swayed this way and that, the tap ploughed and skidded, and there was a danger the Angel would end up a complete mess.

"It's so fiddly!" said Angelica. "Will that do?"

"No," said Tonino. "It needs the scroll more unrolled. Some of the words show on our Angel."

Because he was quite right, Angelica lost her temper. "All right! Do it yourself, if you're so clever, you horrible Montana!"

She held the tap out to Tonino and he snatched it from her, quite as angry. "Here," he said, ploughing up a long curl of varnish. "Here's the hanging bit. And the words go sideways. You can see *Carmen pa, Venit ang, Cap* and a lot more, but there won't be room for it."

"Our Angel," said Angelica, "says *cis saeculare, elus cantare* and *virtus data* near the end." Tonino scratched away and took no notice. It was hard enough shaping tiny letters with a thing like a tap, without listening to Angelica arguing. "Well it does!" said Angelica. "I've often wondered why it's not the words we sing—"

The same idea came to both of them. They stared at one another, nose to nose across the scratched varnish.

"*Finding* the words means *looking* for them," said Tonino.

"And they were over our gates all the time! Oh how *stupid*!" exclaimed Angelica. "Come on. We *must* get out now!"

Tonino left the scroll with *Carmen* scraped on it. There was really no room for any more. They dragged the creaking, swaying table across the hole they had made in the floor and set to work underneath it, hacking lumps out of the painted floor. Shortly, they could see a bar of silvery metal stretching from the trap door to the floor underneath them. Tonino forced the end of his candlestick down between the battered cardboard edges and heaved sideways at the metal.

"There's a spell on it," he said.

"Angel of Caprona," Angelica said at the same moment.

And the bar slipped sideways. A big oblong piece of the floor dropped away from in front of their knees and swung, leaving a very deep dark hole.

"Let's get the Hangman's rope," said Angelica.

They edged along to the pile of puppets and disentangled the string from the little gibbet. Tonino tied it to the table leg.

"It's a long way down," he said dubiously.

"It's only a few feet *really*," Angelica said. "And we're not heavy enough to hurt. I went all floppy when you kicked me off the stage and—well—I didn't break anything anyway."

Tonino let Angelica go first, swinging down into the dark space like an energetic blue monkey. *Crunch* went the shoddy table. *Creeeak*. And it swayed towards the leg where the rope was tied.

"Angel of Caprona!" Tonino whispered.

The table plunged, one corner first, down into the space. The cardboard room rattled. And, with a rending and creaking of wood, the table stuck, mostly in the hole, but with one corner out and wedged against the sides. There was a thump from below. Tonino was fairly sure he was stuck in the room for good now.

"I'm down," Angelica whispered up. "You can pull the rope up. It nearly reaches the floor."

Tonino leaned over and fumbled the string up from the table leg. He was sure there had been a miracle. That leg ought to have broken off, or the table ought to have gone down the hole. He whispered "Angel of Caprona!" again as he slid down under the table into the dark.

The table creaked hideously, but it held together. The string burned Tonino's hands as he slid, and then it was suddenly not there. His feet hit the floor almost at once. "Oof!" he went. His feet felt as if they had been knocked up through his legs.

Down there, they were standing on the shiny floor of a Palace room. The towering walls of the Punch and Judy show were on three sides of them. Instead of a back wall, there was a curtain, intended to hide the puppet-master, and very dim light was coming in around its edges. They pulled one end of the curtain aside. It felt coarse and heavy, like a sack. Behind it was the wall of the room. The puppet show had evidently been simply pushed away to one side. There was just space for Angelica and Tonino to squeeze past the ends of the show, into a large room lit by moonlight falling in strong silver blocks across its shiny floor.

It was the same room where the court had watched the Punch and Judy show. The puppet show had not been put away. Tonino thought of the time he and Angelica had tottered on the edge of the stage, looking into nothingness. They could have been killed. That seemed another miracle. Then, they must have been in some kind of storeroom. But, when the Duchess was so mysteriously taken ill, no one had bothered to put them back there.

The moonlight glittered on the polished face of the Angel, high up on the other side of the room, leaning out over some big double doors. There were other doors, but Tonino and Angelica set out, without hesitation, towards the Angel. Both of them took it for a guide.

"Oh bother!" said Angelica, before they reached

the first block of moonlight. "We're still small. I thought we'd be the right size as soon as we got out, didn't you?"

Tonino's one idea was to get out, whatever his size. "It'll be easier to hide like this," he said. "Someone in your Casa can easily turn you back." He pulled the Hangman's cloak around him and shivered. It was colder out in the big room. He could see the moon through the big windows, riding high and cold in a wintry dark blue sky. It was not going to be fun running through the streets in a red nightgown.

"But I *hate* being this small!" Angelica complained. "We'll never be able to get downstairs."

She was right to complain, as Tonino soon discovered. It seemed a mile across the polished floor. When they reached the double doors, they were tired out. High above them, the carved Angel dangled a scroll they could not possibly read, and no longer looked so friendly. But the doors were open a crack. They managed to push the crack wider by leaning their backs against the edge of both doors. It was maddening to think they could have opened them with one hand if only they had been the proper size.

Beyond was an even bigger room. This one was full of chairs and small tables. The only advantage of being doll-sized was that they could walk under every piece of furniture in a straight line to the far-too-distant door. It was like trudging through a golden moonlit forest, where every tree had an elegant swan-bend to its trunk. The floor seemed to be marble.

Before they reached the door, they were quarrelling again from sheer tiredness.

"It's going to take all *night* to get out of here!" Angelica grumbled.

"Oh shut up!" said Tonino. "You make more fuss about things than my Aunt Gina!"

"Is your Aunt Gina bruised all over because you hit her?" Angelica demanded.

When they came to the half-open door at last, there was only another room, slightly smaller. This one had a carpet. Gilded sofas stood about like Dutch barns, and large frilly armchairs. Angelica gave a wail of despair.

Tonino stood on tiptoe. There seemed to be cushions on some of the seats. "Suppose we hid under a cushion for the night?" he suggested, trying to make peace.

Angelica turned on him furiously. "Stupid! No wonder you're slow at spells! We may be small, but they'll find us *because* of that. We must *stink* of magic. Even my baby brother could find us, and he may be a baby but he's cleverer than you!"

Tonino was too angry to answer. He simply marched away into the carpet. At first it was a relief to his sore feet, but it soon became another trial. It was like walking through long, tufty grass—and anyone who has done that for a mile or so will know how tiring that can be. On top of that, they had to keep going around puffy armchairs that seemed as big as houses, frilly footstools and screens as big as hoardings. Some of these things would have made good hiding places, but they were both too angry and frightened to suggest it.

Then, when they reached the door at last, it was shut. They threw themselves against the hard wood. It did not even shake.

"Now what?" said Tonino, leaning his back against it. The moon was going down by now. The carpet was in darkness. The bars of moonlight from the far-off windows only touched the tops of armchairs, or picked out the gold on the sofa backs, or the glitter from a shelf of colored glass vases. It would be quite dark soon.

"There's an Angel over there," Angelica said wearily.

She was right. Tonino could just see it, as colored flickers on wood, lit by moonlight reflected off the shelf of glass vases. There was another door under the Angel, or rather a dark space, because that door was wide open. Too tired even to speak, Tonino set off again, across another mile of tufty carpet, past beetling cliffs of furniture, to the other side of the room.

By the time they reached that open door, they were so tired that nothing seemed real anymore. There were four steps down beyond the door. Very well. They went down them somehow. At the bottom was an even more brutally tufted carpet. And the window here was the other side from the moon. It was quite dark.

Angelica sniffed the darkness. "Cigars."

It could have been scillas for all Tonino cared. All he wanted was the next door. He set off, feeling around the walls for it, with Angelica stumbling after. They bumped into one huge piece of furniture, felt their way around it, and banged into another, which stuck even farther into the room. And so they went, stumbling and banging, climbing across two rounded metal bars, wading in carpet, until they arrived at the four steps again. It was quite a small room—for the Palace—and it had only one door. Tonino felt for the first step, as high as his head, and did not think he had the strength to get up them again. The Angel had not been a guide after all.

"That part that stuck out," said Angelica. "I don't know what it was, but it was hollow, like a box. Shall we risk hiding in it?"

"Let's find it," said Tonino.

They found it, or something like it, by walking into it. It was a steep-sided box which came up to their armpits. There was a large piece of metal, like a very wide door knocker, hung on the front of it. When they felt inside, they felt sheets of stiff leather, and crisper stuff that was possibly paper.

"I think it's an open drawer," said Tonino.

Angelica did not answer. She simply climbed in. Tonino heard her flapping and crackling among the paper—if it was paper. Well! he thought. And it was Angelica who said they smelled of magic. But he was so tired that he climbed in too, and fell into a warm crumply nest where Angelica was already asleep. Tonino was almost too tired by now to care if they were found or not. But he had the sense to drag a piece of parchment over them both before he went to sleep too.

12

TONINO WOKE UP feeling chilly and puzzled. The light was pale and yellow because his sheet seemed to be over his face. Tonino gazed up at it, thinking it was a surprisingly flat, stiff sheet. It had large black letters on it too. His eyes traveled along the letters. *DECLARATION OF WAR (Duplicate Copy)*, he read.

Then he knew, with a jump, that he was nine inches high and lying in a drawer in the Palace. And it was light! Someone would find them. In fact, someone nearly had. That was what had woken him. He could hear someone moving about the room, making obscure thumps and shuffles, and occasionally whistling a snatch of the *Angel of Caprona*. Whoever it was had reached the drawer now. Tonino could hear the floor creak under him and a dress rustling, loud and near. He moved his head, gently and stiffly, and found Angelica's frightened face resting on crumpled paper an inch or so away. The rustling dress proved the person was a woman. It must be the Duchess looking for them.

"That Duke!" said the person, in a voice no Duchess would use. "There never was such an untidy man!" Her breathing came suddenly nearer. Before either Tonino or Angelica could think what to do, the drawer moved. Helplessly, they were shunted inwards, feet first, into darkness, and the drawer shut with a bang behind their heads.

"Help!" whispered Angelica.

"Ssh!"

The maid was still in the room. They could hear her move something, and then a tinkle of notes as she dusted a piano. Then a bump. And finally nothing. When they were quite sure she was gone, Angelica whispered, "What do we do now?"

There was room to sit up in the drawer, but not much else. Above their heads was a slit of light where the drawer met the desk, or whatever it was, and no way of opening it. But they could see quite well. Light was coming in at the back, beyond their feet. They tried bracing their hands against the wood overhead and heaving, but the drawer was made of solid, spicy-smelling wood and they could not budge it.

"We keep being shut in places without doors!" Angelica cried out. And she went floundering through the papers to the back of the drawer, where the light came in. Tonino crawled after her.

As soon as they got there, they realized this was the way out. The end of the drawer was lower than the front, and it did not reach the back of the wooden desk it was part of. There was quite a big gap there. When they put their heads into the space, they could see the ends of the other drawers above theirs going up like a ladder, and a slit of daylight at the top.

They squeezed through into the gap and climbed, side by side. It was as easy as climbing a ladder. They were one drawer away from the slit of daylight—which was going to be a tight squeeze—when they heard someone else in the room.

"They came down here, madam," said a lady's voice.

"Then we've caught them," replied the Duchess. "Look very carefully."

Tonino and Angelica hung from the back of the drawers by their fingers and toes, not daring to move. Silk dresses rustled as the Duchess and her lady moved around the room.

"There's nothing this end at all, madam,"

"And I swear this window hasn't been opened," said the Duchess. "Open all the drawers in the desk."

There was a sharp rumble above Tonino's head. Dusty white light flooded down from the open top drawer. Papers were loudly tossed over. "Nothing," said the lady. The top drawer slammed in again. Tonino and Angelica had been hanging on to the second drawer. They climbed down to the next as fast and quietly as they could. The second drawer rumbled open, and slammed shut, nearly deafening them. The drawer they were on jerked. Luckily, it was stiff. The lady tugged and rattled at it, and that gave Tonino and Angelica just time to climb frantically up to the second drawer again and cling there. And there they hung, in the dark narrow space, while the lady opened the third drawer, slammed it shut, and pulled out the bottom drawer. They craned over their arms and watched the white light flood in from below.

"Look at this!" cried the lady. "They've been here! It's like a mouse nest!"

Silks rustled as the Duchess hurried over. "Curse it!" she said. "Not long ago too! I can smell them even through the cigars. Quick! They can't be far away. They must have got out before the room was cleaned."

The drawer rumbled in, bringing dusty darkness with it. There was a flurry of silks as the two women hurried away up the steps to the room with the armchairs, and the quiet, firm *clap* of the door closing.

"Do you think it's a trap?" Angelica whispered.

"No," said Tonino. He was sure the Duchess had not guessed where they were. But they were shut in this room now, by the sound, and he had no idea how they would get the door open.

All the same, even a shut room was great open spaces compared with the narrow slit at the back of the drawers. Angelica and Tonino pushed and squeezed and forced themselves through the narrow daylight slit, and finally crawled out on the top of a writing desk. Before their eyes had got used to the light, Tonino stubbed his toe on a vast pen like a telegraph pole and then tripped over a paper knife like an ivory plank. Angelica bumped into a china ornament standing at the back of the desk. It swayed. She swayed. She flung her arms around it. When her eyes stopped watering, she found she was hugging a china Mr. Punch, nose, red nightgown and all, about the same height as she was. There was a china Judy standing at the other end of the desk.

"We can't get away from these things!" she said.

The desk was covered in smooth red leather, very easy on the feet, and held a huge white blotter, which was even more comfortable to walk on. A chair with a matching red seat stood in front of the desk. Tonino saw they could easily jump down onto it. Even more easily, they could climb down the handles of the drawers. On the other hand, the piano the maid had dusted stood right beside the desk, and the window was around the corner from the piano. To reach the window was only a long stride from the piano. Though the window was shut, it had quite an easy-looking catch, if only they could reach it.

"Look!" said Angelica, pointing disgustedly.

A whole row of Punch and Judys stood along the top of the piano. Two were puppets on stands, very old and valuable by the look of them; two more were actually made of gold; and two others were rather arty clay models, which made Punch look like a leering ordinary man and Judy uncomfortably like the Duchess. And the music which was open on the piano was headed *Arnolfini—Punch and Judy Suite.*

"I think this is the Duke's study," said Angelica. And both of them got the giggles.

Still giggling, Tonino stepped onto the piano and started to walk to the window. *Do—ti—so—fa*, went the piano.

"Come back!" Angelica laughed.

Tonino came back—*fa—so—ti—do*—nearly in hysterics.

The door of the room opened and someone hurried down the steps. Angelica and Tonino could think of nothing better to do than stand stiffly where they were, hoping to be taken for more Punch and Judys. And, luckily, the man who came in was busy and worried. He slapped a pile of papers on the desk, without so much as glancing at the two new puppets, and hurried out again, gently closing the door behind him.

"Phew!" said Angelica.

They walked around to the front of the papers and looked at them curiously. The top one said:

Report of Campaign at 08.00 hours. Summary: Troops advancing on all fronts to repel invasion. Heavy Artillery and Reservists moving up in support. Pisan front reports heavy losses. Fleet sighted—Pisan?—steaming for mouth of Voltava.

"We're at war!" said Tonino. "Why?"

"Because the Duchess has got us, of course," said Angelica. "And our families daren't make war-spells. Tonino, we must get *out*. We must tell them where the words to the *Angel* are!"

"But why does the Duchess want Caprona beaten?" Tonino said.

"I don't know," said Angelica. "There's something wrong about her, I know that. Aunt Bella said there was an awful fuss when the Duke decided to marry her. Nobody likes her."

"Let's see if we can open the window," said Tonino. He set off along the piano again. *DO-ti-so-fa-me-re*—

"Quiet!" said Angelica.

Tonino discovered that, if he put each foot down very slowly, the notes did not sound. He was halfway along the keyboard, and Angelica had one foot stretched out to follow, when they heard someone opening the door again. There was no time to be careful. Angelica fled back to the desk. Tonino, with a terrible discord, scrambled across the black notes and squeezed behind the music on the stand.

He was only just in time. When he looked—he was standing with his feet and head sideways, like an Ancient Egyptian—the Duke of Caprona himself was standing in front of the desk. Tonino thought the Duke seemed both puzzled and sad. He was tapping the *Report of Campaign* against his teeth and did not seem to notice Angelica standing between the Punch and the Judy on his desk, although Angelica's eyes were blinking against the glitter from the Duke's buttons.

"But I didn't declare war!" the Duke said to himself. "I was watching that puppet show. How could I—?" He sighed and bit the *Report* worriedly between two rows of big shiny teeth. "Is my mind going?" he asked. He seemed to be talking to Angelica. She had the sense not to answer. "I must go and ask Lucrezia," the Duke said. He flung the *Report* down at Angelica's feet and hurried out of the study.

Tonino slid cautiously down the piano lid onto the keys again—*ker-pling*. Angelica was now standing at the end of the piano, pointing at the window. She was speechless with horror.

Tonino looked—and for a moment he was as frightened as Angelica. There was a brown monster glaring at him through the glass, wide-faced, wide-eyed and shaggy. The thing had eyes like yellow lamps.

Faintly, through the glass, came a slightly irritable request to pull himself together and open the window.

"Benvenuto!" shouted Tonino.

"Oh—it's only a cat," Angelica quavered. "How terrible it must feel to be a mouse!"

"Just a cat!" Tonino said scornfully. "That's Benvenuto." He tried to explain to Benvenuto that it was not easy to open windows when you were nine inches high.

Benvenuto's impatient answer was to shove Tonino's latest magic exercise book in front of Tonino's mind's eye, open at almost the first page.

"Oh, thanks," Tonino said, rather ashamed. There were three opening-spells on that page, and none of them had stuck in his head. He chose the easiest, shut his eyes so that he could read the imaginary page more clearly, and sang the spell.

Gently and easily, the window swung open, letting in a gust of cold wind. And Benvenuto came in with the wind, almost as lightly. As Benvenuto trod gently up the scale towards him, Tonino had another moment when he knew how mice felt. Then he forgot it in the gladness of seeing Benvenuto. He stretched his arms wide to rub behind Benvenuto's horny ears. Benvenuto put his sticky black nose to Tonino's face, and they both stood, delighted, holding down a long humming discord on the piano.

Benvenuto said that Paolo was not quick enough; he could not make him understand where Tonino was. Tonino must send Paolo a message. Could Tonino write this size?

"There's a pen on the desk here," Angelica called. And Tonino remembered her saying she could understand cats.

Rather anxiously, Benvenuto wanted to know if Tonino minded him talking to a Petrocchi.

The question astonished Tonino for a moment. He had clean forgotten that he and Angelica were supposed to hate one another. It seemed a waste of time, when they were both in such trouble. "Not at all," he said.

"Do get off that piano, both of you," said Angelica. "The humming's horrible."

Benvenuto obliged, with one great flowing

leap. Tonino struggled after him with his elbows hooked over the piano lid, pushing himself along against the black notes. By the time he reached the desk, Benvenuto and Angelica had exchanged formal introductions, and Benvenuto was advising them not to try getting out of the window. The room was three floors up. The stonework was crumbling, and even a cat had some trouble keeping his feet. If they would wait, Benvenuto would fetch help.

"But the Duchess—" said Tonino.

"And the Duke," said Angelica. "This is the Duke's study."

Benvenuto considered the Duke harmless on his own. He thought they were in the safest place in the Palace. They were to stay hidden and write him a note small enough to carry in his mouth.

"Wouldn't it be better if we tied it around your neck?" Angelica asked.

Benvenuto had never submitted to anything around his neck, and he was not going to start now. Anyway, someone in the Palace might see the message.

So Tonino put one foot on the *Report of Campaign* and succeeded, by heaving with both hands, in tearing off a corner of it. Angelica passed him the huge pen, which he had to hold in both hands, with the end resting on his shoulder. Then she stood on the paper to keep it steady while Tonino wielded the pen. It was such hard work, that he kept the message as short as possible. *In Duke's*

Palace. Duchess enchantress. T.M. & A.P.

"Tell them about the words to the *Angel*," said Angelica. "Just in case."

Tonino turned the paper over and wrote *Words to* Angel *on Angel over gate. T & A.* Then, exhausted with heaving the pen up and down, he folded the piece of paper with that message inside and the first one outside, and trod it flat. Benvenuto opened his mouth. Angelica winced at that pink cavern with its arched wrinkly roof and its row of white fangs, and let Tonino place the message across Benvenuto's prickly tongue. Benvenuto gave Tonino a loving glare and sprang away. He struck one ringing chord from the piano, around middle C, made the slightest thump on the windowsill, and vanished.

Tonino and Angelica were staring after him and did not notice, until it was too late, that the Duke had come back.

"Funny," said the Duke. "There's a new Punch now, as well as a new Judy."

Tonino and Angelica stood stiff as posts, one on each end of the blotter, in agonizingly uncomfortable attitudes.

Fortunately, the Duke noticed the open window. "Blessed maids and their fresh air!" he grumbled, and went over to shut it. Tonino seized the opportunity to stand on both feet, Angelica to uncrick her neck. Then they both jumped. An unmistakable gunshot cracked out, from somewhere below. And another. The Duke bent out of the window and seemed to be watching something.

"Poor pussy," he said. He sounded sad and resigned. "Why couldn't you keep away, puss? She hates cats. And they make such a din, too, shooting them." Another shot cracked out, and then several more. The Duke stood up, shaking his head sadly. "Ah well," he said, as he shut the window. "I suppose they do eat birds."

He came back across the study. Tonino and Angelica could not have moved if they tried. They were both too stricken.

The Duke's face folded into shiny wrinkles. He had noticed the corner torn from the *Report*. "I've been eating paper now!" he said. His sad, puzzled face turned towards Tonino and Angelica. "I think I do forget things," he said. "I talk to myself. That's a bad sign. But I really don't remember you two at all. At least, I remember the new Judy, but," he said to Tonino, "I don't remember you at all. How did you get here?"

Tonino was far too upset about Benvenuto to think. After all, the Duke really was speaking to him. "Please, sir," he said, "I'll explain——"

"Shut *up*!" snapped Angelica. "I'll say a spell!"

"——only please tell me if they shot my cat," said Tonino.

"I think so," said the Duke. "It looked as if they got it." Here he took a deep breath and turned his eyes carefully to the ceiling, before he looked at Tonino and Angelica again. Neither of them moved. Angelica was glaring at Tonino, promising him spells unimaginable if he said another word.

And Tonino knew he had been an utter idiot anyway. Benvenuto was dead and there was no point in moving—no point in anything.

The Duke, meanwhile, slowly pulled a large handkerchief out of his pocket. A slightly crumpled cigar came out with it and flopped on the desk. The Duke picked it up and put it absent-mindedly between his glistening teeth. And then he had to take it out again to wipe his shiny face. "Both of you spoke," he said, putting the handkerchief away and fetching out a gold lighter. "You know that?" he said, putting the cigar back into his mouth. He gave a furtive look around, clicked the lighter, and lit the cigar. "You are looking," he said, "at a poor dotty Duke." Smoke rolled out with his words, as much smoke as if the Duke had been a dragon.

Angelica sneezed. Tonino thought he was going to sneeze. He drew a deep breath to stop himself and burst out coughing.

"Ahah!" cried the Duke. "Got you!" His large wet hands pounced, and seized each of them around the legs. Holding them like that, firmly pinned to the blotter, he sat down in the chair and bent his triumphant shiny face until it was level with theirs. The cigar, cocked out of one side of his mouth, continued to roll smoke over them. They flailed their arms for balance and coughed and coughed. "Now what are you?" said the Duke. "Another of her fiendish devices for making me think I'm potty? Eh?"

"No we're not!" coughed Tonino, and Angelica

coughed, "Oh, please stop that smoke!"

The Duke laughed. "The old Chinese cigar-torture," he said gleefully, "guaranteed to bring statues to life." But his right hand moved Tonino, stumbling and swaying, across the blotter to Angelica, where his left hand gathered him in. His right hand took the cigar out of his mouth and laid it on the edge of the desk. "Now," he said. "Let's have a look at you."

They scrubbed their streaming eyes and looked fearfully up at his great grinning face. It was impossible to look at all of it at once. Angelica settled for his left eye, Tonino for his right eye. Both eyes bulged at them, round and innocent, like Old Niccolo's.

"Bless me!" said the Duke. "You're the spell-makers' children who were supposed to come to my pantomime! Why didn't you come?"

"We never got an invitation, Your Grace," Angelica said. "Did you?" she asked Tonino.

"No," Tonino said mournfully.

The Duke's face sagged. "So that's why it was. I wrote them myself too. That's my life in a nutshell. None of the orders I give ever get carried out, and an awful lot of things get done that I never ordered at all." He opened his hand slowly. The big warm fingers peeled damply off their legs. "You feel funny wriggling about in my hand," he said. "There, if I let you go, will you tell me how you got here?"

They told him, with one or two forced pauses

when he took a puff at his cigar and set them coughing again. He listened wonderingly. It was not like explaining things to a huge grown-up Duke. Tonino felt as if he was telling a made-up story to his small cousins. From the way the Duke's eyes popped, and the way he kept saying "Go on!" Tonino was sure the Duke was believing it no more than the little Montanas believed the story of Giovanni the Giant Killer.

Yet, when they had finished, the Duke said, "That Punch and Judy show started at eight-thirty and went on till nine-fifteen. I know, because there was a clock just over you. They say I declared war at nine o'clock last night. Did either of you notice me declaring war?"

"No," they said. "Though," Angelica added sourly, "I was being beaten to death at the time and I might not have noticed."

"My apologies," said the Duke. "But did either of you hear gunfire? No. But firing started around eleven and went on all night. It's still going on. You can see it, but not hear it, from the tower over this study. Which means another damn spell, I suppose. And I think I'm supposed to sit here and not notice Caprona being blown to pieces around me." He put his chin in his hands and stared at them miserably. "I know I'm a fool," he said, "but just because I love plays and puppet theaters, I'm not an idiot. The question is, how do we get you two out of here without Lucrezia knowing?"

Tonino and Angelica were almost too surprised

and grateful to speak. And while they were still trying to say thank you, the Duke jumped upright,
staring pop-eyed.

"She's coming! I've got an instinct. Quick! Get
in my pockets!"

He turned around sideways to the desk and
held one pocket of his coat stretched against it,
between two fingers. Angelica hastily lifted the
pocket flap and slid down between the two layers of
cloth. The Duke stubbed out his cigar on the edge of
the desk and popped it in after her. Then he turned
around and held the other pocket open for Tonino.
As Tonino crouched down in fuzzy darkness, he
heard the door open and the voice of the Duchess.

"My lord, you've been smoking cigars in here
again."

13

❧❦

PAOLO WOKE UP that morning knowing that he was going to have to look for Tonino himself. If his father, and Rinaldo, and then Rosa and Marco, all refused to try, then there was no use asking anyone else.

He sat up and realized that the Casa was full of unusual noises. Below in the yard, the gate was open. He could hear the voices of Elizabeth, Aunt Anna, Aunt Maria and Cousin Claudia, who were bringing the day's bread.

"Just look at the Angel!" he heard his mother say. "Now what did that?"

"It's because we've stopped our spells," said Cousin Claudia.

Following that came a single note of song from Aunt Anna, cut off short with a squeak. Aunt Maria said angrily, "No spells, Anna! Think of Tonino!"

This was intriguing, but what really interested Paolo were the noises behind the voices: marching feet, orders being shouted, a drum beating, horses' hooves, heavy rumbling and some cursing. Paolo shot out of bed. It must be the army.

"Hundreds of them," he heard Aunt Anna say.

"Most of them younger than my Domenico," said Aunt Maria. "Claudia, take this basket while I shut the gate. All going to face three armies without a war-scrip between them. I could cry!"

Paolo shot along the gallery, pulling on his jacket, and hurried down the steps into the cold yellow sunlight. He was too late. The gate was barred and the war noises shut out. The ladies were crossing the yard with their baskets.

"Where do you think you're going?" Elizabeth called to him. "No one's going out today. There's going to be fighting. The schools are all closed."

They put down their baskets to open the kitchen door. Paolo saw them recoil, with cries of dismay.

"Good Lord!" said Elizabeth.

"Don't anyone tell Gina!" said Aunt Maria.

At the same moment, someone knocked heavily at the Casa gate.

"See who that is, Paolo," called Aunt Anna.

Paolo went under the archway and undid the flap of the peephole. He was pleased to have this chance to see the army, and pleased that the schools were shut. He had not intended to go to school today anyway.

There was a man in uniform outside, who shouted, "Open and receive this, in the name of the Duke!" Behind him, Paolo caught glimpses of shiny marching boots and more uniforms. He unbarred the gate.

Meanwhile, it became plain that Aunt Gina was not to be kept away from the kitchen. Her feet clattered on the stairs. There was a stunned pause. Then the whole Casa filled with her voice.

"Oh my God! Mother of God! *Insects!*" It even drowned the noise of the military band that was marching past as Paolo opened the gate.

The man outside thrust a sheet of paper at Paolo and darted off to hammer on the next door. Paolo looked at it. He had a mad idea that he had just been handed the words to the *Angel*. After that, he went on staring, oblivious alike of Aunt Gina— who was now screaming what she was going to do to Lucia—and of the great gun that went rumbling past, pulled by four straining horses.

> *State of Caprona,* Paolo read, *Form FR3*
> *Call Up of Final Reservists. The following*
> *to report to the Arsenal for immediate duty*
> *at 03.00 hrs, January 14th, 1979:*
> *Antonio Montana, Lorenzo Montana,*
> *Piero Montana, Ricardo Montana,*
> *Arturo Montana (ne Notti), Carlo Montana,*
> *Luigi Montana, Angelo Montana,*
> *Luca Montana, Giovanni Montana,*
> *Piero Iacopo Montana, Rinaldo Montana,*
> *Domenico Montana, Francesco Montana.*

That was everyone! Paolo had not realized that even his father was a Final Reservist.

"Shut the gate, Paolo!" shrieked Aunt Maria.

Paolo was about to obey, when he remembered that he had not yet looked at the Angel. He dodged outside and stared up, while half a regiment of infantry marched past behind him. It looked as if, in the night, every pigeon in Caprona had chosen to sit on that one golden carving. It was plastered with bird droppings. They were particularly thick, not unnaturally, on the outstretched arm holding the scroll, and the scroll was a crusty white mass. Paolo shuddered. It seemed like an omen. He did not notice one of the marching soldiers detach himself from the column and come up behind him.

"I should close the gate, if I were you," said Chrestomanci.

Paolo looked up at him and wondered why people looked so different in uniform. He pulled himself together and dragged the two halves of the gate shut. Chrestomanci helped him slot the big iron bars in to lock it. As he did, he said, "I was at the Casa Petrocchi around dawn, so there's no great need for explanations. But I would like to know what's the matter in the kitchen this time."

Paolo looked. Eight baskets piled high with round tan-colored loaves stood outside the kitchen. There were agitated noises from inside it, and a curious long droning sound. "I think it's Lucia's spell again," he said.

He and Chrestomanci set off across the yard. Before they had gone three steps, the aunts burst out of the kitchen and rushed towards him. Antonio and the uncles hurried down from the gallery, and cousins arrived from everywhere else. Aunt Francesca surged out of the Saloon. She had spent the night there, and looked as if she had. Chrestomanci was soon in the middle of a crowd and holding several conversations at once.

"You were quite right to call me," he said to Rosa, and to Aunt Francesca, "Old Niccolo is good for years yet, but you should rest." To Elizabeth and Antonio, he said, "I know about Tonino," and to Rinaldo, "This is my fourth uniform today. There's heavy fighting in the hills and I had to get through somehow. What possessed the Duke," he asked the uncles, "to declare war so soon? I could have got help from Rome if he'd waited." None of them knew, and they all told him so at once. "I know," said Chrestomanci. "I know. No war-spells. I think our enemy enchanter has made a mistake over Tonino and Angelica. If it does nothing else, it allows me a free hand." Then, as the clamor showed no sign of abating, he said, "By the way, the Final Reserve has been called up," and nodded to Paolo to give the paper to Antonio.

In the sober hush that this produced, Chrestomanci pushed his way to the kitchen and put his head inside. "My goodness me!" Paolo heard him murmur.

Paolo ducked under all the people crowding round Antonio and looked into the kitchen under Chrestomanci's elbow. He looked into a wall of insects. The place was black with them, and glittering, and crawling, and dense with different humming. Flies of all kinds, mosquitoes, wasps and midges filled the airspace. Beetles, ants, moths and a hundred other crawling things occupied the floor and shelves and sink. Peering through the buzzing clouds, Paolo was almost sure he saw a swarm of locusts on the cooking stove. It was even worse than he had imagined the Petrocchi kitchen when he was little.

Chrestomanci drew a deep breath. Paolo suspected he was trying not to laugh. They both looked around for Lucia, who was standing on one leg among the breadbaskets, wondering whether to run away. "I am sure," Chrestomanci said to her—he *was* trying not to laugh; he had to start again. "I am sure people have talked·to you about misusing spells. But—just out of interest—what did you use?"

"She used her own words to the *Angel of Caprona*!" Aunt Maria said, bursting angrily out of the crowd. "Gina's nearly out of her mind!"

"All the children did it," Lucia said defiantly. "It wasn't only me."

Chrestomanci looked at Paolo, and Paolo nodded. "A considerable tribute to the powers of the younger Montanas," said Chrestomanci. He turned and snapped his fingers into the buzzing, crawling kitchen. Not much happened. The air cleared enough for Paolo to see that it was indeed locusts on the cooker, but that was all. Chrestomanci's eyebrows went up a little. He tried again. This time nothing happened at all. He retreated from the buzzing, looking thoughtful.

"With all due respect," he said to Paolo and

Lucia, "to the *Angel of Caprona*, it should not be this powerful on its own. I'm afraid this spell will just have to wear itself out." And he said to Aunt Maria, "No wonder the enemy enchanter is so much afraid of the Casa Montana. Does this mean there won't be any breakfast?"

"No, no. We'll make it in the dining room," Aunt Maria said, looking very flustered.

"Good," said Chrestomanci. "There's something I have to say to everyone, when they're all there."

And when everyone was gathered around the tables to eat plain rolls and drink black coffee made over the dining room fire, Chrestomanci stood in front of the fire, holding a coffee cup, and said, "I know few of you believe Tonino is not in the Casa Petrocchi, but I swear to you he is not, and that Angelica Petrocchi is also missing. I think you are quite right to stop making spells until they are found, but I want to say this: even if I found Tonino and Angelica this minute, all the spells of the Casa Montana and the Casa Petrocchi are not going to save Caprona now. There are three armies, and the fleet of Pisa, closing in on her. The *only thing* which is going to help you is the true words to the *Angel of Caprona*. Have you all understood?"

They all had. Everyone was silent. Nobody spoke for some time. Then Uncle Lorenzo began grumbling. Moths had got into his Reservist uniform. "Someone took the spell out," he complained. "I shan't be fit to be seen."

"Does it matter?" asked Rinaldo. His face was very white and he was not having anything but coffee. "You'll only be seen dead anyway."

"But that's just it!" said Uncle Lorenzo. "I don't want to be seen dead in it!"

"Oh be quiet!" Domenico snapped at him. Uncle Lorenzo was so surprised that he stopped talking. Breakfast finished in gloomy murmurs.

Paolo got up and slid behind the bench where Chrestomanci was sitting. "Excuse me, sir. Do you know where Tonino is?"

"I wish I did," said Chrestomanci. "This enchanter is good. So far, I have only two clues. Last night, when I was coming up through Siena, somebody worked two very strange spells somewhere ahead of me."

"Tonino?" Paolo said eagerly.

Chrestomanci shook his head. "The first one was definitely Angelica. She has what you might call an individual style. But the other one baffled me. Do you think your brother is capable of working anything strong enough to get through an enchanter's spells? Angelica did it through sheer weirdness. Could Tonino, do you think?"

"I shouldn't think so," said Paolo. "He doesn't know many spells, but he always gets them right and they work—"

"Then it remains a mystery," said Chrestomanci. He sighed. Paolo thought he looked tired.

"Thanks," he said, and slipped off, carefully thinking careless thoughts about what would he do now school was closed. He did not want anyone to notice what he meant to do.

He slipped through the coach house, past the crumpled horses and coachman, past the coach, and opened the little door in the wall at the back. He was half through it, when Rosa said doubtfully, at the front of the coach house, "Paolo? Are you in there?"

No, I'm not, Paolo thought, and shut the little door after him as gently as he knew how. Then he ran.

By this time, there were hardly any soldiers in the streets, and hardly anyone else either. Paolo ran past yellow houses, heavily shuttered, in a quiet broken by the uneasy ringing of bells. From time to time, he thought he could hear a dull, distant noise—a sort of booming, with a clatter in its midst. Wherever the houses opened out and Paolo could see the hills, he saw soldiers—not as soldiers, but as crawling, twinkling lines, winding upwards—and some puffs of smoke. He knew Chrestomanci was right. The fighting was very near.

He was the only person about in the Via Cantello. The Casa Petrocchi was as shuttered and barred as the Casa Montana. And their Angel was covered with birdlime too. Like the Montanas, they had stopped making spells. Which showed, thought Paolo, that Chrestomanci was right about Angelica too. He was much encouraged by that as he hammered on the rough old gate.

There was no sound from inside, but, after a second or so, a white cat jumped to the top of the gate, and crouched in the gap under the archway, looking down with eyes even bluer than Paolo's.

Those eyes reminded Paolo that his own eyes were likely to give him away. He did not think he dared disguise them with a spell, in case the Petrocchis noticed. So he swallowed, told himself that he had to find the one person who was likely to help him look for Tonino, and said to the cat, "Renata. Could I speak to Renata?"

The white cat stared. Maybe it made some remark. Then it jumped down inside the Casa, leaving Paolo with an uncomfortable feeling that it knew who he was. But he waited. Before he had quite decided to go away again, the peephole was unlatched. To his relief, it was Renata's pointed face that looked through the bars at him.

"Whoops!" she said. "I see why Vittoria fetched *me*. What a relief you came!"

"Come and help find Tonino and Angelica," said Paolo. "Nobody will listen."

"Ung." Renata pulled a strip of her red hair into her mouth and bit it. "We're forbidden to go out. Think of an excuse."

"Your teacher's ill and scared of the war and wants us to sit with her," said Paolo.

"That might do," said Renata. "Come in while I ask." Paolo heard the gate being unbarred. "Her name's Mrs. Grimaldi," Renata whispered, holding the gate open for him. "She lives in the Via Sant' Angelo and she's ever so ugly, in case they ask. Come in."

Considerably to his amazement, Paolo entered the Casa Petrocchi, and was even more amazed not to be particularly frightened. He felt as if he was about to do an exam, keyed up, and knowing he was in for it, but that was all.

He saw a yard and a gallery so like his own that he could almost have believed he had been magically whisked back home. There were differences, of course. The gallery railings were fancy wrought-iron, with iron leopards in them at intervals. The cats that sat sunning themselves on the waterbutts were mostly ginger or tabby—whereas in the Casa Montana, Benvenuto had left his mark, and the cats were either black or black and white. And there was a gush of smell from the kitchen—frying onions—the like of which Paolo had not smelled since Lucia cast her unlucky spell.

"Mother!" shouted Renata.

But the first person who appeared was Marco. Marco was galloping down the steps from the gallery with a pair of long shiny boots in one hand, and a crumpled red uniform over his arm. "Mother!" Marco bellowed, in the free and easy way people always bellow for their mothers. "Mother! There's moth in my uniform! Who took the spell out of it?"

"Stupid!" Renata said to him. "We put every single spell away last night." And she said to Paolo, "That's my brother Marco."

Marco turned indignantly to Renata. "But moths take months—!" And he saw Paolo. It was hard to tell which of them was more dismayed.

At that moment, a red-haired, worried-looking lady came across the yard, carrying a little boy. The baby had black hair and the same bulging forehead as Angelica. "I don't know, Marco," she said. "Get Rosa to mend it. What is it, Renata?"

Marco interrupted. "Rosa," he said, looking fixedly at Paolo, "is with her *sister*. Who's your friend, Renata?"

Paolo could not resist. "I'm Paolo Andretti," he said wickedly. Marco rewarded him with a look which dared him to say another word.

Renata was relieved, because she now knew what to call Paolo. "Paolo wants me to come and help look after Mrs. Grimaldi. She's ill in bed, Mother."

Paolo could see by the way Marco's eyes went first wide and then almost to slits, that Marco was extremely alarmed by this and determined to stop Renata. But Paolo could not see how Marco could do anything. He could not give away that he knew who Paolo was without giving away himself and Rosa too. It made him want to laugh.

"Oh poor Mrs. Grimaldi!" said Mrs. Petrocchi. "But, Renata, I don't think—"

"Doesn't Mrs. Grimaldi realize there's a war on?" Marco said. "Did Paolo tell you she was ill?"

"Yes," Paolo said glibly. "My mother's great friends with Mrs. Grimaldi. She's sorry for her because she's so ugly."

"And of course she knows about the war," Renata said. "I kept telling you, Marco, how she dives under her desk if she hears a bang. She's scared stiff of guns."

"And it's all been too much for her, Mother says," Paolo added artistically.

Marco tried another tack. "But why does Mrs. Grimaldi want *you*, Renata? Since when have you been teacher's pet?"

Renata, who was obviously as quick as Paolo, said, "Oh, I'm not. She just wants me to amuse her with some spells—"

At this, Mrs. Petrocchi and Marco both said, "You're not to use spells! Angelica—"

"—but of course I won't," Renata continued smoothly. "I'll just sing songs. She likes me to sing. And Paolo's going to read to her out of the Bible. Do say we can go, Mother. She's lying in bed all on her own."

"Well—" said Mrs. Petrocchi.

"The streets aren't safe," said Marco.

"There was no one about at all," Paolo said, giving Marco a look to make him watch it. Two could play at that.

"Mother," said Renata, "you are going to mend Marco's uniform, aren't you?"

"Yes, yes, of course," said Mrs. Petrocchi.

Renata at once took this as permission to go with Paolo. "Come on, Paolo," she said, and raced under Marco's nose to what was obviously the coach house. Paolo whizzed after her.

Marco, however, was not defeated. Before Renata's hand was on the latch of the big door, an obvious uncle was leaning over the gallery. "Renata! Be a good girl and find me my tobacco." An obvious aunt shot out of the kitchen. She looked like Aunt Gina with red hair, and she hooted in the same way. "Renata! Have you taken my good knife?" Two young cousins shot out of another door. "Renata, you said you'd play dressing up!" and Mrs. Petrocchi, looking anxious and undecided, was holding the baby boy out, saying, "Renata, you'll have to mind Roberto while I'm sewing."

"I can't stop now!" Renata shouted back. "Poor Mrs. Grimaldi!" She wrenched open the big door and pushed Paolo inside. "What's going on?" she whispered.

It was obvious to Paolo what was going on. It was so like the Casa Montana. Marco had broadcast—not an alarm, because he dared not—a sort of general uneasiness about Renata. "Marco's trying to stop us," he said.

"I know *that*," Renata said, hurrying him past the sleek Petrocchi coach and—to Paolo's interest— past four black cardboard horses as crumpled and muddy as the Casa Montana ones. "*Why* is he? How does he know?"

Behind them was a perfect clamor of Petrocchi voices, all wanting Renata. "He just does," Paolo said. "Be quick!"

The small door to the street had a big stiff key. Renata took it in both hands and struggled to turn it. "Does he know *you*?" she said sharply.

Like an answer, Marco's voice sounded from behind the coach. "Renata!" Then, much more softly, "Paolo—Paolo Montana, come here!"

The door came open. "Run, if you're coming!" Paolo said. They shot out into the street, both running hard. Marco came to the door and shouted something, but he did not seem to be following. Nevertheless, Paolo kept on running, which forced Renata to run too. He did not want to talk. He wanted to absorb the shock of Marco. Marco Andretti was really Marco Petrocchi—he must be Guido's eldest son! Rosa Montana and Marco Petrocchi. How did they do it? How ever did they *manage* it? he kept wondering. And also—more soberly—How ever will they get away with it?

"All right. That will do," Renata panted. By this time they had crossed the Corso and were down beside the river, trotting along empty quaysides towards the New Bridge. Renata slowed down, and Paolo did too, quite breathless. "Now," she said, "tell me how Marco knew you, or I won't come a step farther."

Paolo looked at her warily. He had already discovered that Renata was, as Aunt Gina would say, sharp enough to cut herself, and he did not like the way she was looking at him. "He saw me at the Palace of course," Paolo said.

"No he didn't," said Renata. "He drove the coach. He knows your name *and* he knows why you came, doesn't he? How?"

"I think he must have been standing behind us

on the Art Gallery steps, and we didn't see him in the fog," said Paolo.

Renata's shrewd eyes continued the look Paolo did not like. "Good try," she said. Paolo tried to break off the look by turning and sauntering on along the quays. Renata followed him, saying, "And I was meant to get all embarrassed and not ask any more. You're sharp enough to cut yourself, Mr. Montana. But what a pity. Marco wasn't in the fight. They wanted him for the single combat, that's how I know, and he wasn't there, so Papa had to do it. And I can tell that you don't want me to know how Marco knows you. And I can tell Marco doesn't, or he'd have stopped me going by saying who you were. So—"

"You're the one who's going to cut yourself," Paolo said over his shoulder, "by being too clever. I don't know how Marco knew me, but he was being kind not say—" He stopped. He sniffed. He was level with an alleyway, where a peeling blue house bulged out onto the jetty. Paolo felt the air around that alley with a sense he hardly knew he had, inborn over generations of spell-making. A spell had been set here—a strong spell, not long ago.

Renata came up behind. "You're not going to wriggle out—" She stopped too. "Someone made a spell here!"

"Was it Angelica? Can you tell?" Paolo asked.

"Why?" said Renata.

Paolo told her what Chrestomanci had said. Her face went red, and she prodded with her toe at a mooring chain in the path. "Individual style!" she said. "Him and his jokes! It's not Angelica's fault. She was born that way. And it's not everyone who can get a spell to work by doing everything wrong. I think she's a sort of back-to-front genius, and I told the Duchess of Caprona so when she laughed, too!"

"But is the spell hers?" asked Paolo. He could hear gunfire, from somewhere down the river, mixed with the dull booming from the hills. It was a blunt, bonking *clomp, clomp*, like a giant chopping wood. His head went up to listen as he said, "I know it's not Tonino. His feel careful."

"No," said Renata, and her head was up too. "It's a bit stale, isn't it? And it doesn't feel very nice. The war sounds awfully close. I think we ought to get off the quays."

She was probably right. Paolo hesitated. He was sure they were hot on the trail. The stale spell had a slight sick feeling to it, which reminded him of the message in the yard last night.

And while he hesitated, the war seemed suddenly right on top of them. It was deafening, brazen, horrible. Paolo thought of someone holding one end of an acre of sheet metal and flapping it, or of gigantic alarm clocks. But that did not do justice to the noise. Nor did it account for some huge metallic screeches. He and Renata ducked and put their hands to their ears, and enormous things whirled above them. They went on, whatever they were, out above the river. Paolo and Renata crouched on the quay, staring at them.

They flapped across in a group—there were at least eight of them—gonging and screeching. Paolo thought first of flying machines and then of the Montana winged horse. There seemed to be legs dangling beneath the great black bodies, and their metal wings were whirling furiously. Some of them were not flying so well. One lost height, despite madly clanging with its wings, and dropped into the river with a splash that threw water all over the New Bridge and spattered Renata and Paolo. Another one lost height and whirled its iron tail for balance. Paolo recognized it as one of the iron griffins from the Piazza Nuova, as it, too, fell into a spout of water.

Renata began to laugh. "Now that *is* Angelica!" she said. "I'd know her spells anywhere."

They leaped up and raced for the long flight of stairs up to the Piazza Nuova. The din from the griffins was still drowning all but the nearest gunfire. Renata and Paolo ran up the steps, turning round at every landing to see what was happening to the rest of the griffins. Two more came down in the river. A further two plunged into the gardens of rich villas. But the last two were going well. When Paolo next looked, they seemed to be struggling to gain altitude in order to get over the hills beyond the Palace. The distant clanging was fast and furious, and the metal wings a blur.

Paolo and Renata turned and climbed again. "What is it? A call for help?" panted Paolo.

"Must be," gasped Renata. "Angelica's spells—always—mad kind of reasonableness."

An echoing clang brought them whirling around. Another griffin was down, but they did not see where. Fascinated, they watched the efforts of the last one. It had now reached the marble front of the Duke's Palace, and it was not high enough to clear it. The griffin seemed to know. It put out its claws and seemed to be clutching at the zig-zag marble battlements. But that did no good. They saw it, a distant black blot, go sliding down the colored marble facade—they could even hear the grinding—down and down, until it crashed onto the roof of the marble gateway, where it drooped and lay still. Above it, even from here, they could see two long lines of scratches, all down the front of the Palace.

"Wow!" said Paolo.

He and Renata climbed up into the strangely bare Piazza Nuova. It was now nothing but a big paved platform surrounded by a low wall. At intervals around the wall were the snapped-off stumps of the griffins' pedestals, each with a broken green or crimson plaque lying beside it. In the middle, what had been a tangled griffin fountain was now a jet of water from a broken pipe.

"Just look at all these spells she's broken!" exclaimed Renata. "I didn't think she could do anything this strong!"

Paolo looked across at the scratched Palace, rather enviously. There were spells in the marble to stop that kind of thing. Angelica must have broken them all. The odd thing was that he could not feel the spell. The Piazza Nuova ought to have reeked of magic, but it just felt empty. He stared around, puzzled. And there, trotting slowly and wearily along the low wall, was a familiar brown shape with a trailing bush of a tail.

"Benvenuto!" he said.

For a moment, it looked as if Benvenuto was going to walk straight past Paolo, as he so often did. But that must have been because he was tired. He stopped. He glared urgently at Paolo. Then he carefully opened his mouth and spat out a small folded scrap of paper. After that, he lay down and lost interest in the world. Paolo could see his brown sides heaving when he picked up the paper.

Renata looked over Paolo's shoulder as Paolo— rather disgustedly, because it was wet—unfolded the paper. The writing was definitely Tonino's, though it was far too small. And, though Paolo did not know it, not much of Tonino's message had survived. He and Renata read:

ords to Angel on Angel over

It was small wonder that Paolo and Renata misunderstood. From the Piazza Nuova, now the griffins were gone, an Angel was clearly visible. It stood, golden and serene, guarding a Caprona which was already surrounded in the smoke from gunfire, on top of the great dome of the Cathedral.

"Do you think we can get up there?" said Paolo.

Renata's face was white. "We'd better try. But I warn you, I'm no good at heights."

They hurried down among the red roofs and golden walls, leaving Benvenuto asleep on the wall. After a while, Benvenuto picked himself up and trotted away, restored. It took more than a few ill-aimed rifles to finish Benvenuto.

When Paolo and Renata reached the cobbled square in front of the Cathedral, the great bell in the bell tower beside it was tolling. People were gathering into the church to pray for Caprona, and the Archbishop of Caprona himself was standing by the door blessing everyone who entered. Renata and Paolo joined the line. It seemed the easiest way to get in. They had nearly reached the door, when Marco dashed into the square towing Rosa. Rosa saw Renata's hair and pointed. She was too blown to speak. Marco grinned. "Your spell wins," he said.

14

✦

THE WARM POCKET holding Tonino swayed and swooped as the Duke stood up. "Of course I smoked a cigar," he said to the Duchess, injured. "Anyone would smoke a cigar if they found they'd declared war without knowing they had and knew they were bound to be beaten." His voice came rumbling to Tonino's ears through his body, more than from outside.

"I've told you it's bad for your health," said the Duchess. "Where are you going?"

"Me? Oh," said the Duke. The pockets swooped, then swooped again, as he climbed the steps to the door. "Off to the kitchens. I feel peckish."

"You could send for food," said the Duchess, but she did not sound displeased. Tonino knew she had guessed they had been in the study all along and wanted the Duke out of it while she found them.

He heard the door shut. The pocket swung rhythmically as the Duke walked. It was not too bad once Tonino was used to it. It was a large pocket. There was almost room in it for Tonino, and the

Duke's lighter, and his handkerchief, and another cigar, and some string, and some money, and a rosary, and some dice. Tonino made himself comfortable with the handkerchief as a cushion and wished the Duke would not keep patting at him to see if he was there.

"Are you all right in there?" the Duke rumbled at last. "Nobody about. You can stick your heads out. I thought of the kitchens because you didn't seem to have had any breakfast."

"You are kind," Angelica's voice came faintly. Tonino worked himself to his feet and put his head out under the flap of the pocket. He still could not see Angelica—the Duke's generous middle was in the way—but he heard her say, "You keep rather a lot of things in your pockets, don't you? Do you happen to know what I've got stuck to my foot?"

"Er—toffee, I suspect," said the Duke. "Please oblige me by eating it."

"Thanks," Angelica said doubtfully.

"I say," said Tonino. "Why didn't the Duchess know we were in your pockets? She could smell us before."

The Duke's loud laugh rumbled through him. The gilded wall Tonino could see began to jolt upward, and upward, and upward. The Duke was walking downstairs. "Cigars, lad!" the Duke said. "Why do you think I smoke them? She can't smell anything through them, and she hates that. She tried setting a spell on me to make me stop once, but I got so bad-tempered she had to take it off."

"Excuse me, sir," came Angelica's voice from the other side of the Duke. "Won't someone notice if you walk downstairs talking to yourself?"

The Duke laughed again. "Not a soul! I talk to myself all the time—and laugh, too, if something amuses me. They all think I'm potty anyway. Now, have you two thought of a way to get you out of here? The safest way would be to fetch your families here. Then I could hand you over in secret, and she'd be none the wiser."

"Can't you just send for them?" Tonino suggested. "Say you need them to help in the war."

"She'd smell a rat," said the Duke. "She says your war-charms are all washed up anyway. Think of something that's nothing to do with the war."

"Special effects for another pantomime," Tonino suggested, rather hopelessly. But he could see that even the Duke was not likely to produce a play while Caprona was being invaded.

"I know," said Angelica. "I shall cast a spell."

"No!" said Tonino. "Anything might happen!"

"That doesn't matter," said Angelica. "My family would know it's me, and they'd come here like a shot."

"But you might turn the Duke green!" said Tonino.

"I really wouldn't mind," the Duke put in mildly.

He came to the bottom of the stairs and went with long, charging strides through rooms and corridors of the Palace. Angelica and Tonino each held on to an edge of their pockets and shouted arguments around him.

"But you could help me," said Angelica, "and your part would go right. Suppose we made it a calling-charm to fetch all the rats and mice in Caprona to the Palace. If you did the calling, we'd fetch something."

"Yes, but what would it be?" said Tonino.

"We could make it in honor of Benvenuto," shouted Angelica, hoping to please him.

But Tonino thought of Benvenuto lying somewhere on a Palace roof and became more obstinate than ever. He shouted that he was not going to do anything so disrespectful.

"Are you telling me you can't do a calling-spell?" shrieked Angelica. "Even my baby brother—"

They were shouting so loudly that the Duke had to tell them to shush twice. The military man hurrying up to the Duke stared slightly. "No need to stare, Major," the Duke said to him. "I said Shush and I meant Shush. Your boots squeak. What is it?"

"I'm afraid the forces of Caprona are in retreat in the south, Your Grace," said the soldier. "And our coastal batteries have fallen to the Pisan fleet."

Both pockets drooped as the Duke's shoulders slumped. "Thank you," he said. "Report to me personally next time you have news." The Major saluted and went, glancing at the Duke once or twice over his shoulder. The Duke sighed. "There goes another one who thinks I'm mad. Didn't you two say you were the only ones who knew where to find the words to the *Angel*?"

Tonino and Angelica put their heads out of his pockets again. "Yes," they said.

"Then," said the Duke, "will you please agree on a spell. You really must get out and get those words while there's still some of Caprona left."

"All right," said Tonino. "Let's call mice." He had not seen it was so urgent.

So the Duke stood in a wide window bay and lit the cigar stub from under Angelica with the lighter from under Tonino, to cover up the spell. Tonino leaned out of his pocket and sang, slowly and carefully, the only calling-spell he knew. Angelica stood in the other pocket with her arms upraised and spoke, quickly, confidently and—quite certainly—wrong. Afterwards, she swore it was because she nearly laughed.

Another man approached. Tonino thought it was one of the courtiers who had watched the puppet show, but he was never sure, because the Duke flipped his pocket flaps down over their heads and began singing himself.

> *"Merrily his music ringing,*
> *See an Angel cometh singing . . ."*

roared the Duke. Even Angelica did not sing so much out of tune. Tonino had the greatest difficulty in keeping up his own song. And it was certainly around then that the spell seemed to go wrong. Tonino had the sudden feeling that his words were pulling a great weight.

The Duke broke off his abominable singing to say, "Ah, Pollio, there's nothing like a good song while Caprona burns! Nero did it, and now me."

"Yes, Your Grace," the man said feebly. They heard him scuttle away.

"And he's *sure* I'm mad," said the Duke. "Finished?"

Just then, Tonino's words came loose, with a sort of jerk, and he knew the spell had worked in some way or another. "Yes," he said.

But nothing seemed to happen. The Duke said philosophically that it would take a mouse quite a while to run from the Corso to the Palace, and strode on to the kitchens. They thought he was mad there, too, Tonino could tell. The Duke asked for two bread rolls and two pats of butter and solemnly put one into each pocket. No doubt they thought he was madder still when he remarked to no one: "There's a cigar cutter in my right pocket that spreads butter quite well."

"Indeed, Your Grace?" they heard someone say dubiously.

Just then, someone rushed in screaming about the griffins from the Piazza Nuova. They were flying across the river, straight for the Palace. There was a general panic. Everyone screamed and yammered and said it was an omen of defeat. Then someone else rushed in yelling that one griffin had actually reached the Palace and was sliding down the marble front. There was more outcry. The next thing, everyone said, the great gold Angel from the Cathedral would fly away too.

Tonino was taking advantage of the confusion to bash a piece off his roll with the Duke's lighter, when the Duke bellowed, *"Nonsense!"* There was sudden quiet. Tonino dared not move, because everyone was certainly looking at the Duke.

"Don't you see?" said the Duke. "It's just an enemy trick. But we in Caprona don't frighten that easily, do we? Here—you—go and fetch the Montanas. And you go and get the Petrocchis. Tell them it's urgent. Tell as many of them to come as possible. I shall be in the North gallery." And he went striding off there, while Angelica and Tonino jigged against bread and tried not to tread in the butter.

When he got to the gallery, the Duke sat down on a window seat. Angelica and Tonino stood half out of his pockets and managed to eat their bread and butter. The Duke amiably handed the cigar cutter from one to the other and, in between whiles, seemed lost in thought, staring at the white puffs of shells bursting on the hills behind Caprona.

Angelica was inclined to be smug. "I told you," she said to Tonino, "my spells always work."

"Iron griffins," said Tonino, "aren't mice."

"No, but I've never done anything as big as that before," said Angelica. "I'm glad it didn't knock the Palace down."

The Duke said gloomily, "The guns of Pisa are going to do that soon. I can see gunboats on the river, and I'm sure they aren't ours. I wish your families would be quick."

But it was half an hour before a polite footman came up to the Duke, causing him to flip his pocket flaps down and scatter buttery crumbs in all directions. "Your Grace, members of the Montana and Petrocchi families are awaiting you in the Large Reception Saloon."

"Good!" said the Duke. He leaped up and ran so fast that Tonino and Angelica had to brace their feet on the seams of his pockets and hang on hard to the edges. They lost their footing several times, even though the Duke tried to help them by holding his pockets as he ran. They felt him clatter to a stop. "Blast!" he said. "This is always happening!"

"What?" asked Tonino breathlessly. He felt jerked out of shape.

"They've told me the wrong room!" said the Duke and set off again on another swaying, jolting run. They felt him dive forward through a doorway. His pockets swung. Then they swung the other way as he slid and stopped. "Lucrezia, this is too bad! Is this why you always tell me the wrong room?"

"My lord," came the coldest voice of the Duchess from some way off, "I can't answer for the slackness of the footmen. What is the matter?"

"This," said the Duke. "These—" They felt him shaking. "Those were the Montanas and the Petrocchis, weren't they? Don't fob me off, Lucrezia. I sent for them. I know."

"And what if they were?" said the Duchess, rather nearer. "Do you wish to join them, my lord?"

They felt the Duke backing away. "No. No indeed! My dear, your will is always my pleasure. I—I just want to know why. They only came about some griffins."

The Duchess's voice moved away again as she answered. "Because, if you must know, Antonio Montana recognized me."

"But—but—" said the Duke, laughing uneasily, "everyone knows you, my dear. You're the Duchess of Caprona."

"I mean, he recognized me for what I am," said the Duchess from the distance. The sound of a door shutting followed.

"Look!" said the Duke in a shaky whisper. "Just look!" While he was still saying it, Angelica and Tonino were bracing their feet on the seams of his pockets and pushing their heads out from under the flaps.

They saw the same polished room where they had once waited and eaten cakes, the same gilded chairs and angelic ceiling. But this time the polished floor was littered with puppets. Puppets lay all over it, limp grotesque things, scattered this way and that as people might lie if they had suddenly fallen. They were in two groups. Otherwise there was no way of telling which puppet was who. There were Punches, Judys, Hangmen, Sausage-men, Policemen, and an odd Devil or so, over and over again. From the numbers, it looked as if both families had realized

that Tonino and Angelica were behind the mysterious griffins and had sent nearly every grown-up in
the Casas.

Tonino could not speak. Angelica said, "That
hateful woman! Her mind seems to run on puppets."

"She sees people that way," the Duke said miserably. "I'm sorry, both of you. She's been too many
for us. Terrible female! I can't think why I married
her—but I suppose that was a spell too."

"Do you think she suspects you've got us?"
Tonino asked. "She must be wondering where we
are."

"Maybe, maybe," said the Duke. He marched
up and down the room, while they leaned out of his
pockets and looked down at the crowd of strewn
floppy puppets. "She doesn't care now, of course,"
he said. "She's done for both families anyway. Oh, I
am a fool!"

"It's not your fault," said Angelica.

"Oh, but it is," said the Duke. "I never show the
slightest resolution. I always take the easiest way—
What is it?" Darkness descended as he flipped his
pocket flaps down.

"Your Grace," said the Major whose boots
squeaked, "the Pisan fleet is landing men down
beyond the New Quays. And our troops to the south
are being rolled back into the suburbs."

They felt the Duke droop. "Almost done, in
fact," he said. "Thanks— No, wait, Major! Could
you be a good fellow and go to the stables and order
out my coach? The lackeys have all run away, you

know. Ask for it at the door in five minutes."

"But, Your Grace—" said the Major.

"I intend to go down into the city and speak with the people," said the Duke. "Give them what's-it-called. Moral support."

"A very fine aim, sir," said the Major, with a great deal more warmth. "In five minutes, sir." His boots went squeaking swiftly off.

"Did you hear that?" said the Duke. "He called me 'sir'! Poor fellow. I told him a set of whoppers and he couldn't take his eyes off all those puppets, but he called me 'sir,' and he'll get that coach and he won't tell her. Cardboard box!"

The hangings whipped by as the Duke charged through a doorway into another room. This one had a long table down the middle. "Ah!" said the Duke, and charged towards a stack of boxes by the wall. The boxes proved to have wine glasses in them, which the Duke proceeded feverishly to unload on to the table.

"I don't understand," Tonino said.

"Box," said the Duke. "We can't leave your families behind, for her to revenge herself on. I'm going to be resolute for once. I'm going to get in the coach and go, and dare her to stop me." So saying, he stormed back to the reception room with the empty box and knelt down to collect the puppets. Angelica was bounced on the floor as his coat swung. "Sorry," said the Duke.

"Pick them up gently," said Tonino. "It hurts if you don't."

Tenderly and hastily, using both hands for each puppet, the Duke packed the puppets in layers in the cardboard box. In the process, Montanas got very thoroughly mixed with Petrocchis, but there was no way of preventing that. All three of them were expecting the Duchess to come in any moment. The Duke kept looking nervously around and then muttering to himself, "Resolute!" He was still muttering it when he set off, awkwardly carrying the cardboard box in his arms. "Funny to think," he remarked, "that I'm carrying almost every spell-maker in Caprona at the moment."

Boots squeaked towards them. "Your coach is waiting, sir," said the voice of the Major.

"Resolute," said the Duke. "I mean, thank you. I shall think of you in heaven, Major, since I'm sure that's where most of us are going soon. Meanwhile, can you do two more things for me?"

"Sir?" said the Major alertly.

"First, when you think of the Angel of Caprona, what do you think of?"

"The song or the figure, sir?" the Major asked, more wary now than alert.

"The figure."

"Why—" The Major was becoming sure that the Duke was mad again. "I—I think of the golden Angel on the Cathedral, Your Grace."

"Good man!" the Duke cried out. "So do I! The other thing is, can you take this box and stow it in my coach for me?" Neither Tonino nor Angelica could resist peeping out to see how the Major took this request. Unfortunately, his face was hidden behind the box as the Duke thrust it at him. They felt they had missed a rare sight. "If anyone asks," the Duke said, "it's gifts for the war-weary people."

"Yes, Your Grace." The Major sounded amused and indulgent, humoring the Duke in his madness, but they heard his boots squeaking briskly off.

"Thank the lord!" said the Duke. "I'm not going to be caught with them. I can feel her coming."

Thanks to the Duke's charging run, it was some minutes before the Duchess caught up with them. Tonino, squinting out under the flap, could see the great marble entrance hall when the Duke skidded to a stop. He dropped the flap hastily when he heard the cold voice of the Duchess. She sounded out of breath but triumphant.

"The enemy is by the New Bridge, my lord. You'll be killed if you go out now."

"And I'll be killed if I stay here too," said the Duke. He waited for the Duchess to deny this, but she said nothing. They heard the Duke swallow. But his resolution held. "I'm going," he said, a mite squeakily, "to drive down among my people and comfort their remaining hours."

"Sentimental fool," said the Duchess. She was not angry. It was what she thought the Duke was.

This made the Duke bluster. "I may not be a good ruler," he said, "but this is what a good ruler should do. I shall—I shall pat the heads of children and join in the singing of the choir."

The Duchess laughed. "And much good may it

do you, particularly if you sing," she said. "Very well. You can get killed down there instead of up here. Run along and pat heads."

"Thank you, my dear," the Duke said humbly. He surged forward again, *thump, thump, thump*, down marble steps. They heard the sound of hooves on gravel and felt the Duke shaking. "Let's go, Carlo," he said. "What is it? What are you pointing—? Oh yes. So it is a griffin. How remarkable. Drive on, can't you." He surged upwards. Coach-springs creaked and a door clapped shut. The Duke surged down. They heard him say "Oh good!" as he sat, and the rather-too-familiar sound of cardboard being hit, as he patted the box on the seat beside him. Then the coach started, with a shrilling of wheels on gravel and a battering of hooves. They felt the Duke sigh with relief. It made them bounce. "You can come out now," said the Duke.

They climbed cautiously out onto his wide knees. The Duke kindly moved over to the window so that they could see out. And the first thing that met their eyes was an iron griffin, very crumpled and bent, lying in quite a large crater in the Palace yard.

"You know," said the Duke, "if my Palace wasn't going to be broken up anyway by Pisans, or Sienese, or Florentines, I'd get damages off you two. The other griffin has scraped two great ditches all down my facade." He laughed and patted at his glossy face with his handkerchief. He was still very nervous.

As the coach rolled out of the yard onto the

road, they heard gunfire. Some of it sounded near, a rattle of shots from below by the river. Most of it was far and huge, a long grumble from the hills. The bangs were so close together that the sound was nearly continuous, but every so often, out of the grumble, came a very much nearer *clap-clap-clap*. It made all three of them jump each time.

"We *are* taking a pounding," the Duke said unhappily.

The coach slowed down. They could hear the prim voice of the coachman among the other noise. "I fear the New Bridge is under fire, Your Grace. Where exactly are we bound?"

The Duke pushed down the window. The noise doubled. "The Cathedral. Go upriver and see if we can cross by the Old Bridge." He pushed the window shut. "Phew! I don't envy Carlo up there on the box!"

"Why are we going to the Cathedral?" Angelica asked anxiously. "We want to look at the Angels on our Casas."

"No," said the Duke. "She'll have thought of those. That's why I asked the Major. It seems to me that the one place where those words are always safe and always invisible *must* be on the Cathedral Angel. You think of it at once, but it's up there and far away, so you forget it."

"But it's *miles* up!" said Angelica.

"It's got a scroll, though," said Tonino. "And the scroll looks to be more unrolled than the ones on our Angels."

"I'm afraid it's bound to be about the only place she might have forgotten," said the Duke.

They rattled along briskly, except for one place, where there was a shell crater in the road. Somehow, Carlo got them around it.

"Good man, Carlo," said the Duke. "About the one good man she hasn't got rid of."

The noise diminished a little as the coach went down to the river and the Piazza Martia—at least, Angelica and Tonino guessed that was where it was; they found they were too small to see any great distance. They could tell they were on the Old Bridge, by the rumble under the wheels and the little shuttered houses on either side. The Duke several times craned around, whistled and shook his head, but they could not see why. They recognized the Cathedral, when the coach wheeled towards it across the cobbles, because it was so huge and snowy white. Its great bell was still tolling. A large crowd, mostly of women and children, was slowly moving towards its door. As the coach drew up, it was near enough for Tonino and Angelica to see the Archbishop of Caprona in his spreading robes, standing at the door, sprinkling each person with holy water and murmuring a blessing.

"Now there's a brave man," said the Duke. "I wish I could do as well. Look, I'll pop you two out of this door and then get out of the other one and keep everyone busy while you get up on the dome. Will that do?" He had the door nearest the Cathedral open as he spoke.

Tonino and Angelica felt lost and helpless. "But what shall we do?"

"Climb up there and read out those words," said the Duke. He leaned down, encircled them with his warm wet hands, and planted them out on the cold cobbles. They stood shivering under the vast hoop of the coach wheel. "Be sensible," he whispered down to them. "If I ask the Archbishop to put up ladders, she'll guess." That of course was quite true. They heard him surge to the other door and that door crash open.

"He always does everything so *hugely*," Angelica said.

"People of Caprona!" shouted the Duke. "I've come here to be with you in your hour of sorrow. Believe me, I didn't choose what has happened today—"

There was a mutter from the crowd, even a scatter of cheering. "He's doing it quite well," said Angelica.

"We'd better do our bit," said Tonino. "There's only us left now."

15

❧ ⋅ ❦

TONINO AND ANGELICA PATTERED over to the vast
marble cliff of the Cathedral and doubtfully
approached a long, sloping buttress. That was the
only thing they could see which gave them some
chance of climbing up. Once they were close to it,
they saw it was not difficult at all. The marble
looked smooth, but, to people as small as they were,
it was rough enough to give a grip to their hands
and feet.

They went up like monkeys, with the cold air
reviving them. The truth was that, though they had
had an eventful morning, it had also been a restful
and stuffy one. They were full of energy and they
weighed no more than a few ounces. They were
scarcely panting as they scampered up the long cold
slope of the lowest dome. But there the rest of the
Cathedral rose before them, a complicated glacier of
white and rose and green marble. They could not
see the Angel at all.

Neither of them knew which way to climb next.

They hung on to a golden cross and stared up. And there, brown-black hair and white fur hurtled up to them. Gold eyes glared and blue eyes gazed. A black nose and a pink nose dabbed at them.

"Benvenuto!" shouted Tonino. "Did you—?"

"Vittoria!" cried Angelica, and threw her arms round the neck of the white cat.

But the cats were hasty and very worried. Things tumbled into their heads, muddled, troubled things about Paolo and Renata, Marco and Rosa. Would Tonino and Angelica please come on, and hurry!

They began an upward scamper which they would never have believed possible. With the cats to guide them, they raced up long lead groins, and over rainbow buttresses, like dizzy bridges, to higher domes. Always the cats implored them to hurry, and always they were there if the footing was difficult. With his hand on Benvenuto's wiry back, Tonino went gaily up marble glacis and through tiny drainholes hanging over huge drops, and raced up high curving surfaces, where the green marble ribs of a dome seemed as tall as a wall beside him. Even when they began the long toil up the slope of the great dome itself, neither of them was troubled. Once, Angelica stumbled and saved herself by catching hold of Vittoria's silky tail; and once Benvenuto took Tonino's red nightgown in his teeth and heaved him aside from a deep drain. But up here it was rounded and remote. Tonino felt as if he was on the surface of the moon, in spite of the pale winter sky overhead and the wind singing. The rumble of guns was almost beyond the scope of his small ears.

At last, they scrambled between fat marble pillars onto the platform at the very top of the dome. And there was the golden Angel above them. The Angel's tremendous feet rested on a golden pedestal rather higher than Tonino's normal height. There was a design around the pedestal, which Tonino absently took in, of golden leopards entwined with winged horses. But he was looking up beyond, to the Angel's flowing robes, the enormous wings outspread to a width of twenty feet or more, the huge hand high above his head, raised in blessing, and the other hand flung out against the sky, further away still, holding the great unrolled scroll. Far above that again, shone the Angel's vast and tranquil face, unheedingly beaming its blessing over Caprona.

"He's enormous!" Angelica said. "We'll never get up to that scroll, if we tried all day!"

The cats, however, were nudging and hustling at them, to come to a place farther around the platform. Wondering, they trotted around, almost under the Angel's scroll. And there was Paolo's head above the balustrade, with his hair blown back in a tuft and his face exceedingly pale. He had one arm clutched over the marble railing. The other stretched away downward. Tonino peered between the marble pillars to see why. And there was the miserable humped huddle of Renata hanging on to Paolo.

"But she's terrified of heights!" said Angelica. "How *did* she get this high?"

Vittoria told Angelica she was to get Renata up at once.

Angelica stuck her upper half out between the pillars. Being small certainly had its advantages. Distances which were mercilessly huge to Renata and Paolo were too far away to worry Angelica. The dome was like a whole small world to her.

Paolo said, carefully patient, "I can't hold on much longer. Do you think you can have another try?" The answer from Renata was a sobbing shudder.

"Renata!" shouted Angelica.

Renata's scared face turned slowly up. "Something's happened to my eyes now! You look tiny."

"I am tiny!" yelled Angelica.

"Both of them are!" Paolo said, staring at Tonino's head.

"Pull me up quick," said Renata. The size of Angelica and Tonino so worried Renata and Paolo that both of them forgot they were hundreds of feet in the air. Paolo heaved on Renata and Renata shoved at Paolo, and they scrambled over the marble rail in a second. But there, Renata looked up at the immense golden Angel and had an instant relapse. "Oh—oh!" she wailed and sank down in a heap against the golden pedestal.

Tonino and Angelica huddled behind her. The warmth of climbing had worn off. They were feeling the wind keenly through their scanty night-shirts.

Benvenuto leaped across Renata to them. Something else had to be done, and done quickly.

Tonino went again and looked through the marble pillars, where the dome curved away and down like an ice field with ribs of green and gold. There, coming into view over the curve, was a bright red uniform, making Marco's carroty hair look faded and sallow against it. The uniform went with Marco's hair even less well than the crimson he had worn as a coachman. Tonino knew who Marco was in that instant. But that bothered him less than seeing Marco flattened to the surface and looking backwards, which Tonino was sure was a mistake. Beyond Marco's boots, fair hair was wildly blowing. Rosa's flushed face came into sight.

"I'm all *right*. Look after yourself," Rosa said.

Benvenuto was beside Tonino. They were to come up quicker than that. It was important.

"Get Rosa and Marco up here quickly!" Tonino shrieked to Paolo. He did not know if he had caught the feeling from the cats or not, but he was sure Rosa and Marco were in danger.

Paolo went unwillingly to the railing and flinched at the height. "They've been following us and shouting the whole way," he said. "Get up here quickly!" he shouted.

"Thank you very much!" Marco shouted back. "Whose fault is it we're up here anyway?"

"Is Renata all right?" Rosa yelled.

Angelica and Tonino pushed themselves between the pillars. "Hurry up!" they screamed.

The sight of them worked on Rosa and Marco as it had done on Renata and Paolo. They stared at the two tiny figures, and got to their feet as they stared. Then, stooping over, with their hands hanging, they came racing up the last of the curve for a closer look. Marco tumbled over the rail and said, as he was pulling Rosa over, "I couldn't believe my eyes at first! We'd better do a growing-spell before—"

"Get down!" said Paolo. Benvenuto's message was so urgent that he had caught it too. Both cats were crouching, stiff and low, and even Benvenuto's flat ears were flattened. Rosa stooped down. Marco grudgingly went on one knee.

"Look here, Paolo—" he began.

A savage gale hit the dome. Freezing wind shrieked across the platform, howled in the spaces between the marble pillars, and scoured across the curve of the dome below. The Angel's wings thrummed with it. It brought stabs of rain and needles of ice, hurling so hard that Tonino was thrown flat on his face. He could hear ice rattling on the Angel and spitting on the dome. Paolo snatched him into shelter behind himself. Renata feebly scrabbled about until she found Angelica and dragged her into shelter by one arm. Marco and Rosa bowed over. It was quite clear that anyone climbing the dome would have been blown off.

The wind passed, wailing like a wolf. They raised their heads into the sun.

The Duchess was standing on the platform in front of them. She had melting ice winking and trickling from her hair and from every fold of her marble-gray dress. The smile on her waxy face was not pleasant.

"Oh no," she said. "The Angel is not going to help anyone this time. Did you think I'd forgotten?"

Marco and Rosa looked up at the Angel's golden arm holding the great scroll above them. If they had not understood before, they knew now. From their suddenly thoughtful faces, Tonino knew they were finding spells to use on the Duchess.

"Don't!" squeaked Angelica. "She's an enchantress!"

The Duchess's lips pursed in another unpleasant little smile. "More than that," she said. She pointed up at the Angel. "Let the words be removed from the scroll," she said.

There was a click from the huge golden statue, followed by a grating sound, as if a spring had been released. The arm holding the scroll began to move, gently and steadily downwards, making the slightest grinding noise as it moved. They could hear it easily, in spite of a sudden clatter of gunfire from the houses beyond the river. Downwards and inwards, traveled the Angel's arm, until it stopped with a small *clunk*. The scroll now hung, flashing in the sun, between them and the Duchess. There were large raised letters on it. *Angelus*, they saw. *Capronensi populo*. It was as if the Angel were holding it out for them to read.

"Exactly," said the Duchess, though Tonino thought, from the surprised arch of her eyebrows, that this was not at all what she expected. She pointed again at the scroll, with a long white finger like a white wax pencil. "Erase," she said. "Word by word."

Their heads all tipped anxiously as they looked at the lines of writing. The first word read *Carmen*. And, sure enough, the golden capital C was sinking slowly away into the metal background. Paolo moved. He had to do something. The Duchess glanced at him, a contemptuous flick of the eyebrows. Paolo found he was twisted to the spot, with jabbing cramp in both legs.

But he could still speak, and he remembered what Marco and Rosa had said last night. Without daring to draw breath, he screamed as loud as he could. *"Chrestomanci!"*

There was more wind. This was one keen blaring gust. And Chrestomanci was there, beyond Renata and the cats. There was so little room on the platform that Chrestomanci rocked, and quickly took hold of the marble balustrade. He was still in uniform, but it was muddy and he looked extremely tired.

The Duchess whirled around and pointed her long finger at him. "You! I misled you!"

"Oh you did," Chrestomanci said. If the Duchess had hoped to catch him off balance, she was too late. Chrestomanci was steady now. "You led me a proper wild-goose chase," he said, and put out one hand, palm forward, towards her pointing finger. The long finger bent and began dripping white, as if it were wax indeed. The Duchess stared at it, and then looked up at Chrestomanci almost imploringly. "No," Chrestomanci said, sounding very tired. "I think you've done enough harm. Take your true form, please." He beckoned at her, like someone sick of waiting.

Instantly, the Duchess's body was seething out of shape. Her arms gathered inwards. Her face lengthened, and yet still remained the same waxy, sardonic face. Whiskers sprang from her upper lip, and her eyes lit red, like bulging lamps. Her marble skirts turned white, billowed and gathered soapily to her ankles, revealing her feet as long pink claws. And all the time, she was shrinking. Two teeth appeared at the end of her lengthened white face. A naked pink tail, marked in rings like an earthworm, snaked from behind the soapy bundle of her skirts and lashed the marble floor angrily. She shrank again.

Finally, a huge white rat with eyes like red

marbles, leaped to the marble railing and crouched, chittering and glaring with its humped back twitching.

"The White Devil," said Chrestomanci, "which the Angel was sent to expel from Caprona. Right, Benvenuto and Vittoria. She's all yours. Make sure she never comes back."

Benvenuto and Vittoria were already creeping forward. Their tails swept about and their eyes stared. They sprang. The rat sprang too, off the parapet with a squeal, and went racing away down the dome. Benvenuto raced with it, long and low, keeping just beside the pink whip of its tail. Vittoria raced the other side, a snowy sliver making the great rat look yellow, running at the rat's shoulder. They saw the rat turn and try to bite her. And then, suddenly, the three were joined by a dozen smaller rats, all running and squealing. They only saw them for an instant, before the whole group ran over the slope of the dome and disappeared.

"Her helpers from the Palace," said Chrestomanci.

"Will Vittoria be safe?" said Angelica.

"She's the best ratter in Caprona, isn't she?" said Chrestomanci. "Apart from Benvenuto, that is. And by the time the Devil and her friends get to the ground, they'll have every cat in Caprona after them. Now—"

Tonino found he was the right size again. He clung to Rosa's hand. Beyond Rosa, he could see

Angelica, also the right size, shivering and pulling her flimsy blue dress down over her knees, before she grabbed for Marco's hand. The wind was far worse on a larger body. But what made Tonino grab at Rosa was not that. The dome was not world-sized any more. It was a white hummock wheeling in a gray-brown landscape. The hills around Caprona were pitilessly clear. He could see flashes of flame and running figures which seemed to be almost beside him, or just above him, as if the tiny white dome had reeled over on its side. Yet the houses of Caprona were immeasurably deep below, and the river seemed to stand up out of them. The New Bridge appeared almost overhead, suffused in clouds of smoke. Smoke rolled in the hills and swirled giddily out of the downside-upside houses beyond the Old Bridge, and, worst of all, the boom and clap, the rattle and yammer of guns was now nearly deafening. Tonino no longer wondered what had scared Renata and Paolo so. He felt as if he was spinning to his death.

He clung to Rosa's hand and looked desperately up at the Angel. That at least was still huge. The scroll, which it still held patiently towards them, was almost as big as the side of a house.

"—Now," said Chrestomanci, "the best thing you can do, all of you, is to sing those words, quickly."

"What? Me too?" said Angelica.

"Yes, all of you," said Chrestomanci.

They gathered, the six of them, against the marble parapet, facing the golden scroll, with the New Bridge behind them, and began, somewhat uncertainly, to fit those words to the tune of the *Angel of Caprona*. They matched like a glove. As soon as they realized this, everyone sang lustily. Angelica and Renata stopped shivering. Tonino let go of Rosa's hand, and Rosa put her arm over his shoulders instead. And they sang as if they had always known those words. It was only a version of the usual words in Latin, but it was what the tune had always asked for.

> *"Carmen pacis saeculare*
> *Venit Angelus cantare,*
> *Et deorsum pacem dare*
> *Capronensi populo.*
>
> *"Dabit pacem eternalem,*
> *Sine morbo immortalem,*
> *Sine pugna triumphalem,*
> *Capronensi populo.*
>
> *"En diabola albata*
> *De Caprona expulsata,*
> *Missa pax et virtus data*
> *Capronensi populo."*

When they had finished, there was silence. There was not a sound from the hills, or the New

Bridge, or the streets below. Every noise had stopped. So they were all the more startled at the tinny slithering with which the Angel slowly rolled up the scroll. The shining outstretched wings bent and settled against the Angel's golden shoulders, where the Angel gave them a shake to order the feathers. And that noise was not the sound of metal, but the softer rattling of real pinions. It brought with it a scent of such sweetness that there was a moment when they were not aware of anything else.

In that moment, the Angel was in flight. As the huge golden wings passed over them, the scent came again and, with it, the sound of singing. It seemed like hundreds of voices, singing tune, harmony and descant to the *Angel of Caprona*. They had no idea if it was the Angel alone, or something else. They looked up and watched the golden figure wheel and soar and wheel, until it was only a golden glint in the sky. And there was still utter silence, except for the singing.

Rosa sighed. "I suppose we'd better climb down." Renata began to shiver again at the thought.

Chrestomanci sighed too. "Don't worry about that."

They were suddenly down again, on solid cobbles, in the Cathedral forecourt. The Cathedral was once more a great white building, the houses were high, the hills were away beyond, and the people surrounding them were anything but quiet. Everyone was running to where they could see the Angel, flashing in the sun as he soared. The Archbishop was in tears, and so was the Duke. They were wringing one another's hands beside the Duke's coach.

And Chrestomanci had brought them to earth in time to see another miracle. The coach began to work and bounce on its springs. Both doors burst open. Aunt Francesca squeezed out of one, and Guido Petrocchi fell out after her. From the other door tumbled Rinaldo and the red-haired Petrocchi aunt. After them came mingled Montanas and Petrocchis, more and more and more, until anyone could see that the coach could not possibly have held that number. People stopped crowding to see the Angel and crowded to look at the Duke's coach instead.

Rosa and Marco looked at one another and began to back away among the spectators. But Chrestomanci took them each by a shoulder. "It'll be all right," he said. "And if it isn't, I'll set you up in a spell-house in Venice."

Antonio disentangled himself from a Petrocchi uncle and hurried with Guido towards Tonino and Angelica. "Are you all right?" both of them said. "Was it you who fetched the griffins—?" They broke off to stare coldly at one another.

"Yes," said Tonino. "I'm sorry you were turned into puppets."

"She was too clever for us," said Angelica. "But be thankful you got your proper clothes back afterwards. Look at us. We—"

They were pulled apart then by aunts and cousins, fearing they were contaminating one another, and hurriedly given coats and sweaters by uncles. Paolo was swept away from Renata too, by Aunt Maria. "Don't go near her, my love!"

"Oh well," said Renata, as she was pulled away too. "Thanks for helping me up the dome, anyway."

"Just a moment!" Chrestomanci said loudly. Everyone turned to him, respectful but irritable. "If each spell-house," he said, "insists on regarding the other as monsters, I can promise you that Caprona will shortly fall again." They stared at him, Montanas and Petrocchis, equally indignant. The Archbishop looked at the Duke, and both of them began to edge towards the shelter of the Cathedral porch.

"What are you talking about?" Rinaldo said aggressively. His dignity was damaged by being a puppet anyway. The look in his eye seemed to promise cowpats for everyone—with the largest share for Chrestomanci.

"I'm talking about the Angel of Caprona," said Chrestomanci. "When the Angel alighted on the Cathedral, in the time of the First Duke of Caprona, bearing the safety of Caprona with him, history clearly states that the Duke appointed two men—Antonio Petrocchi and Piero Montana—to be keepers of the words of the Angel and therefore keepers of the safety of Caprona. In memory of this, each Casa has an Angel over its gate, and the great Angel stands on a pedestal showing the Petrocchi leopard entwined with the Montana winged horse." Chrestomanci pointed upwards.

"If you don't believe me, ask for ladders and go and see. Antonio Petrocchi and Piero Montana were fast friends, and so were their families after them. There were frequent marriages between the two Casas. And Caprona became a great city and a strong State. Its decline dates from that ridiculous quarrel between Ricardo and Francesco."

There were murmurs from Montanas and Petrocchis alike, here, that the quarrel was not ridiculous.

"Of course it was," said Chrestomanci. "You've all been deceived from your cradles up. You've let Ricardo and Francesco fool you for two centuries. What they really quarreled about we shall never know, but I know they both told their families the same lies. And you have all gone on believing their lies and getting deeper and deeper divided, until the White Devil was actually able to enter Caprona again."

Again there were murmurs. Antonio said, "The Duchess *was* the White Devil, but—"

"Yes," said Chrestomanci. "And she has gone for the moment, because the words were found and the Angel awakened by members of both families. I suspect it could only have been done by Montanas and Petrocchis united. The rest of you could have sung the right words separately, until you were all blue in the face, and nothing would have happened. The Angel respects only friendship. The young ones of both families are luckily less bigoted than the rest of you. Marco and Rosa have even had the courage to fall in love and get married—"

Up till then, both families had listened—restively, it was true, because it was not pleasant to be lectured in front of a crowd of fellow citizens, not to speak of the Duke and the Archbishop—but they had listened. But at this, pandemonium broke out.

"*Married!*" screamed the Montanas. "She's a *Montana!*" screamed the Petrocchis. Insults were yelled at Rosa and at Marco. Anyone who wished to count would have found no less than ten aunts in tears at once, and all cursing as they wept. Rosa and Marco were both white. It needed only Rinaldo to step up to Marco, glowering, and he did. "This scum," he said to Rosa, "knocked me down and cut my head open. And you marry it!"

Chrestomanci made haste to get between Marco and Rinaldo. "I'd hoped someone would see reason," he said to Rosa. He seemed very tired. "It had better be Venice."

"Get out of my way!" said Rinaldo. "You double-dealing sorcerer!"

"Please move, sir," said Marco. "I don't need to be shielded from an idiot like him."

"Marco," said Chrestomanci, "have you thought what two families of powerful magicians could do to you and Rosa?"

"Of course we have!" Marco said angrily, trying to push Chrestomanci aside.

But a strange silence fell again, the silence of the Angel. The Archbishop knelt down. Awed people crowded to one side or another of the Cathedral yard. The Angel was returning. He came from far off down the Corso, on foot now, with his wing tips brushing the cobbles and the chorus of voices swelling as he approached. As he passed through the Cathedral court, it was seen that in every place where a feather had touched the stones there grew a cluster of small golden flowers. Scent gushed over everyone as the Angel drew near and halted by the Cathedral porch, towering and golden.

There he turned his remote smiling face to everyone present. His voice was like one voice singing above many. "Caprona is at peace. Keep our covenant." At that he spread his wings, making them all dizzy with the scent. And he was next seen moving upwards, over lesser domes and greater, to take his place once more on the great dome, guarding Caprona in the years to come.

This is really the end of the story, except for one or two explanations.

Marco and Rosa had to tell their story many times, at least as often as Tonino and Angelica told theirs. Among the first people they told it to was Old Niccolo, who was lying restlessly in bed and only kept there because Elizabeth sat beside him all the time. "But I'm quite well!" he kept saying.

So, in order to keep him there, Elizabeth had first Tonino and then Rosa and Marco come and tell him their stories.

Rosa and Marco had met when they were both

working on the Old Bridge. Falling in love and deciding to marry had been the easiest part, over in minutes. The difficulty was that they had to provide themselves with a family each which had nothing to do with either Casa. Rosa contrived a family first. She pretended to be English. She became very friendly with the English girl at the Art Gallery— the same Jane Smith that Rinaldo fancied so much. Jane Smith thought it was a great joke to pretend to be Rosa's sister. She wrote long letters in English to Guido Petrocchi, supposed to be from Rosa's English father, and visited the Casa Petrocchi herself the day Rosa was introduced there.

Rosa and Marco planned the introductions carefully. They used the pear-tree spell—which they worked together—in both Casas, to Jane's amusement. But the Petrocchis, though they liked the pear-tree, were not kind to Rosa at first. In fact, some of Marco's aunts were so unpleasant that Marco was quite disgusted with them. That was why Marco was able to tell Antonio so vehemently that he hated the Petrocchis. But the aunts became used to Rosa in time. Renata and Angelica became very fond of her. And the wedding was held just after Christmas.

All this time, Marco had been unable to find anyone to act as a family for him. He was in despair. Then, only a few days before the wedding, his father sent him with a message to the house of Mario Andretti, the builder. And Marco discovered that the Andrettis had a blind daughter. When

Marco asked, Mario Andretti said he would do anything for anyone who cured his daughter.

"Even then, we hardly dared hope," said Marco. "We didn't know if we could cure her."

"And apart from that," said Rosa, "the only time we dared both go there was the night after the wedding."

So the wedding was held in the Casa Petrocchi. Jane Smith helped Rosa make her dress and was a bridesmaid for her, together with Renata, Angelica and one of Marco's cousins. Jane thoroughly enjoyed the wedding and seemed, Rosa said dryly, to find Marco's cousin Alberto at least as attractive as Rinaldo, whereas Rosa and Marco could think of almost nothing but little Maria Andretti. They hurried to the Andrettis' house as soon as the celebrations were over.

"And I've never known anything so difficult," said Rosa. "We were at it all night—"

Elizabeth was unable to contain herself here. "And I never even knew you were out!" she said.

"We took good care you didn't," said Rosa. "Anyway, we hadn't done anything like that before, so we had to look up spells in the University. We tried seventeen and none of them worked. In the end we had to make up one of our own. And all the time, I was thinking: suppose this doesn't work on the poor child either, and we've played with the Andrettis' hopes."

"Not to speak of our own," said Marco. "Then our spell worked. Maria yelled out that the room

was all colors and there were things like trees in it—
she thought people looked like trees—and we all
jumped about in the dawn, hugging one another.
And Andretti was as good as his word, and did his
brother act so well here that I told him he ought to
be on the stage."

"He took *me* in," Old Niccolo said, wonderingly.

"But someone was bound to find out in the end,"
said Elizabeth. "What did you mean to do then?"

"Just hoped," said Marco. "We thought perhaps
people might get used to it—"

"In other words, you behaved like a couple of
young idiots," said Old Niccolo. "What is that terrible stench?" And he leaped up and raced out onto
the gallery to investigate, with Elizabeth, Rosa and
Marco racing after him to stop him.

The smell, of course, was the kitchen-spell
again. The insects had vanished and a smell of
drains had taken their place. All day long, the
kitchen belched out stinks, which grew stronger
towards evening. It was particularly unfortunate,
because the whole of Caprona was preparing to
feast and celebrate. Caprona was truly at peace. The
troops from Florence, and Pisa and Siena, had all
returned home—somewhat bewildered and wondering how they had been beaten—and the people
of Caprona were dancing in the streets.

"And we can't even cook, let alone celebrate!"
wailed Aunt Gina.

Then an invitation arrived from the Casa

Petrocchi. Would the Casa Montana be pleased to join in the celebrations at the Casa Petrocchi? It was a trifle stiff, but the Casa Montana did please. What could be more fortunate? Tonino and Paolo suspected that it was Chrestomanci's doing. The only difficulty was to stop Old Niccolo getting out of bed and going with the rest of them. Everyone said Elizabeth had done enough. Everyone, even Aunt Francesca, wanted to go. Then, more fortunately still, Uncle Umberto turned up, and old Luigi Petrocchi with him. They said they would sit with Old Niccolo—and on him if necessary. They were too old for dancing.

So everyone else went to the Casa Petrocchi, and it proved a celebration to remember. The Duke was there, because Angelica had insisted on it. The Duke was so grateful to be invited that he had brought with him as much wine and as many cakes as his coach would hold, and six footmen in a second coach to serve it.

"The Palace is awful," he said. "No one in it but Punch and Judys. Somehow I don't fancy them like I used to."

What with the wine, the cakes, and the good food baked in the Casa Petrocchi kitchen, the evening became very merry. Somebody found a barrel organ and everyone danced to it in the yard. And, if the six footmen forgot to serve cakes and danced with the rest, who was to blame them? After all, the Duke was dancing with Aunt Francesca—a truly formidable sight.

Tonino sat with Paolo and Renata beside a charcoal brazier, watching the dancing. And while they sat, Benvenuto suddenly emerged from the shadows and sat down by the brazier, where he proceeded to give himself a fierce and thorough wash.

They had done a fine, enjoyable job on that white rat, he informed Tonino, as he stuck one leg high above his gnarled head and subjected it to punishing tongue work. She'd not be back again.

"But is Vittoria all right?" Renata wanted to know.

Fine, was Benvenuto's answer. She was resting. She was going to have kittens. They would be particularly good kittens because Benvenuto was the father. Tonino was to make sure to get one for the Casa Montana.

Tonino asked Renata for a kitten then and there, and Renata promised to ask Angelica. Whereupon, Benvenuto, having worked over both hind legs, wafted himself onto Tonino's knees, where he made himself into a tight brown mat and slept for an hour.

"I wish I could understand him," said Paolo. "He tried to tell me where you were, but all I did was see a picture of the front of the Palace."

"But that's how he always tells things!" said Tonino. He was surprised Paolo had not known. "You just have to read his pictures."

"What's he saying now?" Renata asked Paolo.

"Nothing," said Paolo. "Snore, snore." And they all laughed.

Sometime later, when Benvenuto had woken up and drifted off to try his luck in the kitchen, Tonino wandered into a room nearby, without quite knowing why he did. As soon as he got inside, though, he knew it was no accident. Chrestomanci was there, with Angelica and Guido Petrocchi, and so was Antonio. Antonio was looking so worried that Tonino braced himself for trouble.

"We were discussing you, Tonino," said Chrestomanci. "You helped Angelica fetch the griffins, didn't you?"

"Yes," said Tonino. He remembered the damage they had done and felt alarmed.

"And you helped in the kitchen-spell?" asked Chrestomanci.

Tonino said "Yes" again. Now he was sure there was trouble.

"And when you hanged the Duchess," Chrestomanci said, to Tonino's confusion, "how did you do that?"

Tonino wondered how he could be in trouble over that too, but he answered, "By doing what the puppet show made me do. I couldn't get out of it, so I had to go along with it, you see."

"I do," said Chrestomanci, and he turned to Antonio rather triumphantly. "You see? And that was the White Devil! What interests me is that it was someone else's spell each time." Then before Tonino could be too puzzled, he turned back to him. "Tonino," he said, "it seems to me that you have a new and rather useful talent. You may not be able to work many spells on your own, but you seem to be able to turn other people's magic to your own use. I think if they had let you help on the Old Bridge, for instance, it would have been mended in half a day. I've been asking your father if he'd let you come back to England with me, so that we could find out just what you can do."

Tonino looked at his father's worried face. He hardly knew what to think. "Not for good?" he said.

Antonio smiled. "Only for a few weeks," he said. "If Chrestomanci's right, we'll need you here badly."

Tonino smiled too. "Then I don't mind," he said.

"But," said Angelica, "it was me who fetched the griffins really."

"What were you really fetching?" asked Guido.

Angelica hung her head. "Mice." She looked resigned when her father roared with laughter.

"I wanted to talk about you too," said Chrestomanci. He said to Guido, "Her spells always work, don't they? It occurs to me you might learn from Angelica."

Guido scratched his beard. "How to turn things green and get griffins, you mean?"

Chrestomanci picked up his glass of wine. "There are risks, of course, to Angelica's methods. But I meant she can show you that a thing need not be done in the same old way in order to work. I think, in time, she will make you a whole new set of spells. Both houses can learn from her." He raised his wine glass. "Your health, Angelica. Tonino. The Duchess thought she was getting the weakest members of both Casas, and it turned out quite the opposite."

Antonio and Guido raised their glasses too. "I'll say this," said Guido. "But for you two, we wouldn't be celebrating tonight."

Angelica and Tonino looked at each other and made faces. They felt very shy and very, very pleased.

.

WITCH WEEK

EDITOR'S NOTE

Late one night in 1605, a soldier named Guy Fawkes was caught with some two tons of gunpowder that he had smuggled into a cellar beneath the Houses of Parliament in London. Fawkes was arrested, tried, and executed for his part in the Gunpowder Plot—a failed conspiracy to blow up King James I and most of his government the very next day, November 5. Centuries later, English people still set off fireworks, light bonfires, and burn "Guys" in effigy to celebrate November 5 as Guy Fawkes Day.

1

❧❦

THE NOTE SAID: *SOMEONE IN THIS CLASS IS A WITCH*. It was written in capital letters in ordinary blue ballpoint, and it had appeared between two of the geography books Mr. Crossley was marking. Anyone could have written it. Mr. Crossley rubbed his ginger moustache unhappily. He looked out over the bowed heads of Class 6B and wondered what to do about it.

He decided not to take the note to the head-mistress. It was possibly just a joke, and Miss Cadwallader had no sense of humor to speak of. The person to take it to was the deputy head, Mr. Wentworth. But the difficulty there was that Mr. Wentworth's son was a member of 6B—the small boy near the back who looked younger than the rest was Brian Wentworth. No. Mr. Crossley decided to ask the writer of the note to own up. He would explain just what a serious accusation it was and leave the rest to the person's conscience.

Mr. Crossley cleared his throat to speak. Some of 6B looked up hopefully but Mr. Crossley had changed his mind then. It was journal time, and journal time was only to be interrupted for a serious emergency. Larwood House was very strict about that rule. Larwood House was very strict about a lot of things, because it was a boarding school run by the government for witch-orphans and children with other problems. The journals were to help the children with their problems. They were supposed to be strictly private. Every day, for half an hour, every pupil had to confide his or her private thoughts to their journals, and nothing else was done until everyone had. Mr. Crossley admired the idea heartily.

But the real reason that Mr. Crossley changed his mind was the awful thought that the note might be true. Someone in 6B could easily be a witch. Only Miss Cadwallader knew who exactly in 6B was a witch-orphan, but Mr. Crossley suspected that a lot of them were. Other classes had given Mr. Crossley feelings of pride and pleasure in being a schoolmaster; 6B never did. Only two of them gave him any pride at all: Theresa Mullett and Simon Silverson. They were both model pupils. The rest of the girls tailed dismally off until you came to empty chatterers like Estelle Green, or that dumpy girl, Nan Pilgrim, who was definitely the odd one out. The boys were divided into groups. Some had the sense to follow Simon Silverson's example, but quite as many clustered around that bad boy Dan Smith, and others again admired that tall Indian boy Nirupam Singh. Or they were loners like Brian Wentworth and that unpleasant boy Charles Morgan.

Here Mr. Crossley looked at Charles Morgan and Charles Morgan looked back, with one of the blank, nasty looks he was famous for. Charles wore glasses, which enlarged the nasty look and trained it on Mr. Crossley like a double laser beam. Mr. Crossley looked away hastily and went back to worrying about the note. Everyone in 6B gave up hoping for anything interesting to happen and went back to their journals.

28 October 1981, Theresa Mullett wrote in round, angelic writing. *Mr. Crossley has found a note in our geography books. I thought it might be from Miss Hodge at first, because we all know Teddy is dying for love of her, but he looks so worried that I think it must be from some silly girl like Estelle Green. Nan Pilgrim couldn't get over the vaulting horse again today. She jumped and stuck halfway. It made us all laugh.*

Simon Silverson wrote: *28. 10. 81. I would like to know who put that note in the geography books. It fell out when I was collecting them and I put it back in. If it was found lying about we could all be blamed. This is strictly off the record of course.*

I do not know, Nirupam Singh wrote musingly, *how anyone manages to write much in their journal, since everyone knows Miss Cadwallader reads them all during the holidays. I do not write my secret thoughts. I will now describe the Indian rope trick which I saw in India before my father came to live in England . . .*

Two desks away from Nirupam, Dan Smith chewed his pen a great deal and finally wrote, *Well*

I mean it's not much good if you've got to write your secret feelings, what I mean is it takes all the joy out of it and you don't know what to write. It means they aren't secret if you see what I mean.

I do not think, Estelle Green wrote, *that I have any secret feelings today, but I would like to know what is in the note from Miss Hodge that Teddy has just found. I thought she scorned him utterly.*

At the back of the room, Brian Wentworth wrote, sighing, *Timetables just ran away with me, that is my problem. During geography I planned a bus journey from London to Baghdad via Paris. Next lesson I shall plan the same journey via Berlin.*

Nan Pilgrim meanwhile was scrawling, *This is a message to the person who reads our journals. Are you Miss Cadwallader, or does Miss Cadwallader make Mr. Wentworth do it?* She stared at what she had written, rather taken aback at her own daring. This kind of thing happened to her sometimes. Still, she thought, there were hundreds of journals and hundreds of daily entries. The chances of Miss Cadwallader reading this one had to be very small—particularly if she went on and made it really boring. *I shall now be boring,* she wrote. *Teddy Crossley's real name is Harold, but he got called Teddy out of the hymn that goes "Gladly my cross I'd bear." But of course everyone sings "Crossley my glad-eyed bear." Mr. Crossley is glad-eyed. He thinks everyone should be upright and honorable and interested in geography. I am sorry for him.*

But the one who was best at making his journal

boring was Charles Morgan. His entry read, *I got up. I felt hot at breakfast. I do not like porridge. Second lesson was woodwork but not for long. I think we have games next.*

Looking at this, you might think Charles was either very stupid or very muddled, or both. Anyone in 6B would have told you that it had been a chilly morning and there had been cornflakes for breakfast. Second lesson had been PE, during which Nan Pilgrim had so much amused Theresa Mullett by failing to jump the horse, and the lesson to come was music, not games. But Charles was not writing about the day's work. He really was writing about his secret feelings, but he was doing it in his own private code so that no one could know.

He started every entry with *I got up.* It meant, I hate this school. When he wrote *I do not like porridge,* that was actually true, but porridge was his code word for Simon Silverson. Simon was porridge at breakfast, potatoes at lunch, and bread at tea. All the other people he hated had code words too. Dan Smith was cornflakes, cabbage, and butter. Theresa Mullett was milk.

But when Charles wrote *I felt hot,* he was not talking about school at all. He meant he was remembering the witch being burned. It was a thing that would keep coming into his head whenever he was not thinking of anything else, much as he tried to forget it. He had been so young that he had been in a stroller. His big sister Bernadine had been pushing him while his mother carried the shopping, and they had been crossing a road where there was a view down into the Market Square. There were crowds of people down there, and a sort of flickering. Bernadine had stopped the stroller in the middle of the street in order to stare. She and Charles had just time to glimpse the bonfire starting to burn, and they had seen that the witch was a large fat man. Then their mother came rushing back and scolded Bernadine on across the road. "You mustn't look at witches!" she said. "Only awful people do that!" So Charles had only seen the witch for an instant. He never spoke about it, but he never forgot it. It always astonished him that Bernadine seemed to forget about it completely. What Charles was really saying in his journal was that the witch came into his head during breakfast, until Simon Silverson made him forget again by eating all that toast.

When he wrote *woodwork second lesson,* he meant that he had gone on to think about the second witch—which was a thing he did not think about so often. *Woodwork* was anything Charles liked. They only had woodwork once a week, and Charles had chosen that for his code on the very reasonable grounds that he was not likely to enjoy anything at Larwood House any oftener than that. Charles had liked the second witch. She had been quite young and rather pretty, in spite of her torn skirt and untidy hair. She had come scrambling across the wall at the end of the garden and stumbled down the rockery to the lawn, carrying her smart shoes in one hand. Charles had been nine years old then, and he was minding his little brother on the lawn. Luckily for the witch, his parents were out.

Charles knew she was a witch. She was out of breath and obviously frightened. He could hear the yells and police whistles in the house behind. Besides, who else but a witch would run away from the police in the middle of the afternoon in a tight skirt? But he made quite sure. He said, "Why are you running away in our garden?"

The witch rather desperately hopped on one foot. She had a large blister on the other foot, and both her stockings were laddered. "I'm a witch," she panted. "Please help me, little boy!"

"Why can't you magic yourself safe?" Charles asked.

"Because I can't when I'm this frightened!" gasped the witch. "I tried, but it just went wrong! *Please,* little boy—sneak me out through your house and don't say a word, and I'll give you luck for the rest of your life. I promise."

Charles looked at her in that intent way of his which most people found blank and nasty. He saw she was speaking the truth. He saw, too, that she understood the look as very few people seemed to. "Come in through the kitchen," he said. And he led the witch, hobbling on her blister in her laddered stockings, through the kitchen and down the hall to the front door.

"Thanks," she said. "You're a love." She smiled at him while she put her hair right in the hall mirror, and after she had done something to her skirt that may have been witchcraft to make it seem untorn again, she bent down and kissed Charles. "If I get away, I'll bring you luck," she said. Then she put her smart shoes on again and went away down the front garden, trying hard not to limp. At the front gate, she waved and smiled at Charles.

That was the end of the part Charles liked. That was why he wrote *but not for long* next. He never saw the witch again, or heard what had happened to her. He ordered his little brother never to say a word about her—and Graham obeyed, because he always did everything Charles said— and then he watched and waited for any sign of the witch or any sign of luck. None came. It was next to impossible for Charles to find out what might have happened to the witch, because there had been new laws since he glimpsed the first witch burning. There were no more public burnings. The bonfires were lit inside the walls of jails instead, and the radio would simply announce: "Two witches were burned this morning inside Holloway Jail." Every time Charles heard this kind of announcement he thought it was *his* witch. It gave him a blunt, hurtful feeling inside. He thought of the way she had kissed him, and he was fairly sure it made you wicked too, to be kissed by a witch. He gave up expecting to be lucky. In fact, to judge from the amount of bad luck he had had, he thought the witch must have been caught almost straightaway. For the blunt, hurtful feeling he had when the radio announced a burning made him refuse to do anything his parents told him to do. He just gave them his steady stare instead. And each time he stared, he knew they thought he was being nasty. They did not understand it the way the witch did. And, since Graham imitated everything Charles did, Charles's parents very soon decided Charles was a problem child and leading Graham astray. They arranged for him to be sent to Larwood House, because it was quite near.

When Charles wrote *games,* he meant bad luck. Like everyone else in 6B, he had seen Mr. Crossley had found a note. He did not know what was in the note, but when he looked up and caught Mr. Crossley's eye, he knew it meant bad luck coming.

Mr. Crossley still could not decide what to do about the note. If what it said was true, that meant inquisitors coming to the school. And that was a thoroughly frightening thought. Mr. Crossley sighed and put the note in his pocket. "Right, everyone," he said. "Put away your journals and get into line for music."

As soon as 6B had shuffled away to the school hall, Mr. Crossley sped to the staff room, hoping to find someone he could consult about the note.

He was lucky enough to find Miss Hodge there. As Theresa Mullett and Estelle Green had observed, Mr. Crossley was in love with Miss Hodge. But of course he never let it show. Probably the one person in the school who did not seem to know was Miss Hodge herself. Miss Hodge was a small neat person who wore neat gray skirts and blouses and her hair was even neater and smoother than Theresa Mullett's. She was busy making neat stacks of books on the staff room table, and she went on making them all the time Mr. Crossley was telling her excitedly about the note. She spared the note one glance.

"No, I can't tell who wrote it either," she said.

"But what shall I do about it?" Mr. Crossley pleaded. "Even if it's true, it's such a spiteful thing to write! And suppose it *is* true. Suppose one of them is—" He was in a pitiable state. He wanted so badly to attract Miss Hodge's attention, but he knew that words like *witch* were not the kind of words one used in front of a lady. "I don't like to say it in front of you."

"I was brought up to be sorry for witches," Miss Hodge remarked calmly.

"Oh, so was I! We all are," Mr. Crossley said hastily. "I just wondered how I should handle it—"

Miss Hodge lined up another stack of books. "I think it's just a silly joke," she said. "Ignore it. Aren't you supposed to be teaching 4C?"

"Yes, yes. I suppose I am," Mr. Crossley agreed miserably. And he was forced to hurry away without Miss Hodge's having looked at him once.

Miss Hodge thoughtfully squared off another stack of books, until she was sure Mr. Crossley had gone. Then she smoothed her smooth hair and hurried away upstairs to find Mr. Wentworth.

Mr. Wentworth, as deputy head, had a study

where he wrestled with the schedules and various other problems Miss Cadwallader gave him. When Miss Hodge tapped on the door, he was wrestling with a particularly fierce one. There were seventy people in the school orchestra. Fifty of these were also in the school choir and twenty of those fifty were in the school play. Thirty boys in the orchestra were in various football teams, and twenty of the girls played hockey for the school. At least a third played basketball as well. The volleyball team were all in the school play. Problem: How do you arrange rehearsals and practices without asking most people to be in three places at once? Mr. Wentworth rubbed the thin patch at the back of his hair despairingly. "Come in," he said. He saw the bright, smiling, anxious face of Miss Hodge, but his mind was not on her at all.

"So spiteful of someone, and so awful if it's true!" he heard Miss Hodge saying. And then, merrily, "But I think I have a scheme to discover who wrote the note—it must be someone in 6B. Can we put our heads together and work it out, Mr. Wentworth?" She put her own head on one side, invitingly.

Mr. Wentworth had no idea what she was talking about. He scratched the place where his hair was going and stared at her. Whatever it was, it had all the marks of a scheme that ought to be squashed. "People only write anonymous notes to make themselves feel important," he said experimentally. "You mustn't take them seriously."

"But it's the perfect scheme!" Miss Hodge protested. "If I can explain—"

Not squashed yet, whatever it is, thought Mr. Wentworth. "No. Just tell me the exact words of this note," he said.

Miss Hodge instantly became crushed and shocked. "But it's awful!" Her voice fell to a dramatic whisper. "It says someone in 6B is a witch!"

Mr. Wentworth realized that his instinct had been right. "What did I tell you?" he said heartily. "That's the sort of stuff you can only ignore, Miss Hodge."

"But someone in 6B has a very sick mind!" Miss Hodge whispered.

Mr. Wentworth considered 6B, including his own son, Brian. "They all have," he said. "Either they'll grow out of it, or we'll see them all riding around on broomsticks in the sixth grade." Miss Hodge started back. She was genuinely shocked at this coarse language. But she hastily made herself laugh. She could see it was a joke. "Take no notice," said Mr. Wentworth. "Ignore it, Miss Hodge." And he went back to his problem with some relief.

Miss Hodge went back to her stacks of books, not as crushed as Mr. Wentworth supposed she was. Mr. Wentworth had made a joke to her. He had never done that before. She must be getting somewhere. For—and this was a fact not known to Theresa Mullett or Estelle Green—Miss Hodge intended to marry Mr. Wentworth. He was a widower. When Miss Cadwallader retired, Miss Hodge was sure Mr. Wentworth would be head of Larwood House. This suited Miss Hodge, who had her old father to consider. For this, she was quite willing to put up with Mr. Wentworth's bald patch and his tense and harrowed look. The only drawback was that putting up with Mr. Wentworth also meant putting up with Brian. A little frown wrinkled Miss Hodge's smooth forehead at the thought of Brian Wentworth. Now there was a boy who quite deserved the way the rest of 6B were always on to him. Never mind. He could be sent away to another school.

Meanwhile, in music, Mr. Brubeck was asking Brian to sing on his own. 6B had trailed their way through "Here We Sit like Birds in the Wilderness." They had made it sound like a lament. "I'd prefer a wilderness to this place," Estelle Green whispered to her friend Karen Grigg. Then they sang "Cuckaburra Sits in the Old Gum Tree." That sounded like a funeral dirge. "What's a cuckaburra?" Karen whispered to Estelle.

"Another kind of bird," Estelle whispered back. "Australian."

"No, no, *no*!" shouted Mr. Brubeck. "Brian is the only one of you who doesn't sound like a cockerel with a sore throat!"

"Mr. Brubeck must have birds on the brain!" Estelle giggled. And Simon Silverson, who believed, strongly and sincerely, that nobody was worthy of praise except himself, gave Brian a scathingly jeering look.

But Mr. Brubeck was far too addicted to music to take any notice of what the rest of 6B thought. "'The Cuckoo Is a Pretty Bird,'" he announced. "I want Brian to sing this to you on his own."

Estelle giggled, because it was birds again. Theresa giggled too, because anyone who stood out for any reason struck her as exceedingly funny. Brian stood up with the song book in his hands. He was never embarrassed. But instead of singing, he read the words out in an incredulous voice.

"'The cuckoo is a pretty bird, she singeth as she flies. She bringeth us good tidings, she telleth us no lies.' Sir, why are all these songs about birds?" he asked innocently. Charles thought that was a shrewd move of Brian's, after the way Simon Silverson had looked at him.

But it did Brian no good. He was too unpopular. Most of the girls said, *"Brian!"* in shocked voices. Simon said it jeeringly.

"Quiet!" shouted Mr. Brubeck. "Brian, get on and sing!" He struck notes on the piano.

Brian stood with the book in his hands, obviously wondering what to do. It was clear that he would be in trouble with Mr. Brubeck if he did not sing, and that he would be hit afterward if he did. And while Brian hesitated, the witch in 6B took a hand. One of the long windows of the hall flew open with a clap and let in a stream of birds. Most of them were ordinary birds: sparrows, starlings, pigeons, blackbirds, and thrushes, swooping around the hall in vast numbers and shedding feathers and droppings as they swooped. But among the beating wings were two curious furry creatures with large pouches, which kept uttering violent laughing sounds, and the red and yellow thing swooping among a cloud of sparrows and shouting "Cuckoo!" was clearly a parrot.

Luckily, Mr. Brubeck thought it was simply the wind which had let the birds in. The rest of the lesson had to be spent in chasing the birds out again. By that time, the laughing birds with pouches had vanished. Evidently the witch had decided they were a mistake. But everyone in 6B had clearly seen them. Simon said importantly, "If this happens again, we all ought to get together and—"

At this, Nirupam Singh turned around, towering among the beating wings. "Have you any proof that this is not perfectly natural?" he said.

Simon had not, so he said no more.

By the end of the lesson, all the birds had been sent out of the window again, except the parrot. The parrot escaped to a high curtain rail, where no one could reach it, and sat there shouting "Cuckoo!" Mr. Brubeck sent 6B away and called the caretaker to get rid of it. Charles trudged away with the rest, thinking that this must be the end of the games he had predicted in his journal. But he was quite wrong. It was only the beginning.

And when the caretaker came grumbling along with his small white dog trailing at his heels, to get rid of the parrot, the parrot had vanished.

2

THE NEXT DAY was the day Miss Hodge tried to
find out who had written the note. It was also the
worst day either Nan Pilgrim or Charles Morgan
had ever spent at Larwood House. It did not begin
too badly for Charles, but Nan was late for breakfast.

She had broken her shoelace. She was told off
by Mr. Towers for being late, and then by a monitor.
By this time, the only table with a place was one
where all the others were boys. Nan slid into the
place, horribly embarrassed. They had eaten all the
toast already, except one slice. Simon Silverson took
that slice as Nan arrived. "Bad luck, fatso." From
further down the table, Nan saw Charles Morgan
looking at her. It was meant to be a look of sympathy, but, like all Charles's looks, it came out like a
blank double-barreled glare. Nan pretended not to
see it and did her best to eat wet, pale scrambled egg
on its own.

At lessons, she discovered that Theresa and her
friends had started a new craze. That was a bad

sign. They were always more than usually pleased
with themselves at the start of a craze—even though
this one had probably started so that they need not
think of witches or birds. The craze was white knitting, white and clean and fluffy, which you kept
wrapped in a towel so that it would stay clean. The
classroom filled with mutters of, "Two purl, one
plain, twist two . . ."

But the day really got into its evil stride in the
middle of the morning, during PE. Larwood House
had that every day, like the journals. 6B joined with
6C and 6D, and the boys went running in the field,
while the girls went together to the gym. The climbing ropes were let down there.

Theresa and Estelle and the rest gave glad cries
and went shinnying up the ropes with easy swinging pulls. Nan tried to lurk out of sight against the
wall bars. Her heart fell with a flop into her gym
shoes. This was worse even than the vaulting horse.
Nan simply could not climb ropes. She had been
born without the proper muscles or something.

And, since it was that kind of day, Miss Phillips
spotted Nan almost at once. "Nan, you haven't had
a turn yet. Theresa, Delia, Estelle, come on down
and let Nan have her turn on the ropes." Theresa
and the rest came down readily. They knew they
were about to see some fun.

Nan saw their faces and ground her teeth. This
time, she vowed, she would do it. She would climb
right up to the ceiling and wipe that grin off
Theresa's face. Nevertheless, the distance to the

ropes seemed several hundred shiny yards. Nan's legs, in the floppy divided skirts they wore for gym, had gone mauve and wide, and her arms felt like weak pink puddings. When she reached the rope, the knot on the end of it seemed to hang rather higher than her head. And she was supposed to stand on that knot somehow.

She gripped the rope in her fat, weak hands and jumped. All that happened was that the knot hit her heavily in the chest and her feet dropped sharply to the floor again. A murmur of amusement began among Theresa and her friends. Nan could hardly believe it. This was ridiculous—worse than usual! She could not even get off the floor now. She took a new grip on the rope and jumped again. And again. And again. And she leaped and leaped, bounding like a floppy kangaroo, and still the knot kept hitting her in the chest and her feet kept hitting the floor. The murmurs of the rest grew into giggles and then to outright laughter. Until at last, when Nan was almost ready to give up, her feet somehow found the knot, groped, gripped, and hung on. And there she clung, upside down like a sloth, breathless and sweating, from arms which did not seem to work anymore. This was terrible. And she still had to climb up the rope. She wondered whether to fall off on her back and die.

Miss Phillips was beside her. "Come on, Nan. Stand up on the knot."

Somehow, feeling it was superhuman of her, Nan managed to lever herself upright. She stood there, wobbling gently around in little circles, while Miss Phillips, her face level with Nan's trembling knees, kindly and patiently explained for the hundredth time exactly how to climb a rope.

Nan clenched her teeth. She *would* do it. Everyone else did. It must be possible. She shut her eyes to shut out the other girls' grinning faces and did as Miss Phillips told her. She took a strong and careful grip on the rope above her head. Carefully, she put the rope between the top of one foot and the bottom of the other. She kept her eyes shut. Firmly, she pulled with her arms. Crisply, she pulled her feet up behind. Gripped again. Reached up again, with fearful concentration. Yes, this was it! She was doing it at last! The secret must be to keep your eyes shut. She gripped and pulled. She could feel her body easily swinging upward toward the ceiling, just as the others did it.

But, around her, the giggles grew to laughter, and the laughter grew into screams, then shouts, and became a perfect storm of hilarity. Puzzled, Nan opened her eyes. All around her, at knee level, she saw laughing red faces, tears running out of eyes, and people doubled over yelling with mirth. Even Miss Phillips was biting her lip and snorting a little. And small wonder. Nan looked down to find her gym shoes still resting on the knot at the bottom of the rope. After all that climbing, she was still standing on the knot.

Nan tried to laugh too. She was sure it had been very funny. But it was hard to be amused. Her only consolation was that, after that, none of the other girls could climb the ropes either. They were too weak with laughing.

The boys, meanwhile, were running around and around the field. They were stripped to little pale blue running shorts and splashing through the dew in big spiked shoes. It was against the rules to run in anything but spikes. They were divided into little groups of laboring legs. The quick group of legs in front, with muscles, belonged to Simon Silverson and his friends, and to Brian Wentworth. Brian was a good runner in spite of his short legs. Brian was prudently trying to keep to the rear of Simon, but every so often the sheer joy of running overcame him and he went ahead. Then he would get bumped and jostled by Simon's friends, for everyone knew it was Simon's right to be in front.

The group of legs behind these were paler and moved without enthusiasm. These belonged to Dan Smith and his friends. All of them could have run at least as fast as Simon Silverson, but they were saving themselves for better things. They loped along easily, chatting among themselves. Today, they kept bursting into laughter.

Behind these again labored an assorted group of legs: mauve legs, fat legs, bright white legs, legs with no muscles at all, and the great brown legs of Nirupam Singh, which seemed too heavy for the rest of Nirupam's skinny body to lift. Everyone in the group was too breathless to talk. Their faces wore assorted expressions of woe.

The last pair of legs, far in the rear, belonged to Charles Morgan. There was nothing particularly wrong with Charles's legs, except that his feet were in ordinary school shoes and soaked through. He was always behind. He chose to be. This was one of the few times in the day when he could be alone to think. He had discovered that, as long as he was thinking of something else, he could keep up his slow trot for hours. And think. The only interruptions he had to fear were when the other groups came pounding past him and he was tangled up in their efforts for a few seconds. Or when Mr. Towers, encased in his nice warm tracksuit, came loping up alongside and called ill-advised encouragements to Charles.

So Charles trotted slowly on, thinking. He gave himself over to hating Larwood House. He hated the field under his feet, the shivering autumn trees that dripped on him, the white goalposts, and the neat line of pine trees in front of the spiked wall that kept everyone in. Then, when he swung around the corner and had a view of the school buildings, he hated them more. They were built of a purplish sort of brick. Charles thought it was the color a person's face would go if he was choking. He thought of the long corridors inside, painted caterpillar green, the thick radiators which were never warm, the brown classrooms, the frosty white dormitories, and the smell of school food, and he was almost in an ecstasy of hate. Then he looked at the groups of legs straggling around the field ahead, and he hated all the people in the school most horribly of all.

Upon that, he found he was remembering the witch being burned. It swept into his head unbidden, as it always did. Only today, it seemed worse than usual. Charles found he was remembering things he had not noticed at the time: the exact shape of the flames, just leaping from small to large, and the way the fat man who was a witch had bent sideways away from them. He could see the man's exact face, the rather blobby nose with a wart on it, the sweat on it, and the flames shining off the man's eyes and the sweat. Above all, he could see the man's expression. It was astounded. The fat man had not believed he was going to die until the moment Charles saw him. He must have thought his witchcraft could save him. Now he knew it could not. And he was horrified. Charles was horrified too. He trotted along in a sort of trance of horror.

But here was the smart red tracksuit of Mr. Towers loping along beside him. "Charles, what are you doing running in walking shoes?"

The fat witch vanished. Charles should have been glad, but he was not. His thinking had been interrupted, and he was not private anymore.

"I said why aren't you wearing your spikes?" Mr. Towers said.

Charles slowed down a little while he wondered what to reply. Mr. Towers trotted springily beside him, waiting for an answer. Because he was not thinking anymore, Charles found his legs aching and his chest sore. That annoyed him. He was even more annoyed about his spikes. He knew Dan Smith had hidden them. That was why that group was laughing. Charles could see their faces craning over their shoulders as they ran, to see what he was telling Mr. Towers. That annoyed him even more. Charles did not usually have this kind of trouble, the way Brian Wentworth did. His double-barreled nasty look had kept him safe up to now, if lonely. But he foresaw he was going to have to think of something more than just looking in future. He felt very bitter.

"I couldn't find my spikes, sir."

"How hard did you look?"

"Everywhere," Charles said bitterly. Why don't I say it was them? he wondered. And knew the answer. Life would not be worth living for the rest of the term.

"In my experience," said Mr. Towers, running and talking as easily as if he were sitting still, "when a lazy boy like you says everywhere, it means nowhere. Report to me in the locker room after school and find those spikes. You stay there until you find them. Right?"

"Yes," said Charles. Bitterly, he watched Mr. Towers surge away from him and run up beside the next group to pester Nirupam Singh.

He hunted for his spikes again during break. But it was hopeless. Dan had hidden them somewhere really cunning. At least, after break, Dan Smith had something else to laugh about besides Charles. Nan Pilgrim soon found out what. As Nan came into the classroom for lessons, she was greeted by Nirupam. "Hello," said Nirupam. "Will you do your rope trick for me too?"

Nan gave him a glare that was mostly astonishment and pushed past him without replying. How did he know about the ropes? she thought. The girls just never talked to the boys! How *did* he know?

But next moment, Simon Silverson came up to Nan, barely able to stop laughing. "My dear Dulcinea!" he said. "What a charming name you have! Were you called after the Archwitch?" After that, he doubled up with laughter, and so did most of the people nearby.

"Her name really is Dulcinea, you know," Nirupam said to Charles.

This was true. Nan's face felt to her like a balloon on fire. Nothing else, she was sure, could be so large and so hot. Dulcinea Wilkes had been the most famous witch of all time. No one was supposed to know Nan's name was Dulcinea. She could not think how it had leaked out. She tried to stalk loftily away to her desk, but she was caught by person after person, all laughingly calling out, "Hey, Dulcinea!" She did not manage to sit down until Mr. Wentworth was already in the room.

6B usually paid attention during Mr. Wentworth's lessons. He was known to be absolutely merciless. Besides, he had a knack of being interesting, which made his lessons seem shorter than other teachers'. But today, no one could keep their mind on Mr. Wentworth. Nan was trying not to cry. When, a year ago, Nan's aunts had brought her to Larwood House, even softer, plumper, and more timid than she was now, Miss Cadwallader had promised that no one should know her name was Dulcinea. Miss Cadwallader had *promised*! So how had someone found out? The rest of 6B kept breaking into laughter and excited whispers. Could Nan Pilgrim be a witch? Fancy anyone being called Dulcinea! It was as bad as being called Guy Fawkes! Halfway through the lesson, Theresa Mullett was so overcome by the thought of Nan's name that she was forced to bury her face in her knitting to laugh.

Mr. Wentworth promptly took the knitting away. He dumped the clean white bundle on the desk in front of him and inspected it dubiously. "What is it about this that seems so funny?" He unrolled the towel—at which Theresa gave a faint yell of dismay—and held up a very small fluffy thing with holes in it. "Just what is this?"

Everyone laughed.

"It's a bootee!" Theresa said angrily.

"Who for?" retorted Mr. Wentworth.

Everyone laughed again. But the laughter was short and guilty, because everyone knew Theresa was not to be laughed at.

Mr. Wentworth seemed unaware that he had performed a miracle and made everyone laugh at Theresa, instead of the other way around. He cut the laughter even shorter by telling Dan Smith to come out to the blackboard and show him two triangles that were alike. The lesson went on. Theresa kept muttering, "It's not funny! It's just not funny!" Every time she said it, her friends nodded sympathetically, while the rest of the class kept looking at Nan and bursting into muffled laughter.

At the end of the lesson, Mr. Wentworth uttered a few unpleasant remarks about mass punishments if people behaved like this again. Then, as he turned to leave, he said, "And by the way, if Charles Morgan, Nan Pilgrim, and Nirupam Singh haven't already looked at the main notice board, they should do so at once. They will find they are down for lunch on high table."

Both Nan and Charles knew then that this was not just a bad day—it was the worst day ever. Miss Cadwallader sat at high table with any important visitors to the school. It was her custom to choose three pupils from the school every day to sit there with her. This was so that everyone should learn proper table manners, and so that Miss Cadwallader should get to know her pupils. It was rightly considered a terrible ordeal. Neither Nan nor Charles had ever been chosen before. Scarcely able to believe it, they went to check with the notice board. Sure enough it read: *Charles Morgan 6B, Dulcinea Pilgrim 6B, Nirupam Singh 6B.*

Nan stared at it. So that was how everyone knew her name! Miss Cadwallader had forgotten. She had forgotten who Nan was and everything she had promised, and when she came to stick a pin in the register—or whatever she did to choose people for high table—she had simply written down the names that came under her pin.

Nirupam was looking at the notice too. He had been chosen before, but he was no less gloomy than Charles or Nan. "You have to comb your hair and get your blazer clean," he said. "And it really is true you have to eat with the same kind of knife or fork that Miss Cadwallader does. You have to watch and see what she uses all the time."

Nan stood there, letting other people looking at the notices push her about. She was terrified. She suddenly knew she was going to behave very badly on high table. She was going to drop her dinner, or scream, or maybe take all her clothes off and dance among the plates. And she was terrified, because she knew she was not going to be able to stop herself.

She was still terrified when she arrived at high table with Charles and Nirupam. They had all combed their heads sore and tried to clean from the fronts of their blazers the dirt which always mysteriously arrives on the fronts of blazers, but they all felt grubby and small beside the stately company at high table. There were a number of teachers, and the bursar, and an important-looking man called Lord Something-or-other, and tall, stringy Miss Cadwallader herself. Miss Cadwallader smiled at them graciously and pointed to three empty chairs at her left side. All of them instantly dived for the chair furthest away from Miss Cadwallader. Nan, much to her surprise, won it, and Charles won the chair in the middle, leaving

Nirupam to sit beside Miss Cadwallader.

"Now we know that won't do, don't we?" said Miss Cadwallader. "We always sit with a gentleman on either side of a lady, don't we? Dulcimer must sit in the middle, and I'll have the gentleman I haven't yet met nearest me. Clive Morgan, isn't it? That's right."

Suddenly, Charles, Nan, and Nirupam changed places. They stood there, while Miss Cadwallader was saying grace, looking out over the heads of the rest of the school, not very far below, but far enough to make a lot of difference. Perhaps I'm going to faint, Nan thought hopefully. She still knew she was going to behave badly, but she felt very odd as well—and fainting was a fairly respectable way of behaving badly.

She was still conscious at the end of grace. She sat down with the rest, between the glowering Charles and Nirupam. Nirupam had gone pale yellow with dread. To their relief, Miss Cadwallader at once turned to the important lord and began making gracious conversation with him. The ladies from the kitchen brought around a tray of little bowls and handed everybody one.

What was this? It was certainly not a usual part of school dinner. They looked suspiciously at the bowls. They were full of yellow stuff, not quite covering little pink things.

"I believe it may be prawns," Nirupam said dubiously. "For a starter."

Here Miss Cadwallader reached forth a gracious hand. Their heads at once craned around to see what implement she was going to eat out of the bowl with. Her hand picked up a fork. They picked up forks too. Nan poked hers cautiously into her bowl. Instantly she began to behave badly. She could not stop herself. "I think it's custard," she said loudly. "Do prawns mix with custard?" She put one of the pink things into her mouth. It felt rubbery. "Chewing gum?" she asked. "No, I think they're jointed worms. Worms in custard."

"Shut up!" hissed Nirupam.

"But it's not custard," Nan continued. She could hear her voice saying it, but there seemed no way to stop it. "The tongue-test proves that the yellow stuff has a strong taste of sour armpits, combined with—yes—just a touch of old drains. It comes from the bottom of a dustbin."

Charles glared at her. He felt sick. If he had dared, he would have stopped eating at once. But Miss Cadwallader continued gracefully forking up prawns—unless they really were jointed worms—and Charles did not dare do differently. He wondered how he was going to put this in his journal. He had never hated Nan Pilgrim particularly before, so he had no code word for her. Prawn? Could he call her prawn? He choked down another worm—prawn, that was—and he wished he could push the whole bowlful in Nan's face.

"A clean yellow dustbin," Nan announced.

"The kind they keep the dead fish for biology in."

"Prawns are eaten curried in India," Nirupam said loudly.

Nan knew he was trying to shut her up. With a great effort, by cramming several forkfuls of worms—prawns, that was—into her mouth at once, she managed to stop herself from talking. She could hardly bring herself to swallow the mouthful, but at least it kept her quiet. Most fervently, she hoped that the next course would be something ordinary, which she would not have any urge to describe, and so did Nirupam and Charles.

But alas! What came before them in platefuls next was one of the school kitchen's more peculiar dishes. They produced it about once a month and its official name was hot-pot. With it came tinned peas and tinned tomatoes. Charles's head and Nirupam's craned toward Miss Cadwallader again to see what they were supposed to eat this with. Miss Cadwallader picked up a fork. They picked up forks too, and then craned a second time, to make sure that Miss Cadwallader was not going to pick up a knife as well and so make it easier for everyone. She was not. Her fork dove gracefully under a pile of tinned peas. They sighed, and found both their heads turning towards Nan then in a sort of horrified expectation.

They were not disappointed. As Nan levered loose the first greasy ring of potato, the urge to describe came upon her again. It was as if she was possessed. "Now the aim of this dish," she said, "is to use up leftovers. You take old potatoes and soak them in washing-up water that has been used at least twice. The water must be thoroughly scummy." It's like the gift of tongues! she thought. Only in my case it's the gift of foul-mouth. "Then you take a dirty old tin and rub it around with socks that have been worn for a fortnight. You fill this tin with alternate layers of scummy potatoes and catfood, mixed with anything else you happen to have. Old doughnuts and dead flies have been used in this case—"

Could his code word for Nan be hot-pot? Charles wondered. It suited her. No, because they only had hot-pot once a month—fortunately—and, at this rate, he would need to hate Nan practically every day. Why didn't someone stop her? Couldn't Miss Cadwallader hear?

"Now these things," Nan continued, stabbing her fork into a tinned tomato, "are small creatures that have been killed and cleverly skinned. Notice, when you taste them, the slight, sweet savor of their blood—"

Nirupam uttered a small moan and went yellower than ever.

The sound made Nan look up. Hitherto, she had been staring at the table where her plate was, in a daze of terror. Now she saw Mr. Wentworth sitting opposite her across the table. He could hear her perfectly. She could tell from the expression on his face. Why doesn't he stop me? she thought. Why do they let me go on? Why doesn't somebody do something, like a thunderbolt strike me, or eternal detention? Why don't I get under the table and crawl away? And, all the time, she could hear herself talking. "These did in fact start life as peas. But they have since undergone a long and deadly process. They lie for six months in a sewer, absorbing fluids and rich tastes, which is why they are called processed peas. Then—"

Here, Miss Cadwallader turned gracefully to them. Nan, to her utter relief, stopped in mid-sentence. "You have all been long enough in the school by now," Miss Cadwallader said, "to know the town quite well. Do you know that lovely old house in High Street?"

They all three stared at her. Charles gulped down a ring of potato. "Lovely old house?"

"It's called the Old Gate House," said Miss Cadwallader. "It used to be part of the gate in the old town wall. A very lovely old brick building."

"You mean the one with a tower on top and windows like a church?" Charles asked, though he could not think why Miss Cadwallader should talk of this and not processed peas.

"That's the one," said Miss Cadwallader. "And it's such a shame. It's going to be pulled down to make way for a supermarket. You know it has a king-pin roof, don't you?"

"Oh," said Charles. "Has it?"

"And a queen-pin," said Miss Cadwallader.

Charles seemed to have got saddled with the conversation. Nirupam was happy enough not to talk, and Nan dared do no more than nod intelligently, in case she started describing the food again. As Miss Cadwallader talked, and Charles was forced to answer while trying to eat tinned tomatoes—no, they were *not* skinned mice!—using just a fork, Charles began to feel he was undergoing a particularly refined form of torture. He realized he needed a hate-word for Miss Cadwallader too. Hot-pot would do for her. Surely nothing as awful as this could happen to him more than once a month? But that meant he had still not got a code word for Nan.

They took the hot-pot away. Charles had not eaten much. Miss Cadwallader continued to talk to him about houses in the town, then about stately homes in the country, until the pudding arrived. It was set before Charles, white and bleak and swimming, with little white grains in it like the corpses of ants—Lord, he was getting as bad as Nan Pilgrim! Then he realized it was the ideal word for Nan.

"Rice pudding!" he exclaimed.

"It *is* agreeable," Miss Cadwallader said, smiling. "And so nourishing." Then, incredibly, she reached to the top of her plate and picked up a fork. Charles stared. He waited. Surely Miss Cadwallader was not going to eat runny rice pudding with just a fork? But she was. She dipped the fork in and brought it up, raining weak white milk.

Slowly, Charles picked up a fork too and turned to meet Nan's and Nirupam's incredulous faces. It was just not possible.

Nirupam looked wretchedly down at his brimming plate. "There is a story in the *Arabian Nights*," he said, "about a woman who ate rice with a pin, grain by grain." Charles shot a terrified look at Miss Cadwallader, but she was talking to the lord again. "She turned out to be a ghoul," Nirupam said. "She ate her fill of corpses every night."

Charles's terrified look shot to Nan instead. "Shut up, you fool! You'll set her off again!"

But the possession seemed to have left Nan by then. She was able to whisper, with her head bent over her plate so that only the boys could hear, "Mr. Wentworth's using his spoon. Look."

"Do you think we dare?" said Nirupam.

"I'm going to," said Charles. "I'm hungry."

So they all used their spoons. When the meal was at last over, they were all dismayed to find Mr. Wentworth beckoning. But it was only Nan he was beckoning. When she came reluctantly over, he said, "See me at four in my study." Which was, Nan felt, all she needed. And the day was still only half over.

3

THAT AFTERNOON, Nan came into the classroom to find a broom laid across her desk. It was an old tatty broom, with only the bare minimum of twigs left in the brush end, which the groundsman sometimes used to sweep the paths. Someone had brought it in from the groundsman's shed. Someone had tied a label to the handle: *Dulcinea's Pony.* Nan recognized the round, angelic writing as Theresa's.

Amid sniggers and titters, she looked around the assembled faces. Theresa would not have thought of stealing a broom on her own. Estelle? No. Neither Estelle nor Karen Grigg was there. No, it was Dan Smith, by the look on his face. Then she looked at Simon Silverson and was not so sure. It could not have been both of them because they never, ever did anything together.

Simon said to her, in his suavest manner, grinning all over his face, "Why don't you hop on and have a ride, Dulcinea?"

"Yes, go on. Ride it, Dulcinea," said Dan.

Next moment, everyone else was laughing and yelling at her to ride the broom. And Brian Wentworth, who was only too ready to torment other people when he was not being a victim himself, was leaping up and down in the gangway between the desks, screaming, "Ride, Dulcinea! Ride!"

Slowly, Nan picked up the broom. She was a mild and peaceable person who seldom lost her temper—perhaps that was her trouble—but when she did lose it, there was no knowing what she would do. As she picked up the broom, she thought she just meant to stand it haughtily against the wall. But, as her hands closed around its knobby handle, her temper left her completely. She turned around on the jeering, hooting crowd, filled with roaring rage. She lifted the broom high above her head and bared her teeth. Everyone thought that was funnier than ever.

Nan meant to smash the broom through Simon Silverson's laughing face. She meant to bash in Dan Smith's head. But, since Brian Wentworth was dancing and shrieking and making faces just in front of her, it was Brian she went for. Luckily for him, he saw the broom coming down and leaped clear. After that, he was forced to back away up the gangway and then into the space by the door, with his arms over his head, screaming for mercy, while Nan followed him, bashing like a madwoman.

"Help! Stop her!" Brian screamed, and backed

into the door just as Miss Hodge came through it carrying a large pile of English books. Brian backed into her and sat down at her feet in a shower of books. "Ow!" he yelled.

"What is going on?" asked Miss Hodge.

The uproar in the room was cut off as if with a switch. "Get up, Brian," Simon Silverson said righteously. "It was your own fault for teasing Nan Pilgrim."

"Really! Nan!" said Theresa. She was genuinely shocked. "Temper, temper!"

At that, Nan nearly went for Theresa with the broom. Theresa was only saved by the fortunate arrival of Estelle Green and Karen Grigg. They came scurrying in with their heads guiltily lowered and their arms wrapped around bulky bags of knitting wool. "Sorry we're late, Miss Hodge," Estelle panted. "We had permission to go shopping."

Nan's attention was distracted. The wool in the bags was fluffy and white, just like Theresa's. Why on earth, Nan wondered scornfully, did everyone have to imitate Theresa?

Miss Hodge took the broom out of Nan's unresisting hands and propped it neatly behind the door. "Sit down, all of you," she said. She was very put out. She had intended to come quietly into a nice quiet classroom and galvanize 6B by confronting them with her scheme. And here they were galvanized already, *and* with a witch's broom. There was clearly no chance of catching the writer of the note or the witch by surprise. Still, she did not like to let a good scheme go to waste.

"I thought we would have a change today," she said, when everyone was settled. "Our poetry book doesn't seem to be going down very well, does it?" She looked brightly round the class; 6B looked back cautiously. Some of them felt anything would be better than being asked to find poems beautiful. Some of them felt it depended on what Miss Hodge intended to do instead. Of the rest, Nan was trying not to cry, Brian was licking a scratch on his arm, and Charles was glowering. Charles liked poetry because the lines were so short. You could think your own thoughts in the spaces around the print.

"Today," said Miss Hodge, "I want you all to do something yourselves."

Everyone recoiled. Estelle put her hand up. "Please, Miss Hodge. I don't know how to write poems."

"Oh, I don't want you to do that," said Miss Hodge. Everyone relaxed. "I want you to act out some little plays for me." Everyone recoiled again. Miss Hodge took no notice and explained that she was going to call them out to the front in pairs, a boy and a girl in each, and every pair was going to act out the same short scene. "That way," she said, "we shall have fifteen different pocket dramas." By this time, most of 6B were staring at her in wordless despair. Miss Hodge smiled around them and prepared to galvanize them. Really, she thought, her scheme might go quite well after all. "Now, we

316

must choose a subject for our playlets. It has to be something strong and striking, with passionate possibilities. Suppose we act a pair of lovers saying good-bye?" Somebody groaned, as Miss Hodge had known somebody would. "Very well. Who has a suggestion?"

Theresa's hand was up, and Dan Smith's.

"A television star and her admirer," said Theresa.

"A murderer and a policeman making him confess," said Dan. "Are we allowed to torture?"

"No, we are not," said Miss Hodge, at which Dan lost interest. "Anyone else?"

Nirupam raised a long thin arm. "A salesman deceiving a lady over a car."

Well, Miss Hodge thought, she had not really expected anyone to make a suggestion that would give them away. She pretended to consider. "We-ell, so far the most dramatic suggestion is Dan's. But I had in mind something really tense, which we all know about quite well."

"We all know about murder," Dan protested.

"Yes," said Miss Hodge. She was watching everyone like a hawk now. "But we know even more about stealing, say, or lying, or witchcraft, or—" She let herself notice the broomstick again, with a start of surprise. It came in handy after all. "I know! Let us suppose that one of the people in our little play is suspected of being a witch, and the other is an inquisitor. How about that?"

Nothing. Not a soul in 6B reacted, except Dan.

"That's the same as my idea," he grumbled. "And it's no fun without torture."

Miss Hodge made Dan into suspect number one at once. "Then you begin, Dan," she said, "with Theresa. Which are you, Theresa—witch or inquisitor?"

"Inquisitor, Miss Hodge," Theresa said promptly.

"It's not fair!" said Dan. "I don't know what witches do!"

Nor did he, it was clear. And it was equally clear that Theresa had no more idea what inquisitors did. They stood woodenly by the blackboard. Dan stared at the ceiling, while Theresa stated, "You are a witch." Whereupon Dan told the ceiling, "No I am not." And they went on doing this until Miss Hodge told them to stop. Regretfully, she demoted Dan from first suspect to last, and put Theresa down there with him, and called up the next pair.

Nobody behaved suspiciously. Most people's idea was to get the acting over as quickly as possible. Some argued a little, for the look of the thing. Others tried running about to make things seem dramatic. And first prize for brevity certainly went to Simon Silverson and Karen Grigg. Simon said, "I know you're a witch, so don't argue."

And Karen replied, "Yes, I am. I give in. Let's stop now."

By the time it came to Nirupam, Miss Hodge's list of suspects was all bottom and no top. Then

Nirupam put on a terrifying performance as inquisitor. His eyes blazed. His voice alternately roared and fell to a sinister whisper. He pointed fiercely at Estelle's face. "Look at your evil eyes!" he bellowed. Then he whispered, "I see you, I feel you, I know you—you *are* a witch!" Estelle was so frightened that she gave a real performance of terrified innocence. But Brian Wentworth's performance as a witch outshone even Nirupam. Brian wept, he cringed, he made obviously false excuses, and he ended kneeling at Delia Martin's feet, sobbing for mercy and crying real tears.

Everyone was astonished, including Miss Hodge. She would dearly have liked to put Brian at the top of her list of suspects, as either the witch or the one who wrote the note. But how bothersome for her plans if she had to go to Mr. Wentworth and say it was Brian. No, she decided. There was no genuine feeling in Brian's performance, and the same went for Nirupam. They were both just good actors.

Then it was the turn of Charles and Nan. Charles had seen it coming for some time now, that he would be paired with Nan. He was very annoyed. He seemed to be haunted by her today. But he did not intend to let that stop his performance from being a triumph of comic acting. He was depressed by the lack of invention everyone except Nirupam had shown. Nobody had thought of making the inquisitor funny. "I'll be inquisitor," he said quickly.

But Nan was still smarting from the broom-stick. She thought Charles was getting at her and glared at him. Charles, on principle, never let anyone glare at him without giving his nastiest double-barreled stare in return. So they shuffled to the front of the class looking daggers at one another.

There Charles beat at his forehead. "Emergency!" he exclaimed. "There are no witches for the autumn bonfires. I shall have to find an ordinary person instead." He pointed at Nan. "You'll do," he said. "Starting from now, you're a witch."

Nan had not realized that the acting had begun. Besides, she was too hurt and angry to care. "Oh, no, I'm not!" she snapped. "Why shouldn't you be the witch?"

"Because I can prove you're a witch," Charles said, trying to stick to his part. "Being an inquisitor, I can prove anything."

"In that case," said Nan, angrily ignoring the fine acting, "we'll both be inquisitors, and I'll prove you're a witch too! Why not? You have four of the most evil eyes I ever saw. And your feet smell."

All eyes turned to Charles's feet. Since he had been forced to run around the field in the shoes he was wearing now, they were still rather wet. And, being warmed through, they were indeed exuding a small but definite smell.

"Cheese," murmured Simon Silverson.

Charles looked angrily down at his shoes. Nan had reminded him that he was in trouble over his missing running shoes. And she had spoiled his act-ing. He hated her. He was in an ecstasy of hate again. "Worms and custard and dead mice!" he said. Everyone stared at him, mystified. "Tinned peas soaked in sewage!" Charles said, beside himself with hatred. "Potatoes in scum. I'm not surprised your name's Dulcinea. It suits you. You're quite dis-gusting!"

"And so are you!" Nan shouted back at him. "I bet it was you who did those birds in music yes-terday!" This caused shocked gasps from the rest of 6B.

Miss Hodge listened, fascinated. This was real feeling all right. And *what* had Charles said? It was clear to her now why the rest of 6B had clustered so depressingly at the bottom of her list of suspects. Nan and Charles were at the top of it. It was obvi-ous. They were always the odd ones out in 6B. Nan must have written the note, and Charles must be the witch in question. And now let Mr. Wentworth pour scorn on her scheme!

"Please, Miss Hodge, the bell's rung," called a number of voices.

The door opened and Mr. Crossley came in. When he saw Miss Hodge, which he had come early in order to do, his face became a deep red, most interesting to Estelle and Theresa. "Am I interrupt-ing a lesson, Miss Hodge?"

"Not at all," said Miss Hodge. "We had just fin-ished. Nan and Charles, go back to your places." And she swept out of the room, without appearing to notice that Mr. Crossley had leaped to hold the door open for her.

Miss Hodge hurried straight upstairs to Mr. Wentworth's study. She knew this news was going to make an impression on him. But there, to her annoyance, was Mr. Wentworth dashing downstairs with a box of chalk, very late for a lesson with 3A.

"Oh, Mr. Wentworth," panted Miss Hodge. "Can you spare a moment?"

"Not a second. Write me a memo if it's urgent," said Mr. Wentworth, dashing on down.

Miss Hodge reached out and seized his arm. "But you must! You know 6B and my scheme about the anonymous note—"

Mr. Wentworth swung around on the end of her clutching hands and looked up at her irritably. "What about what anonymous note?"

"My scheme worked!" Miss Hodge said. "Nan Pilgrim wrote it, I'm sure. You must see her—"

"I'm seeing her at four o'clock," said Mr. Wentworth. "If you think I need to know, write me a memo, Miss Hodge."

"Eileen," said Miss Hodge.

"Eileen who?" said Mr. Wentworth, trying to pull his arm away. "You mean two girls wrote this note?"

"My name is Eileen," said Miss Hodge, hanging on.

"Miss Hodge," said Mr. Wentworth, "3A will be breaking windows by now!"

"But there's Charles Morgan too!" Miss Hodge cried out, feeling his arm pulling out of her hands. "Mr. Wentworth, I swear that boy recited a spell! Worms and custard and scummy potatoes, he said. All sorts of nasty things."

Mr. Wentworth succeeded in tearing his arm loose and set off downstairs again. His voice came back to Miss Hodge. "Slugs and snails and puppy-dogs' tails. Write it all down, Miss Hodge."

"Bother!" said Miss Hodge. "But I *will* write it down. He *is* going to notice!" She went at once to the staff room, where she spent the rest of the lesson composing an account of her experiment, in writing almost as round and angelic as Theresa's.

Meanwhile, in the 6B classroom, Mr. Crossley shut the door behind Miss Hodge with a sigh. "Journals out," he said. He had come to a decision about the note, and he did not intend to let his feelings about Miss Hodge interfere with his duty. So, before anyone could start writing in a journal and make it impossible for him to interrupt, he made 6B a long and serious speech. He told them how malicious and sneaky and unkind it was to write anonymous accusations. He asked them to consider how they would feel if someone had written a note about them. Then he told them that someone in 6B had written just such a note.

"I'm not going to tell you what was in it," he said. "I shall only say it accused someone of a very serious crime. I want you all to think about it while you write your journals, and after you've finished,

I want the person who wrote the note to write me another note confessing who they are and why they wrote it. That's all. I shan't punish the person. I just want them to see what a serious thing they have done."

Having said this, Mr. Crossley sat back to do some marking, feeling he had settled the matter in a most understanding way. In front of him, 6B picked up their pens. Thanks to Miss Hodge, everyone thought they knew exactly what Mr. Crossley meant.

29 October, wrote Theresa. *There is a witch in our class. Mr. Crossley just said so. He wants the witch to confess. Mr. Wentworth confiscated my knitting this morning and made jokes about it. I did not get it back till lunchtime. Estelle Green has started knitting now. What a copycat that girl is. Nan Pilgrim couldn't climb the ropes this morning and her name is Dulcinea. That made us laugh a lot.*

29.10.81. Mr. Crossley has just talked to us very seriously, Simon Silverson wrote, *very seriously, about a guilty person in our class. I shall do my best to bring that person to justice. If we don't catch them we might all be accused. This is off the record of course.*

Nan Pilgrim is a witch, Dan Smith wrote. *This is not a private thought because Mr. Crossley just told us. I think she is a witch too. She is even called after the famous witch, but I can't spell it. I hope they burn her where we can see.*

Mr. Crossley has been talking about serious accusations, Estelle wrote. *And Miss Hodge has been making us all accuse one another. It was quite frightening. I hope none of it is true. Poor Teddy went awfully red when he saw Miss Hodge but she scorned him again.*

While everyone else was writing the same sort of things, there were four people in the class who were writing something quite different.

Nirupam wrote, *Today, no comment. I shall not even think about high table.*

Brian Wentworth, oblivious to everything, scribbled down how he would get from Timbuktu to Uttar Pradesh by bus, allowing time for road-works on Sundays.

Nan sat for a considerable while wondering what to write. She wanted desperately to get some of today off her chest, but she could not at first think how to do it without saying something personal. At last she wrote, in burning indignation, *I do not know if 6B is average or not, but this is how they are. They are divided into girls and boys with an invisible line down the middle of the room and people only cross that line when teachers make them. Girls are divided into real girls (Theresa Mullett) and imitations (Estelle Green). And me. Boys are divided into real boys (Simon Silverson), brutes (Daniel Smith), and unreal boys (Nirupam Singh). And Charles Morgan. And Brian Wentworth. What makes you a real girl or boy is that no one laughs at you. If you are imitation or unreal, the rules give you a right to exist provided you do what the real ones or brutes say. What makes you into me or Charles Morgan is that the rules allow all the girls to be better than me and all the boys better than Charles*

Morgan. They are allowed to cross the invisible line to prove this. Everyone is allowed to cross the invisible line to be nasty to Brian Wentworth.

Nan paused here. Up to then she had been writing almost as if she was possessed the way she had been at lunch. Now she had to think about Brian Wentworth. What was it about Brian that put him below even her? *Some of Brian's trouble,* she wrote, *is that Mr. Wentworth is his father, and he is small and perky and irritating with it. Another part is that Brian is really good at things and comes top in most things, and he ought to be the real boy, not Simon. But SS is so certain he is the real boy that he has managed to convince Brian too.* That, Nan thought, was still not quite it, but it was as near as she could get. The rest of her description of 6B struck her as masterly. She was so pleased with it that she almost forgot she was miserable.

Charles wrote, *I got up, I got up, I GOT UP.* That made it look as if he had sprung eagerly out of bed, which was certainly not the case, but he had so hated today that he had to work it off somehow. *My running shoes got buried in cornflakes. I felt very hot running around the field and on top of that I had lunch on high table. I do not like rice pudding. We have had games with Miss Hodge and rice pudding and there are still about a hundred years of today to go.* And that, he thought, about summed it up.

When the bell rang, Mr. Crossley hurried to pick up the books he had been marking in order to get to the staff room before Miss Hodge left it.

And stared. There was another note under the pile of books. It was written in the same capitals and the same blue ballpoint as the first note. It said: *HA HA. THOUGHT I WAS GOING TO TELL YOU. DIDN'T YOU?*

Now what do I do? wondered Mr. Crossley.

4

❖

AT THE END OF LESSONS, there was the usual stampede to be elsewhere. Theresa and her friends, Delia, Heather, Deborah, Julia, and the rest, raced to the lower school girls' playroom to grab the radiators there, so that they could sit on them and knit. Estelle and Karen hurried to get the chillier radiators in the corridor, and sat on them to cast on their stitches. Simon led his friends to the labs, where they added to Simon's collection of honor marks by helping tidy up. Dan Smith left his friends to play football without him, because he had business in the shrubbery, watching the senior boys meeting their senior girl friends there. Charles crawled reluctantly to the locker room to look for his running shoes again. Nan went, equally reluctantly, up to Mr. Wentworth's study.

There was someone else in with Mr. Wentworth when she got there. She could hear voices and see two misty shapes through the wobbly glass in the door. Nan did not mind. The longer the interview was put off the better. So she hung about in the passage for nearly twenty minutes, until a passing monitor asked her what she was doing there.

"Waiting to see Mr. Wentworth," Nan said. Then, of course, in order to prove it to the monitor, she was forced to knock at the door.

"Come in!" bawled Mr. Wentworth.

The monitor, placated, passed on down the passage. Nan put out her hand to open the door, but, before she could, it was pulled open by Mr. Wentworth himself and Mr. Crossley came out, rather red and laughing sheepishly.

"I still swear it wasn't there when I put the books down," he said.

"Ah, but you know you didn't look, Harold," Mr. Wentworth said. "Our practical joker relied on your not looking. Forget it, Harold. So there you are, Nan. Did you lose your way here? Come on in. Mr. Crossley's just going."

He went back to his desk and sat down. Mr. Crossley hovered for a moment, still rather red, and then hurried away downstairs, leaving Nan to shut the door. As she did so, she noticed that Mr. Wentworth was staring at three pieces of paper on his desk as if he thought they might bite him. She saw that one was in Miss Hodge's writing and that the other two were scraps of paper with blue capital letters on them, but she was much too worried on her own account to bother about pieces of writing.

"Explain your behavior at high table," Mr. Wentworth said to her.

Since there really was no explanation that Nan could see, she said, in a miserable whisper, "I can't, sir," and looked down at the parquet floor.

"Can't?" said Mr. Wentworth. "You put Lord Mulke off his lunch for no reason at all! Tell me another. Explain yourself."

Miserably, Nan fitted one of her feet exactly into one of the parquet oblongs in the floor. "I don't know, sir. I just said it."

"You don't know, you just said it," said Mr. Wentworth. "Do you mean by that that you found yourself speaking without knowing you were?"

This was meant to be sarcasm, Nan knew. But it seemed to be true as well. Carefully, she fitted her other shoe into the parquet block which slanted towards her first foot, and stood unsteadily, toe to toe, while she wondered how to explain. "I didn't know what I was going to say next, sir."

"Why not?" demanded Mr. Wentworth.

"I don't know," Nan said. "It was like—like being possessed."

"*Possessed!*" shouted Mr. Wentworth. It was the way he shouted just before he suddenly threw chalk at people. Nan went backward to avoid the chalk which came next. But she forgot that her feet were pointing inward and sat down heavily on the floor. From there, she could see Mr. Wentworth's surprised face, peering at her over the top of his desk. "What did that?" he said.

"Please don't throw chalk at me!" Nan said.

At that moment, there was a knock at the door

and Brian Wentworth put his head around it into the room. "Are you free yet, Dad?"

"No," said Mr. Wentworth.

Both of them looked at Nan sitting on the floor. "What's she doing?" Brian asked.

"She says she's possessed. Go away and come back in ten minutes," Mr. Wentworth said. "Get up, Nan."

Brian obediently shut the door and went away. Nan struggled to her feet. It was almost as difficult as climbing a rope. She wondered a little how it felt to be Brian, with your father one of the teachers, but mostly she wondered what Mr. Wentworth was going to do to her. He had on his most harrowed, worried look, and he was staring again at the three papers on his desk.

"So you think you're possessed?" he said.

"Oh no," Nan said. "All I meant was it was *like* it. I knew I was going to do something awful before I started, but I didn't know what until I started describing the food. Then I tried to stop and I couldn't somehow."

"Do you often get taken that way?" Mr. Wentworth asked.

Nan was about to answer indignantly No, when she realized that she had gone for Brian with the witch's broom in exactly the same way straight after lunch. And many and many a time, she had impulsively written things in her journal. She fitted her shoe into a parquet block again, and hastily took it away. "Sometimes," she said, in a low, guilty mutter. "I do sometimes—when I'm angry with people—I write what I think in my journal."

"And do you write notes to teachers too?" asked Mr. Wentworth.

"Of course not," said Nan. "What would be the point?"

"But someone in 6B has written Mr. Crossley a note," said Mr. Wentworth. "It accused someone in the class of being a witch."

The serious, worried way he said it made Nan understand at last. So that was why Mr. Crossley had talked like that and then been to see Mr. Wentworth. And they thought Nan had written the note. "The unfairness!" she burst out. "How *can* they think I wrote the note *and* call me a witch too! Just because my name's Dulcinea!"

"You could be diverting suspicion from yourself," Mr. Wentworth pointed out. "If I asked you straight out—"

"I am *not* a witch!" said Nan. "And I didn't write that note. I bet that was Theresa Mullett or Simon Silverson. They're both born accusers! Or Daniel Smith," she added.

"Now, I wouldn't have picked on Dan," Mr. Wentworth said. "I wasn't aware he could write."

The sarcastic way he said that showed Nan that she ought not to have mentioned Theresa or Simon. Like everyone else, Mr. Wentworth thought of them as the real girl and the real boy. "Someone accused *me*," she said bitterly.

"Well, I'll take your word for it that you didn't

write the note," Mr. Wentworth said. "And next time you feel a possession coming on, take a deep breath and count up to ten, or you may be in serious trouble. You have a very unfortunate name, you see. You'll have to be very careful in future. How did you come to be called Dulcinea? Were you called after the Archwitch?"

"Yes," Nan admitted. "I'm descended from her."

Mr. Wentworth whistled. "And you're a witch-orphan too, aren't you? I shouldn't let anyone else know that, if I were you. I happen to admire Dulcinea Wilkes for trying to stop witches being persecuted, but very few other people do. Keep your mouth shut, Nan—and don't ever describe food in front of Lord Mulke again either. Off you go now."

Nan fumbled her way out of the study and plunged down the stairs. Her eyes were so fuzzy with indignation that she could hardly see where she was going. "What does he take me for?" she muttered to herself as she went. "I'd rather admit to being descended from—from Attila the Hun or—or Guy Fawkes. Or anyone."

It was around that time that Mr. Towers, who had stood over Charles while Charles hunted unavailingly for his running shoes in the boys' locker room, finally smothered a long yawn and left Charles to go on looking by himself. "Bring them to me in the staff room when you've found them," he said.

Charles sat down on a bench, alone among gray lockers and green walls. He glowered at the slimy gray floor and the three odd football boots that always lay in one corner. He looked at nameless garments withering on pegs. He sniffed the smell of sweat and old socks. "I hate everything," he said. He had searched everywhere. Dan Smith had found a really cunning place for those shoes. The only way Charles was going to find them was by Dan telling him where they were.

Charles ground his teeth and stood up. "All right. Then I'll ask him," he said. Like everyone else, he knew Dan was in the shrubbery spying on seniors. Dan made no secret of it. He had got his uncle to send him a pair of binoculars so that he could get a really close view. And the shrubbery was only around the corner from the locker room. Charles thought he could risk going there, even if Mr. Towers suddenly came back. The real risk was from the seniors in the shrubbery. There was an invisible line around the shrubbery, just like the one Nan had described between the boys and the girls in 6B. Anyone younger than a senior who got found in the shrubbery could be most thoroughly beaten up by the senior who found them. Still, Charles thought, as he set off, Dan was not a senior either. That should help.

The shrubbery was a messy tangle of huge evergreen bushes, with wet grass in between. Charles's almost-dry shoes were soaked again before he found Dan. He found him quite quickly. Since it was a cold evening and the grass was so wet, there were only two pairs of seniors there, and they were all in the most trodden part, on either side of a mighty laurel bush. Ah! thought Charles. He crept to the laurel bush and pushed his face in among the wet and shiny leaves. Dan was there, among the dry branches inside.

"Dan!" whispered Charles.

Dan took his binoculars from his eyes with a jerk and whirled around. When he saw Charles's face leaning in among the leaves at him, beaming its nastiest double-barreled glare, he seemed almost relieved. "Pig off!" he whispered. "Magic out of here!"

"What have you done with my spikes?" said Charles.

"Whisper, can't you?" Dan whispered. He peered nervously through the leaves at the nearest pair of seniors. Charles could see them too. They were a tall, thin boy and a very fat girl—much fatter than Nan Pilgrim—and they did not seem to have heard anything. Charles could see the thin boy's fingers digging into the girl's fat where his arm was around her. He wondered how anyone could enjoy grabbing, or watching, such fatness.

"Where have you hidden my spikes?" he whispered.

But Dan did not care, as long as the seniors had not heard. "I've forgotten," he whispered. Beyond the bush, the thin boy leaned his head against the fat girl's head. Dan grinned. "See that? Mixing the breed." He put his binoculars to his eyes again.

Charles spoke a little louder. "Tell me where

you've put my spikes, or I'll shout that you're here."

"Then they'll know you're here too, won't they?" Dan whispered. "I told you, magic off!"

"Not till you tell me," said Charles.

Charles saw that he had no option but to raise a yell and fetch the seniors into the bush. While he was wondering whether he dared, the second pair of seniors came hurrying around the laurel bush. "Hey!" said the boy. "There's some juniors in that bush. Sue heard them whispering."

"Right!" said the thin boy and the fat girl. And all four seniors dived at the bush.

Charles let out a squawk of terror and ran. Behind him, he heard cracking branches, leaves swishing, grunts, crunchings, and most unladylike threats from the senior girls. He hoped Dan had been caught. But even while he was hoping, he knew Dan had gotten away. Charles was in the open. The seniors had seen him and it was Charles they were after. He burst out of the shrubbery with all four of them after him. With a finger across his nose to hold his glasses on, he pelted for his life around the corner of the school.

There was nothing in front of him but a long wall and open space. The lower school door was a hundred yards away. The only possible place that was any nearer was the open door of the boys' locker room. Charles bolted through it without thinking. And skidded to a stop, realizing what a fool he had been. The seniors' feet were hammering around the corner, and the only way out of the locker room was the open door he had come in by. All Charles could think of was to dodge behind that door and stand there flat against the wall, hoping. There he stood, flattened and desperate, breathing in old sock and mildew and trying not to pant, while four pairs of feet slid to a stop outside the door.

"He's hiding in there," said the fat girl's voice.

"We can't go in. It's boys'," said the other girl. "You two go and bring him out."

There were breathless grunts from the two boys, and two pairs of heavy feet tramped in through the doorway. The thin boy, by the sound, tramped into the middle of the room. His voice rumbled around the concrete space.

"Where's he gotten to?"

"Must be behind the door," rumbled the other. The door was pulled aside. Charles stood petrified at the sight of the senior it revealed. This one was huge. He towered over Charles. He even had a sort of moustache. Charles shook with terror.

But the little angry eyes, high up above the moustache, stared down through Charles, seemingly at the floor and the wall. The bulky face twitched in annoyance. "Nope," said the senior. "Nothing here."

"He must have made it to the lower school door," said the thin boy.

"Magicking little witch!" said the other.

And, to Charles's utter amazement, the two of them tramped out of the locker room. There was some annoyed exclaiming from the two girls outside, and then all four of them seemed to be going away. Charles stood where he was, shaking, for quite a while after they seemed to have gone. He was sure it was a trick. But, five minutes later, they had still not come back. It was a miracle of some kind!

Charles tottered out into the middle of the room, wondering just what kind of miracle it was that could make a huge senior look straight through you. Now he knew it had happened, Charles was sure the senior had not been pretending. He really had not seen Charles standing there.

"So what did it?" Charles asked the nameless hanging clothes. "Magic?"

He meant it to be a scornful question, the kind of thing you say when you give the whole thing up. But, somehow, it was not. As he said it, a huge, terrible suspicion which had been gathering, almost unnoticed, at the back of Charles's head, like a headache coming on, now swung to the front of his mind, like a headache already there. Charles began shaking again.

"No," he said. "It wasn't that. It was something else!"

But the suspicion, now it was there, demanded to be sent away at once, now, completely. "All right," Charles said. "I'll prove it. I know how. I hate Dan Smith anyway."

He marched up to Dan's locker and opened it. He looked at the jumble of clothes and shoes inside. He had searched his locker twice now. He had searched all of them twice. He was sick of looking in lockers. He took up Dan's spiked running shoes, one in each hand, and backed away with them to the middle of the room.

"Now," he said to the shoes, "you vanish." He tapped them together, sole to spiked sole, to make it clear to them. "Vanish," he said. "Abracadabra." And, when nothing happened, he threw both shoes into the air, to give them every chance. "Hey presto," he said.

Both shoes were gone, in midair, before they reached the slimy floor.

Charles stared at the spot where he had last seen them. "I didn't mean it," he said hopelessly. "Come back."

Nothing happened. No shoes appeared.

"Oh well," said Charles. "Perhaps I did mean it."

Then, very gently, almost reverently, he went over and shut Dan's locker. The suspicion was gone. But the certainty which hung over Charles in its place was so heavy and so hideous that it made him want to crouch on the floor. He was a witch. He would be hunted like the witch he had helped and burned like the fat one. It would hurt. It would be horrible. He was very, very scared—so scared it was like being dead already, cold, heavy, and almost unable to breathe.

Trying to pull himself together, he took his glasses off to clean them. That made him notice that he was, actually, crouching on the floor beside Dan's locker. He dragged himself upright. What should he do? Might not the best thing be to get it over now, and go straight to Miss Cadwallader and confess?

That seemed an awful waste, but Charles could not seem to think of anything else to do. He shuffled to the door and out into the chilly evening. He had always known he was wicked, he thought. Now it was proved. The witch had kissed him because she had known he was evil too. Now he had grown so evil that he needed to be stamped out. He wouldn't give the inquisitors any trouble, not like some witches did. Witchcraft must show all over him anyway. Someone had already noticed and written that note about it. Nan Pilgrim had accused him of conjuring up all those birds in music yesterday. Charles thought he must have done that without knowing he had, just as he had made himself invisible to the seniors just now. He wondered how strong a witch he was. Were you more wicked, the stronger you were? Probably. But weak or powerful, you were burned just the same. And he was in nice time for the autumn bonfires. It was nearly Halloween now. By the time they had legally proved him a witch, it would be November 5, and that would be the end of it.

He did not know it was possible to feel so scared and hopeless.

Thinking and thinking, in a haze of horror, Charles shuffled his way to Miss Cadwallader's room. He stood outside the door and waited, without even the heart to knock. Minutes passed. The door opened. Seeing the misty oblong of bright light, Charles braced himself.

"So you didn't find them?" said Mr. Towers.

Charles jumped. Though he could not see what Mr. Towers was doing here, he said, "No, sir."

"I'm not surprised, if you took your glasses off to look," said Mr. Towers.

Tremulously, Charles hooked his glasses over his ears. They were ice cold. He must have had them in his hand ever since he took them off to clean. Now that he could see, he saw he was standing outside the staff room, not Miss Cadwallader's room at all. Why was that? Still he could just as easily confess to Mr. Towers. "Please, I deserve to be punished, sir. I—"

"Take a black mark for that," Mr. Towers said coldly. "I don't like boys who crawl. Now, either you can pay for a new pair of shoes, or you can write five hundred lines every night until the end of the term. Come to me tomorrow morning and tell me which you decide to do. Now get out of here."

He slammed the door of the staff room in Charles's face. Charles stood and looked at it. That was a fierce choice Mr. Towers had given him. And a black mark. But it had jolted his horror off sideways somehow. He felt his face going red. What a fool he was! Nobody knew he was a witch. Instinct had told him this, and taken his feet to the staff room instead of to Miss Cadwallader. But only luck had saved him confessing to Mr. Towers. He had better not be that stupid again. As long as he kept his mouth shut and worked no more magic, he would be perfectly safe. He almost smiled as he trudged off to supper.

But he could not stop thinking about it. Around and around and around, all through supper. How wicked was he? Could he do anything about it? Was it enough just not to do any magic? Could you go somewhere and be de-magicked, like clothes were dry-cleaned? If not, and he was found out, was it any use running away? Where did witches run to, after they had run through people's backyards? Was there any certain way of being safe?

"Oh magic!" someone exclaimed, just beside him. "I left my book in the playroom!" Charles jumped and hummed, like the school gong when it was hit, at the mere word.

"Don't swear," said the monitor in charge.

Then Theresa Mullett, from the end of the table, called out in a way that was not quite jeering, "Nan, won't you do something interesting and miraculous for us? We know you can." Charles jumped and hummed again.

"No, I can't," said Nan.

But Theresa, and Delia Martin too, kept on asking. "Nan, high table's got some lovely bananas. Won't you say a spell and fetch them over?"

"Nan, I feel like some ice cream. Conjure some up."

"Nan, do you really worship the devil?"

Each time they said any of these things, Charles jumped and hummed. Though he knew it was entirely to his advantage to have everyone think Nan Pilgrim was the witch, he wanted to scream at the girls to stop. He was very relieved, halfway through supper, when Nan jumped up and stormed out of the dining room.

Nan went straight to the deserted library. Very well, she thought. If everyone was so sure she was guilty, she could at least take advantage of it and do something she had always wanted to do and never dared to do before. She took down the encyclopedia and looked up Dulcinea Wilkes. Curiously enough, the fat book fell open at that page. It seemed as if a lot of people at Larwood House had taken an interest in the Archwitch. If so, they had all been as disappointed as Nan. The laws against witchcraft were so severe that most information about Nan's famous ancestress was banned. The entry was quite short.

WILKES, DULCINEA. 1760–1790. Notorious witch, known as the Archwitch. Born in Steeple Bumpstead, Essex, she moved to London in 1781, where she soon became well known for her nightly broomstick flights around St. Paul's and the Houses of Parliament. Brooms are still sometimes call "Dulcinea's Ponies." Dulcinea took a leading part in the Witches' Uprising of 1789. She was arrested and burned, along with the other leaders. While she was burning, it is said that the lead on the roof of St. Paul's melted and ran off the dome. She continued to be burned in effigy every bonfire day until 1845, when the practice was discontinued owing to the high price of lead.

Nan sighed and put the encyclopedia back. When the bell rang, she went slowly to the classroom to do the work that had been set during the day. It was called devvy at Larwood House; no one knew why. Everyone else was there when Nan arrived. The room was full of the slap of exercise books around Brian Wentworth's head and Brian squealing. But the noise stopped as Nan came in, showing that Mr. Crossley had come in behind her.

"Charles Morgan," said Mr. Crossley. "Mr. Wentworth wants to see you."

Charles dragged his mind with a jolt from imaginary flames whirling around him. He got up and trudged off, like a boy in a dream, along corridors and through swinging doors to the part of the school where teachers who lived in the school had their private rooms. He had only been to Mr. Wentworth's room once before. He had to tear his mind away from thoughts of burning and look at the names on the doors. He supposed Mr. Wentworth wanted him because of his beastly shoes. Blast and magic Dan Smith! He knocked on the door.

"Come in!" said Mr. Wentworth.

He was sitting in an armchair smoking a pipe. The room was full of strong smoke. Charles was surprised to see how shabby Mr. Wentworth's room was. The armchair was worn out. There were holes in the soles of Mr. Wentworth's slippers, and holes in the hearthrug the slippers rested on. But the gas fire was churning away comfortably and the room was beautifully warm compared with the rest of school.

"Ah, Charles." Mr. Wentworth laid his pipe in an ashtray that looked like Brian's first attempt at pottery. "Charles, I was told this afternoon that you might be a witch."

5

CHARLES HAD THOUGHT, in the locker room, that he had been as frightened as a person could possibly be. Now he discovered this was not so. Mr. Wentworth's words seemed to hit him heavy separate blows. Under the blows, Charles felt as if he were dissolving and falling away somewhere far, far below. He thought at first he was falling somewhere so sickeningly deep that the whole of his mind had become one long horrible scream. Then he felt he was rising up as he screamed. The shabby room was blurred and swaying, but Charles could have sworn he was now looking down on it from somewhere near the ceiling. He seemed to be hanging there, screaming, looking down on the top of his own head, and the slightly bald top of Mr. Wentworth's head, and the smoke writhing from the pipe in the ashtray. And that terrified him too. He must have divided into two parts. Mr. Wentworth was bound to notice.

To his surprise, the part of himself left standing on the worn carpet answered Mr. Wentworth quite normally. He heard his own voice, with just the right amount of amazement and innocence, saying, "Who, me? I'm not a witch, sir."

"I didn't say you were, Charles," Mr. Wentworth replied. "I just said someone said you were. From the account I was given, you had a public row with Nan Pilgrim, in the course of which you spoke of worms and dead mice, and a number of other unpleasant things."

The part of Charles left standing on the carpet answered indignantly, "Well I did. But I was only saying some of the things *she* said at lunch. You were there, sir. Didn't you hear her, sir?" Meanwhile, the part of Charles hovering near the ceiling was thanking whatever lucky stars looked after witches that Mr. Wentworth had chanced to sit opposite Nan Pilgrim at high table.

"I did," said Mr. Wentworth. "I recognized your reference at once. But my informant thought you were reciting a spell."

"But I wasn't, sir," protested the part of Charles on the carpet.

"But you sounded as if you were," Mr. Wentworth said. "You can't be too careful, Charles, in these troubled times. It sounds as if I'd better explain the position to you."

He picked up his pipe to help him in the explanation. In the way of pipes, it had gone out by then. Mr. Wentworth struck matches and puffed, and struck more matches and puffed. Smoke does not seem to mean fire where pipes are concerned. Mr.

Wentworth used ten matches before the pipe was alight. As Charles watched, it dawned on him that Mr. Wentworth did not think he was a witch. Nor did Mr. Wentworth seem to have noticed the odd way he had split into two. Perhaps the part of him hovering near the ceiling was imaginary, and simply due to panic. As Charles thought this, he found the part of him near the ceiling slowly descending into the part of him standing normally on the carpet. By the time Mr. Wentworth risked putting his pipe out again by pressing the matchbox down on it, Charles found himself in one piece. He was still fizzing all over with terror, it is true, but he was feeling nothing like so peculiar.

"Now, Charles," said Mr. Wentworth. "You know witchcraft has always been illegal. But I think it's true to say that the laws against it have never been as strict as they are now. You've heard of the Witches' Uprising of course, in 1789, under the Archwitch Dulcinea Wilkes?"

Charles nodded. Everyone knew about Dulcinea. It was like being asked if you knew about Guy Fawkes.

"Now that," said Mr. Wentworth, "was a respectable sort of uprising in its way. The witches were protesting against being persecuted and burned. Dulcinea said, reasonably enough, that they couldn't help being born the way they were, and they didn't want to be killed for something they couldn't help. She kept promising that witches would use their powers only for good, if people

348

would stop burning them. Dulcinea wasn't at all the awful creature everyone says, you know. She was young and pretty and clever—but she had a terribly hot temper. When people wouldn't agree not to burn witches, she lost her temper and worked a number of huge and violent spells. That was a mistake. It made people absolutely terrified of witchcraft, and when the uprising was put down, there were an awful lot of bonfires and some really strict laws. But you'll know all that."

Charles nodded again. Apart from the fact that he had been taught that Dulcinea was an evil old hag, and a stupid one, this was what everyone knew.

"But," said Mr. Wentworth, pointing his pipe at Charles, "what you may not know is that there was another, much more unpleasant uprising, just before you were born. Surprised? Yes, I thought you were. It was hushed up rather. The witches leading it were all unpleasant people, and their aim was to take over the country. The main conspirators were all civil servants and army generals, and the leader was a cabinet minister. You can imagine how scared and shocked everyone was at that."

"Yes, sir," said Charles. He had almost stopped being frightened by now. He found himself trying to imagine the prime minister as a witch. It was an interesting idea.

Mr. Wentworth put his pipe in his mouth and puffed out smoke expressively. "The minister was burned in Trafalgar Square," he said. "And Parliament passed the Witchcraft Emergency Act in an effort to stamp out witches for good. That act, Charles, is still in force today. It gives the inquisitors enormous powers. They can arrest someone on the mere suspicion of witchcraft—even if they're only your age, Charles."

"My age?" Charles said hoarsely.

"Yes. Witches keep on being born," said Mr. Wentworth. "And it was discovered that the minister's family had known he was a witch since he was eleven years old. A lot of research has been done since on witches. There are a hundred different kinds of witch-detectors. But most of the research has been towards discovering when witches first come into their powers, and it seems that most witches start at around your age, Charles. So, these days, the inquisitors keep a special eye on all schools. And a school like this one, where at least half the pupils are witch-orphans anyway, is going to attract their notice at once. Understand?"

"No, sir," said Charles. "Why are you telling me?"

"Someone thought you recited a spell," Mr. Wentworth said. "Think, boy! If I hadn't happened to know what you were really saying, you'd be under arrest by now. So now you'll have to be extra specially careful. Now do you see?"

"Yes, sir," said Charles. He was almost frightened again.

"Then off you go, back to devvy," said Mr. Wentworth. Charles turned around and trudged over the threadbare carpet to the door. "And

Charles," called Mr. Wentworth. Charles turned around. "Take a black mark to remind you to be careful," said Mr. Wentworth.

Charles opened the door. Two black marks in one evening! If you got three black marks in a week, you went to Miss Cadwallader and were in real trouble. Two black marks! Both for things which were not his fault! Charles turned around while he was closing the door and directed the full force of his nastiest double-barreled glare at Mr. Wentworth. He was seething.

He trudged up the corridor to the swinging door, still seething. The swinging door swung as he reached it, and, to his surprise, Miss Hodge came through it. Miss Hodge did not live in school. As Estelle had speedily found out and told everyone, she lived with her old father in town. She was not usually here in the evenings at all.

"Charles!" said Miss Hodge. "How convenient! Have you been seeing Mr. Wentworth?"

It did not occur to Charles to wonder how Miss Hodge knew that. In his experience, teachers always knew far too much anyway. "Yes," he said.

"Then you can tell me which his room is," said Miss Hodge.

Charles pointed out the room and applied his shoulder to the swinging door. He had just forced his way out into the corridor beyond, when it swung again and again let Miss Hodge through.

"Charles, are you sure Mr. Wentworth was there? He didn't answer when I knocked."

"He was sitting by his fire," Charles said.

"Then perhaps I knocked at the wrong door," Miss Hodge said. "Can you come and show me? Would you mind very much?"

Yes, I would mind, Charles thought. He sighed and went back through the swinging door with Miss Hodge. Miss Hodge seemed pleased to have his company, which surprised him a little.

Miss Hodge was thinking how fortunate it was she had met Charles. Since the afternoon, she had been thinking carefully. And she saw that her next and most certain move towards marrying Mr. Wentworth was to go to him and impulsively take back her accusation against Charles. It was unpleasant to think of anyone being burned, even if Charles did have the most evil glare of any boy she knew. She would look so generous. And here she was, actually with Charles, to prove she bore him no malice.

Charles looked at Mr. Wentworth's name on the door and wondered how Miss Hodge could have gotten the wrong room.

"Oh," said Miss Hodge. "It was the right door. That's his name."

She knocked, and knocked again, with golden visions of her romance with Mr. Wentworth growing as, together, they tried to protect Charles from the clutches of the inquisitors. But there was no answer from the room. She turned to Charles in perplexity.

"Maybe he's gone to sleep," Charles said. "It was warm in there."

"Suppose we open the door and take a peep?" Miss Hodge said, fluttering a little.

"You do it," said Charles.

"No, you," said Miss Hodge. "I'll take all responsibility."

Charles sighed, and opened Mr. Wentworth's door for the second time that evening. A gust of cold, smoky air blew in their faces. The room was dark, except for a faint glow from the cooling gas fire. Even that vanished when Miss Hodge imperiously switched on the light and stood fanning the smoke away from her.

"Dear, dear," she said, looking around. "That man needs a woman's hand here. Are you sure he was here, Charles?"

"Just this minute," Charles said doggedly, but horror was beginning to descend on him. It was almost as if Mr. Wentworth had never been. He walked over to the bald patch of carpet in front of the fire and felt the fire. It was quite hot. Mr. Wentworth's pipe was lying in the pottery ashtray still, and that was warm too, but cooling in the icy air from the open window. Perhaps, Charles thought hopefully, Mr. Wentworth had just felt tired and gone to bed. There was a door in the opposite wall, beyond the blowing curtains of the window, which was probably the door to his bedroom.

But Miss Hodge boldly walked over and opened that door. It was a cupboard, stuffed with schoolbooks. "He didn't go this way," she said. "Has he a bedroom along the corridor, do you know?"

"He must have," said Charles. But he knew Mr. Wentworth had not gone down the corridor. He could not have come out of this room without Charles seeing him as he went to the swinging door, or Miss Hodge seeing him as she pushed past Charles the other way. There was only one other possibility. Charles had looked daggers at Mr. Wentworth. He had given him his very nastiest glare. And that glare had caused Mr. Wentworth to disappear, just as Dan's running shoes had disappeared. It was what they called the Evil Eye.

"I don't think there's any point in waiting," Miss Hodge said discontentedly. "Oh well. I can speak to him tomorrow."

Charles was only too glad to go. He was only too glad to accompany Miss Hodge down to the door where she had left her bicycle. He talked to her most politely all the way. It kept his mind off what he had done. And he thought that if he talked hard enough and made himself truly charming, Miss Hodge might not realize that Charles had been the last person to set eyes on Mr. Wentworth.

They talked of poems, football, bicycles, the caretaker's dog, and Mr. Hodge's garden. The result was that Miss Hodge mounted her bicycle and rode off, thinking that Charles Morgan was a very nice child once you got to know him. It made it all the better that she intended to withdraw her accusation against him. A teacher, she told herself, should always try to get to know her pupils.

Charles puffed out a big sigh of relief and trudged off again, weighted with new guilt. By the time he reached the classroom, nearly all the others had finished their work and were trooping off to choir practice. Charles had the room to himself, apart from Nan Pilgrim, who also seemed to be behindhand. They did not speak to one another, of course, but it was doubtful that either did much work. Nan was thinking miserably that if only she *was* a witch like Dulcinea Wilkes, she would not mind what anyone said. Charles was thinking about Mr. Wentworth.

First the birds in music, now Mr. Wentworth. Being invisible to the senior didn't count, because no one knew about that. What terrified Charles was that he would seem to keep using witchcraft by accident, where it showed. If only he could stop himself doing that, then he still might have a chance. Miss Hodge might give him an alibi over Mr. Wentworth, if he went on being nice to her. But how did you stop yourself working magic?

"This has been an awful day," Nan said, as she packed up to leave. "I'm so glad it's nearly over."

Charles stared at her, wondering how she knew. Then he packed up and left too. He was very much afraid that today was not over for him yet, by a long way. He had heard the inquisitors usually came for you in the night. So they would come for him, as soon as someone discovered Mr. Wentworth was missing. Charles thought about Mr. Wentworth all the time he was washing. He had rather liked Mr.

Wentworth on the whole. He felt very bad about him. Perhaps the way to stop himself doing it again, to Mr. Crossley or someone, was to think hard about how it felt to be burned. It would hurt.

It hurts to be burned, he repeated to himself as he undressed. *It hurts to be burned.* He was shivering as he climbed into bed, and not only from the cold air in the long Spartan dormitory.

Brian Wentworth was being beaten up again a few beds along from him. Brian was crouching on his bed with his arms over his head, while Simon Silverson and his friends hit him with their pillows. They were laughing, but they meant it too. "Show off!" they were saying. "Bootlicker! Show off!"

Up till then, Charles had always been almost glad he was in this dormitory, and not in the one next door like Nirupam, where Dan Smith ruled with his friends from 6C and 6D. Now he wondered whether to sneak off and sleep in the lower school boys' playroom. Brian's yells—for Brian could never be hit quietly—kept cutting through Charles's miserable meditations and reminding him what he had done to Brian's father. It grew so bothersome that Charles nearly got out of bed and joined in hitting Brian too, just to relieve his feelings. But by this time he had gathered the reason for the pillows. Mr. Brubeck had asked Brian to sing a solo at the school concert, and Brian had unwisely agreed. Everyone else knew that it was Simon's right to sing solo.

This meant that hitting Brian would be sucking up to Simon. That Charles would not do. He went back to his desperate wonderings. There was no way of keeping Mr. Wentworth's disappearance secret that he could see. But there was quite a chance that no one would realize Charles had done it. So, if only he could think of some surefire way of stopping himself working magic by accident—that was it! Sure fire. It hurts to be burned.

Charles got out of bed. He unhooked his glasses from his bedrail, hooked them on his ears, and thumped across to the flurry of pillows.

"Can I borrow the emergency candle for five minutes?" he said loudly to Simon.

Simon of course was dormitory monitor. He paused in belaboring Brian and became official. "The candle's only for emergencies. What do you want it for?"

"You'll see if you give it to me," said Charles.

Simon hesitated, torn between curiosity and his usual desire never to give anyone anything. "You'll have to tell me what you want it for first. I can't let you have it for no reason."

"I'm not going to tell you," said Charles. "Just give it to me."

Simon considered. Long experience of Charles Morgan had shown him that when Charles said he was not going to tell, nothing would make him tell, not pillows or even wild horses. His curiosity, as Charles had hoped, was thoroughly aroused. "If I give it to you," he said righteously, "I shall be breaking the rules. You owe me compensation for risking getting into trouble, you know."

This was only to be expected. "What do you want?" said Charles.

Simon smiled graciously, wondering how great Charles's need was. "Your pocket money every week for the rest of term," he said. "How about that?"

"Too much," said Charles.

Simon turned away and picked up his pillow again. "Take it or leave it," he said. "That's my final offer."

"I'll take it," said Charles, hating Simon.

Simon turned back to him in astonishment. He had expected Charles either to protest or give up asking. His friends stared at Charles, equally astonished. In fact, by this time, nobody was hitting Brian anymore. Here was something really odd going on. Even Brian was staring at Charles. How could anyone want a candle that much? "Very well," Simon said. "I'll accept your offer, Charles. But remember you promised in front of witnesses. You'd better pay up."

"I'll pay up," said Charles. "Every week when Mr. Crossley gives us our money. Now give me the candle."

Simon, with busy efficiency, fetched his key ring from his blazer and unlocked the cupboard on the wall where the first-aid kit and the candle were kept. If a miracle happened, Charles thought, and the inquisitors did not come for him after all, he had put himself in a true mess now. No pocket money until Christmas. That meant he could not pay for new running shoes. He would have to write five hundred lines every day for Mr. Towers. But he did not really believe he would be around to do that very long. Everyone said the inquisitors found witches whatever they did.

Simon put the candle in his hands. It was unlit, in a white enamel candle holder. Charles looked at it. He looked up to see Simon and all the other boys, even Brian, grinning.

"You forgot to ask for matches," Simon pointed out.

Charles looked at him. He glared. He did more than glare. It was the nastiest look he had ever given anyone. He hoped it would shrivel Simon on the spot.

All that happened was that Simon stepped backward from him. Even so, he looked as superior as ever. "But I'll give you the matches free," he said. "It's all part of the service." He tossed a box of matches toward Charles.

Charles put the candlestick down on the floor. With everyone staring at him, he struck a match and lit the candle. He knelt down beside it. *It hurts to be burned,* he thought. *It hurts to be burned.* He put out his finger and held it in the small yellow flame.

"Why on earth are you doing that?" asked Ronald West.

Charles did not answer. For a second, he thought the flame was not going to burn him. It just felt warm and wet. Then, quite suddenly, it was hot and it hurt very much indeed. It hurt, as Charles had expected, in quite a different way from cutting yourself or stubbing your toe. This was a much nastier pain, sharp and dull together, which brought Charles's back out in goose pimples and jangled the nerves all the way up his arm. Imagine this all over you, he thought. *It hurts to be burned.* He took hold of his wrist with his other hand and held it hard to stop himself snatching his finger out of the pain. *It hurts to be burned.* It did hurt too. It was making sweat prickle out just beneath his eyes.

"It must be for a dare or a bet," he heard Simon saying. "Which is it? Tell, or I'll put the candle away again."

"A bet," Charles answered at random. *It hurts to be burned. It hurts to be burned.* He thought this over and over, intent on branding it into his brain—or into whatever part of him it was that did magic. *It hurts to be*—Oh, it hurts!—*hurts to be burned.*

"Some people," Simon remarked, "make awfully stupid bets."

Charles ignored him and tried to keep his jerking finger steady. It was trying to jump out of the flame of its own accord. The finger was now red, with a white band across the red. He could hear a funny noise, a sort of tiny frizzling, as if his skin were frying. Then, suddenly, he could bear no more. He found himself snatching his finger away and blowing out the candle. The boys watching him all let out a sigh, as if they had been holding their breath.

"I suppose," Simon said discontentedly, as

Charles handed him the candle back, "you make more money on this bet than you owe me now."

"No, I don't," Charles said quickly. He was afraid Simon would be after that money too. Simon was quite capable of telling Mr. Crossley about the candle if Charles did not pay. "I don't get anything. The bet was to burn my finger right off."

The monitor on duty appeared in the doorway, shouting, "Lights out! No more talking!"

Charles got into bed, sucking his burned finger, hoping and praying that he had now taught himself not to work magic by accident. His tongue could feel a big pulpy blister rising between the first and second joint of his finger. It hurt more than ever.

Simon said, out of the darkness, "I always knew Charles Morgan was mad. What a brainless thing to do!"

Ronald West said, "You don't expect brains in an animal."

"Animals have more sense," said Geoffrey Baines.

"Charles Morgan," said Simon, "is a lower life form."

These kinds of comments went on for some time. It was perfectly safe to talk because there was always such a noise from the next dormitory. Charles lay and waited for them to stop. He knew he was not going to sleep. Nor did he. Long after Simon and his friends had fallen silent, long after two monitors and the master in charge had come along and shut up the boys next door, Charles lay stiff as a log of wood, staring up into the shadows.

He was frightened—terrified. But the terror was now a dreary long-distance kind of terror, which he was sure he was going to feel all the time, for the rest of his life now. Suppose by some miracle, no inquisitors came for him; then he was going to be afraid that they would, every minute of every day, for years and years. He wondered if you learned to get used to it. He hoped so, because at this moment he felt like springing out of bed and confessing, just to get it over. What would Simon say if Charles jumped up shouting, "I'm a witch!" Probably he would think Charles was mad. It was funny that Simon had not disappeared too. Charles sucked his finger and puzzled over that. He certainly hated Simon enough. He had not hated Mr. Wentworth at all really—or only in the way you hate any master who gives you a black mark you do not deserve. Perhaps witchcraft had to be sort of clinical to work properly.

Then Charles thought of his other troubles. Two black marks in one day. No running shoes. No money. Five hundred lines a day. And none of it was his fault! It was not his fault he had been born a witch, either, for that matter. It was all so unfair! He wished he did not have to feel so guilty about Mr. Wentworth on top of it all. *It hurts to be burned.*

Charles's thoughts slowly grew less connected after this point. He realized afterward that he must have been asleep. But if it was sleep, it was only a light horrified doze, in which his thoughts kept on clanking about in his head, as if he were a piece of machinery with the switch jammed to ON. But he did not know he had been asleep. It seemed to him at the time that he sat up in bed after thinking things out in a perfectly orderly way. It was all quite obvious. He was a witch. He dared not be found out. Therefore he had to use some more witchcraft in order not to be found out. In other words, he had better go somewhere private like the toilets downstairs and conjure up first Mr. Wentworth and then his running shoes.

6

⚜

CHARLES GOT UP. He remembered to put on his glasses. He even thought of arranging his bedclothes in heaps to make it look as if he were still in bed. He could see to do that by the dim light shining in from the corridor. By that light, he could see to creep past the sleeping humps of all the other boys. He crept out into the corridor, which seemed light as day by comparison.

There was a lot of noise coming from the next dormitory. There was rustling, and some heavy thumps, followed by some giggles hurriedly choked off. Charles stopped. It sounded as if they were having one of their midnight feasts in there. The thumps would be the floorboards coming up so that they could get at their hidden food. It was a bad time to wander about. If the master in charge heard the noise, Charles would be caught too.

But the corridor remained empty. After a while, Charles dared to go on. He went along the corridor and down the dark pit of the concrete stairs at the end. It was cold. The heating, which was never warm anyway, was turned down for the night. The chill striking up through Charles's bare feet and in through his pajamas served to wake him up a little. He wondered if it was the pain in his finger which had awakened him in the first place. It was throbbing steadily. Charles held it against the cold wall to soothe it and, while his feet felt their way from stair to cold stair, he tried to plan what he would do. Mr. Wentworth was obviously the most important one to get back—if he could. But he did need those running shoes too.

"I'll practice on the shoes," Charles muttered. "If I get those, I'll try for Mr. Wentworth."

He stumbled off the end of the stairs and turned left towards the toilets. They were in a cross-passage down at the end. Charles was halfway to the corner, when the cross-passage became full of dull moving light. A half-lit figure loomed there, swinging a giant torch. The moving light caught the small white creature trundling at the figure's heels. The caretaker and his dog were on their way to inspect the toilets for vandals.

Charles turned and tiptoed the other way. The passage promptly filled with a shrill yap, like one very small clap of thunder. The dog had heard him. Charles ran. Behind him, he heard the caretaker shout, "Who's there?" and come clattering along the passage.

Charles ran. He ran past the end of the stairs, hoping the caretaker would think he had gone up them again, and went on, with his arms out in front of him, until he met the swinging door beyond. Gently, he pushed the door open a small way. Softly, he slid around it, holding the edge of the door so that it would not thump shut and give him away. Then he stood there hoping.

It was no good. The caretaker was not fooled. A muzz of light grew in the glass of the door. The shadow of the stair rails swung across it and fell away, and the light went on growing brighter as the caretaker advanced.

Charles let the door go and ran again, thumping along dark corridors until he had no idea where he was and could hardly breathe. He shook off the caretaker, but he lost himself. Then he ran around a corner and blinked in the orange light from a far-off streetlight shining through a window. Beyond the window was the unmistakable door of the lower school boys' playroom. Even in that dim light, Charles knew the kick marks at the bottom of the door, and the cracked glass in the upper panel where Nirupam Singh had tried to hit Dan Smith and missed. It seemed like home just then. There were worse places to practice magic in, Charles thought. He opened the door and crept in.

In the faint light, someone else jumped around to face him.

Charles jumped back against the door. He squeaked. The other person squeaked. "Who are you?" they both said at once. Then Charles found the light switch. He moved it down and then back up in one swift waggle, dazzling both of them. What he saw made him lean against the door, confounded, blinking green darkness. The other person was Brian Wentworth. That was odd enough. But the oddest thing, in that dazzling moment of light, was that Charles had clearly seen that Brian was in tears. Charles was amazed. Brian, as was well known, never cried. He shrieked and yowled and yelled for mercy when he was hit, but he had never, ever been known to shed tears. Charles went very quickly from amazement to horror. For it clearly took something out of the ordinary to make Brian cry—and that thing must be that Brian had discovered his father was mysteriously missing.

"I came down to make it all right again," Charles said guiltily.

"What can *you* do?" said Brian's voice out of the dark, thick and throaty with crying. "The only reason you're better off than me is because you glare at people and they leave you alone. I wish I had a dirty look like yours. Then I could stop them getting at me and hitting me all the time!"

He began crying again, loud jerky sobs. Charles could hear the crying move off into the middle of the playroom, but he could not see Brian at first for the green dazzle. He really could not believe Brian minded being hit that much. It happened so often that Brian must be thoroughly used to it. By this time, he could see that Brian was crouching in the center of the concrete floor. Charles went over and crouched down facing him.

"Is that the only thing that's the matter?" he inquired cautiously.

"Only!" said Brian. "Only thing! What else do you want them to do? Tear me apart limb from limb or something! Sometimes I wish they would. I'd be dead then. I wouldn't have to put up with them getting at me then, hour after hour, day after day! I hate this school!"

"Yes," Charles said feelingly. "So do I." It gave him wonderful pleasure to say it, but it did not help bring the subject around to the disappearance of Mr. Wentworth. He took a deep breath to encourage himself. "Er—have you seen your father—?"

Brian broke in, almost with a scream. "Of *course* I've been to my magicking father! I go to him nearly every day and ask him to let me leave this place. I went to him this afternoon and asked him. I said why couldn't I go to Forest Road School, like Stephen Towers does, and you know what he said? He said Forest Road was a private school and he couldn't afford it. Couldn't afford it!" Brian said bitterly. "I ask you! *Why* can't he afford it, if Mr. Towers can? He must get paid twice as much as Mr. Towers! I bet he earns almost as much as Miss Cadwallader. And he says he can't afford it!"

Charles wondered. He remembered the threadbare hearthrug and the holes in Mr. Wentworth's slippers. That looked like poverty to him. But he supposed it could be meanness. And that brought him back to his guilt. With Mr. Wentworth gone, Brian would have to stay at Larwood House forever.

"But have you seen your father since then?" he asked.

"No," said Brian. "He told me not to keep coming whining to him." And he began to cry again.

So Brian had not found out yet. Charles felt huge relief. There was still time to get Mr. Wentworth back. But that meant that it really was only being got at which was making Brian so unhappy. Despite the evidence, that surprised Charles. Brian always seemed so perky and unconcerned.

Brian was talking again, through his sobs. "Whatever I do," he said, "they get at me. I can't help my father being a teacher here! I can't help being good at things! I didn't *ask* Mr. Brubeck to give me a solo to sing. He just did. But of course magicking Simon Silverson thinks *he* ought to sing it. That's the thing I hate most," Brian said vehemently. "The way everyone does what Simon Silverson says!"

"I hate him too," said Charles. "Badly."

"Oh it doesn't matter how *we* feel," Brian said. "Simon's word is law. It's like that game—you know, *Simon Says*—where you have to do things if they say *Simon Says* first. And what is he anyway? A stuck up—"

"Prat," said Charles, "who sucks up to teachers—"

"With golden hair and a saintly expression. Don't forget the smug look," said Brian.

"Who could?" said Charles. "He kicks you in the pants, and then looks as if it's your fault his foot came up."

He was enjoying this. But he stopped enjoying it when Brian said, "Thanks for stopping them from hitting me this evening. What gave you the idea of burning your finger like that? And trust Simon Silverson to rip you off all your money just for a candle!" Brian hesitated a second and then added, "I suppose I'd better pay you half of it."

Charles managed to stop himself backing away. That would be really unkind. But what was he to do now? Brian clearly thought Charles had come downstairs in order to comfort him. Probably he would expect Charles to be his friend in the future. Well, Charles supposed, he had deserved it. This was what you got for putting the Evil Eye on people's fathers. But quite apart from Mr. Wentworth, quite apart from the fact that Brian was lowest of the low in 6B, even quite apart from the fact that Charles did not like Brian, Charles knew he could not be friends with anyone now. He was a witch. He could get anyone who was friends with him arrested too.

"You mustn't pay me anything," he said. "You don't owe me a thing."

Brian seemed distinctly relieved. "Then I'll tell you something instead," he said. "I've had enough of this place. If my father won't take me away, I'm going to *run* away."

"Where to?" said Charles. He had thought about running away himself, a while back, but he had had to give up the idea because there was nowhere to run away to.

"No idea," said Brian. "I shall just go."

"Don't be a fool," said Charles. This was one friendly thing he could say at least. "You have to plan it properly. If you just go, they'll call in tracker dogs and bring you straight back. Then you'll be punished."

"But I'll go mad if I stay here!" Brian said hysterically. Then he appeared to stop and consider, with his teeth chattering. "I think I see a way," he said.

By this time, both of them were shivering. It was cold in the playroom. Charles wondered how he could make Brian go back to bed without going himself. He could not think of a way. So they both went on crouching face to face in the middle of the concrete floor, until there was a sudden little pattering outside the cracked door. Both of them jumped.

"Caretaker's dog," whispered Charles.

Brian giggled. "Stupid creature. It looks just like Theresa Mullett's knitting."

Charles, before he could stop himself, gave a shriek of laughter. "It does! It does!"

"Shut up!" hissed Brian. "The caretaker's coming!"

Sure enough, the cracked glass of the door was showing misty torchlight. The dog began yapping furiously on the other side of it. It knew they were there.

Brian and Charles sprang up and fled, through the playroom and out its other door. As it thumped shut behind them, the cracked door thumped open and the hollow playroom echoed with the dog's little thunderclaps. Without a word, Charles ran one way and Brian ran another. Where Brian went, Charles never knew. He heard the second door thump open as he ran, and the patter of tiny feet behind him. Charles held his glasses on and ran desperately. It was just like the seniors in the shrubbery. What made everyone chase *him*? Did he smell of witch, or something?

He found an outside door, but it was locked. He pelted on. Behind him, in the distance, he could hear the caretaker bawling to his dog to come back. That made the dog hesitate. Charles, quite terrified by now, put on a spurt and hurled himself through the next door he came to.

There was a feeling of large cold space inside this door. Charles went forward a few cautious steps and hit his foot with a clang on a row of steel chairs. He stood frozen, waiting to be discovered. He could hardly hear for the blood banging in his ears at first. Then he found he could hear the dog yapping again, somewhere quite far off. It seemed to have lost him. At the same time, he found he could see the faint shapes of huge windows, high up, beyond the chairs. He was in the school hall.

It came to Charles that he was not going to get a better opportunity than this. Better summon up his shoes at once. No—forget the shoes. Mr. Wentworth was far more urgent. Get Mr. Wentworth, and when Mr. Wentworth appeared, perhaps Charles could put in a word about Brian.

It was at this point that Charles realized that he dared not fetch Mr. Wentworth back. If Mr. Wentworth did not know who had made him vanish, he *would* know as soon as he arrived back and found Charles.

"Flaming witches!" Charles moaned. "Why didn't I think?"

The dog, not too distant, gave another yap. Hunted and undecided, Charles shuffled forward and fell across more chairs. He was in a perfect maze of chairs. He stood where he was and tried to think.

He could still get the shoes, he thought. He could say he was sleepwalking with worry about them when the caretaker found him. Uncertainly, he held up both arms. That dog was definitely coming nearer again.

"Shoes," Charles said hurriedly, and his voice cracked with fear and cold and lack of breathe. "Shoes. Come to me. Hey presto. Abracadabra. Shoes, I say!" The dog sounded almost outside the hall door now. Charles made dragging movements with his hands and then crossed them over his chest. "Shoes!"

A thing that, by the sound, could have been a shoe, fell on the chair next to him. Despite the yapping dog, Charles grinned with pleasure. The second shoe fell on the other side of him. Charles put out groping hands to find them. And two more fell on his head. Several more flopped down near his feet. Now he could hear shoes dropping down all around him. He seemed to be in the center of a rain of shoes. And the dog was scrabbling at the door now as it yapped. A Wellington boot, by the feel, hit Charles on the shoulder as he turned and groped along the chairs, stumbling over gym shoes, football boots, and lace-ups, with more and more dropping around him as he groped.

The caretaker was nearly at the door now. Charles could see the torchlight advancing through the glass. It helped him find his way. For he knew there was no question of any nonsense about sleep-walking now. He had to get out, and fast. He floundered among the pattering, flopping shoes, between the rows of chairs to the side of the hall, where he bolted for the door that the teachers came in by. Pitch dark descended on the other side of that door. Charles supposed he was in the staff room, but he never knew for sure. Stumbling, with his hands held out in front of him, dreamlike with panic, he fell over a stool. As he picked himself up, he remembered his second witch, the one who came through the garden. He should have thought about her earlier, he realized, as he knocked into a pile of books. She had said you couldn't work magic when you were frightened. She was right. Something had gone very wrong out there in the hall. Obviously, Charles thought, having a mad tangle with a coat of some kind, you needed to be cool and collected to be sure of getting it right. Oh thank Heaven! Here was a door.

Charles plunged out of the door and found

himself not far from the main stairs. He fled up them. As he went, his thumb found the fat painful blister on his finger and he rubbed it as he ran upward. What a waste! What an utter waste of money! Burning his finger seemed to have taught him nothing at all. And here was the beautiful, welcoming green night light of the dormitory corridors. Not far now.

Charles did not remember getting into bed. His last clear thought was to wonder whether Brian had come back or whether he had run away on the spot. When the clanging bell dragged him awake in the morning, he had a sort of feeling that he had gone to sleep on the dormitory floor near the end of Brian's bed. But no. He was in his own bed. His glasses were hooked on the bedrail. He began to hope he had dreamed last night. But, long before he was awake enough to sit up and yawn, the room filled with indignant voices.

"I can't find my shoes!"

"I say, what's happened to all our shoes?"

"My slippers aren't here either!"

As Charles managed to sit up, Simon said, "Are you a shoe thief now, Brian?" and smacked Brian's head in a jolly, careless way, to show he did not think Brian was capable of being anything so enterprising. Brian was kneeling up in bed, looking as sleepy as Charles felt. He did not answer Simon or look at Charles.

In the next dormitory, they had no shoes either. And a senior could be heard coming down the corridor, shouting, "Hey! Have you lot pinched our shoes?"

Everyone was annoyed. Everyone thought there was a practical joke going on. Charles just hoped they would go on thinking that. Everyone was forced to go without shoes and slither around in socks. Charles's shoes were missing too—he was glad he seemed to have been that thorough, and he was just dragging on a second pair of socks, when rumor spread along the corridor. In the way of rumors, it was quite mysterious. Nobody knew who started it.

"We're to go down to the hall. All the shoes are there."

Charles joined the slithering rush for the hall. That rush was joined in the downstairs passage by all the girls, also in socks, also making for the hall. The seniors naturally occupied the door of the hall. Everyone from the lower school streamed outside into the quadrangle to look through the hall windows. There, everyone's first reaction was simple awe.

A school with six hundred pupils owns an awful lot of shoes. There would be twelve hundred even if everyone simply had one pair. But at Larwood House, everyone had to have special shoes for almost everything they did. So you had to add to that number all the gym shoes, running shoes, tennis shoes, trainers, dancing shoes, spare shoes, best shoes, sandals, football boots, hockey boots, Wellington boots, and galoshes. The number of shoes is swiftly in thousands. Add to those all the shoes owned by the staff, too: Miss Cadwallader's characteristic footgear with heels like cottonreels; the cook's extra-wide fitting; the groundsman's hobnails; Mr. Crossley's handmade suede; Mr. Brubeck's brogues; the matron's sixteen pairs of stiletto heels; someone's purple fur boots; and even the odd pair of riding boots; not to speak of many more. And you have truly formidable numbers. The chairs in the hall were buried under a monstrous mountain of shoes.

Amid the general marveling, Theresa's voice was heard. "If this is someone's idea of a joke, I don't think it's funny. My bedsocks are all muddy!" She was wearing blue fluffy bedsocks over her school socks.

After this, there was something of a free-for-all. People scrambled in through doors and windows and slithered on the pile of shoes, digging for shoes they thought were theirs—or, failing that, simply a pair that would fit.

Until a voice began bellowing, "OUT! GET OUT ALL OF YOU! LEAVE ALL THE SHOES THERE!"

Charles was pushed backwards by the rather slower rush to leave the hall, and had to crane to see who was shouting. It was Mr. Wentworth. Charles was so amazed that he stopped moving and was left by a sort of eddy inside the hall, just by the door. From there, he could clearly see Mr. Wentworth walking down the edge of the pile of shoes. He was wearing his usual shabby suit, but his feet were completely bare. Otherwise there was nothing wrong with him at all. After him came Mr. Crossley in bright yellow socks and Mr. Brubeck with a large hole in the heel of his left sock. After them came the caretaker. After him of course trundled the caretaker's dog, which was manifestly wishing to raise a leg against the pile of shoes.

"I don't know who done it!" the caretaker was protesting. "But I know there was people sneaking around my building half the night. The dog nearly caught one, right in this very hall."

"Did you come in here and investigate?" Mr. Wentworth said.

"Door was shut," said the caretaker. "Thought it was locked."

Mr. Wentworth turned from him in disgust. "Someone was pretty busy in here all last night," he said to Mr. Crossley, "and he didn't even look!"

"Thought it was locked," repeated the caretaker.

"Oh shut up!" snapped Mr. Wentworth. "And stop your dog peeing on that shoe. It's Miss Cadwallader's."

Charles slipped out into the corridor, trying to keep the grin on his face down to decent proportions. Mr. Wentworth was all right. He must have slipped off to bed after all last night, while Miss Hodge was asking Charles the way. And, better still, everyone thought the shoes had arrived in the hall quite naturally. Charles could have danced and sung.

But here was Dan Smith beside him. That sobered Charles somewhat. "Hey," said Dan. "Did those seniors catch you last night?"

"No, I ran away," Charles replied airily.

"You must have run pretty fast!" said Dan. It was grudging, but it was praise, coming from Dan. "Know anything about who did these shoes?" Dan asked, jerking his head toward the hall.

Charles would dearly have loved to say it was him and watch the respect grow on Dan's face. But he was not that much of a fool. "No," he said.

"I do," said Dan. "It was the witch in our class, I bet."

Mr. Wentworth appeared in the doorway of the hall. There were loud shushings up and down the packed corridor. "Breakfast is going to be late," Mr. Wentworth shouted. He looked very harrowed. "You can't expect the kitchen staff to work without shoes. You are all to go to your classrooms and wait there. Meanwhile, teachers and sixth graders are going to be working hard laying all the shoes out in the main quadrangle. When you are called—*when* you are called, understand?—you are to come by classes and pick out the shoes which are yours. Off you all go. Sixth grade stay behind."

Everyone milled off in a reluctant crowd. Charles was so pleased with himself that he risked grinning at Brian. But Brian was staring dreamily at the wall and did not notice. He did not move or even yell when Simon slapped him absentmindedly around the head. "Where's Nan Pilgrim?" Simon asked, laughing. "Turned herself invisible?"

Nan was keeping out of the way, lurking in the top corridor by the girls' bathrooms. From there, she had an excellent view of the quadrangle being covered with row upon row of shoes, and the kitchen ladies tiptoeing about the rows in stockings looking for their workshoes. It did not amuse her. Theresa's friend Delia Martin and Estelle's friend Karen Grigg had already made it quite plain that they thought it was Nan's doing. The fact that these two normally did not speak to one another, or to Nan either, only seemed to make it worse.

7

BREAKFAST WAS READY before 6B had been called to find their shoes. Theresa was forced to walk through the corridors in her blue bedsocks. They were, by this time, quite black underneath, which upset her considerably. Breakfast was so late that assembly was cancelled. Instead, Miss Cadwallader stood up in front of high table, with her face all stringy with displeasure and one foot noticeably damp, and made a short speech.

"A singularly silly trick has been played on the school," she said. "The people who played it no doubt think it very funny, but they must be able to see by now what a stupid and dishonorable thing they have done. I want them to be honorable now. I want them to come to me and confess. And I want anyone else who knows or suspects who did it to be equally honorable and come and tell me what they know. I shall be in my study all morning. That is all."

"What is honorable," Nirupam said loudly, as everyone stood up, "about going and telling tales?"

By saying that, he did Nan a service, whether he meant to or not. No one in 6B wanted a name for telling tales. Nobody went to Miss Cadwallader. Instead, they all went out into the quadrangle, where a little freezing drizzle of rain was now falling, and walked up and down the rows of damp footgear, finding their shoes. Nan was forced to go too.

"Oh look! Here comes Archwitch Dulcinea," said Simon.

"Why did you do it to your own shoes too, Dulcinea? Thought it would look more innocent, did you?"

And Theresa said, "Really, Nan! My bedsocks are ruined! It isn't funny!"

"Do something really funny now, Nan," Karen Grigg suggested.

"Hurry up!" Mr. Crossley shouted from the shelter of the porch. Everyone at once became very busy turning over shoes. The only one who did not was Brian. He simply wandered about, staring into space. In the end, Nirupam found his shoes for him and bundled them into Brian's lax arms.

"Are you all right?" Nirupam asked him.

"Who? Me? Oh yes," Brian said.

"Are you sure? One of your eyes is sort of set sideways," Nirupam said.

"Is it?" Brian asked vaguely, and wandered off.

Nirupam turned severely to Simon. "I think you hit him on the head once too often."

Simon laughed, a little uneasily. Nirupam was a

head taller than he was. "Nonsense! There's nothing in his head to get hurt."

"Well, you watch it," said Nirupam, and might have said more, except that they were interrupted by an annoyed outcry from Dan Smith.

"I'll get someone for this!" Dan was shouting. He was very pale and cross after last night's midnight feast, and he looked quite savage. "I'll get them even if they're a magicking senior. Someone's gone off with my running shoes! I can't find them anywhere."

"Look again, carefully!" Mr. Crossley bawled from the porch.

This was a queer fact. Dan searched up and down the rows, and so did Charles, until their socks were soaked and their hair was trickling rain, but neither Dan's spikes nor Charles's were there. By this time, 7A, 7B, and 7C had been allowed out to collect their shoes too before they all got too wet, and almost the only footgear left was the three odd football boots, the riding boots, and a pair of luminous green trainers that nobody seemed to want. Dan uttered such threats that Charles was glad that it did not seem to occur to Dan that this had anything to do with Charles Morgan.

But it meant that Charles had to go to Mr. Towers next and confess that his running shoes had still not turned up. He was fed up as he stood and trickled rain outside the staff room. After all his trouble!

"I did look, sir," he assured Mr. Towers.

Mr. Towers glanced at Charles's soaking hair and rain-dewed glasses. "Anyone can stand in the rain," he said. "Are you paying for new ones or writing lines?"

"Doing lines," Charles said resentfully.

"In detention every evening until Christmas then," Mr. Towers said. The idea seemed to please him. "Wait." He dodged back into the staff room and came out again with a fat old book. "Here," he said, handing the book to Charles. "Copy five hundred lines of this out every evening. It will show you what a real schoolboy should be like. When you've copied it all, I'll give you the sequel."

Charles stood in front of the staff room and looked at the book. It was called *The Pluckiest Boy in School*. It smelled of mildew. Inside, the pages were furry and brownish, and the first line of the story went: *"What ripping fun!" exclaimed Watts Minor. "I'm down for scrum half this afternoon!"*

Charles looked from this to the fat, transparent, and useless blister on his finger and felt rather ill. "Magicking hell," he said.

"Good morning, Charles," said Miss Hodge, tripping toward the staff room, all fresh and unaware. "That looks like a nice old book. I'm glad to see you doing some serious reading at last."

She was most disconcerted to receive one of Charles's heaviest double-barreled glares. What a moody boy he was to be sure! she thought as she neatly stripped off her raincoat. She was equally surprised to find the staff room in some kind of uproar, with a pile of boots and shoes in the middle. Still, there was Mr. Wentworth at last, flying past on his way somewhere else. Miss Hodge stood in his way.

"Oh, Mr. Wentworth, I want to apologize for making that accusation against Charles Morgan." That was pretty generous of her, she thought, after the way Charles had just looked at her. She smiled generously at Mr. Wentworth.

To her annoyance, Mr. Wentworth simply said, "I'm glad to hear it," and brushed past her quite rudely. But he did have a lot on his mind, Miss Hodge realized, when Mr. Crossley told her excitedly all about the shoes. She did not hold it against Mr. Wentworth. She collected books—they had gotten spilled all over the floor somehow—and went off to give 6B another English lesson.

She arrived to find Simon Silverson holding aloft *The Pluckiest Boy in School.* "Listen to this!" he was saying. *"Swelling with pride, Watts Minor gazed into the eyes of his one true friend. Here was a boy above all, straight alike in body and mind—"*

Theresa and Delia were screaming with laughter, with their faces buried in their knitting. Charles was glaring blue murder.

"Really, Simon!" said Miss Hodge. "That was unworthy of you." Simon looked at her in astonishment. He knew he never did anything unworthy. "But, Charles," said Miss Hodge, "I do think you made rather an unfortunate choice of book." For the second time that day, Charles turned his glare on her. Miss Hodge flinched. Really, if she had not known now that Charles was a nice boy underneath, that glare of his would make her think seriously of the Evil Eye.

Nirupam held up his long arm. "Are we going to do acting again?" he asked hopefully.

"No, we are not," Miss Hodge said, with great firmness. "Get out your poetry books."

The lesson, and the rest of the morning, dragged past. Theresa finished her second bootee and cast on stitches for a sweater. Estelle knitted quite a lot of a baby's bonnet. Brian gave up staring at the wall and instead seemed to be attacked by violent industry. Whenever anyone looked at him, he was scribbling furiously in a different exercise book.

Charles sat and brooded, rather surprised at the things going on in his mind. He was not frightened at all now. He seemed to be accepting the fact he was a witch quite calmly after all. No one had noticed. They all thought the witch was Nan Pilgrim, because of her name, which suited Charles very well. But the really strange thing was the way he had stopped being worried by the witch he had seen being burned. He tried remembering him, cautiously at first, then boldly, when he found it did not bother him. Then he went on to the second witch, who came over the wall. Neither troubled him now. They were in the past: they were gone. It was like having a toothache that suddenly stops. In the peace that came with this, Charles saw that his mind must have been trying to tell him he was going to grow up a witch. And now that he knew, it stopped nagging him. Then, to see if this made him frightened, he thought of inquisitors. It hurts to be burned, he thought, and looked at his fat blister. It had taught him something after all. And that was: Don't get found out.

Good, thought Charles. And turned his mind to what he was going to do to Simon Silverson. Dan Smith next, but Simon definitely first. What could he do to Simon that would be worth nearly a whole term's pocket money? It was difficult. It had to be something bad enough, and yet with no connection with Charles. Charles was quite stumped at first. He wanted it to be artistic. He wanted Simon to suffer. He wanted everyone else to know about it, but not to know it was Charles who did it. What *could* he do?

The last lesson before lunch was the daily PE. Today, it was the boys' turn in the gym. They were to climb ropes too. Charles sat by the wallbars and pretended to tie his gym shoe. Unlike Nan, he could get up a rope if he wanted, but he did not want to. He wanted to sit and think what to do to Simon. Simon, of course, was one of the first to the ceiling. He saw Charles and shouted something down. The result was that someone from 6C came and dug Charles in the back.

"Simon says you're to stop lazing about."

"Simon says that, does he?" said Charles. He stood up. He was inspired. It was something Brian had said last night. That game, *Simon Says*. Suppose it was not just a game. Suppose everything Simon said really came true. At the very worst it ought to be pretty funny. At best, people might even think Simon was a witch.

Charles went up a rope. He dragged himself up it, nice and slow and gentle, so that he could go on thinking. He was obviously not going to be able to stand anywhere near Simon to put the spell on him. Someone would notice. But instinct told Charles that this was not the kind of magic you could work at a distance. It was too strong and personal. What he needed, in order to do it safely, was something which was not Simon himself, but something which belonged to Simon so personally that any witchcraft worked on it would work on Simon at the same time—a detachable piece of Simon, really. What removable parts had Simon? Teeth, toenails, finger-nails, hair? He could hardly go up to Simon and pull any of those off him. Wait a minute! Hair. Simon combed his hair this morning. With any luck, there might be some hair stuck in Simon's comb.

Charles slid jubilantly down the rope—so fast that he was reminded again that it hurts to be burned. He had to blow on his hands to cool them. After lunch was the time. He could sneak up to the dormitory then.

After lunch proved to be important for Nan too. At lunch, she managed to escape Karen Grigg and Delia Martin by sitting at a table full of much older girls who did not seem to know Nan was there. They towered over her, talking of their own things. The food was almost as bad as yesterday, but Nan felt no urge to describe it. She rather wished she was dead. Then it occurred to her that if any of 6B went and told a teacher she was a witch, she would be dead, quite soon after that. She realized at once that she did not wish she was dead. That made her feel better. No one had gone to a teacher yet, after all. "It's only their usual silliness," she told herself. "They'll forget about it by Christmas. I'll just have to keep out of their way till they do."

Accordingly, after lunch, Nan sneaked upstairs to lurk in the passage outside the girls' bathrooms again. But Karen Grigg had been keeping tabs on her. She and Theresa appeared in the passage in front of Nan. When Nan turned around to make off, she found Delia and the other girls coming along the passage from the other end.

"Let's go in this bathroom," Theresa suggested. "We want to ask you something, Nan."

Nan could tell there was an ordeal coming. For a moment, she wondered whether to charge Theresa and Karen like a bull and burst past them. But they would only catch her tonight in the dormitory. Best get it over. "Okay," she said, and sauntered into the bathroom as if she did not care.

Almost at the same moment, Charles hastened furtively into the boys' dormitory. White and clean and cold, the beds stood like rows of deserted icebergs, each with its little white locker at its side. Charles hurried to Simon's. It was locked. Simon was an inveterate locker of things. Even his watch had a little key to lock it on his wrist. But Charles did not let that bother him. He held out his hand imperiously in front of the locked door. "Comb," he said. "Abracadabra."

Simon's comb came gliding out through the white wooden surface, like a fish swimming out of milk, and darted fishlike into Charles's hand. It was beautiful. Better still, there were three of Simon's curly golden hairs clinging to the teeth of the comb. Charles carefully pulled them off. He held the hairs in the finger and thumb of his left hand and carefully ran his right finger and thumb down the length of them. And down again. Over and over, he did it. "Simon Says," he whispered to them. "Simon Says, Simon Says. Whatever Simon says is true."

After about a minute, when he had done it often enough to give him the feeling that the spell was going to take, Charles carefully threaded the hairs back into the comb again. He did not intend to leave any evidence against himself. He had just finished, when Brian said, from behind him, "I want a bit of help from you, Charles."

Charles jumped as if Brian had shot him. He bent over, in white horror, to hide the comb in his hand and, with terrible guilty haste, gave it a push toward the locker. It went in, to his surprise, not quite like a fish this time—more like a comb being pushed through a door—but at least it went. "What do you want?" Charles said ungraciously to Brian.

"Take me down to the matron in the sick bay," Brian said.

It was a school rule that a person who felt ill had to find another person to take them to the matron. It had been made because, before that, the sick bay had been crowded with healthy people trying to get an afternoon off. The idea was that you could not deceive your friends. It did not work very well. Estelle Green, for instance, got Karen to take her to the matron at least twice a week. As far as Charles could see, Brian looked his usual pink and perky self, just like Estelle.

"You don't look ill to me," he said. He wanted to find Simon and see if the spell was working.

"How about this then?" said Brian. To Charles's surprise, he suddenly turned pale. He stared vaguely at the wall, with one eye pointing inward slightly. "This is it," Brian said. "Don't I look rather as if I'd been hypnotized?"

"You look as if you've been hit on the head," Charles said rudely. "Get Nirupam to take you."

"He looked after me this morning," said Brian. "I want as many witnesses as possible. I helped you last night. You help me now."

"You didn't help me last night," said Charles.

"Yes, I did," said Brian. "You came in and you went to sleep on the floor, just at the end of my bed. I got you in your bed. I even hooked your glasses on your bedrail for you." And he looked at Charles, very meaningfully.

Charles stared back. Brian was so thin and small that it was hard to believe he could lift anyone into bed. But, whether it was true or not, Charles realized that Brian had gotten him over a barrel. He knew Charles had been up last night. He had caught him with Simon's comb in his hands just now. Charles could not see why Brian wanted to go to the matron, but that was his own affair. "All right," he said. "I'll take you."

Inside the bathroom, on the other side of the quadrangle, the girls crowded in around Nan. "Where's Estelle?" asked Theresa.

"Outside, keeping watch," said Karen. "That's all she would do."

"What's this about?" Nan asked aggressively.

"We want you to do some proper witchcraft," said Theresa. "Here, where we can see you. We've none of us seen any before. And we know you can. Come on. We won't give you away."

The other girls joined in. "Come on, Nan. We won't tell."

The bathroom was a very public one. There were six baths in it, in a row. As the girls all crowded forward, Nan backed away, down the space between two of the baths. This was evidently just what they had wanted. Delia said, "That's it." Heather said, "Fetch it out." And Karen bent and pulled the groundsman's old broom out from under the left-hand bath. Julia and Deborah seized it and propped it across the two baths in front of Nan, penning her in. Nan looked from it to them.

"We want you to get on it and fly about," Theresa explained.

"Everyone knows that's what witches do," said Karen.

"We're asking you very nicely," said Theresa.

Typical Theresa double-think, Nan thought angrily. She was not asking her nicely. It was a smiling jeer. But if anyone asked Theresa afterward, she would say, with honest innocence, that she had been perfectly kind.

"We can prove you're a witch anyway, if you won't," Theresa said kindly.

"Yes, everyone knows that witches don't drown," said Delia. "You can put them right under water and they stay alive."

At this cue, Karen leaned over and put the plug in the nearest bath. Heather turned on the cold tap, just a little trickle, to show Nan they meant business.

"You know perfectly well," Nan said, "that I'm not a witch, and I can't fly on this broomstick. It's just an excuse to be nasty!"

"Nasty?" said Theresa. "Who's being nasty? We're asking you quite politely to ride the broomstick." Behind her, the tap trickled steadily into the bath.

"You can fetch all the shoes here again if you like," Delia said. "We don't mind which."

"But you've got to do *something*," said Karen. "Or how would you like a nice deep cold bath with all your clothes on?"

Nan was annoyed enough by that to put one leg over the broomstick in order to climb out and get at

Karen. Seeing it, Theresa gave a delighted jump and a giggle. "Oh, she's going to ride!"

The rest of them joined in. "She's going to ride it! Ride it, Nan!"

Very red in the face, Nan stood astride the broom and explained, "I am not going to ride. I do not know how to ride. You know I can't. I know I can't. Look. Look at me. I am sitting on the broomstick." Unwisely, she sat. It was extremely uncomfortable and she was forced to bounce upright again. This amused everyone highly. Angrier than ever, Nan shouted, "How *can* I ride a broomstick? I can't even climb a rope!"

They knew that. They were falling about laughing, when Estelle burst in, screaming with excitement. "Come and look, come and look! *Look* at what Simon Silverson's doing!"

This caused a stampede to the door, to look out of the windows in the corridor. Nan heard cries of "Good heavens! Just look at that!" This was followed by a further stampede as everyone raced off down to the quadrangle.

Nan was left astride an old broom propped on two baths.

"Thank goodness!" was the first thing she said. She had been precious near crying. "Stupid hussies!" she said next. "As if I could ride this thing. Look at it!" She jogged the broom. "Just an old broom!" Then she noticed the water still trickling into the bath behind her. She leaned sideways and back and turned off the tap.

That was the moment the old broom chose to rise sharply to the ceiling.

Nan shrieked. She was suddenly dangling head-down over a bath of cold water. The broom staggered a bit under her weight, but it went on climbing, swinging Nan right over the water. Nan bent her leg as hard as she could over its knobby stick, and managed to clench one hand in its sparse brushwood end. The broom reached the ceiling and leveled out. It did not leave room for Nan to climb on top of it, even if she had possessed the muscles. Blood thudded in her head from hanging upside down, but she did not dare let go.

"Stop it!" she squealed at the broom. "Please!"

It took no notice. It simply went on a solemn, lopsided, bumping flight all around the bathroom, with Nan dangling desperately underneath it and getting this-way-and-that glimpses of hard white baths frighteningly far below.

"I'm glad this didn't happen while the others were here," she gasped. "I must look a right idiot!" She began to laugh. She must look so silly. "Do go down," she said to the broom. "Suppose someone else comes in here."

The broom seemed struck by this. It gave a little start and slanted steeply down towards the floor. As soon as the floor was near enough, Nan clutched the handle in both hands and tried to unhook her leg. A mistake. The broom went steeply up again and hovered where it was just too high for Nan to dare to fall off. But her arms were getting tired and she had to do something. Wriggling and squirming, she managed to kick herself over, until she was more or less lying along the knobby handle, looking down at the row of baths. She hooked her feet on the brush and stayed there, panting.

Now what was she to do? This broom seemed determined to be ridden. There was a sad feeling about it. Once, long ago, it had been ridden, and it missed its witch.

"But that's all very well," Nan said to it. "I really daren't ride you now. Don't you understand? It's illegal. Suppose I promise to ride you tonight. Would you let me down then?"

There was a hesitating sort of hover to the broom.

"I swear to," said Nan. "Listen, I tell you what. You fly me down the passage to our dormitory. That will make a bit of a flight at least. Then you can hide yourself on top of the cupboard, right at the back. No one will see you there. And I'll promise to take you out tonight. What do you say?"

Though the broom could not speak, it evidently meant Yes! It turned and swept through the bathroom doorway in a glad swoop that made Nan seasick. It sped down the passage. She had to shut her eyes in order not to see the walls whirling by. It made a hair-raising turn into the dormitory. And it stopped there with such a jerk that Nan nearly fell around underneath it again.

"I see I shall have to train you," she gasped.

The broom gave an indignant buck and a bounce.

"I mean you'll have to train me," Nan said quickly. "Go down now. I have to get off you."

The broom hovered, questioning.

"I promised," Nan said.

At that, the broom came sweetly to the ground, and Nan was able to get off, very wobbly in the legs. As soon as she was off, the broom fell to the floor, lifeless. "You poor thing!" Nan said. "I see. You need a rider to move at all. All right. Let's get you on top of the cupboard."

In this way, she missed the first manifestation of the *Simon Says* spell. Charles missed it too. Neither of them discovered how Simon first found out that everything he said came true. Charles left Brian with a thermometer in his mouth, staring cross-eyed at the wall, and trudged back to the quadrangle to find an excited group around Simon. At first, Charles thought that the brightness flaring at Simon's feet was simply the sun shining off a puddle. But it was not. It was a heap of gold coins. People were passing him pennies and stones and dead leaves.

To each thing as he took it, Simon said, "This is a gold coin. This is another gold coin." When that got boring he said, "This is a *rare* gold coin. These are pieces of eight. This is a doubloon . . ."

Charles shoved his way to the front of the crowd and watched, utterly disgusted. Trust Simon to turn things to his own advantage! Gold chinked down on the heap. Simon must have been a millionaire by this time.

With a great clatter of running feet, the girls arrived. Theresa, with her knitting bag hanging on her arm, pushed her way to the front, beside Charles. She was so astonished at the size of the pile of gold that she crossed the invisible line and spoke to Simon.

"How are you *doing* it, Simon?"

Simon laughed. He was like a drunk person by this time. "I've got the Golden Touch!" he said. Of course this immediately became the truth. "Just like that king in the story. Look." He reached for Theresa's knitting. Theresa indignantly snatched the knitting away and gave Simon a push at the same time. The result was that Simon touched her hand.

The knitting fell on the ground. Theresa screamed, and stood holding her hand out, and then screamed again because her hand was too heavy to hold up. It dropped down against her skirt, a bright golden metal hand, on the end of an ordinary human arm.

Out of the shocked silence which followed, Nirupam said, "Be very careful what you say, Simon."

"Why?" said Simon.

"Because everything you say becomes true," Nirupam said.

Evidently, Simon had not quite seen the extent of his powers. "You mean," he said, "I haven't got the Golden Touch." Instantly, he hadn't. "Let's test this," he said. He bent down and picked up Theresa's knitting. It was still knitting, in a slightly muddy bag.

"Put it down!" Theresa said faintly. "I shall go to Miss Cadwallader."

"No, you won't," said Simon, and that was true too. He looked at the knitting and considered. "This knitting," he announced, "is really two little caretaker's dogs."

The bag began to writhe about in his hands. Simon hurriedly dropped it with a sharp chink, onto the heap of gold. The bag heaved. Little shrill yappings came from inside it, and furious scrabbling. One little white bootee-dog burst out of it, shortly followed by a second. They ran on little minute legs, down the heap of gold and in among people's legs. Everyone got rather quickly out of their way. Everyone turned and watched as the two tiny white dogs went running and running into the distance across the quadrangle.

Theresa started to cry. "That was my knitting, you beast!"

"So?" Simon said, laughing.

Theresa lifted up her golden hand with her ordinary one and hit him with it. It was stupid of her, because she risked breaking her arm, but it was certainly effective. It nearly knocked Simon out. He sat down heavily on his heap of gold. "Ow!" said Theresa. "And I hope that hurt!"

"It didn't," said Simon, and got up smiling and, of course, unhurt.

Theresa went for him again, double-handed.

Simon skipped aside. "You haven't got one golden hand," he said.

There was suddenly space where Theresa's heavy golden hand had been. Her arm ended in a round pink wrist. Theresa stared at it. "How shall I knit?" she said.

"I mean," Simon said carefully, "that you have two ordinary hands."

Theresa looked at her two perfectly ordinary human hands and burst into strange, artificial-sounding laughter. "Somebody kill him for me!" she said.

"Quickly!"

Nobody offered to. Everybody was too shattered. Delia took Theresa's arm and led her tenderly away. The bell rang for afternoon lessons as they went.

"This is marvelous fun!" Simon said. "From now on, I'm all in favor of witchcraft."

Charles trudged off to lessons, wondering how he could cancel the spell.

8

❦

SIMON ARRIVED LATE for lessons. He had been making sure his heap of gold was safe. "I'm sorry, sir," he said to Mr. Crossley. And sorry he was. Tears came into his eyes, he was so sorry.

"That's all right, Simon," Mr. Crossley said kindly, and everyone else felt compelled to look at Simon with deep sympathy.

You can't win with people like Simon, Charles thought bitterly. Anyone else would have been in bad trouble by now. And it was exasperating the way nobody so much as dreamed of accusing Simon of witchcraft. They kept looking at Nan Pilgrim instead.

Nan felt much the same about Theresa. Theresa arrived ten minutes after Simon, very white and sniffing rather. She was led in tenderly by Delia, and received almost as much sympathy as Simon. "Just gave her an aspirin and sent her away!" Nan heard Delia whisper indignantly to Karen. "I do think she ought to have been allowed to lie down, after all she's been through!"

What about all *I've* been through? Nan thought. No, it was Theresa's right to be in the right, as much as it was Simon's.

Nan had been given the full story by Estelle. Estelle was always ready to talk in class, and she was particularly ready now that Karen seemed to have joined Theresa's friends. She knitted away under her desk at her baby's bonnet, and whispered and whispered. Nor was she the only one. Mr. Crossley kept calling for quiet, but the whispers and rustling hardly abated at all. Notes kept arriving on Nan's desk. The first to arrive was from Dan Smith.

Make me the same as Simon and I'll be your friend forever, it said.

Most of the other notes said the same. All were very respectful. But one note was different. This one said, *Meet me around the back after lessons. I think you need help and I can advise you.* It was not signed. Nan wondered about it. She had seen the writing before, but she did not know whose it was.

She supposed she did need help. She really was a witch now. No one but a witch could fly a broomstick. She knew she was in danger and she knew she should be terrified. But she was not. She felt happy and strong, with a happiness and strength that seemed to be welling up from deep inside her. She kept remembering the way she had started to laugh when the broomstick went flying round the bathroom with herself dangling underneath it, and the way she seemed to understand by instinct what the broom wanted. Hair-raising as it had been, she had enjoyed it thoroughly. It was like coming into her birthright.

"Of course, Simon always said you were a witch," Estelle whispered.

That reduced Nan's joy a little. There was another witch in 6B, she did not doubt that. And that witch had, for some mad reason, made everything Simon said come true. He must be one of Simon's friends. And it was quite possible that Simon, while he was under the spell, had happened to say that Nan was a witch. So of course she would have become one.

Nan refused to believe it. She *was* a witch. She wanted to be one. She came from a long line of witches, stretching back beyond even Dulcinea Wilkes herself. She felt she had a *right* to be a witch.

All this while, Mr. Crossley was trying to give 6B a geography lesson. He had gotten to the point where he was precious near giving up and giving everyone detention instead. He had one last try. He could see that the unrest was centering on Simon, with a subcenter around Nan, so he tried to make use of it by asking Simon questions.

"Now the geography of Finland is very much affected by the last Ice Age. Simon, what happens in an Ice Age?"

Simon dragged his mind away from dreams of gold and glory. "Everything is very cold," he said. A blast of cold air swept through the room, making everyone's teeth chatter. "And goes on getting colder, I suppose," Simon added unwisely. The air in the room swiftly became icy. 6B's breath rolled out in steam. The windows misted over and froze, almost at once, into frosty patterns. Icicles began to grow under the radiators. Frost whitened the desks.

There was a chorus of shivers and groans, and Nirupam hissed, "*Watch* it!"

"I mean everything gets very hot," Simon said hastily.

Before Mr. Crossley had time to wonder why he was shivering, the cold was replaced by tropical heat. The frost slid away down the windows. The icicles tinkled off the radiators. For an instant, the room seemed fine and warm, until the frozen water evaporated. This produced a thick, steamy fog. In the murk, people were gasping. Some faces turned red, others white, and sweat ran on foreheads, adding to the fog.

Mr. Crossley put a hand to his forehead, thinking he might be getting the flu. The room seemed so dim suddenly. "Some theories do say that an Ice Age starts with extreme heat," he said uncertainly.

"But I say everything is normal for this time of year," Simon said, desperately trying to adjust the temperature.

Instantly it was. The classroom reverted to its usual way of being not quite warm enough, though still a little damp. Mr. Crossley found he felt better. "Stop talking nonsense, Simon!" he said angrily.

Simon, with incredulity, realized that he might get into trouble. He tried to pass the whole thing off in his usual lordly way. "Well, sir, nobody really knows a thing about Ice Ages, do they?"

"We'll see about that," Mr. Crossley said grimly. And of course nobody did. When he came to ask Estelle to describe an Ice Age, Mr. Crossley found himself wondering just why he was asking about something which did not exist. No wonder Estelle looked so blank. He rounded back on Simon. "Is this a joke of some kind? What are you thinking of?"

"Me? I'm not thinking of anything!" Simon said defensively. With disastrous results.

Ah! This is more like it! Charles thought, watching the look of complete vacancy growing on Simon's face.

Theresa saw Simon's eyes glaze and his jaw drop and jumped to her feet with a scream. "Stop him!" she screamed. "Kill him! Do something to him before he says another word!"

"Sit down, Theresa," said Mr. Crossley.

Theresa stayed standing up. "You wouldn't believe what he's done already!" she shouted. "And now look at him. If he says a word in that state—"

Mr. Crossley looked at Simon. The boy seemed to be pretending to be an idiot now. What was the matter with everyone? "Take that look off your face, Simon," he said. "You're not that much of a fool."

Simon was now in a state of perfect blankness. And in that state, people have a way of picking up and echoing anything that is said to them. "Not that much of a fool," he said slurrily. The vacancy of his face was joined by a look of deep cunning. Perhaps that was just as well, Charles thought. There was no doubt that Theresa had a point.

"Don't *speak* to him!" Theresa shouted. "Don't you understand? It's every word he says! And—" She swung around and pointed at Nan. "It's all *her* fault!"

Before lunch, Nan would have quailed in front of Theresa's pointing finger and everyone's eyes turned on her. But she had ridden a broomstick now, and things were different. She was able to look scornfully at Theresa. "What nonsense!" she said.

Mr. Crossley was forced to agree that Nan was right. "Don't be ridiculous, Theresa," he said. "I told you to sit down." And he relieved his feelings by giving both Theresa and Simon an hour in detention.

"Detention!" Theresa exclaimed, and sat down with a bump. She was outraged.

Simon, however, uttered a cunning chuckle. "You think you've got me, don't you?" he said.

"Yes, I do," said Mr. Crossley. "Make it an hour and a half."

Simon opened his mouth to say something else. But here Nirupam intervened. He leaned over and whispered to Simon, "You're very clever. Clever people keep their mouths shut."

Simon nodded slowly, with immense, stupid wisdom. And, to Charles's disappointment, he seemed to take Nirupam's advice.

"Get your journals out," Mr. Crossley said

wearily. There should be some peace now at least, he thought.

People opened their journals. They spread today's page in front of them. They picked up pens. And, at that point, even those who had not realized already, saw that there was almost nothing they dared write down. It was most frustrating. Here they were, with real, interesting events going on for once, and plenty of things to say, and almost none of it was fit for Miss Cadwallader's eyes. People chewed pens, shifted, scratched their heads, and stared at the ceiling. The most pitiable ones were those who were planning to ask Nan to endow them with the Golden Touch, or instant fame, or some other good thing. If they described any of the magic Nan was thought to have done, she would be arrested for witchcraft, and they would have killed the goose that laid the golden eggs.

Nan Pilgrim is not really a witch, Dan Smith wrote, after much hard thinking. He had rather a stomachache after last night's midnight feast and it made his mind go slow. *I never thought she was really, it was just Mr. Crossley having a joke. There was a practical joke this morning, it must have been hard work pinching everyone's shoes like that and then someone pinched my spikes and got me really mad. The caretakers dog peed*—And there Dan stopped, remembering Miss Cadwallader would read this too. Got quite carried away there, he thought.

No comment again today, Nirupam wrote swiftly. *Someone is riding for a fall. Not that I blame them for this afternoon, but the shoes were silly.* He put down his pen and went to sleep. He had been up half the night eating buns from under the floorboards.

My bedsocks were ruined, Theresa complained in her angel-writing. *My knitting was destroyed. Today has been awful. I do not want to tell tales and I know Simon Silverson is not in his right mind but someone should do something. Teddy Crossley is useless and unfair and Estelle Green always thinks she knows best but she can't keep her knitting clean. The matron was unfair too. She sent me away with an aspirin and she let Brian Wentworth lie down and I was really ill. I shall never speak to Nan Pilgrim again.*

Most people, though they could not attain Theresa's eloquence, managed to write something in the end. But three people still sat staring at blank paper. These were Simon, Charles, and Nan.

Simon was very cunning. He was clever. He was thoroughly suspicious of the whole thing. They were trying to catch him out somehow. The safest and cleverest thing was not to commit anything to writing. He was sure of that. On the other hand, it would not do to let everyone know how clever he had gone. It would look peculiar. He ought to write just one thing. So, after more than half an hour of deep thought, he wrote: *Doggies.* It took him five minutes. Then he sat back, confident that he had fooled everyone.

Charles was stumped because he simply had no code for most of the things which had happened. He knew he had to write something, but the more he tried to think, the more difficult it seemed. At one point, he almost went to sleep like Nirupam. He pulled himself together. Think! Well, he could not write *I got up* for a start, because he had almost enjoyed today. Nor could he write *I didn't get up* because that made no sense. But he had better mention the shoes, because everyone else would. And he could talk about Simon under the code of potatoes. Mr. Towers could get a mention too.

It was nearly time for the bell before Charles sorted all this out. Hastily he scrawled: *Our shoes all went to play games. I thought about potatoes having hair hanging on a rope. I have games with a bad book.* As Mr. Crossley told them to put away their journals, Charles thought of something else and dashed it down. *I shall never be hot again.*

Nan wrote nothing at all. She sat smiling at her empty page, feeling no need to describe anything. When the bell went, as a gesture, she wrote down the date: October 30. Then she shut her journal.

The instant Mr. Crossley left the room, Nan was surrounded. "You got my note?" People clamored at her. "Can you make it that whenever I touch a penny it turns to gold? Just pennies."

"Can you make my hair go like Theresa's?"

"Can you give me three wishes every time I say Buttons?"

"I want big muscles like Dan Smith."

"Can you get us ice cream for supper?"

"I need good luck for the rest of my life."

Nan looked over at where Simon sat, hunched up with cunning and darting shrewd, stupid looks at Nirupam, who was sitting watchfully over him. If it was Simon who was responsible, there was no knowing when he would say something to cancel her witchcraft. Nan refused to believe it *was* Simon, but it was silly to make rash promises, whatever had made her a witch.

"There isn't time to work magic now," she told the clamoring crowd. And when that brought a volley of appeals and groans, she shouted, "It takes *hours,* don't you understand? You don't only have to mutter spells and brew potions. You have got to go out and pick strange herbs, and say stranger incantations, at dawn and full moon, before you can even begin. And when you've done all that, it doesn't necessarily work right away. Most of the time, you have to fly around and around the smoking herbs all night, chanting sounds of unutterable sweetness, before anything happens at all. Now do you see?" Utter silence greeted this piece of invention. Much encouraged, Nan added, "Besides, what have any of you done to deserve me going to all that trouble?"

"What indeed?" Mr. Wentworth asked, from behind her. "What exactly is going on here?"

Nan spun around. Mr. Wentworth was right in the middle of the room and had probably heard every word. Around her, everyone was slinking back to their seats. "That was my speech for the school concert, sir," she said. "Do you think it's any good?"

"It has possibilities," said Mr. Wentworth. "But it will need a little more working up to be quite good enough. Math books out, please."

Nan sank down into her seat, weak with relief. For one awful moment, she had thought Mr. Wentworth might have her arrested.

"I said math books out, Simon," Mr. Wentworth said. "Why are you giving me that awful cunning look? Is it such a peculiar thing to ask?"

Simon considered this. Nirupam, and a number of other people, doubled their legs under their chairs, ready to spring up and gag Simon if necessary. Theresa once more jumped to her feet.

"Mr. Wentworth, if he says another word, I'm not staying!"

Unfortunately, this attracted Simon's attention. "You," he said to Theresa, "stink."

"He seems to have spoken," said Mr. Wentworth. "Get out and stand in the corridor, Theresa, with a black mark for bad behavior. Simon can have another, and the rest of us will have a lesson."

Theresa, redder in the face than anyone had ever seen her, raced for the door. She could not, however, beat the truly awful smell which rolled off her and filled the room as she ran.

"Pooh!" said Dan Smith.

Somebody kicked him, and everybody looked nervously at Mr. Wentworth to see if he could smell it too. But, as often happens to people who smoke a pipe, Mr. Wentworth had less than the average sense of smell. It was not for five minutes, during which he had written numerous things on the board and said many more, none of which 6B were in a fit state to attend to, that he said, "Estelle, put down that gray bag you're knitting and open a window, will you? There's rather a smell in here. Has someone let off a stink bomb?"

Nobody answered. Nirupam resourcefully passed Simon a note, saying, *Say there is no smell in here.*

Simon spelled it out. He considered it carefully, with his head on one side. He could see there was a trick in it somewhere. So he cunningly decided to say nothing.

Luckily, the open window, though it made the room almost as cold as Simon's Ice Age, did slowly disperse the smell. But nothing could disperse it from Theresa, who stood in the passage giving out scents of sludge, kippers, and old dustbins until the end of afternoon school.

When the bell had rung and Mr. Wentworth swept from the room, everyone relaxed with a groan. No one had known what Simon was going to say next. Even Charles had found it a strain. He had to admit that the results of his spell had taken him thoroughly by surprise.

Meanwhile, Delia and Karen, with most of Theresa's main friends, were determined to retrieve Theresa's honor. They surrounded Simon. "Take that smell off her at once," Delia said. "It's not funny. You've been on her all afternoon, Simon Silverson!"

Simon considered them. Nirupam leaped up so quickly that he knocked over his desk, and tried to put his hand over Simon's mouth. But he got there too late. "You girls," said Simon, "all stink."

The result was almost overpowering. So was the noise the girls made. The only girls who escaped were the lucky few, like Nan, who had already left the room. It was clear something had to be done. Most people were either smelling or choking. And Simon was slowly opening his mouth to say something else.

Nirupam left off trying to pick up his desk and seized hold of Simon by his shoulders. "You can break this spell," he said to him. "You could have stopped it straight away if you had any brain at all. But you would be greedy."

Simon looked at Nirupam in slow, dawning annoyance. He was being accused of being stupid. Him! He opened his mouth to speak.

"Don't *say* anything!" everyone near him shouted.

Simon gazed around at them, wondering what trick they were up to now. Nirupam shook him. "Say this after me," he said. And, when Simon's dull, cunning eyes turned to him, Nirupam said, slowly and loudly, "Nothing I said this afternoon came true. Go on. Say it."

"*Say* it!" everyone yelled.

Simon's slow mind was not proof against all this yelling. It gave in. "Nothing I said this afternoon came true," he said obediently.

The smell instantly stopped. Presumably everything else was also undone, because Simon at once became his usual self again. He had almost no memory of the afternoon. But he could see Nirupam was taking unheard-of liberties. He looked at Nirupam's hands, one on each of his shoulders, in surprise and annoyance. "Get off!" he said. "Take your face away."

The spell was still working. Nirupam was forced to let go and stand back from Simon. But, as soon as he had, he plunged back again and once more took hold of Simon's shoulders. He stared into Simon's face like a great dark hypnotist. "Now say," he said, "'Nothing I say is going to come true in the future.'"

Simon protested at this. He had great plans for the future. "Now, look here!" he said. And of course Nirupam did. He looked at Simon with such intensity that Simon blinked as he went on with his protest. "But I'll fail every exam I ever ta-a-a-ake—!" His voice faded out into a sort of hoot, as he realized what he had said. For Simon loved passing exams. He collected A's and ninety percents as fervently as he collected honor marks. And what he had just said had stopped all that.

"Exactly," said Nirupam. "Now you've *got* to say it. Nothing I say—"

"Oh, all right. Nothing I say is going to come true in the future," Simon said peevishly.

Nirupam let go of him with a sigh of relief and went back to pick up his desk. Everyone sighed.

Charles turned sadly away. Well, it had been good while it lasted.

"What's the matter?" Nirupam asked, catching sight of Charles's doleful face as he stood his desk on its legs again.

"Nothing," Charles said. "I—I've got detention." Then, with a good deal more pleasure, he turned to Simon. "So have you," he said.

Simon was scandalized. "What? I've never had detention all the time I've been at this school!"

It was explained to him that this was untrue. Quite a number of people were surprisingly ready to give Simon details of how he had rendered himself mindless and gained an hour and a half of detention from Mr. Crossley. Simon took it in very bad part and stormed off muttering.

Charles was about to trudge away after Simon, when Nirupam caught his arm. "Sit on the back bench," he said. "There's a store of comics in the middle, on the shelf underneath."

"Thanks," said Charles. He was so unused to people being friendly that he said it with enormous surprise and almost forgot to take Mr. Towers's awful book with him.

He trudged towards the old lab, where detention was held, and shortly found himself trudging behind Theresa Mullett. Theresa was proceeding towards detention, looking wronged and tragic, supported by a crowd of her friends, with Karen Grigg in addition.

"It's only for an hour," Charles heard Karen say consolingly.

"A whole *hour*!" Theresa exclaimed. "I shall never forgive Teddy Crossley for this! I hope Miss Hodge kicks him in the teeth!"

In order not to go behind Theresa's procession the whole way, Charles turned off halfway through the quadrangle and went by the way that was always called "around the back." It was a grassy space which had once been a second quadrangle. But the new labs and the lecture room and the library had been built in the space, sticking out into the grass at odd angles, so that the space had been pared down to a zigzag of grassy passage, where, for some reason, there was always a piercing wind blowing. It was a place where people only went to keep out of the way. So Charles was not particularly surprised to see Nan Pilgrim loitering about there. He prepared to glare at her as he trudged by. But Nan got in first with a very unfriendly look and moved off around the library corner.

I'm glad it wasn't Charles Morgan who wrote me that note, Nan thought, as Charles went on without speaking. I don't want any help from *him*.

She loitered out into the keen wind again, wondering if she needed help from anyone. She still felt a strong, confident inner witchiness. It was marvelous. It was like laughter bubbling up through everything she thought. She could not believe that it might be only Simon's doing. On the other hand, no one knew better than Nan how quickly inner confidence could drain away. Particularly if someone like Theresa laughed at you.

Another person was coming. Brian Wentworth this time. But he scurried by on the other side of the passage, to Nan's relief. She did not think Brian could help anyone. And—this place seemed unusually popular this evening—here was Nirupam Singh now, wandering up from the other direction, looking rather pleased with himself.

"I took the spell off Simon Silverson," he said to Nan. "I got him to say nothing he said was true."

"Good," said Nan. She wandered away around the library corner again. Did this mean she was no longer a witch then? She poked with one foot at the leaves and crisp packets the wind had blown into the corner. She could test it by turning them into something, she supposed.

But Nirupam had followed her around the corner. "No, wait," he said. "It was me that sent you that note."

Nan found this extremely embarrassing. She pretended to be very interested in the dead leaves. "I don't need help," she said gruffly.

Nirupam smiled and leaned against the library wall as if he were sunning himself. Nirupam had rather a strong personality, Nan realized. Though the sun was thin and yellow and the wind was whirling crisp packets about, Nirupam gave out such a strong impression of basking that Nan almost felt warm. "Everyone thinks you're a witch," he said.

"Well I *am*," Nan insisted, because she wanted to be sure of it herself.

"You shouldn't admit it," said Nirupam. "But it makes no difference. The point is, it's only a matter of time before someone goes to Miss Cadwallader and accuses you."

"Are you sure? They all want me to do things," said Nan.

"Theresa doesn't," said Nirupam. "Besides, you can't please everybody. Someone will get annoyed before long. I know this, because my brother tried to please all the servants. But one of them thought my brother was giving more to the other servants and told the police. And my brother was burned in the streets of Delhi."

"I'm sorry—I didn't know," said Nan. She looked across at Nirupam. His profile was like a chubby hawk, she thought. It looked desperately sad.

"My mother was burned too, for trying to save him," Nirupam said. "That was why my father came to this country, but things are just the same here. What I want to tell you is this—I have heard of a witches' underground rescue service in England. They help accused witches to escape, if you can get to one of their branches before the inquisitors come. I don't know where they send you, or whom to ask, but Estelle does. If you are accused, you must get Estelle to help."

"Estelle?" Nan said. She thought of Estelle's soft brown eyes and soft wriggly curls, and of Estelle's irritating chatter, and of Estelle's even more irritating way of imitating Theresa. She could not see Estelle helping anyone.

"Estelle is rather nice," said Nirupam. "I come around here and talk to her quite often."

"You mean Estelle talks to *you*," said Nan.

Nirupam grinned. "She does talk a lot," he agreed. "But she will help. She told me she likes you. She was sad you didn't like her."

Nan gaped. Estelle? It was not possible. No one liked Nan. But, now she remembered, Estelle had refused to come and threaten to drown her in the bathroom. "All right," she said. "I'll ask her. Thanks. But are you *sure* I'll be accused?"

Nirupam nodded. "There is this, you see. There are at least two other witches in 6B—"

"Two?" said Nan. "I mean, I know there's *one* more. It's obvious. But why *two*?"

"I told you," said Nirupam, "I've had experience of witches. Each one has their own style. It's like the way everyone's writing is different. And I tell you that it was not the same person who did the birds in music and the spell on Simon today. Those are two quite different outlooks on life. But both those people must know they have been very silly to do anything at all, and they will both be wanting to put the blame on you. It could well be one of them who accuses you. So you must be very careful. I will do my part and warn you if I hear of any trouble coming. Then you must ask Estelle to help you. Do you see now?"

"Yes, and I'm awfully grateful," said Nan.

Regretfully, she saw she did not dare try turning the dead leaves into anything. And, in spite of her promise to the old broom, she had better not ride it again. She was quite frightened. Yet she still felt the laughing confidence bubbling up inside, even though there might not be anything now to be confident about. Watch it! she told herself. You must be mad!

9

❧❧

THE OLD LAB was not used for anything much except detention. But there was still a faint smell of old science clinging to it, from generations of experiments which had gone wrong. Charles slid onto the splintery back bench and propped Mr. Towers's awful book against the stump of an old gas pipe. The comics were there, stacked on the shelf underneath, just below a place where someone had spent industrious hours carving *Cadwallader is a bag* on the bench top. The rest of the people in the room were all at the front. They were mostly from 5B or 5C, and probably did not know about the comics.

Simon came in. Charles gave him a medium-strength glare to discourage him from the back bench. Simon went and sat haughtily in the very middle of the middle bench. Good. Then Mr. Wentworth came in. Not so good. Mr. Wentworth was carefully carrying a steaming mug of coffee, which everyone in the room looked at with mute envy. It would *have* to be Mr. Wentworth! Charles thought resentfully.

Mr. Wentworth set his cup of coffee carefully down on the teacher's bench and looked around to see who was doing time. He seemed surprised to see Simon and not at all surprised to see Charles. "Anyone need paper for lines?" he asked.

Charles did. He went up with most of 5B and was handed a lump of someone's old exam. The exam had used only one side of the paper, so, Charles supposed, it made sense to use the other side for lines. But it did, all the same, seem like a deliberate way of showing people how pointlessly they were wasting time here. Wasting wastepaper. And Charles could tell, as Mr. Wentworth gave the paper out, that he was in his nastiest and most harrowed mood.

Not good at all, Charles thought, as he slid back behind the back bench. For, though Charles had not particularly thought about it, it was obvious to him that he was going to use witchcraft to copy out Mr. Towers's awful book. What was the point of being a witch if you didn't make use of it? But he would have to go carefully with Mr. Wentworth in this mood.

The door opened. Theresa made an entry with her crowd of supporters.

Mr. Wentworth looked at them. "Come in," he said. "So glad you were able to make it, all of you. Sit down, Delia. Find a seat, Karen. Heather, Deborah, Julia, Theresa, and the rest can no doubt all squeeze in around Simon."

"*We* haven't got detention, sir," Delia said.

"We just came to bring Theresa," Deborah explained.

"Why? Didn't she know the way?" said Mr. Wentworth. "Well, you all have detention now—"

"But, sir! We only came—!"

"—unless you get out this second," said Mr. Wentworth.

Theresa's friends vanished. Theresa looked angrily at Simon, who was sitting in the place she would otherwise have chosen, and carefully selected a place at the end of the bench just behind him. "This is all your fault," she whispered to Simon.

"Drop dead!" said Simon.

It was, Charles thought, rather a pity that Nirupam had managed to break the *Simon Says* spell.

Silence descended, the woeful, restless silence of people who wish they were elsewhere. Mr. Wentworth opened a book and picked up his coffee. Charles waited until Mr. Wentworth seemed thoroughly into his book, and then brought out his ballpoint pen. He ran his finger and thumb down it, just as he had done with Simon's hair, down and down again. Write lines, he thought to it. Write five hundred lines out of this book. Write lines. Then, very grudgingly, he wrote out the first sentence for it— *"What ripping fun!" exclaimed Watts Minor. "I'm down for scrum half this afternoon!"*—to show it what to do. Then he cautiously let go of it. And the pen not only stood where he had left it but began to write industriously. Charles arranged Mr. Towers's book so that it would hide the scribbling pen. Then, with a sigh of satisfaction, he fetched out one of the comics and settled down as comfortably as Mr. Wentworth.

Five minutes later, he thought a thunderbolt hit him.

The pen fell down and rolled on the floor. The comic was snatched away. His right ear was in agony. Charles looked up—mistily, because his glasses were now hanging from his left ear—to find Mr. Wentworth towering over him. The pain in his ear was from the excruciatingly tight grip Mr. Wentworth had on it.

"Get up," Mr. Wentworth said, dragging at the ear.

Charles got up perforce. Mr. Wentworth led him, like that, by the ear, with his head painfully on one side, to the front of the room. Halfway there, Charles's glasses fell off his other ear. He almost didn't have the heart to catch them. In fact, he only saved them by reflex. He was fairly sure he would not be needing them much longer.

At the front, he could see just well enough to watch Mr. Wentworth cram the comic one-handed into the wastepaper basket. "Let that teach you to read comics in detention!" Mr. Wentworth said. "Now come with me." He led Charles, still by the ear, to the door. There, he turned around and spoke to the others in the room. "If anyone so much as stirs," he said, "while I'm gone, he or she will be here for double time, every night till Christmas."

Upon this, he towed Charles outside.

He towed Charles some distance up the covered way outside. Then he let go of Charles's ear, took hold of his shoulders, and commenced shaking him. Charles had never been shaken like that. He bit his tongue. He thought his neck was breaking. He thought the whole of him was coming apart. He grabbed his left hand in his right one to try and hold himself together—and felt his glasses snap into two pieces. That was it, then. He could hardly breathe when Mr. Wentworth at last let go of him.

"I warned you!" Mr. Wentworth said, furiously angry. "I called you to my room and purposely warned you! Are you a complete fool, boy? How much more frightened do you have to be? Do you need to be in front of the inquisitors before you stop?"

"I—" gasped Charles. "I—" He had never known Mr. Wentworth could be this angry.

Mr. Wentworth went on, in a lifting under-tone that was far more frightening than shouting, "Three times—three times today to *my* knowl-edge—you've used witchcraft. And the Lord knows how many times I *don't* know about. Are you *trying* to give yourself away? Have you the *least* idea what risk you run? What kind of a show-off are you? *All* the shoes in the school this morning—"

"That—that was a mistake, sir," Charles panted. "I—I was trying to find my spikes."

"A *stupid* thing to waste witchcraft on!" said Mr. Wentworth. "And not content with a public display like that, you *then* go and cast spells on Simon Silverson!"

"How did you know that was me?" said Charles.

"One look at your face, boy. And what's more, you were sitting there letting the unfortunate Nan Pilgrim take the blame. I call that thoroughly selfish and despicable! And now this! Writing lines where anyone could see you! You are lucky, let me tell you, boy, *very* lucky not to be down at the police station at this moment, waiting for the inquisitor. You *deserve* to be there. Don't you?" He shook Charles again. "Don't you?"

"Yes, sir," said Charles.

"And you will be," said Mr. Wentworth, "if you do one more thing. You're to forget about witchcraft, understand? Forget about magic. Try to be normal, if you know what that means. Because I promise you that if you do it again, you will be *really* in trouble. Is that clear?"

"Yes, sir," said Charles.

"Now get back in there and write properly!" Mr. Wentworth shoved Charles in front with one hand, and Charles could feel that hand shaking with anger. Frightening though that was, Charles was glad of it. He could barely see a thing without his glasses. When Mr. Wentworth burst back with him into the old lab, the room was just a large fuzzy blur. But he could tell everyone was looking at him. The air was thick with people thinking, I'm glad it wasn't me!

"Get back to your seat," Mr. Wentworth said,

and let go of Charles with a sharp push.

Charles felt his way through swimming colored blurs, down to the other end of the old lab. Those crooked white squares must be the book and the old exam paper. But his pen, he remembered, had fallen on the floor. How was he to find it, in this state, let alone write with it?

"What are you standing there for?" Mr. Wentworth barked at him. "Put your glasses on and get back to work!"

Charles jumped with terror. He found himself diving for his seat, and hooking his glasses on as he dived. The world clicked into focus. He saw his pen lying almost under his feet and bent to pick it up. But surely, he thought, as he was half under the bench, his glasses had been in two pieces? He had heard a dreadfully final snapping noise. He thought he had felt them come apart. He put his hand up hurriedly and felt his glasses—there was no point taking them off and looking, because then he would not be able to see. They felt all right. Entire and whole. Either he had made a mistake, or the plastic had snapped and not the metal inside. Much relieved, Charles sat up with the pen in his hand.

And stared at what it had written by itself. *I am Watts down scrum Minor ripping this fun afternoon. I fun Minor am half this afternoon Watts* . . . and so on, for two whole pages. It was no good. Mr. Towers was bound to notice. Charles sighed and began writing. Perhaps he *should* stop doing witchcraft. Nothing seemed to go right.

Consequently, the rest of the evening was rather quiet. Charles sat in devvy running his thumb over the fat cushion of blister on his finger, not wanting to give up witchcraft and knowing he dared not go on. He felt such a mixture of regret and terror that it quite bewildered him. Simon was subdued too. Brian Wentworth was back, sitting scribbling industriously, with one eye still turned slightly inward, but Simon seemed to have lost his desire to hit Brian for the time being. And Simon's friends followed Simon's lead.

Nan kept quiet also, because of what Nirupam had said, but, however hard she reasoned with herself, she could not get rid of that bubbling inner confidence. It was still with her in the dormitory that night. It stayed, in spite of Delia, Deborah, Heather, and the rest, who began on her in their usual way.

"It was a bit much, that spell on Simon!"

"Really, Nan, I know we asked you, but you should *think* first."

"Look what he did to Theresa. And she lost her knitting over it."

And Nan, instead of submitting or apologizing, as she usually did, said, "What's put it into your pretty little heads that that spell was mine?"

"Because we know you're a witch," said Heather.

"Of course," said Nan. "But what gave you the idea I was the only one? You think, Heather, instead of just opening your little pink mouth and letting words trickle out. I told you, it takes *time* to make a spell. I told you about picking herbs and flying around and chanting, didn't I? And I left out the way you have to catch bats. That takes ages, even on a fast modern broomstick, because bats are so good at dodging. And you were with me in the bathroom, and with me all the time all this last week, and you *know* I haven't had time to catch bats or pick herbs, and you've *seen* I haven't been muttering and incantating. So you see? It wasn't me."

She could tell they were convinced, because they all looked so disappointed. Heather muttered, "And you said you couldn't fly that broomstick!" but she said nothing more. Nan was pleased. She seemed to have shut them up without losing her reputation as a witch.

All except Karen. Karen was newly admitted to the number of Theresa's friends. That made her very zealous. "Well, I think you should work a spell now," she said. "Theresa's lost a pair of bootees she spent hours knitting, and I think the least you can do is get them back for her."

"No trouble at all," Nan said airily. "But does Theresa want me to try?"

Theresa finished buttoning her pajamas and turned away to brush her hair. "She's not going to try, Karen," she said. "I should be *ashamed* to get my knitting back that way!"

"Lights out," said a monitor at the door. "Do these belong to anyone? The caretaker found them in his dog's basket." She held up two small gray fluffy things with holes in them.

The look everyone gave Nan, as Theresa went to claim her bootees, made Nan wonder if she had been wise to talk like that. And I don't even really know if I'm still a witch, she thought, as she got into bed. I'll keep my mouth shut in the future. And that broomstick stays on top of the cupboard. I don't care if I did promise it.

Right in the middle of the night, she was awakened by something prodding at her. Nan, in her sleep, rolled out of the way, and rolled again, until she woke up in the act of falling out of bed. There was a swift swishing noise. Something she only dimly saw in the near-dark dived over her and then dived under her. Nan woke up completely to find herself six feet off the floor and doubled over the broomstick, with her head hanging down one side and her feet the other. The knobby handle was a painful thing to be draped over. Nevertheless, Nan began to laugh. I *am* a witch after all! she thought joyfully.

"Put me down, you big fraud!" she whispered. "You were just playing for sympathy, pretending you needed a rider, weren't you? Put me down and go and fly yourself!"

The broomstick's answer was to rise up to the ceiling. Nan's bed looked like a small dim oblong from there. She knew she would miss it if she tried to jump off.

"You big bully!" she said. "I know I promised, but that was before—"

The broom drifted suggestively towards the

window. Nan became alarmed. The window was open because Theresa believed in fresh air. She had visions of herself being carted over the countryside, draped over the stick in nothing but pajamas. She gave in.

"All right. I'll fly you. But let me go down and get some blankets first. I'm not going to go like this!"

The broom whirled around and swooped back to Nan's bed. Nan's legs flew out and she landed on the mattress with a bounce. The broom did not trust her in the least. It hovered over her while she dragged the pink school blankets from her bed, and as soon as she had wrapped them around her, it made quite sure of her by darting underneath her and swooping up to the ceiling again. Nan was thrown backwards. She nearly ended hanging underneath again.

"Go carefully!" she whispered. "Let me get settled."

The broom hovered impatiently while Nan tried to balance herself and get comfortable. She did not dare take too long over it. All the swooping and whispering were disturbing the other girls. Quite a few of them were turning over and murmuring crossly. Nan tried to sit on the broom and toppled over sideways. She got tangled in her blankets. In the end, she simply fell forward on her face and settled for lying along the handle again, in a bundle of blanket, with her feet hooked up on the brush.

Before she had even gotten comfortable like

that, the broomstick swooped to the window, nudged it further open, and darted outside. There was pitch black night out there. It was cold, with a drizzle of rain falling. Nan wrinkled her face against it and tried to get used to being high up. The broom flew with a strange choppy movement, not altogether pleasant for a person lying on her face.

Nan talked, to take her mind off it. "How is this," she said, "for romantic dreams come true? I always thought of myself flying a broomstick on a warm summer night, outlined against an enormous moon, with a nightingale or so singing its head off. And look at us!" Underneath her, the broomstick jerked. It was obviously a shrug.

"Yes, I daresay it is the best we can do," Nan said. "But I don't feel very glamorous like this, and I'm getting wet. I bet Dulcinea Wilkes used to *sit* on her broom, gracefully, sidesaddle probably, with her long hair flowing out behind. And because it was London, she probably wore an elegant silk dress, with lots of lacy petticoats showing from underneath. Did you know I was descended from Dulcinea Wilkes?"

The rippling underneath her might have been the broom's way of nodding. But it could have been laughing at the contrast.

Nan found she could see in the dark now. She looked down and blenched. The broomstick felt very flimsy to be this high. It had soared and turned while she was talking, so that the square shapes of the school were a long way below and to one side.

The pale spread of the playing field was directly underneath, and beyond that Nan could see the entire town, filling the valley ahead. The houses were all dark, with orange chains of streetlights in between. And in spite of the drifting drizzle, Nan could see as far as the blackness of Larwood Forest on the hill opposite.

"Let's fly over the forest," she said.

The broom swept off. Once you got used to it, it really would be a nice feeling, Nan told herself firmly, blinking against the drizzle. Secret, silent flight. It was in her blood. She held the end of the broom handle in both hands and tried to point it at the town. But the broom had other ideas. It wanted to go around the edge of the town. The result was that they flew sideways, jolting a little.

"Fly over the houses," said Nan.

The broom gave a shake that nearly sent her tumbling off. No.

"I suppose someone might look up and see us," Nan agreed. "All right. You win again. Bully." And it occurred to her that her dreams of flying against a huge full moon were really the most arrant romantic nonsense. No witch in her senses would do that, for fear the inquisitors might see her.

So they swooped over fields, and across the main road in a rush of rain. The rain at first came at Nan's face in separate drops out of the orange haze made by the streetlights. Then it was just wetness out of darkness, as they reached Larwood Forest, and the wetness brought a smell with it of autumn leaves and mushroom. But even a dark wood is not quite black at night. Nan could see paler trees, which still had yellow leaves, and she could clearly see mist caused by the rain smoking out above the trees. Some of it seemed to be real smoke. Nan smelled fire distinctly. A wet fire, burning smokily.

She suddenly felt rather quiet. "I say, that can't be a bonfire, can it? If it's after midnight, it is Halloween, isn't it?"

The idea seemed to upset the broom. It stopped with a jerk. For a second, its front end tipped downwards as if it were thinking of landing. Nan had to grip hard in order not to slide off head first. Then it began actually flying backwards, wagging its brush in agitated sweeps, so that Nan's feet were swirled from side to side.

"Stop it!" she said. "I shall be sick in a minute!"

They did, she knew, sometimes burn witch's brooms with the witch they belonged to. So she was not surprised when the broom swung around, away from the smell of smoke, and began flying back towards the school, in a stately sort of way, as if that was the way it had meant to go all along.

"You don't fool me," she said. "But you can go back if you want. I'm soaked."

The broom continued on its wet and stately way, high above the fields and the main road, until the pale flatness of the playing field appeared beneath them once more. Nan was just thinking that she would be in bed any minute now, when a new notion seemed to strike the broom. It dived a sickening fifty feet and put on speed. Nan found herself hurtling over the field, about twenty feet up, and oozing off backwards with the speed. She hung on and shouted to it to stop. Nothing she said made any difference. The broom continued to hurtle.

"Oh really!" Nan gasped. "You are the most willful thing I've ever known! Stop!"

The rain beat in her face, but she could see something ahead now, all the same. It was something dark against the grass, and it was quite big, too big for a broom, although it was flying too, floating gently away across the field. The broom was racing towards it. As they plunged on, Nan saw that the thing was flat underneath, with the shape of a person on top of it. It got bigger and bigger. Nan decided it could only be a small carpet with a man sitting on it. She tugged and jerked at the broom handle, but there seemed nothing she could do to stop the broom.

The broom plunged gladly up alongside the dark shape. It *was* a man on a small carpet. The broom swooped around it, wagging its end so hard that Nan bit her tongue. It nuzzled and nudged and jogged at the carpet, jerking Nan this way and that as it went. And the carpet seemed equally delighted to meet the broom. It was jiggling and flapping, and rippling so that the man on top of it was rolled this way and that. Nan shrank down and clung to the broom, hoping that she just looked like a roll of blankets to whoever this witch on a carpet was.

But the man was becoming annoyed by the

antics of the carpet and the broom. "Can't you control that thing yet?" he snapped.

Nan shrank down even further. Her bitten tongue made it hard to speak anyway, and she was almost glad of it. She knew that voice. It was Mr. Wentworth's.

"And I told you never to ride that thing in term time, Brian," Mr. Wentworth said. When Nan still did not say anything, he added, "I know, I know. But this wretched hearthrug insists on going out every night."

This is worse and worse! Nan thought. Mr. Wentworth thought she was Brian. So Brian must be—with a fierce effort, she managed to wrench the broom around, away from the hearthrug. With an even fiercer effort, she got it going again, towards the school. By kicking it hard with her bare toes, she kept it going. When she was some way away, she risked turning around and whispering, "Sorry." She hoped Mr. Wentworth would go on thinking she was Brian.

Mr. Wentworth called something after her as the broomstick lumbered away, but Nan did not even try to hear what it was. She did not want to know. She could still barely believe it. Besides, she needed all her attention to make the broom go. It was very reluctant. It flew across the field in a dismal, trudging way, which reminded Nan irresistibly of Charles Morgan, but at least it went. Nan was pleased to discover that she could control it after all, when she had to.

It made particularly heavy weather of lifting Nan upwards to her dormitory window. She almost believed it groaned. Some of the difficulty may have been real. All Nan's pink school blankets were soaked through by now and they must have weighed a great deal. But Nan remembered what an act the broom had put on in the afternoon and resolved to be pitiless. She drummed with her toes again. Up went the broom through the dark rainy night, up and up the wall, until at last they were outside the half-open dormitory window. Nan helped the broom shoulder the window open wider, and then swooped to the floor on her stomach. What a relief! she thought.

Someone whispered, "I put dry blankets on your bed."

Nan nearly fainted. After a pause to recover, she rolled herself off the broom and knelt up in her sopping blankets. A dim figure in regulation school pajamas was standing in front of her, bending down a little, so that Nan could see the hair was curly. Heather? No, don't be daft! Estelle. "Estelle?" she whispered.

"Hush!" whispered Estelle. "Come and help put these blankets in the airing cupboard. We can talk there."

"But the broom—?" Nan whispered.

"Send it away."

A good idea, Nan thought, if only the broom would obey. She picked it up, shedding soaking blankets as she went, and carried it to the window.

"Go to the groundsman's shed," she told it in a severe whisper, and sent it off with a firm shove. Knowing the kind of broom it was, she would not have been surprised if it had simply clattered to the ground. But it obeyed her, rather to her astonishment—or at least, it flew off into the rainy night.

Estelle was already lugging the heap of blankets to the door. Nan tiptoed to help her. Together they dragged the heap down the passage and into the fateful bathroom. There, Estelle shut the door and daringly turned on the light.

"It'll be all right if we don't talk too loud," she said. "I'm awfully sorry—Theresa woke up while I was making your bed. I had to tell her you'd been sick. I said you were in the bathroom being sick again. Can you remember that if she asks tomorrow?"

"Thanks," said Nan. "That was kind of you. Did I wake you going out?"

"Yes, but it was training mostly," Estelle said. She opened the big airing cupboard. "If we fold these blankets and put them right at the back, no one's going to find them for weeks. They might even be dry by then, but with this school's heating there's no relying on that."

It was not a quick job. They had to take out the piles of pale pink dry blankets stacked in the cupboard, fold the heavy bright pink wet ones, put them in at the back, and then put all the dry ones back to hide them.

"Why did you say training woke you up?"

Nan asked Estelle as they worked.

"Training with the witches' underground escape route," said Estelle. "My mum used to belong to it, and I used to help her. It took me right back, when I heard you going out—though it was usually people coming in that used to wake me up. And I knew you'd be wet when you came back, and need help. Mum brought me up to think of everything like that. We used to have witches coming in on brooms at all hours of the night, poor things. Most of them were as wet as you—and much more frightened, of course. Hold the blanket down with your chin. That's the best way to get it folded."

"Why did your mum send you away to this school?" Nan asked. "You must have been such a help."

Estelle's bright face saddened. "She didn't. The inquisitors sent me. They had a big campaign and broke up all our branch of the organization. My mum got caught. She's in prison now, for helping witches. But"—Estelle's soft brown eyes looked earnestly into Nan's face—"*please* don't say. I couldn't bear anyone else to know. You're the only one I've ever told."

10

>+<

THE NEXT MORNING, Brian Wentworth did not get
up. Simon threw a pillow at him as he lay there, but
Brian did not stir.

"Wakey, wakey, Brian!" Simon said. "Get up,
or I'll strip your bed off." When Brian still did not
move, Simon advanced on his bed.

"Let him alone," Charles said. "He was ill
yesterday."

"Anything you say, Charles," said Simon.
"Your word is my command." And he pulled all the
covers off Brian's bed.

Brian was not in it. Instead, there was a line of
three pillows, artfully overlapped to give the shape
of a body. Everyone gathered around and stared.
Ronald West bent down and looked under the
bed—as if he thought Brian might be there—and
came up holding a piece of paper.

"Here," he said. "This must have come off with
the bedclothes. Take a look!"

Simon snatched the paper from him. Everyone
else craned and pushed to see it too. It was written

in capital letters, in ordinary blue ballpoint, and it said: *HA HA. I HAVE GOT BRIAN WENT-WORTH IN MY POWER. SIGNED, THE WITCH.*

The slightly tense look on Simon's face gave way to righteous concern. He had known at once that Brian's disappearance had nothing to do with him. "We're not going to panic," he said. "Someone get the master on duty."

There was instant emergency. Voices jabbered, rumors roared. Charles fetched Mr. Crossley, since everyone else seemed too astonished to think. After that, Mr. Crossley and monitors came and went, asking everyone when they had last seen Brian. People from the other dormitories crowded in the doorway, calling comments. Everyone was very eager to say something, but nothing very useful came out. A lot of people had noticed Brian was pale and cross-eyed the day before. Somebody said he had been ill and gone to the matron. A number of other people said he had come back later and seemed very busy writing. Everyone swore Brian had gone to bed as usual the night before.

Long before Mr. Crossley had sorted even this much out, Charles was tiptoeing hastily away downstairs. He felt sick. Up to last night, he had supposed Brian was trying to get himself invalided out of school. Now he knew better. Brian had run away, just as he had said he would. And he had taken the advice Charles had given him in the middle of the night before and confused his trail. But what had given Brian the idea of blaming the witch? Could it have been the shoes, and the sight of Charles muttering over some hairs from Simon's comb? Charles was fairly sure it was.

As Charles pushed through the boys in the corridor, he heard the words "witch" and "Nan Pilgrim" coming from all sides. Fine, as long as they went on blaming Nan. But would they? Charles took a look at his burned finger as he went down the stairs. The transparent juicy cushion of blister on it was fatter than ever. *It hurts to be burned.* Charles went the rest of the way down at a crazy gallop. He too remembered Brian scribbling and scribbling during devvy. Brian must have written pages. If there was one word about Charles Morgan in those pages, he was going to make sure no one else saw them. He pelted along the corridors. He flung himself into the classroom, squawking for breath.

Brian's desk was open. Nirupam was bending over it. He did not seem in the least surprised to see Charles. "Brian has been very eloquent," he said. "Come and see."

Behind the raised lid of the desk, Nirupam had lined up six exercise books, each of them open to a double page of hurried blue scrawl. *Help, help, help, help,* Charles read in the first. *The witch has the Evil Eye on me. HELP. I am being dragged away I know not where. HELP. My mind is in thrall. Nameless deeds are being forced upon me. HELP. The world is turning gray. The spell is working. Help* . . . And so on, for the whole two pages.

"There's yards of it!" said Charles.

"I know," said Nirupam, opening Brian's French book. "This is full of it too."

"Does it give names?" Charles asked tensely.

"Not so far," said Nirupam.

Charles was not going to take Nirupam's word for that. He picked up each book in turn and read the scrawl through. *Help. Wild chanting and horrible smells fill my ears. HELP. I can FEEL MYSELF GOING. The witch's will is strong. I must obey. Gray humming and horrible words. HELP. My spirit is being dragged from TIMBUKTU to UTTAR PRADESH. To utter destruction I mean. Help* . . . It went on like this for all six books. Enough of it was in capitals for Charles to be quite sure that Brian had written the note under his bed himself.

After that, he read each of the rest of Brian's books as Nirupam finished with it. It was all the same kind of thing. To Charles's relief, Brian named no names. But there was still Brian's journal, at the bottom of the pile.

"If he's said anything definite, it will be in this," Nirupam said, picking up the journal. Charles reached out for it too. If necessary, he was going to force it out of Nirupam's hands by witchcraft. Or was it better just to make all the pages blank? But did he dare do either? His hand hesitated.

As Charles hesitated, they heard Mr. Crossley's voice out in the corridor. Charles and Nirupam frantically crammed the books back into Brian's desk and shut it. They raced to their own desks, sat down, got out books, and pretended to be busy finishing devvy from the night before.

"You boys should be going along to breakfast now," Mr. Crossley said, when he came in. "Go along."

Both of them had to go, without a chance of looking at Brian's journal. Charles wondered why Nirupam looked so frustrated. But he was too frightened on his own account to bother much about Nirupam's feelings.

In the corridor outside the dining hall, Mr. Wentworth rushed past them, looking even more harrowed than usual. Inside the dining hall, the rumor was going around that the police had just arrived.

"You wait," Simon said knowingly. "The inquisitor will be here before dinner time. You'll see."

Nirupam slid into a seat beside Nan. "Brian has written in all his school books about a witch putting a spell on him," he murmured to her.

Nan hardly needed this to show her the trouble she was in. Karen and Delia had already asked her several times what she had done to Brian. And Theresa had added, not looking at Nan, "Some people can't leave people alone, can they?"

"But he didn't name any names," Nirupam muttered, also not looking at Nan.

Brian didn't need to name names, Nan thought desperately. Everyone else would do that for him. And, if that was not enough, Estelle knew she had been out on the broomstick last night. She looked around for Estelle, but Estelle seemed to be avoiding her. She was at another table. At that, the last traces of witchy inner confidence left Nan completely. For once in her life, she had no appetite for breakfast. Charles was not much better. Whatever he tried to eat, the fat blister on his finger seemed to get in the way.

At the end of breakfast, another rumor went around: The police had sent for tracker dogs.

A short while after this, Miss Hodge arrived, to find the school in an uproar. It took her some time to find out what had happened, since Mr. Crossley was nowhere to be found. When Miss Phillips finally told her, Miss Hodge was delighted. Brian Wentworth had vanished! That is, Miss Hodge thought hastily, it was very sad and worrying of course, but it did give her a real excuse to attract Mr. Wentworth's attention again. Yesterday had been most frustrating. After Mr. Wentworth had brushed aside her generous apology over Charles Morgan, she had not been able to think of any other move towards getting him to marry her. But this was ideal. She could go to Mr. Wentworth and be terribly sympathetic. She could enter into his sorrow. The only difficulty was that Mr. Wentworth was not to be found, any more than Mr. Crossley. It seemed that they were both with the police in Miss Cadwallader's study.

As everyone went into the hall for assembly, they could see a police van in the quadrangle. Several healthy Alsatians were getting out of it, with their pink tongues draped over their large white fangs in a way that suggested they could hardly wait to get on and hunt something. A number of faces turned pale. There was a lot of nervous giggling.

"It doesn't matter if the dogs don't find anything," Simon could be heard explaining. "The inquisitor will simply run his witch-detector over everyone in the class, and they'll find the witch that way."

To Nan's relief, Estelle came pushing along the line and stood next to her. "Estelle—!" Nan began violently.

"Not now," Estelle whispered. "Wait for the singing."

Neither Mr. Wentworth nor Miss Cadwallader came into assembly. Mr. Brubeck and Mr. Towers, who sat in the main chairs instead, did not explain about that, and neither of them mentioned Brian. This seemed to make it all much more serious. Mr. Towers chose his favorite hymn. It was, to Nan's misery, "He Who Would Valiant Be." This hymn always caused Theresa to look at Nan and giggle, when it came to "To be a pilgrim." Nan had to wait for Theresa to do that before she dared to speak to Estelle, and, she thought, Theresa's giggle was rather nastier than usual.

"Estelle," Nan whispered, as soon as everyone had started the second verse. "Estelle, you don't think I went out—last night, the way I did— because of Brian, do you? I swear I didn't."

"I know you didn't," Estelle whispered back. "What would anyone want Brian *for,* anyway?"

"But everyone thinks I did! What shall I *do?*" Nan whispered back.

"It's PE second lesson. I'll show you then," said Estelle.

Charles was also whispering under cover of the singing, to Nirupam. "What are witch-detectors? Do they work?"

"Machines in black boxes," Nirupam said breathily at his hymn book. "And they always find a witch with them."

Mr. Wentworth had talked about witch-detectors too. So, Charles thought, if the rumor was right and the inquisitor got here before lunch-time, today was the end of Charles. Charles hated Brian. Selfish beast. Yes, all right, he had been selfish too, but Brian was even worse. There was only one thing to do now, and that was to run away as well. But those tracker dogs made that nearly impossible.

When they got to the classroom, Brian's desk had been taken away. Charles looked at the empty space in horror. Fingerprints! he thought. Nirupam had gone quite yellow.

"They took it to give the dogs the scent," said Dan Smith. He added thoughtfully, "They're trained to tear people to pieces, those police dogs. I wonder if they'll tear Brian up, or just the witch."

Charles looked at the blister on his finger and realized that burning was not the only thing that hurt. His first thought had been to run away during break. Now he decided to go in PE, next lesson. He wished there were not a whole lesson in between.

That lesson seemed to last about a year. And for most of that lesson, policemen were continually going past the windows with dogs on leads. Back and forth they went. Wherever Brian had gone, they seemed to be finding it hard to pick up his scent.

By this time, Nan's hands were shaking so that she could hardly hold her pen. Thanks to last night, she knew exactly why Brian had left no scent. It was that double-dealing broomstick. It must have flown Brian out before it came and woke her up. Nan was sure of it. She could have taken the police to the exact spot where Brian was. That was no bonfire she had smelled over Larwood Forest last night. It had been Brian's campfire. The broomstick had brought her right over the spot and then realized its mistake. That was why it had gotten so agitated and tried to fly away backwards. She was so angry with Brian for getting her blamed that she wished she really could tell them where he was. But the moment she did that, she proved that she was a witch and incriminated Mr. Wentworth into the bargain. Oh, it was too bad of Brian! Nan just hoped Estelle could think of some kind of rescue before someone accused her, and she started accusing Brian and Mr. Wentworth.

Just before the end of that lesson, the dogs must have found some kind of scent. When the girls walked around the outside of the school on their way to the girls' locker room, to change for PE, there was not a policeman or a dog in sight. As the line of girls went past the shrubbery, Estelle gently took hold of Nan's arm and pulled her towards the bushes. Nan let herself be pulled. She did not know if she was more relieved or more terrified. It was a little early in the day to find seniors in the shrubbery, but even so, surely somebody would notice.

"We have to go into town," Estelle whispered, as they pushed among the wet bushes. "To the Old Gate House."

"Why?" Nan asked, thrusting her way after Estelle.

"Because," Estelle whispered over her shoulder, "the lady there runs the Larwood branch of the witches' escape route."

They came out into the grass beside the huge laurel bush. Nan looked from Estelle's scared face to Estelle's trim blazer and school skirt. Then she looked down at her own plump shape. Different as they were, they were both obviously in Larwood House school uniforms. "But if someone sees us in town, they'll report us to Miss Cadwallader."

"I was hoping," Estelle whispered, "that you might be able to change us into ordinary clothes."

Nan realized that the only witchcraft she had ever done was to fly that broom. She had not the least idea how you changed clothes. But Estelle was relying on her and it really was urgent. Feeling an awful fool, Nan held out both shaking hands and said the first thing remotely like a spell that came into her head.

> "Eeny, meeny, miney, mo,
> Out of uniform we go!"

There was a swirling feeling around her. Estelle was suddenly in a small snowstorm that seemed to be made of little bits of rag. Navy blue rag, then dark rag. The rags settled like burned paper, clinging to Estelle and hanging, and clinging to Nan too. And there they both were in seconds, dressed as witches, in long trailing black dresses, pointed black hats and all.

Estelle clapped both hands to her mouth to stop a giggle. Nan snorted with laughter. "This won't do! Try again," giggled Estelle.

"What do you want to wear?" Nan asked.

Estelle's eyes shone. "Riding clothes," she whispered ardently. "With a red jumper, please."

Nan stretched out her hands again. Now she knew she could do it, she felt quite confident.

> "Agga, tagga, ragga, roast.
> Wear the clothes you want the most."

The rag-storm began again. In Estelle's case, it started black and swirled very promisingly into pale brown and red. Around Nan, it seemed to be turning pink. When the storm stopped, there was Estelle, looking very trim and pretty in jodhpurs, red sweater, and hard hat, with her legs in shiny boots, pointing at Nan with a riding crop and making helpless bursting noises.

Nan looked down at herself. It seemed that the sort of clothes she wanted most was the dress she had imagined Dulcinea Wilkes wearing to ride her broomstick around London in. She was in a shiny pink silk balldress. The full skirt swept the wet grass. The tight pink bodice left her shoulders bare. It had blue bows up the front and lace in the sleeves. No wonder Estelle was laughing! Pink silk was definitely a mistake for someone as plump as Nan. Why pink? she wondered. Probably she had gotten that idea from the school blankets.

She had her hands stretched out to try again, when they heard Karen Grigg shouting outside the shrubbery. "Estelle! *Estelle!* Where are you? Miss Philips wants to know where you've gotten to!"

Estelle and Nan turned and ran. Estelle's clothes were ideal for sprinting through bushes. Nan's were not. She lumbered and puffed behind Estelle, and wet leaves kept showering her bare shoulders with water. Her sleeves got in her way. Her skirt wrapped around her legs and kept catching on bushes. Just at the edge of the shrubbery, the dress got stuck on a twig and tore with such a loud ripping noise that Estelle whirled around in horror.

"Wait!" panted Nan. She wrenched the pink skirt loose and tore the whole bottom part of it off. She wrapped the torn bit like a scarf around her wet shoulders. "That's better."

After that, she could keep up with Estelle quite easily. They slipped through onto the school drive and pelted down it and out through the iron gates. Nan meant to stop and change the pink dress into something else in the road outside, but there was a man sweeping the pavement just beyond the gates. He stopped sweeping and stared at the two of them. A little further on, there were two ladies with shopping bags, who stared even harder. Nan put her head down in acute embarrassment as they walked past the ladies. She had strips of torn pink silk hanging down and clinging to the pale blue stockings she seemed to have changed her socks into. Below that, she seemed to have given herself pink ballet shoes.

"Will you call for me at my ballet class after you've had your riding lesson?" she said loudly and desperately to Estelle.

"I might. But I'm scared of your ballet teacher," Estelle said, playing up bravely.

They got past the ladies, but there were more people further down the road. The further they got into town, the more people there were. By the time they came to the shops, Nan knew she was not going to get a chance to change the pink balldress.

"You look awfully pretty. Really," Estelle said consolingly.

"No, I don't. It's like a bad dream," said Nan.

"In my bad dreams like that, I don't have any clothes on at all," said Estelle.

At last they reached the strange red brick castle which was the Old Gate House. Estelle, looking white and nervous, led Nan up the steps and under the pointed porch. Nan pulled the large bell pull hanging beside the pointed front door. Then they stood under the arch and waited, more nervous than ever.

For a long time, they thought nobody was going to answer the door. Then, after nearly five minutes, it opened, very slowly and creaking a great deal. A very old lady stood there, leaning on a stick, looking at them in some surprise.

Estelle was so nervous by then that she stuttered. "A—a w—way out in the n—name of D—Dulcinea," she said.

"Oh dear!" said the old lady. "My dears, I'm so sorry. The inquisitors broke up the organization here several years ago. If it wasn't for my age, I'd be in prison now. They come and check up on me every week. I daren't do a thing."

They stood and stared at her in utter dismay.

The old lady saw it. "If it's a real emergency," she said, "I can give you a spell. That's all I can think of. Would you like that?"

They nodded, dismally.

"Then wait a moment, while I write it down," said the old lady. She left the front door open and hobbled aside to a table at one side of the dark old hall. She opened a drawer in it and fumbled for some paper. She searched for a pen. Then she looked across at them. "You know, my dears, in order not to attract attention, you really should look as if you were collecting for charity. I can pretend to be writing you a check. Can either of you manage collecting boxes?"

"I can," said Nan. She had almost lost her voice with fright and dismay. She had to cough. She did not dare risk saying spells, standing there on the steps of the old house, up above the busy street. She simply waved a quivering hand and hoped.

Instant weight bore her hand down. A mighty collecting tin dangled from her arm, and another dangled from Estelle's. Each was as big as a tin of paint. Each had a huge red cross on one side and chinked loudly from their nervous trembling.

"That's better," said the old lady, and started, very slowly, to write.

The outsize tins did indeed make Nan and Estelle feel easier while they waited. People passing certainly looked up at them curiously, but most of them smiled when they saw the tins. And they were standing there for quite a long time, because, as well as writing very slowly, the old lady kept calling across to them.

"Do either of you know the Portway Oaks?" she called. They shook their heads. "Pity. You have to go there to say this," said the old lady. "It's a ring of trees just below the forest. I'd better draw you a map then." She drew, slowly. Then she called, "I don't know why they're called the Oaks. Every single tree there is a beech tree." Later still, she called, "Now I'm writing down the way you should pronounce it."

The girls still stood there. Nan was beginning to wonder if the old lady was really in league with the inquisitors and keeping them there on purpose, when the old lady at last folded up the paper and shuffled back to the front door.

"There you are, my dears. I wish I could do more for you."

Nan took the paper. Estelle produced a bright artificial smile. "Thanks awfully," she said. "What does it do?"

"I'm not sure," said the old lady. "It's been handed down in my family for use in emergencies, but no one has ever used it before. I'm told it's very powerful."

Like many old people, the old lady spoke rather too loudly. Nan and Estelle looked nervously over their shoulders at the street below, but nobody seemed to have heard. They thanked the old lady politely and, when the front door shut, they went drearily back down the steps, lugging their huge collecting tins.

"I suppose we'd better use it," said Estelle. "We daren't go back now."

11

❧·❧

CHARLES JOGGED around the playing field towards the groundsman's hut. He hoped anyone who saw him would think he was out running for PE. For this reason, he had changed into his small sky-blue running shorts before he slipped away. When he had time, he supposed he could transform the shorts into jeans or something. But the important thing at the moment was to get hold of that mangy old broom people had been taunting Nan Pilgrim with the other day. If he got to that before anyone noticed he was missing, he could ride away on it and no dog on earth could pick up his trail.

He reached the hut, in its corner beside the kitchen gardens. He crept around it to its door. At the same moment, Nirupam crept around it from the opposite side, also in sky-blue shorts, and stretched out his long arm for the door too. The two of them stared at one another. All sorts of ideas for things to say streamed through Charles's mind, from explaining he was just dodging PE, to accusing Nirupam of kidnapping Brian. In the end, he said none of these things. Nirupam had hold of the doorlatch by then.

"Bags I the broomstick," Charles said.

"Only if there are two of them," said Nirupam. His face was yellow with fear. He pulled open the door and dodged into the hut. Charles dived in after him.

There was not even the one old broomstick. There were flowerpots, buckets, an old roller, a new roller, four rakes, two spades, a hoe, and an old wet mop propped in one of the buckets. And that was all.

"Who took it?" Charles said wildly.

"Nobody brought it back," said Nirupam.

"Oh, magic it all!" said Charles. "What shall we *do*?"

"Use something else," said Nirupam. "Or walk." He seized the nearest spade and stood astride it, bending and stretching his great long legs. "Fly," he told the spade. "Go on, fly, magic you!"

Nirupam had the right idea, Charles saw. A witch surely ought to be able to make anything fly. "I should think a rake would fly better," he said, and quickly grabbed hold of the wet mop for himself. The mop was so old that it had stuck to the bucket. Charles was forced to put one foot on the bucket and pull, before it came loose, and a lot of the head got left behind in the bucket. The result was a stick ending in a scraggly gray stump. Charles seized it and stood astride it. He jumped up and down. "Fly!" he told the mop. "Quick!"

Nirupam threw the spade down and snatched

up the hoe. Together they jumped desperately around the hut. "Fly!" they panted. "Fly!"

In an old, soggy, dispirited way, the mop obeyed. It wallowed up about three feet into the air and wove towards the hut door. Nirupam was wailing in despair, when the hoe took off too, with a buck and a rush, as if it did not want to be left behind. Nirupam shot past Charles with his huge legs flailing. "It works!" he panted triumphantly, and went off in another kangaroo bound towards the kitchen gardens.

They were forbidden to go in the kitchen gardens, but it seemed the most secret way out of school. Charles followed Nirupam through the gate and down the gravel path, both of them trying to control their mounts. The mop wallowed and wove. It was like an old, old person, feebly hobbling through the air. The hoe either went by kangaroo surges, or it slanted and trailed its metal end along the path. Nirupam had to stick his feet out in front in order not to leave a scent on the ground. His eyes rolled in agony. He kept overtaking Charles and dropping behind. When they got to the wall at the end of the garden, both implements stopped. The mop wallowed about in the air. The hoe jittered its end on the gravel.

"They can't go high enough to get over," said Charles. "Now what?"

That might have been the end of their journey, had not the caretaker's dog been sniffing about in the kitchen gardens and suddenly caught their scent. It came racing down the long path towards them, yapping. The hoe and the mop took off like startled cats. They soared over the wall, with Charles and Nirupam hanging on anyhow, and went bucking off down the fields beyond. They raced towards the main road, the mop surging, the hoe plunging and trailing, clearing hedges by a whisker and missing trees by inches. They did not slow down until they had put three fields between them and the caretaker's dog.

"They must hate that dog as much as we do," Nirupam gasped. "Was it you that did the *Simon Says* spell?"

"Yes," said Charles. "Did you do the birds in music?"

"No," said Nirupam, much to Charles's surprise. "I did only one thing, and that was secret, but I daren't stay if the inquisitors are going to bring a witch-detector. They always get you with those."

"What did you do?" said Charles.

"You know that night all our shoes went into the hall," said Nirupam. "Well, we had a feast that night. Dan Smith made me get up the floorboards and get the food out. He says I have no right to be so large and so weak," Nirupam said resentfully, "and I was hating him for it, when I took the boards up and found a pair of running shoes, with spikes, hidden there with the food. I turned those shoes into a chocolate cake. I knew Dan was so greedy that he would eat it all himself. And he did eat it. He didn't let anyone else have any. You may have noticed that he wasn't quite himself the next day."

So much had happened to Charles that particular day, that he could not remember Dan seeming anything at all. He didn't have the heart to explain all the trouble Nirupam had caused him. "Those were my spikes," he said sadly. He wobbled along on the mop rather awed at the thought of iron spikes passing through Dan's stomach. "He must have a digestion like an ostrich!"

"The spikes were turned into cherries," said Nirupam. "The soles were the cream. The shoes as a whole became what is called a Black Forest gâteau."

Here they reached the main road and saw the tops of cars whipping past beyond the hedge. "We'll have to wait for a gap in that traffic," Charles said. "Stop!" he commanded the mop.

"Stop!" Nirupam cried to the hoe.

Neither implement took the slightest notice. Since Charles and Nirupam did not dare put their feet down for fear of leaving a scent for the dogs, they could find no way of stopping at all. They were carried helplessly over the hedge. Luckily, the road was down in a slight dip, and they had just enough height to clear the whizzing cars. Nirupam frantically bent his huge legs up. Charles tried not to let his legs dangle. Horns honked. He saw faces peering up at them, outraged and grinning. Charles suddenly saw how ridiculous they must look, both in their little blue shorts: himself with the disgraceful dirty old mop head wagging behind him; Nirupam lunging through the air in bunny hops, with a look of anguish on his face.

Horns were still sounding as they cleared the hedge on the other side of the road.

"Oh help!" gasped Nirupam. "Make for the woods, quick, before somebody gets the police!"

Larwood Forest was only a short hillside away and, luckily, their panic seemed to get through to the mop and the hoe. Both put on speed. The wagging and slewing of the mop nearly threw Charles off. The hoe helped itself along by digging its metal end fiercely into the ground, so that Nirupam went upwards like someone on a pogo stick, yelping at each leap. Horns were still sounding from the road as first Nirupam, then Charles reached the trees and plunged in among them. By this time, Nirupam was so far ahead that Charles thought he had lost him. Probably just as well, Charles thought. They might be safer going separate ways. But the mop had other ideas. After dithering a bit, as if it had lost the scent, it set off again at top wallow. Charles was wagged around tree trunks and swayed through prickly undergrowth. Finally he was slewed through a bed of nettles. He yelled. Nirupam yelled too, just beyond the nettles. The hoe tipped him off into a blackberry bush and darted gladly towards an old threadbare broomstick which was leaning on the other side of the brambles. At the sight, the mop threw Charles into the nettles and went bouncing flirtatiously towards the broomstick too, looking just like a granny on an outing.

Charles and Nirupam picked themselves bad-temperedly up. They listened. The motorists on the road seemed to have got tired of sounding their horns. They looked. Beyond the jumping hoe and the nuzzling mop, there was a well-made campfire. Behind the fire, concealed by more brambles, was a small orange tent. Brian Wentworth was standing by the tent, glowering at them.

"I thought I'd got at least one of you arrested," Brian said. "Get lost, can't you! Or are you trying to get me caught?"

"No, we are not!" Charles said angrily. "We're— Hey, listen!"

Somewhere uphill, in the thick part of the wood, a dog gave one whirring, excited bark, and stopped suddenly. Birds were clapping up out of the trees. And Charles's straining ears could also hear a rhythmic swishing, as of heavy feet marching through undergrowth.

"That's the police," he said.

"You fools! You've brought them down on me!" Brian said in a screaming whisper. He grabbed the old broom from between the mop and the hoe and, in one practiced jump, he was on the broom and gliding away across the brambles.

"*He* did the birds in music," Nirupam said, and snatched the hoe. Charles seized the mop and both of them set off after Brian, wavering and hopping across the brambles and in among low trees. Charles kept his head down, because branches were raking at his hair, and thought that Nirupam must be right.

Those birds had appeared promptly in time to save Brian's having to sing. And a parrot shouting "Cuckoo!" was exactly Brian's kind of thing.

They were catching up with the broom, not because they wanted to, but because the mop and the hoe were plainly determined to stay with the broom. They must have spent years together in the groundsman's hut and, Charles supposed irritably, they had got touchingly fond of one another. Nothing he or Nirupam could do would make either implement go a different way. Shortly, Brian was gliding among the trees only a few yards ahead of them.

He turned and glared at them. "Leave me alone! You've spoiled my escape and made me lose my tent. Go away!"

"It was the mop and the hoe," said Charles.

"The police are looking for you, not us," Nirupam panted. "What did you expect? You were missing."

"I didn't expect two great idiots crashing about the forest and bringing the police after me," Brian snarled. "Why couldn't you stay in school?"

"If you didn't want us, you shouldn't have written all that rubbish about a witch putting a spell on you," said Charles. "There's an inquisitor coming today because of you."

"Well, you advised me to do it," Brian said.

Charles opened his mouth and shut it again, quite unable to speak for indignation. They were coming to the edge of the woods now. He could see green fields through a mass of yellow hazel leaves, and he tried to turn the mop aside yet again. If they came out of the woods, they would be seen at once. But the mop obstinately followed the broom.

As they forced their way among whippy hazel boughs, Nirupam panted severely, "You ought to be glad to have some friends with you, Brian."

Brian laughed hysterically. "Friends! I wouldn't be friends with either of you if you paid me! Everyone in 6B laughs at you!"

As Brian said this, there was a sudden clamor of dog noises behind them in the wood. A voice shouted something about a tent. It was plain that the police had found Brian's camp. Brian and the broomstick put on speed and surged out into the field beyond. Charles and Nirupam found themselves being dragged anyhow through the hazel boughs as the mop and the hoe tried to keep up.

Scratched and breathless, they were whirled out into the field on the side of the woods that faced the town. Brian was some way ahead, flying low and fast downhill, towards a clump of trees in the middle of the field. The mop and the hoe surged after him.

"I know Brian is nasty, but I had always thought it was his situation before this," Nirupam remarked, in jerks, as the hoe kangaroo-hopped down the field.

Charles could not answer at once, because he was not sure that a person's character could be separated from his situation in quite this way. While he was wondering how you said this kind of thing aboard a speeding, wallowing mop, when you were hanging on with one hand and holding your glasses with the other, Brian reached the clump of trees and disappeared among them. They heard his voice again, shrill and annoyed, echoing out of the trees.

"Is Brian *trying* to bring the police after us?" Nirupam panted.

Both of them looked over their shoulders, expecting men and dogs to come charging out through the edge of the woods. There was nothing. Next moment, they were swishing through low branches covered with carroty beech leaves. The mop and the hoe jolted to a stop. Charles put his nettled legs down and stood up in a windy rustling space surrounded by pewter-colored tree trunks. He stared at Estelle Green, looking as if she had mislaid a horse. He stared at Nan Pilgrim in ragged pink silk, with the broomstick hopping and sidling affectionately around her.

Brian was standing angrily beside them. "Look at this!" he said to Charles and Nirupam. "The place is alive with you lot! Why can't you let a person run away in peace?"

"Will one of you please shut Brian up?" Estelle said, with great dignity. "We are just about to say a spell that will rescue us all."

"These trees are called the Portway Oaks," Nan explained, and bit the inside of her cheek in order not to laugh. Nirupam riding a hoe was one of the funniest things she had ever seen. And Charles

Morgan's mop looked as if he had slain an old-age pensioner. But she knew she and Estelle looked equally silly, and the boys had not laughed at them.

Brian was still talking angrily. Nirupam let the hoe loose to jump delightedly around the broom and clapped one long brown hand firmly over Brian's mouth. "Go ahead," he said.

"And make it quick," said Charles.

Nan and Estelle bent over their fluttering piece of paper again. The old lady had written just one strange word three times at the top of the paper. Under that, as she had told them, she had written, in shaky capitals, how to say this word: KREST-OH-MAN-SEE. After that she had put, *Go to Portway Oaks and say word three times.* The rest of the paper was full of a very wobbly map.

Estelle and Nan pronounced the word together, three times. "Chrestomanci, Chrestomanci, Chrestomanci."

"Is that all?" asked Nirupam. He took his hand from Brian's face.

"Somebody swindled you!" Brian said. "That's no spell!"

It seemed as if a great gust of wind hit the clump of trees. The branches all around them lashed, and creaked with the strain, so that the air was full of the rushing of leaves. The dead orange leaves from the ground leaped in the air and swirled around them all, around and around, as if the inside of the clump were the center of a whirlwind. This was followed by a sudden stillness. Leaves stayed

where they were, in the air, surrounding everyone. No one could see anything but leaves, and there
was not a sound to be heard from anywhere. Then,
very slowly, sound began again. There was a gentle
rustling as the suspended leaves dropped back to the
ground. Where they had been, there was a man
standing.

He seemed utterly bewildered. His first act was
to put his hands up and smooth his hair, which was
a thing that hardly needed doing, since the wind
had not disturbed even the merest wisp of it. It was
smooth and black and shiny as new tar. Having
smoothed his hair, this man rearranged his starched
white shirt cuffs and straightened his already
straight pale gray cravat. After that, he carefully
pulled down his dove-mauve waistcoat and, equally
carefully, brushed some imaginary dust off his
beautiful dove-gray suit. All the while he was doing
this, he was looking from one to the other of the five
of them in increasing perplexity. His eyebrows rose
higher with everything he saw.

They were all thoroughly embarrassed. Nirupam
tried to hide behind Charles as the man looked at
his little blue shorts. Charles tried to slither behind
Brian. Brian tried to knock the mud off the knees of
his jeans without looking as if he was. The man's
eyes turned to Nan. They were bright black eyes,
which did not seem quite as bewildered as the rest
of the man's face, and they made Nan feel that she
would rather have had no clothes on at all than a
ragged pink balldress. The man looked on towards

Estelle, as if Nan were too painful a sight. Nan looked at Estelle too. Estelle, as she set her hard hat straight, was gazing adoringly up into the man's handsome face.

That was all we needed! Nan thought. Evidently this was the kind of man that Estelle fell instantly in love with. So, not only had they somehow summoned up an over-elegant stranger, but they were no nearer being safe and, to crown it all, there would probably be no sense to be had from Estelle from now on.

"Bless my soul!" murmured the man. He was now staring at the mop, the hoe, and the broom, which were jigging about in a little group like an old folks' reunion. "I think you'd *definitely* better go," he said to them. All three implements vanished, with a faint whistling sound. The man turned to Nan. "What are we all doing here?" he said, a little plaintively. "And where are we?"

12

❧⭒❧

A DOG BARKED EXCITEDLY up the hill. Everyone except the stranger jumped.

"I think we must go now, sir," Nirupam said politely. "That was a police dog. They were looking for Brian, but I think they're looking for the rest of us now."

"What do you expect them to do if they find you?" the man asked.

"Burn us," said Charles, and his thumb ran back and forth over the fat blister on his finger.

"We're all witches, you see, except Estelle," Nan explained.

"So if you don't mind us leaving you——" said Nirupam.

"How very barbarous," said the man. "I think it would be much better if the police and their dogs simply didn't see this clump of trees where we all are, don't you?" He looked vaguely around to see what they thought of this idea. Everyone looked dubious, and Brian downright scornful. "I assure you," the man said to Brian, "that if you go into the field outside and look, you will not see these trees any more than the police will. If the word of an enchanter is not enough for you, go out and see for yourself."

"What enchanter?" Brian said rudely. But of course no one dared leave the trees. They all waited, with their backs prickling, while the voices of policemen came slowly nearer. Finally, they seemed to be just outside the trees.

"Nothing," they heard the policeman saying. "Everyone go back and concentrate on the woods. Hills and MacIver, you two go down and see what those motorists by the hedge are waving about. The rest of you get the dogs back to that tent and start again from there."

After that, the voices all went away. Everyone relaxed a little, and Nan even began to hope that the stranger might be some help. But then he went all plaintive again. "Would one of you tell me where we are now?" he said.

"Just outside Larwood Forest," Nan said. "Hertfordshire."

"In England, the British Isles, the world, the solar system, the Milky Way, the Universe," Brian said scornfully.

"Ah yes," said the man. "But which one?" Brian stared. "I mean," the man said patiently, "do you happen to know *which* world, galaxy, universe, et cetera? There happen to be infinite numbers of them, and unless I know which this one is, I shall not find it very easy to help you."

This gave Charles a very strange feeling. He thought of outer space and bug-eyed monsters and his stomach turned over. His eyes ran over the man's elegant jacket, fascinated, trying to make out if there was room under it for an extra pair of arms. There was not. The man was obviously a human being. "You're not really from another world, are you?" he said.

"I am precisely that," said the man. "Another world full of people just like you, running side by side with this one. There are myriads of them. So which one *is* this one?"

As far as most of them knew, the world was just the world. Everyone looked blank, except Estelle. Estelle said shyly, "There is *one* other world. It's the one the witches' rescue people send witches into to be safe."

"Ah!" The man turned to Estelle, and Estelle blushed violently. "Tell me about this safe world."

Estelle shook her head. "I don't know any more," she whispered, overwhelmed.

"Then let's get at it another way," the man suggested. "You tell me all the events that led up to you summoning me here—"

"Is Chrestomanci your name then?" Estelle interrupted in an adoring whisper.

"I'm usually called that. Yes," said the man. "Was it you who summoned me then?"

Estelle nodded. "Some spell!" Brian said jeeringly.

Brian was plainly determined not to help in any

way. He stayed scornfully silent while the rest of them explained the events which had led up to their being here. Nobody told Chrestomanci quite everything. Brian's contemptuous look made it all feel like a pack of lies anyway. Nan did not mention her meeting with Mr. Wentworth on his hearthrug. She felt rather noble not saying anything about that, considering the way Brian was behaving. She did not mention the way she had described the food, either, though Charles did. On the other hand, Charles did not feel the need to mention the *Simon Says* spell. Nirupam told Chrestomanci about that, but he somehow forgot to say that Dan Smith had eaten Charles's shoes. And when the rest of them had finished, Chrestomanci looked at Brian.

"Your narrative now, please," he said politely.

It was a very powerful politeness. Everyone had thought that Brian was not going to tell anything at all, but, grudgingly, he did. First he admitted to causing the birds in music. Then he claimed that Charles had advised him in the night to run away from school and confuse his trail by blaming the witch. And, while Charles was still stuttering with anger over that, Brian coolly explained that he had discovered Charles was a witch the next morning anyway and got Charles to take him to the matron so that the matron could see the effects of the Evil Eye at first hand. Finally, more grudgingly still, he confessed that he had written the anonymous note to Mr. Crossley and started everything. Then, as an afterthought, he turned on Nan.

"And you kept stealing my broomstick, didn't you?"

"It's not yours. It belongs to the school," said Nan.

At the same time, Charles was saying angrily to Chrestomanci, "It's not true I advised him to blame the witch!"

Chrestomanci was staring vaguely up into the beech trees and did not seem to hear. "The situation is quite impossible," he remarked. "Let us all go and see the old lady who used to run the witches' rescue service."

This struck them all as an excellent idea. It was clear the old lady could rescue them if she wanted. They agreed vigorously. Nirupam said, "But the police—"

"Invisibly, of course," said Chrestomanci. He was still obviously thinking of something else. He turned to walk away between the tree trunks, and, as he did so, everyone flicked out of sight. All that could be seen was the rustling circle of autumn beeches. "Come along," said Chrestomanci's voice.

There followed a minute or so of almost indescribable confusion. It started with Nan assuming she had no body and walking into a tree. She was just as solid as ever, and knocked herself quite silly for a second. "Oh, sorry!" she said to the tree. The rest of them somehow forced their way under the low branches and found themselves out in the field. There, the first thing everybody saw was two cars parked almost in the hedge below, and a number of people from the cars leaning over the hedge to talk to two policemen. From the way all the people kept pointing up at the woods, it was clear they were describing how they saw two witches ride across the road on a mop and a hoe. That panicked everyone. They all set off the other way, towards the town, in a hurry. But as soon as they did, they saw that there was no one ahead of them and waited for the rest to catch up. Then they heard someone speak some way ahead, and ran to catch up. But of course they could not tell where the people they were running after were. Shortly, nobody knew where anybody was or what to do about it.

"Perhaps," Chrestomanci's voice said out of the air, "you could all bring yourselves to hold hands? I have no idea where the Old Gate House is, you see."

Thankfully, everyone grabbed for everyone else. Nan found herself holding Brian's hand and Charles Morgan's. She had never thought the time would come when she would be glad to do that. Estelle had managed to be the one holding Chrestomanci's hand. That became clear when the line of them began to move briskly down to the path that led into town and Estelle's voice could be heard in front, piping up in answer to Chrestomanci's questions.

As soon as there was no chance of anyone else hearing them, Chrestomanci began asking a great many questions. He asked who was prime minister, and which were the most important countries, and what was the EEC, and how many world wars there had been. Then he asked about things from history.

Before long, everyone was giving him answers, and feeling a little superior, because it was really remarkable the number of things Chrestomanci seemed not to know. He had heard of Hitler, though he asked Brian to refresh his memory about him, but he had only the haziest notion about Gandhi or Einstein, and he had never heard of Walt Disney or reggae. Nor had he heard of Dulcinea Wilkes. Nan explained about Dulcinea, and found herself saying, with great pride, that she was descended from Dulcinea.

Why am I saying that? she thought, in sudden alarm. I don't really know it's safe to tell him! And yet, as soon as she thought that, Nan began to see why she had said it. It was the way Chrestomanci was asking those questions. It reminded Nan of the time she had kept coming out in a rash, and her aunt had taken her to a very important specialist. The specialist had worn a very good suit, though it was nothing like as beautiful as Chrestomanci's, and he had asked questions in just the same way, trying to get at Nan's symptoms. Remembering this specialist made Nan feel a lot more hopeful. If you thought of Chrestomanci, in spite of his vagueness and his elegance, as a sort of specialist trying to solve their problems, then you could believe that he might just be able to help them. He was certainly a strong and expert witch. Perhaps he could make the old lady send them somewhere really safe.

When the path led them into the busy streets of the town, Chrestomanci stopped asking questions, but it was clear to Nan that he went on finding symptoms. He made everyone stop while he examined a truck parked by the supermarket. It was just an ordinary truck with Leyland on the front of it and Heinz Meanz Beanz on the side, but Chrestomanci murmured "Good Lord!" as if he was really astonished, before dragging them over to look through the windows of the supermarket. Then he towed them up and down in front of some cars. This part was really frightening. The car windows, the hubcaps, and the glass of the supermarket all showed faint, misty reflections of the six of them. They were quite sure some of the people who were shopping would notice any second.

At last, Chrestomanci let Estelle drag him up the street as far as the tatty draper's where nobody ever seemed to buy anything. "How long have you had decimal currency?" he asked. While they were telling him, the misty reflection in the draper's window showed his tall shape bending to look at some packets of tights and a dingy blue nylon nightdress. "What are these stockings made of?"

"Nylon, of course!" snapped Charles. He was wondering whether to let go of Nan's hand and run away.

Estelle, feeling much the same, heaved on Chrestomanci's hand and led them all in a rush to the doorway of the Old Gate House. She dragged them up the steps and hurriedly rang the bell before Chrestomanci could ask any more questions.

"There was no need to disturb her," Chrestomanci remarked. As he said it, the pointed porch dissolved away around them. Instead, they were in an old-fashioned drawing room, full of little tables with bobbly cloths on and ornaments on the cloth. The old lady was reaching for her stick and trying to lever herself out of her chair, muttering something about "An endless stream of callers today!"

Chrestomanci flicked into sight, tall and elegant and somehow very much in place in that old-fashioned room. Estelle, Nan, Charles, Nirupam, and Brian also flicked into sight, and they looked as much out of place as people could be. The old lady sank back in her chair and stared.

"Forgive the intrusion, madam," Chrestomanci said.

The old lady beamed up at him. "What a splendid surprise!" she said. "No one's appeared like this for years! Forgive me if I don't get up. My knees are very arthritic these days. Would you care for some tea?"

"We won't trouble you, madam," said Chrestomanci. "We came because I understand you are a keeper of some kind of way through."

"Yes, I am," said the old lady. She looked dubious. "If you all have to use it, I suppose you have to, but it will take us hours. It's down in the cellar, you see, hidden from the inquisitors under seven tons of coal."

"I assure you, we haven't come to ask you to

heave coal, madam," said Chrestomanci. No, Charles thought, looking at Chrestomanci's white shirt cuffs. It will be us that does that. "What I really need to know," Chrestomanci went on, "is just which world it is on the other side of the way through."

"I haven't seen it," the old lady said regretfully. "But I've always understood that it's a world exactly like ours, only with no witchcraft."

"Thank you. I wonder——" said Chrestomanci. He seemed to have gone very vague again. "What do you know of Dulcinea Wilkes? Was there much witchcraft here before her day?"

"The Archwitch? Good gracious, yes!" said the old lady. "There were witches all over the place long before Dulcinea. I think it was Oliver Cromwell who made the first laws against witches, but it may be before that. Somebody did once tell me that Elizabeth I was probably a witch. Because of the storm which wrecked the Spanish Armada, you know."

Nan watched Chrestomanci nodding as he listened to this and realized that he was collecting symptoms again. She sighed, and wondered whether to offer to start shoveling the coal.

Chrestomanci sighed a little too. "Pity," he said. "I was hoping the Archwitch was the key to the problems here. Perhaps Oliver Cromwell——?"

"I'm afraid I'm not a historian," the old lady said firmly. "And you won't find many people who know much more. Witch history is banned. All those kinds of books were burned long ago."

Charles, who was as impatient as Nan, butted in here. "Mr. Wentworth knows a lot of witch history, but—"

"Yes!" Nan interrupted eagerly. "If you really want to know, you could summon Mr. Wentworth here. He's a witch too, so it wouldn't matter." Here she realized that Brian was giving her a glare almost up to Charles Morgan's standards, and that Charles himself was staring at her wildly. "Yes, he is," she said. "You know he is, Brian. I met him out flying on his hearthrug last night, and he thought I was you on your broomstick."

That explained everything, Charles thought. The night Mr. Wentworth had vanished, he had gone out flying. The window had been wide open and, now he understood, Charles could remember distinctly the bald place in front of the gas fire where the ragged hearthrug had been. And it explained that time in detention, too, when he had thought his glasses were broken. They *were* broken, and Mr. Wentworth had restored them by witchcraft.

"Can't you keep your big mouth shut?" Brian said furiously to Nan. He pointed to Chrestomanci. "How do we know he's safe? For all *we* know, he could be the Devil that you summoned up!"

"Oh, you flatter me, Brian," Chrestomanci said.

The old lady looked shocked. "What an unpleasant thing to say," she said to Brian. "Hasn't anyone told you that the Devil, however he appears, is *never* a perfect gentleman? Quite unlike this Mr.—er—Mr.—?" She looked at Chrestomanci with her eyebrows politely ráised.

"Chrestomanci, madam," he said. "Which reminds me. I wish you would tell me how you came to give Estelle and Nan my name."

The old lady laughed. "Was that what the spell was? I had no idea. It has been handed down in my family from my great-grandmother's time, with strict instructions that it's only to be used in an emergency. And those two poor girls were in such trouble—but I refuse to believe you can be that old, my dear sir."

Chrestomanci smiled. "No. Brian will be sorry to hear that the spell must have been meant to call one of my predecessors. Now. Shall we go? We must go to your school and consult Mr. Wentworth, evidently."

They stared at him, even the old lady. Then, as it dawned on them that Chrestomanci was not going to let them go into the coal cellar to safety, everyone broke out into protest. Brian, Charles, and Nan said, "Oh no! Please!" The old lady said, "Aren't you taking rather a risk?" at the same moment as Nirupam said, "But I told you there's an inquisitor coming to school!" And Estelle added, "Couldn't we just all stay here quietly while *you* go and see Mr. Wentworth?"

Chrestomanci looked from Estelle to Nirupam, to Nan, and then at Brian and Charles. He seemed astounded, and not vague at all. The room seemed to go very quiet and sinister and unloving. "What's all this?" he said. It was so gentle that they all shivered. "I did understand you, didn't I? The five of you, between you, turn your school upside down. You cause what I am sure is a great deal of trouble to a great many teachers and policemen. You summon me a long way from some extremely important business, in a manner which makes it very difficult for me to get back. And now you all propose just to walk out and leave the mess you've made. Is that what you mean?"

"I didn't summon you," said Brian.

"It wasn't our fault," Charles said. "I didn't ask to be a witch."

Chrestomanci looked at him with faint, chilly surprise. "Didn't you?" The way he said it made Charles actually wonder, for a moment, if he had somehow chosen to be born a witch. "And so," said Chrestomanci, "you think your troubles give you a right to get this lady into much worse trouble with the inquisitors? Is that what you all say?"

Nobody said anything.

"I think we shall be going now," Chrestomanci said, "if you would all hold one another's hands again, please." Wordlessly, they all held out hands and took hold. Chrestomanci took hold of Brian's, but, before he took hold of Estelle's in the other hand, he took the old lady's veined and knobby hand and kissed it. The old lady was delighted. She winked excitedly at Nan over Chrestomanci's smooth head. Nan did not even feel up to smiling back. "Lead the way, Estelle," Chrestomanci said, straightening up and taking Estelle's hand. They found themselves invisible again. And, the same instant, they were outside in the street.

Estelle set off toward Larwood House. If it had been anybody else but Estelle in the lead, Charles thought, they might have thought of taking the line of them somewhere else—anywhere else—because Chrestomanci would not know. But Estelle led them straight to school, and everyone else shuffled after, too crushed and nervous to do anything else. Brian was the only one who protested. Whenever there were no people about, his voice could be heard saying that it wasn't *fair*. "What did you girls have to fetch him for?" he kept saying.

By the time they were through the school gates and shuffling up the drive, Brian gave up protesting. Estelle led them to the main door, the grand one, which was only used for parents or visitors like Lord Mulke. There were two police cars parked on the gravel beside it, but they were empty and there was no one about.

Here, in a sharp scuffling of gravel, Brian made a determined effort to run away. To judge by the sounds, and by the way Estelle came feeling her way along Nirupam and Nan, Chrestomanci was after Brian like a shot. Three thumps, and a scatter of small stones, and Chrestomanci suddenly reappeared, beside the nearest police car. He seemed to be on his own, but his right arm was stiffly bent and jerking a little, as the invisible Brian writhed on the end of it.

"I do advise you all to keep quite close to me," he said, as if nothing had happened. "You will only be invisible within ten yards of me."

"I can make myself invisible," Brian's voice said, from beside Chrestomanci's dove-gray elbow. "I'm a witch too."

"Quite probably," Chrestomanci agreed. "But I am not a witch, as it happens. I am an enchanter. And, among other differences, an enchanter is ten times as strong as a witch. Who is at the end of the line now? Charles. Charles, will you be good enough to walk up the steps to the door and ring the bell?"

Charles trudged forward, towing the others behind him, and rang the bell. There seemed nothing else to do.

The door was opened almost at once by the school secretary. Chrestomanci stood there, apparently alone, with his dove-gray suit quite unruffled and not a hair out of place, smiling pleasantly at the secretary. It was hard to believe that he had Brian gripped in one hand and Estelle clinging to the other, and three more people crowded uncomfortably around him. He bowed slightly.

"Name of Chant," he said. "I believe you were expecting me. I'm the inquisitor."

13

❖

THE SCHOOL SECRETARY dissolved into dither. She gushed. It was just as well. Otherwise she might have heard five gasps out of the air around Chrestomanci.

"Oh, *do* come in, inquisitor," the secretary gushed. "Miss Cadwallader is expecting you. And I'm awfully sorry—we seem to have got your name wrong. We were told to expect a Mr. Littleton."

"Quite right," Chrestomanci said blandly. "Littleton is the regional inquisitor. But head office decided the matter was too grave to be merely regional. I'm the divisional inquisitor."

"Oh!" said the secretary, and seemed quite overawed. She ushered Chrestomanci in and through the tiled hall. Chrestomanci stepped after her, slow and stately, in a way that allowed plenty of time for everyone to squeeze around him into the hall and tiptoe beside him across the tiles. The secretary threw wide the door to Miss Cadwallader's study. "Mr. Chant, Miss Cadwallader. The divisional inquisitor." Chrestomanci went into the study even more slowly, lugging Brian and pulling Estelle. Nan and Nirupam squeezed after, and Charles just got in too by jamming himself against the doorpost as the secretary backed reverently out. He did not want to be left outside the circle of invisibility.

Miss Cadwallader sprang forward in a quite unusual flutter and shook hands with Chrestomanci. The rest of them heard Brian thump away sideways as Chrestomanci let go of him. "Oh, good morning, inquisitor!"

"Morning, morning," said Chrestomanci. He seemed to have gone vague again. He looked absently around the room while he was shaking hands. "Nice place you have here, Miss—er—Cudwollander."

This was true. Perhaps on the grounds that she had to persuade government officials and parents that Larwood House was a really good school, Miss Cadwallader had surrounded herself in luxury. Her carpet was like deep crimson grass. Her chairs were purple clouds of softness. She had marble statues on her mantelpiece and large gilt frames around her hundred or so pictures. She had a cocktail cabinet with a little refrigerator built into it and a coffee-maker on top. Her hi-fi and tape deck took up most of one wall. Charles looked yearningly at her vast television with a crinoline doll on top. It seemed years since he had watched any television. Nan gazed at the wall of bright new books. Most of them seemed to be mystery stories. She would have loved to have a closer look at them, but she did not dare let go of Nirupam or Charles in case she never found them again.

"I'm so glad you approve, inquisitor," fluttered Miss Cadwallader. "My room is entirely at your disposal, if you wish to use it to interview children in. I take it that you will need to interview some of the children in 6B?"

"All the children in 6B," Chrestomanci said gravely, "and probably all their teachers too." Miss Cadwallader looked thoroughly dismayed by this. "I shall expect to interview everyone in the school before I'm through," Chrestomanci went on. "I shall stay here for as long as it takes—weeks, if necessary—to get to the bottom of this matter."

By this time, Miss Cadwallader was distinctly pale. She clasped her hands nervously. "Are you sure it's *that* serious, inquisitor? It *is* only a boy in 6B who disappeared in the night. His father happens to be one of our teachers here, which is really why we're so concerned. I know you were told that the boy left a large number of notes accusing a witch of abducting him, but the police have telephoned since to say they have found a camp in the forest with the boy's scent on it. Don't you think the whole thing could be cleared up quite easily and quickly?"

Chrestomanci gravely shook his head. "I have been kept abreast of the facts too, Miss—er—Kidwelly. The boy has still not turned up, has he? One can't be too careful in a case like this. I think someone in 6B knows more about this than you think."

Up to now, everyone listening had been feeling more and more relieved. If Miss Cadwallader had known there were four other people missing besides Brian, she would surely have said so. But their feelings changed at what Miss Cadwallader said next.

"You must interview a girl called Theresa Mullett straightaway, inquisitor, and I think you will find that the matter will be cleared up at once. Theresa is one of our *good* girls. She came to me during break and told me that the witch is almost certainly a child called Dulcinea Pilgrim. Dulcinea is *not* one of our good girls, inquisitor, I'm sorry to say. Some of her journal entries have been very free-spoken and disaffected. She questions everything and makes jokes about serious matters. If you like, I can send for Dulcinea's journal and you can see for yourself."

"I shall read all the journals in 6B," said Chrestomanci, "in good time. But is this all you have to go on, Miss—er—Collander? I can't find a girl a witch simply on hearsay and a few jokes. It's not professional. Have you no other suspects? Teachers, for instance—"

"Teachers here are all above suspicion, inquisitor." Miss Cadwallader said this very firmly, although her voice was a little shrill. "But 6B as a class are not. It is a sad fact, inquisitor, in a school like this, that a number of children come to us as witch-orphans, having had one or both parents burned. There are an unusual number of these in 6B. I would pick out, for your immediate attention,

Nirupam Singh, who had a brother burned, Estelle Green, whose mother is in prison for helping witches escape, and a boy called Charles Morgan, who is almost as undesirable as the Pilgrim girl."

"Dear me! What a poisonous state of affairs!" said Chrestomanci. "I see I must get down to work at once."

"I shall leave you this room of mine to work in then, inquisitor," Miss Cadwallader said graciously. She seemed to have recovered from her flutter.

"Oh, I can't possibly trouble you," Chrestomanci said, quite as graciously. "Doesn't your deputy head have a study I could use?"

Intense relief shone through Miss Cadwallader's stately manner. "Yes, indeed he does, inquisitor. What an excellent idea! I shall take you to Mr. Wentworth myself, at once."

Miss Cadwallader swept out of her room, almost too relieved to be stately. Chrestomanci located Brian as easily as if he could see him, took his arm, and swept off after her. The other four were forced to tiptoe furiously to keep up. None of them wanted to see Mr. Wentworth. In fact, after what Miss Cadwallader had just said, the one thing they all longed to do was to sneak off and run away again. But the instant they got more than ten yards away from Chrestomanci, there they would be, in riding clothes, little blue shorts, and pink balldress, for Miss Cadwallader or anyone else they passed to see. That was enough to keep them all tiptoeing hard, along the corridors and up the stairs.

Miss Cadwallader rapped on the glass of Mr. Wentworth's study. "Come in!" said Mr. Wentworth's voice. Miss Cadwallader threw the door open and made ushering motions to Chrestomanci. Chrestomanci nodded vaguely and once more made a slow and imposing entry, with a slight dragging noise as he pulled the resisting Brian through the doorway. That gave the other four plenty of time to slip inside past Miss Cadwallader.

"I'll leave you with Mr. Wentworth for now, inquisitor," Miss Cadwallader said, in the doorway. Mr. Wentworth, at that, looked up from his schedules. When he saw Chrestomanci, his face went pale, and he stood up slowly, looking thoroughly harrowed. "Mr. Wentworth," said Miss Cadwallader, "this is Mr. Chant, who is the divisional inquisitor. Come to my study for sherry before lunch, both of you, please." Then obviously feeling she had done enough, Miss Cadwallader shut the door and went away.

"Good morning," Chrestomanci said politely.

"G—good morning," said Mr. Wentworth. His hands were trembling and rustling the schedules. He swallowed, loudly. "I—I didn't realize there were divisional inquisitors. New post, is it?"

"Oh, do you not have divisional ones?" Chrestomanci said. "What a shame. I thought it sounded so imposing."

He nodded. Everybody was suddenly visible again. Nan, Charles, and Nirupam all tried to hide behind one another. Brian was revealed tugging crossly to get his arm loose from Chrestomanci, and Estelle was hanging on to Chrestomanci's other hand again. She let go hurriedly and took her hard hat off. But it was quite certain that Mr. Wentworth did not notice any of these things. He backed against the window, staring from Chrestomanci to Brian, and he was more than harrowed now: he was terrified.

"What's going on?" he said. "Brian, what have you lent yourself to?"

"Nothing," Brian said irritably. "He isn't an inquisitor. He's an enchanter or something. It's not my fault he's here."

"What does he want?" Mr. Wentworth said wildly. "I haven't anything I can give him!"

"My dear sir," said Chrestomanci, "please try and be calm. I only want your help."

Mr. Wentworth pressed back against the window. "I don't know what you mean!"

"Yes, you do," Chrestomanci said pleasantly. "But let me explain. I am Chrestomanci. This is the title that goes with my post, and my job is controlling witchcraft. My world is somewhat more happily placed than yours, I believe, because witchcraft is not illegal there. In fact, this very morning I was chairing a meeting of the Walpurgis Committee, in the middle of making final arrangements for the Halloween celebrations, when I was rather suddenly summoned away by these pupils of yours—"

"Is that why you're wearing those beautiful clothes?" Estelle asked admiringly.

Everyone winced a little, except for Chrestomanci, who seemed to think it was a perfectly reasonable question. "Well, no, to be quite honest," he said. "I like to be well dressed, because I am always liable to be called elsewhere, the way you called me. But I have to confess that I have several times been fetched away in my dressing gown, in spite of all my care." He looked at Mr. Wentworth again, obviously expecting him to have calmed down by now. "There are real problems with this particular call," he said. "Your world is all wrong, in a number of ways. That's why I would appreciate your help, sir."

Unfortunately, Mr. Wentworth was by no means calm. "How dare you talk to me like this!" he said. "It's pure blackmail! You'll get no help from me!"

"Now that is unreasonable, sir," Chrestomanci said. "These children are in acute trouble. You are in the same trouble yourself. Your whole world is in even greater trouble. Please, try if you can, to forget that you have been scared for years, both for yourself and Brian, and listen to the questions I am going to ask you."

But Mr. Wentworth seemed unable to be reasonable. Nan looked at him sorrowfully. She had always thought he was such a firm person up till now. She felt quite disillusioned. So did Charles. He remembered Mr. Wentworth's hand on his shoulder, pushing him back into detention. He had thought that hand had been shaking with anger, but he realized now that it had been terror.

"It's a trick!" Mr. Wentworth said. "You're trying to get a confession out of me. You're using Brian. You *are* an inquisitor!"

Just as he said that, there was a little tap at the door, and Miss Hodge came brightly in. She had just given 6B an English lesson—the last one until next Tuesday, thank goodness! Naturally, she had noticed that four other people besides Brian were now missing. At first, she had assumed that they were all being questioned by the inquisitor. They were the obvious ones. But then someone in the staff room had remarked that the inquisitor still hadn't come. Miss Hodge saw at once that this was the excuse she needed to go to Mr. Wentworth and start sympathizing with him about Brian. She came in as soon as she had knocked, to make quite sure that Mr. Wentworth did not get away again.

The room for an instant seemed quite full of people, and poor Mr. Wentworth was looking so upset and shouting at what seemed to be the inquisitor after all. The inquisitor gave Miss Hodge a vague look and then waved his hand, just the smallest bit. After that, there did only seem to be the inquisitor and Mr. Wentworth in the room besides Miss Hodge. But Miss Hodge knew what she had seen. She thought about it while she said what she had come to say.

"Oh, Mr. Wentworth, I'm afraid there are four more people missing from 6B now." And the four people had all been here in the room, Miss Hodge knew. Wearing such peculiar things too. And Brian

had been there as well. That settled it. Mr.
Wentworth might look upset, but he was not sor-
rowing about Brian. That meant that she either
had to think of some other way to get his attention,
or use the advantage she knew she had. The man
who was supposed to be an inquisitor was politely
putting forward a chair for her to sit in. A smooth
villain. Miss Hodge ignored the chair. "I think
I'm interrupting a witches' Sabbath," she said
brightly.

The man with the chair raised his eyebrows as
if he thought she was mad. A very smooth villain.
Mr. Wentworth said, in a strangled sort of way,
"This is the divisional inquisitor, Miss Hodge."

Miss Hodge laughed, triumphantly. "Mr.
Wentworth! You and I both know that there's no
such thing as a divisional inquisitor! Is this man
annoying you? If so, I shall go straight to Miss
Cadwallader. I think she has a right to know that
your study is full of witches."

Chrestomanci sighed and wandered away to
Mr. Wentworth's desk, where he idly picked up one
of the schedules. Mr. Wentworth's eyes followed
him as if Chrestomanci was annoying him very
much, but he said, in a resigned way, "There's
absolutely no point in going to Miss Cadwallader,
Miss Hodge. Miss Cadwallader has known I'm a
witch for years. She takes most of my salary in
return for not telling anyone."

"I didn't know you—!" Miss Hodge began. She
had not realized Mr. Wentworth was a witch too.

That made quite a difference. She smiled more triumphantly than before. "In that case, let me offer you an alliance against Miss Cadwallader, Mr. Wentworth. You marry me, and we'll both fight her."

"Marry you?" Mr. Wentworth stared at Miss Hodge in obvious horror. "Oh no. You can't. I can't—"

Brian's voice said out of the air, "I'm not having *her* as a mother!"

Chrestomanci looked up from the schedules. He shrugged. Brian appeared on the other side of the room, looking as horrified as Mr. Wentworth. Miss Hodge smiled again. "So I was right!" she said.

"Miss Hodge," Mr. Wentworth said, shakily trying to sound calm and reasonable, "I'm sorry to disappoint you, but I can't marry anyone. My wife is still alive. She was arrested as a witch, but she managed to get away through someone's backyard and get to the witches' rescue service. So you see—"

"Well, you'd better pretend she was burned," Miss Hodge said. She was very angry. She felt cheated. She marched up to Mr. Wentworth's desk and took hold of the receiver of Mr. Wentworth's telephone. "You agree to marry me, or I ring the police about you. Now."

"No, please—!" said Mr. Wentworth.

"I mean it," said Miss Hodge. She tried to pick the receiver up off the telephone. It seemed to be stuck. Miss Hodge jiggled it angrily. It gave out a lot of tinkling, but it would not seem to move. Miss

Hodge looked around to find Chrestomanci looking at her in an interested way. "You stop that!" she said to him.

"When you tell me one thing," Chrestomanci said. "You don't seem at all alarmed to find yourself in a roomful of witches. Why not?"

"Of course I'm not," Miss Hodge retorted. "I pity witches. Now will you please allow me to ring the police about Mr. Wentworth? He's been deceiving everyone for years!"

"But my dear young lady," said Chrestomanci, "so have you. The only sort of person who would behave as you do must be a witch herself."

Miss Hodge stared at him haughtily. "I have never used a spell in my life," she said.

"A slight exaggeration," Chrestomanci said. "You used one small spell, to make sure no one knew you were a witch."

Why didn't I think of that? Charles wondered, watching the look of fear and dismay grow in Miss Hodge's face. He was very shaken. He could not get used to the idea that his second witch had probably been Brian's mother.

Miss Hodge once more jiggled the telephone. It was still stuck. "Very well," she said. "I'm not afraid of you. You can disable all the phones in the school if you like, but you won't stop me going and telling everyone I meet about you and Mr. Wentworth and Brian, and the other four, unless Mr. Wentworth agrees to marry me this instant. I think I shall start with Harold Crossley." She made as if to turn away and leave the room. It was clear she meant it.

Chrestomanci sighed and put one finger down on the schedule he was holding, very carefully and precisely, in the middle of one of the rectangles marked *Miss Hodge 6B*. And Miss Hodge was not there anymore. The telephone gave out a small *ting*, and she was gone. At the same moment, Nan, Estelle, Nirupam, and Charles all found themselves visible again. It was clear to them that Miss Hodge was not just invisible in their place. The room felt empty of her, and a small gust of wind ruffling the papers on Mr. Wentworth's desk seemed to prove she was gone.

"Fancy her being a witch!" said Nirupam. "Where is she?"

Chrestomanci examined the schedule. "Er—next Tuesday, I believe. That should give us time to sort out this wretched situation. Unless we are very unlucky, of course." He looked at Mr. Wentworth. "Perhaps you would be ready to help us do that now, sir?"

But Mr. Wentworth sank into the chair behind his desk and covered his face with his hands.

"You never told me Mum got away," Brian said to him accusingly. "And you never said a word about Miss Cadwallader."

"You never told me you intended to go and camp in the forest," Mr. Wentworth said wearily. "Oh Lord! Where shall I get an extra teacher from? I've got to find someone to take Miss Hodge's lessons this afternoon somehow."

Chrestomanci sat in the chair he had put out for Miss Hodge. "It never ceases to amaze me," he said, "the way people always manage to worry about the wrong things. My dear sir, do you realize that you, your son, and four of your pupils are all likely to be burned unless we do something? And here you are worrying about schedules."

Mr. Wentworth lifted his harrowed face and stared past Chrestomanci. "How did she *do* it?" he said. "How does she keep it up? How *can* Miss Hodge be a teacher and not use witchcraft at all? I use it all the time. How else can I have eyes in the back of my head?"

"One of the great mysteries of our time," Chrestomanci agreed. "Now please listen to me. You are aware, I believe, that there is at least one other world besides this one. It seems to be your custom to send escaped witches there. I presume your wife is there. What you may not realize is that these are only two out of a multitude of worlds, all very different from one another. I come from one of the other ones myself."

To everyone's relief, Mr. Wentworth listened to this. "Alternative worlds, you mean?" he said. "There's been some speculation about that. If-worlds, counterfactuals, and so on. You mean they're real?"

"As real as you are," Chrestomanci said.

Nirupam was very interested in this. He doubled himself up on the floor beside Chrestomanci's beautifully creased trousers and said, "They are made from the great events in history, I believe, sir, where it is possible for things to go two ways. It is easiest to understand with battles. Both sides cannot win a battle, so each war makes two possible worlds, with a different side winning. Like the Battle of Waterloo. In our world, Napoleon lost it, but another world at once split off from ours, in which Napoleon won the battle."

"Exactly," said Chrestomanci. "I find that world a rather trying one. Everyone speaks French there and winces at my accent. The only place they speak English there, oddly enough, is in India, where they are very British and eat treacle pudding after their curry."

"I should like that," Nirupam said.

"Everyone to his taste," Chrestomanci said with a slight shudder. "But, as you will see, exactly who won the Battle of Waterloo made a great deal of difference between those two worlds. And that is the rule. A surprisingly small change always alters the new world almost out of recognition. Except in the case of this world of yours, where we all now are." He looked at Mr. Wentworth. "This is what I need your help about, sir. There is something badly wrong with this world. The fact that witches are extremely common, and illegal, should have made as much difference here as it does in my own world, where witches are equally common, but quite legal. But it does not. Estelle, perhaps you can tell us about the world where the witches' rescue service sends witches."

Estelle beamed up at him adoringly from where she was sitting cross-legged on the floor. "The old lady said it was just like this one, only with no witchcraft," she said.

"And that is just the trouble," said Chrestomanci. "I know that world rather well, because I have a young ward who used to belong in it. And since I have been here, I have discovered that events in history here, cars, advertisements, goods in shops, money—everything I can check—are all exactly the same as those in my ward's world. And this is quite wrong. No two worlds are ever this alike."

Mr. Wentworth was attending quite keenly now. He frowned. "What do you think has gone wrong?" And Nan thought, So he *was* finding out symptoms!

Chrestomanci looked around them all, vaguely and dubiously, before he said, "If you'll forgive me saying, your world should not exist." They all stared. "I mean it," Chrestomanci said, apologetically. "I have often wondered why there is so little witchcraft in my ward's world. I see now that it is all in this one. Something—I don't know what—has caused your world to separate from the other one, taking all the witchcraft with it. But instead of breaking off cleanly, it has somehow remained partly joined to the first world, so that it almost *is* that world. I think there has been some kind of accident. You shouldn't get a civilized world where witches are burned. As I said, it ought not to exist. So, as I have been trying to explain to you all along,

Mr. Wentworth, I urgently need a short history of witchcraft, in order to discover what kind of accident happened here. Was Elizabeth I a witch?"

Mr. Wentworth shook his head. "Nobody knows for sure. But witchcraft didn't seem to be that much of a problem in her reign. Witches were mostly just old women in villages then. No—modern witchcraft really started soon after Elizabeth I died. There seems to have been a big increase in about 1606, when the first official bonfires started. The first Witchcraft Edict was passed in 1612. Oliver Cromwell passed more. There had been thirty-four Witchcraft Acts passed by 1760, the year Dulcinea Wilkes—"

But Chrestomanci held up one hand to stop him there. "Thank you. I know about the Archwitch. You've told me what I need to know. The present state of witchcraft began quite suddenly soon after 1600. That means that the accident we're looking for must have happened around then. Have you any idea what it might be?"

Mr. Wentworth shook his head again, rather glumly. "I haven't a notion. But—suppose you did know, what could you do about it?"

"One of two things," said Chrestomanci. "Either we could break this world away completely from the other one, which I don't consider a good idea, because then you would certainly all be burned—" Everybody shuddered, and Charles's thumb found itself running back and forth over the blister on his finger. "Or," said Chrestomanci, "and this is a much better idea, we could put your world back into the other one, where it really belongs."

"What would happen to us if you did?" asked Charles.

"Nothing much. You would simply melt quietly into the people you really are in that world," said Chrestomanci.

Everyone considered this in silence for a moment. "Can that really be done?" Mr. Wentworth asked hopefully.

"Well," said Chrestomanci, "it can, as long as we can find what caused the split in the first place. It will take strong magic. But it *is* Halloween and there ought to be a great deal of magic loose in this world particularly, and we can draw on that. Yes. I'm sure it can be done, though it may not be easy."

"Then let's do it," said Mr. Wentworth. The idea seemed to restore him to his usual self. He stood up, and his eyes roved grimly across the riding clothes, the sky-blue shorts and Brian's jeans, and rested incredulously upon the tattered pink ball-dress. "If you lot think you can appear in class like that," he said. He was back to being a schoolmaster again.

"Er, leave Brian, I think," Chrestomanci said quickly.

"You will have plenty of time to reconsider in detention," Mr. Wentworth finished. Nan, Estelle, Charles, and Nirupam all scrambled hurriedly to their feet. And as soon as they were standing up, they found they were wearing school uniforms. They looked around for Brian, but he did not seem to be there.

"I'm invisible again!" Brian said disgustedly, out of the air.

Chrestomanci was smiling. "Not bad, sir," he said to Mr. Wentworth. Mr. Wentworth looked pleased, and, as he shepherded the four of them to the door, he smiled back at Chrestomanci in quite a friendly way.

"Why is Brian allowed to stay invisible?" Estelle complained, as Mr. Wentworth marched them back toward the classroom.

"Because he gives Chrestomanci an excuse to go on staying here as an inquisitor," Nirupam whispered. "He is supposed to be finding what the witch has done with Brian."

"But don't tell Brian," Charles muttered, as they arrived outside the door of 6B. "He'd spoil it. He's like that." The truth was, he was not so sure he would not spoil things himself if he got the chance. Nothing had been changed. He was still in as much trouble as ever.

14

Mr. Wentworth opened the door and ushered the four of them into the classroom, into a blast of stares and whispers. "I'm afraid I had to kidnap these four," Mr. Wentworth said to Mr. Crossley, who happened to be teaching the rest. "We've been arranging my study for the inquisitor to use."

Mr. Crossley seemed to believe this without question. 6B, to judge from their faces, felt it was an awful letdown. They had expected all four of them to have been arrested. But they made the best of it.

"Mr. Towers is looking for you two," Simon whispered righteously to Nirupam and Charles. And Theresa said to Estelle, "Miss Phillips wants you." Nan was lucky. Miss Phillips never remembered Nan if she could help it.

They had arrived back so late that there was only a short piece of lesson left before lunchtime. When the bell rang for lunch, Charles and Nirupam kept to the thickest crowds. Neither of them wanted Mr. Towers to see them. But Charles had his usual bad luck. Mr. Towers was on duty at the door of the dining hall. Charles was very relieved when he slipped past without Mr. Towers showing any interest in him at all.

Nirupam nudged Charles as they sat down after grace. Chrestomanci was sitting beside Miss Cadwallader at high table, looking bland and vague. Everyone craned to look at him. Word went around that this was the divisional inquisitor.

"I don't fancy getting on the wrong side of him," Dan Smith observed. "You can see that sleepy look's just there to fool you."

"He looks feeble," said Simon. "I'm not going to let him scare me."

Charles craned to look too. He knew what Simon meant, but he was quite sure by now that Chrestomanci's vague look was as deceptive as Dan thought. Mr. Wentworth was up at high table too. Charles wondered where Brian was and how Brian would get any lunch.

Charles turned back to the table to hear Theresa saying, "He is so super looking, he makes me feel quite weak!"

To everyone's surprise, Estelle jumped to her feet and leaned across the table, glaring at Theresa. "Theresa Mullett!" she said. "You just dare be in love with the inquisitor and see what you get! He's mine. I met him first and *I* love him! So you just dare!"

Nobody said a word for a moment. Theresa was too astonished even to giggle. Everyone was so unused to seeing Estelle so fierce that even the monitor in charge could not think what to say.

During the silence, it became clear how Brian was going to get lunch. Charles and Nirupam felt themselves being pushed apart by an invisible body. Both of them were jabbed by invisible elbows as the body climbed onto the bench between them and sat. "You'll have to let me eat off your plates," whispered Brian's voice. "I hope it's not stew."

Luckily, Simon broke the silence just as Brian spoke. He said, in a jeering, not-quite-believing way, "And what took you all so long to arrange for Mr. Feeble Inquisitor?"

From the way everyone looked then, Nan knew nobody had believed Mr. Wentworth's excuse for an instant. She could see most of them suspected something like the truth. Help! thought Nan. "Well we had to put a lot of electric wiring into the study," she invented hastily. "He has to have a bright light arranged to shine into people's faces. It helps break them down."

"Not for electric shocks at all?" Dan asked hopefully.

"Some of it *may* have been," Nan admitted. "There were quite a lot of bare wires, and a sort of helmet thing with electrodes sticking out of it. Charles wired that. Charles is very good with electricity."

"And what else?" Dan asked breathlessly. He was far too fascinated by now to notice he was talking to a girl.

"The walls were all draped in black," invented Nan. "Estelle and I did that."

Lunch was served just then. It was potato pie. This was fortunate for Brian, who dared not use a knife and fork, but not so lucky for Charles and Nirupam. Both of them gave grunts of indignation as a large curved chunk vanished from their plates. Brian had taken a handful from each. They were more annoyed still, when lumps of potato began to flop down between them.

"Don't waste it!" snapped Nirupam.

"Can't you tell where your mouth is?" Charles whispered angrily.

"Yes. But I don't know where my hands are," Brian whispered back. "*You* try, if you think you're so clever!"

While they whispered, Nan was being eagerly questioned by Dan, and forced to invent more and more inquisitor's equipment for Mr. Wentworth's study. "Yes, there *were* these things with little chromium screws," she was saying. "I think you're right—those must have been thumbscrews. But some of them looked big enough to get an arm or a leg in. I don't think he stops at thumbs."

Nirupam dug Brian's invisible side with his elbow. "Listen to this!" he whispered. "It all has to be there if he calls Dan in."

"I'm not a fool," Brian's voice retorted with its mouth full.

"And of course there were a lot of other things we had to hang on the wall. All sizes of handcuffs," Nan went on. She was inspired now and her invention seemed boundless. She just could not seem to stop. Charles began to wonder if one small study could possibly hold all the things she was describing—or even only the half of it that Brian managed to remember.

Fortunately, Estelle, who was far too busy watching Chrestomanci to eat, caused a sudden diversion by shouting out, "Look, look! Miss Cadwallader's only using a fork, and *he's* using a knife and a fork! Oh, isn't he *brave!*"

At that, Nirupam seized the opportunity to try and shut Nan up. He gave her a sinister stare and said loudly, "You realize that the inquisitor will probably be questioning every one of us very searchingly indeed, after lunch is over."

Though Nirupam meant this simply as a warning to Nan, it caused a worried silence. A surprising number of people did not seem very keen on the treacle tart which followed the potato pie. Nirupam seized that opportunity too. He took third and fourth helpings and shared them with Brian.

Straight after lunch, Mr. Wentworth came and marshaled the whole of 6B into alphabetical order. The worried silence became a scared one. From the looks they saw on faces of the rest of the school, the scare was catching. Even seniors looked alarmed as 6B were marched away. They marched upstairs and were lined up half in the passage and half on the stairs, while Mr. Wentworth went into his study to tell Chrestomanci they were ready. Those at the front of the line were able to see that the wavy glass in the door was now black as night.

Then it turned out that Chrestomanci wanted to see them in reverse alphabetical order. They all had to march up and down and around again, so that Heather Young and Ronald West were at the front of the line instead of Geoffrey Barnes and Deborah Clifton. They did it with none of the usual grumbling and scuffling. Even Charles, who was quite certain that they were only marching to give Chrestomanci time to put all Nan's inventions in, found himself a little quiet and queasy, with his thumb rubbing at that blister. Heather and Ronald looked quite ill with terror. Dan Smith—who was third now that Brian was missing—asked Nirupam in an urgent whisper, "What's he going to do with us?"

Nirupam had no more idea than Dan. He had not even known that Chrestomanci really was going to question them. He tried to look sinister. "You'll see." Dan's face went cream-colored.

Chrestomanci did not see people for the same length of time. Heather disappeared into the study for what seemed an endless age, and she came out as frightened as she went in. Ronald was only in for a minute, and he came out from behind the darkened door looking relieved. He leaned across Dan and Nirupam to whisper to Simon, "No problem at all!"

"I knew there wouldn't be," Simon lied loftily.

"Quiet!" bellowed Mr. Wentworth. "Next—Daniel Smith."

Dan Smith was not gone long either, but he did not come out looking as if there were no problem.

His face was more like cheese than cream.

Nirupam was gone for much longer than either Nan or Charles had expected. When he came out, he was frowning and uneasy. He was followed by Simon. There was another endless wait. During it, the bell rang for afternoon lessons, and was followed by the usual surge of hurrying feet. The silence of lessons which came after that had gone on for so long before Simon came out that there was not a soul in 6B who did not feel like an outcast. Simon came out at last. He was an odd color. He would not speak to any of the friends who were leaning out of the line wanting to know what had happened. He just walked to the wall like a sleepwalker and leaned against it, staring into space.

This did not make anyone feel better. Nan wondered what Chrestomanci was doing to people in there. By the time the three girls who came between her and Simon had all come out looking as bad as Heather Young, Nan was so scared that she could hardly make her legs work. But it was her turn. She had to go. She shuffled around the dark door somehow.

Inside, she stood and stared. Chrestomanci had indeed been very busy while 6B marched up and down outside. Mr. Wentworth's study was entirely lined with black curtains. A black carpet Nan had forgotten to invent covered the parquet floor. Hung on the walls and glimmering against the black background were manacles, a noose, festoons of chains, several kinds of scourge, and a cat-o'-nine-tails.

There was a large can in one corner labeled PETROL, DIV. INQ. OFFICE, FOR USE IN TORTURE ONLY.

Chrestomanci himself was only dimly visible behind a huge glittering lamp, which reminded Nan uncomfortably of the light over an operating table. The light from it beamed onto Mr. Wentworth's desk, draped in more black cloth, where there was a sort of jeweler's display of shiny thumbscrews and other displeasing objects. The wired-up helmet was there. So was a bouquet of bare wires, spitting blue sparks. Behind those was a pile of fat black books.

"Can you see anything Brian forgot?" asked the dim shape of Chrestomanci.

Nan began to laugh. "I didn't say the carpet or the petrol!"

"Brian suggested a carpet. And I thought that corner looked a little bare," Chrestomanci admitted.

Nan pointed to the pile of black books. "What are those?"

"Disguised schedules," said Chrestomanci. "Oh—I see what you mean. Obviously they are Acts of Parliament and Witchcraft Edicts, torture manuals, and *The Observer's Guide to Witch-Spotting*. No inquisitor would be without them."

Nan could tell from his voice that he was laughing. "I accuse you of enjoying yourself," she said, "while everyone outside gibbers."

"I confess to that." Chrestomanci came around the desk under the light. He pushed the spitting bunch of wires casually aside—it did not appear to give him any kind of shock—and sat on the black-draped desk so that his face was level with Nan's. She suddenly found it almost impossible to look away. "I accuse you of enjoying yourself too," he said.

"Yes, I have!" Nan said defiantly. "For about the first time since I came to this beastly school!"

Chrestomanci looked at her almost anxiously. "You enjoy being a witch?" Nan nodded vigorously. "And you've enjoyed making things up and describing them—thumbscrews and so on?" Nan nodded again. "Which did you enjoy most?" Chrestomanci asked.

"Oh, being a witch," Nan declared. "It's made me feel—well—just so confident, I suppose."

"Describe the things you've invented so far to do as a witch," said Chrestomanci.

"I—" Nan looked at Chrestomanci, lit from one side by the strong light of the lamp and, from the other, by the flickering wires, and was rather puzzled to find how little she had done as a witch. All she had done, when you came down to it, was to ride a broomstick and to give herself and Estelle the wrong kind of clothes and some decidedly odd collecting tins. "I haven't had much time to do things yet," she said.

"But Charles Morgan has had about the same amount of time, and according to the things people have been telling me, he has been very inventive indeed," Chrestomanci said. "Wouldn't you say that, now that you've been a witch, and got your confidence, you might really prefer describing things even to witchcraft?"

Nan thought about it. "I suppose I would," she said, rather surprised. "If only we didn't have to do it in our journals!"

"Good," said Chrestomanci. "I think I can promise you one really good opportunity to describe things, nothing to do with journals. I told you it would take strong magic to put this world back into the one where it belongs. When I find the way to do it, I shall need everyone's help, in order to harness all the magic there is in the world to make the change. When the time comes, can I rely on you to explain all this?"

Nan nodded. She felt hugely flattered and responsible.

While she was feeling this way, Chrestomanci added, "Just as well you prefer describing things. I'm afraid you won't be a witch when the change comes." Nan stared at him. He was not joking. "I know you are descended from the Archwitch," Chrestomanci said, "but talents don't always descend in the same shape. Yours seem to have come to you in the form of making-up and describing. My advice is to stick with that, if you can. Now name me one character out of history."

Nan blinked at the change of subject. "Er— Christopher Columbus," she said miserably.

Chrestomanci took out a little gold notebook and unclipped a gold pencil. "Would you mind explaining who he was?" he said, a little helplessly.

It was astonishing the way Chrestomanci seemed not to know the most obvious things, Nan thought. She told him all about Christopher Columbus, as kindly as she could, and Chrestomanci wrote it down in his gold notebook. "Admirable," he murmured as he wrote. "Clear and vivid." The result was that Nan went out of the study one half delighted that Chrestomanci thought she was so good at describing things, and the other half desperately sad at not being a witch before long. Dan Smith's friend Lance Osgood, who was next one in, looked hard at Nan's face as she came out and did not know what to make of it.

Lance was not in the study long. Nor was Theresa Mullett, who came next. By this time, Estelle had just gotten up to the top of the stairs, near the end of the line. Estelle craned around the corner as Theresa came out, searching for signs of love in Theresa, but Theresa looked peevish and puzzled. Everyone saw that the inquisitor had not treated Theresa with proper respect. Delia was whispering across to Heather about it when Charles went in.

Charles was not in the least frightened by this time. He was sure by now that Chrestomanci was treating everybody exactly as he or she deserved. He grinned when he saw the study all draped in black, and pushed his glasses up his nose to look at the things hung on the walls.

Chrestomanci was a dim shape behind the lamp and the spitting wires. "You approve?" he said.

"It's not bad," said Charles. "Where's Brian?"

"Over here," said Brian's voice. Two pairs of handcuffs on the black-draped wall lifted and jingled. "How long is this going on? I'm magicking bored already, and you've only gotten to M."

"Why have you got him in here?" Charles asked Chrestomanci. He kept his finger on his glasses in order to give Brian his best double-barreled glare.

"I have my reasons," Chrestomanci said quietly. Quiet though it was, it made Charles feel as if something very cold and rather deadly was crawling down his back. "I want to talk to you," Chrestomanci continued, in the same quiet way, "about your *Simon Says* spell."

The cold spread from Charles's spine right through the rest of him, and settled particularly in his stomach. He knew that this interview was not going to be anything like the joke he had thought it would be. "What about it?" he muttered.

"I can't understand," Chrestomanci said, mild and puzzled and more deadly quiet than ever, "how you forgot to mention that spell. How did it come to slip your mind?"

It was like being embedded in ice. Charles tried to break out of the ice by blustering. "There was no point in telling you. It was only a spell—it wasn't important and Simon deserved it! And Nirupam took it off him anyway!"

"I beg your pardon. I wasn't aware that you had a defense," Chrestomanci said.

Sarcasm like this is hard enough to bear, and even

worse if you know someone like Brian is listening in. Charles mustered another glare. But he found it hard to direct at Chrestomanci, hidden beyond the light, and swung it around at Brian again instead. Or rather, at the handcuffs where Brian might be. "It wasn't that important," he said.

Chrestomanci seemed more puzzled than ever. "Not important? My dear boy, what is so unimportant about a spell that could break the world up? You may know better, of course, but my impression is that Simon could easily have chanced to say something very silly, like—say—'Two and two are five.' If he had, everything to do with numbers would have fallen apart at once. And since everything can be counted, everything would have come apart— the earth, the sun in the sky, the cells in bodies, anything else you can think of. No doubt you have a mind above such things, but I can't help finding that quite important myself."

Charles glowered at the handcuffs to disguise how awful this made him feel. And Brian had heard every word! "I didn't realize—how could I? Simon had it coming to him, anyway. He deserved something." He was rather glad, as he said it, that no one knew he intended to do something to Dan Smith next.

"Simon deserved it?" wondered Chrestomanci. "Simon certainly has a large opinion of himself, but—Brian, you tell us. You have an ego at least as big as Simon's. Do you or Simon deserve to have such power put in your hands?"

"No," Brian's voice said sulkily. "Not to destroy the world."

Charles was cold all through with horror at what he had almost done. But he was not going to admit it. "Nirupam took it off him," he said, "before Simon did anything really."

"Brian seems to be learning," Chrestomanci remarked, "even if you are not, Charles. I grant you that, because magic is forbidden here, nobody has ever taught you what it can do or how to use it. But you could have worked it out. And you are still not thinking. Nirupam did *not* take that spell off Simon. He simply turned it back to front. *Nothing* the poor boy says comes true now. I have had to order him to keep his mouth shut."

"Poor boy!" Charles exclaimed. "You can't be sorry for him!"

"I am," said Brian's voice. "And if I hadn't been in the sick bay, I'd have tried to take it off him myself. I'd have managed better than Nirupam, too!"

"Now there, Charles," said Chrestomanci, "you have an excellent example quite apart from rights and wrongs, of why it is such a bad idea to do things to people. Everyone is now sorry for Simon. Which is not what you want at all, is it?"

"No." Charles looked down at the shadowy black carpet and decided regretfully to think again about Dan Smith. This time he would get it right.

"Make him take the spell off Simon," Brian suggested.

"I doubt if he could," said Chrestomanci. "It's a fearsomely strong thing. Charles must have powers way up in the enchanter class in order to have worked it at all." Charles kept his face turned to the carpet, hoping that would hide the huge smug grin he could feel spreading on his face. "It will take a number of special circumstances to get that spell off Simon," Chrestomanci continued. "For a start, Charles must want to take the spell off. And he doesn't. Do you, Charles?"

"No," said Charles. The idea of Simon having to hold his tongue for the rest of his life gave him such pleasure that he did not bother to listen to all the names Brian began calling him. He held his finger out, into the lamplight, and admired the way the strong light and the spitting wires made patterns in the yellow cushion of blister. Wickedness was branded into him, he thought.

Chrestomanci waited for Brian to run out of names to call Charles. Then he said, "I'm sorry you feel this way, Charles. We are all going to need your help when we try to put this world back where it belongs. Won't you reconsider?"

"Not after the way you went on at me in front of Brian," said Charles. And he went on admiring his blister.

Chrestomanci sighed. "You and Brian are both as bad as one another," he said. "People in Larwood House are always developing into witches, Mr. Wentworth tells me, but he tells me he has had no trouble in stopping any of them giving themselves away, until it came to you and Brian. Brian was so anxious to be noticed that he didn't care if he was burned—"

"Hey!" Brian said indignantly.

So Chrestomanci was trying to make it fair by getting at Brian now, Charles thought. It was a bit late for that. He was not going to help.

"So he is going to have to help, or stay invisible for the rest of his life," Chrestomanci went on. He ignored indignant, miserable noises from Brian and turned to Charles. "You, Charles, seem to have bottled yourself up, hating everything, until your witchcraft came along and blew the stopper off you. Now, either you are going to have to bottle yourself up again or be burned, *or* you are going to have to help us. Since your talent for witchcraft is so strong, it seems certain that in your right world, you will have an equally strong talent for something else, and you should find that easier. So which do you choose?"

Lose his witchcraft? Charles pressed one finger to his glasses and glared through the strong light at Chrestomanci. He did not think he even hated Simon or Dan as much as he hated Chrestomanci. "I'm going to go on being a witch! So there!"

The dim shape of Chrestomanci shrugged behind the light. "Warlock is the usual term for people who mess about the way you do. Very well. Now name me one historical personage, please."

"Jack the Ripper," snarled Charles.

The gold notebook flashed in the lamplight.

"Thank you," said Chrestomanci. "Send the next person in as you go out."

As Charles turned and trudged to the door, Brian began calling him names again.

"Brian," Chrestomanci said quietly, "I told you I would take your voice away, and I shall if you speak to anyone else."

Typical! Charles thought angrily. He tore open the door, wondering what he dared do to Nan and Estelle for calling Chrestomanci here, and found himself staring into Delia Martin's face. He must have looked quite frightening. Delia went white. She actually spoke to him. "What's he like?"

"Magicking horrible!" Charles said loudly. He hoped Chrestomanci heard him.

15

❖·❖

THE REST OF 6B shuffled slowly in and out of the study. Some came out white, some came out relieved. Estelle came out misty-eyed and beaming.

"Really!" said Theresa. "Some people!"

Estelle shot her a look of utter scorn and went up to Nan. She put both hands around one of Nan's ears and whispered wetly, "He says that where we're going, my mum won't be in prison!"

"Oh good!" said Nan, and she thought, in sudden excitement, *my* mum will still be alive, then!

Chrestomanci himself came out of the study with Geoffrey Barnes, who was last, and exchanged a deep look with Mr. Wentworth. Nan could tell that he had not found out how to change the world. She saw they were both worried.

"Right. In line and back to the classroom," shouted Mr. Wentworth. He was looking so harrowed, and hurried them down the stairs so fast, that Nan knew Chrestomanci's luck was running out. Perhaps the real inquisitor had arrived by now. The bell for the end of the first lesson rang as 6B marched through the corridors, which increased the urgent feeling. Other classes hurried past them, and gave them looks of pitying curiosity.

Simon's friends kept trying to talk to him as they went. Simon shook his head madly and pointed to his mouth. "He knows who the witch is, but his lips are sealed," Ronald West said wisely.

This caused Delia and Karen to skip out of line and walk beside Simon. "Tell us who the witch is, Simon," they whispered. "We won't say." The more Simon shook his head, the more they asked.

"Quiet!" barked Mr. Wentworth.

Everyone filed into the classroom. There stood Mr. Crossley, expecting to sit with 6B while they wrote their journals.

"You'd better treat this as a free period, Harold," Mr. Wentworth said to him. Mr. Crossley nodded, highly pleased, and went off to the staff room, hoping to catch Miss Hodge there.

"Poor Teddy," Estelle whispered to Nan. "He doesn't know she's in next Tuesday. Mind you, I don't think she'd ever have him anyway."

Chrestomanci came into the classroom, looking suave and vague. No one could have guessed from the look of him that time was running out and he was probably just as anxious as Mr. Wentworth. He coughed for attention. He got instant silence, complete and attentive. Mr. Wentworth looked a little envious.

"This is a miserable affair," Chrestomanci said. "We have a witch in our midst. And this witch has cast a spell on Simon Silverson—"

The room rustled with people turning to look at Simon. Charles glowered. Simon was looking almost happy again. He was in the limelight, where he belonged.

"Now, most unfortunately," Chrestomanci went on, "someone made a well-meant but misguided effort to break the spell and turned it back to front." Nirupam looked morbid. "You can't blame this person," said Chrestomanci, "but the result is most unhappy. It was a very strong spell. Everything Simon now says does not only *not* happen, but it never *has* happened. I have had to warn Simon not to open his mouth until we get to the bottom of the matter."

As he said this, Chrestomanci's eyes turned, vaguely and absently, towards Charles. Charles gave his blankest and nastiest look in reply. If Chrestomanci thought he could make him take the spell off this way, Chrestomanci could just think again. What Charles did not notice was that Chrestomanci's eyes moved towards Nan after that. Nobody else noticed at all, because three people had put their hands up: Delia, Karen, and Theresa. Delia spoke for all three.

"Mr. Inquisitor, sir, we told you who the witch is. It's Nan Pilgrim."

Estelle's desk went over with a crash. Books, journal, papers, and knitting skidded in all directions. Estelle stood in the middle of them, red with anger. "It is *not* Nan Pilgrim!" she shouted. "Nan never harmed anyone in her life! It's you lot that do the harm, spreading tales all the time, you and Theresa and Karen. And I'm ashamed I was ever friends with Karen!"

Nan put her hot face in her hands. Estelle was a bit too loyal for comfort.

"Pick that desk up, Estelle," said Mr. Wentworth.

Simon forgot himself and opened his mouth to make a jeering comment. Chrestomanci's eyes just happened to glance at him. Simon's mouth shut with a snap and his eyes popped.

And that was all the notice Chrestomanci took of the interruption. "If you will all attend," he said. Everyone did, immediately. "Thank you. Before we name the witch, I want you all to give the name of a second historical personage. You in the front, you begin—er—um—Theresa—er—Fish."

Everyone had already given one name. Everyone was convinced that the inquisitor would know the witch by the name they gave. It was obviously important not to name anybody wicked. So Theresa, although she was offended by the way the inquisitor got her name wrong, thought very carefully indeed. And, as usually happens, her mind was instantly filled with all the villains in history. She sat there dumbly, running through Burke and Hare, Crippen, Judas Iscariot, Nero, and Torquemada, and quite unable to think of anybody good.

"Come along—er—Tatiana," said Chrestomanci.

"Theresa," said Theresa. And then, with inspiration, "*Saint* Theresa, I mean."

Chrestomanci wrote that down in his gold notebook and pointed to Delia. "Saint George," said Delia.

"Didn't exist in any world," said Chrestomanci. "Try again."

Delia racked her brains and eventually came up with Lady Godiva. Chrestomanci's pointing finger moved on around the class, causing everyone the same trouble. Villains poured through their minds—Attila the Hun, Richard III, Lucrezia Borgia, Joseph Stalin—and when they did manage to think of anyone less villainous, it always seemed to be people like Anne Boleyn or Galileo, who had been put to death. Most people did not like to mention those either, though Nirupam, because he knew Chrestomanci was not really an inquisitor, took a risk and said Charles I. Chrestomanci turned to Mr. Wentworth after most names were mentioned, and Mr. Wentworth told him who they were. Most of 6B could not think why the inquisitor needed to do that, unless it was to prove that Mr. Wentworth was a mastermind, but Nan thought, He's collecting symptoms again. Why? Somebody in history must be very important, I think.

Charles watched Chrestomanci's finger point toward him. He thought, You don't get me like that! "Saint Francis," he said. Chrestomanci's finger simply moved on to Dan Smith.

Dan was stumped. "Please, sir, I've got a stomachache. I can't think.".

The finger went on pointing.

"Oh," said Dan. "Er—Dick Turpin."

This evoked a gasp from 6B, and a near-groan of disappointment when Chrestomanci's finger moved on, across the gangway, and pointed to Estelle.

Estelle had picked up her desk and most of her books by now, but her knitting wool had rolled under several desks and come unwound as it went. Estelle was on her knees reeling it in, grayer than ever, and did not notice. Nan leaned down and poked her. Estelle jumped. "Is it me now? Sorry. Guy Fawkes—has anyone had Guy Fawkes yet?" She went back to her wool.

"One moment," said Chrestomanci. A curious hush seemed to grow in the room. "Can you tell me about Guy Fawkes?"

Estelle looked up again. Everyone was looking at her, wondering if she was the witch, but Estelle was only thinking about her wool. "Guy Fawkes?" she said. "They put him on a bonfire for blowing up the Houses of Parliament."

"Blowing them *up*?" said Chrestomanci. "But Guy Fawkes never managed to blow up Parliament in any world I ever heard of!"

Simon opened his mouth to say Estelle was quite right, and shut it again hastily. Estelle nodded. A number of people called out, "Yes, sir. He did, sir!"

Chrestomanci looked at Mr. Wentworth. Mr. Wentworth said, "In 1605, Guy Fawkes was smuggled into the Parliament cellars with some kegs of gunpowder, in order to blow up the government and the king. But he seems to have made a mistake. The gunpowder blew up in the night and destroyed both Houses, without killing anyone. Guy Fawkes got out unhurt, but they caught him almost at once."

It sounded like all the other times Mr. Wentworth had told Chrestomanci a piece of history, but somehow it was not. Chrestomanci's eyes had a special gleam, very bright and black, and he looked straight at Nan as he remarked, "A mistake, eh? That doesn't surprise me. That fellow Fawkes never could get anything right. So this is the world where he got things wronger even than usual." He pointed at Nan.

"Richard the Lionheart," said Nan. And she thought, He's got it! Guy Fawkes is the reason our world went different. But why? He'll want me to describe it and I don't know why. She thought and thought, while Chrestomanci was collecting names no one needed now from the rest of 6B. November 5, 1605. All Nan could remember was something her mother had once said, long ago, before the inquisitor took her away. Mum had said November 5 was the last day of Witch Week. Witch Week began on Halloween, and today was Halloween. Did that help? It must do, though Nan could not see how. But she knew she was right, and that

Chrestomanci *had* found the answer, because he had such a smooth, pleased look as he stood beside Mr. Wentworth.

"Now," he said. "We shall reveal the witch."

He had gone vague again. He was slowly fetching a slim golden case from a dove-gray pocket and, if he was looking at anyone, it was at Charles now. Good, thought Nan. He's giving me time to think. And Charles thought, All right. Reveal me then. But I'm still not going to help.

Chrestomanci held the flat gold box out so that everyone could see it. "This," he said, "is the very latest modern witch-finder. Look at it carefully." Charles did. He was almost certain that the witch-finder was a gold cigarette case. "When I let go of this machine," Chrestomanci said, "it will travel by itself through the air, and it will point to everyone in turn, except Simon. When it points to a witch, it is programmed to make a noise. I want the witch it points to to come and stand beside me."

6B stared at the gold oblong, tense and excited. There were gasps. It had bobbled in Chrestomanci's hand. Chrestomanci let go of it and it stayed in the air, bobbing about by itself. Charles glowered. He understood. Brian. Brian was going to carry it invisibly around. That did it! If Chrestomanci thought he could get around Charles by giving Brian all the fun, he was going to be really disappointed.

The bobbing case upended itself. Charles saw it split open a fraction along the top edge, as Brian took a quick peep to see if it was indeed a cigarette case. It was. Charles glimpsed white cigarettes in it.

"Off you go," Chrestomanci said to it.

The gold box shut with a loud snap, making everybody jump, and then traveled swiftly to the first desk. It stopped level with Ronald West's head. It gave out a shrill beeping sound. Everybody jumped again, including Ronald and the gold box.

"Come out here," Chrestomanci said.

Ronald, looking quite dumbfounded, got out of his desk and stumbled towards Chrestomanci. "I never—!" he protested.

"Yes, you are, you know," Chrestomanci said. And he said to the gold box, "Carry on."

A little uncertainly, the box traveled to Geoffrey Barnes. It beeped again. Chrestomanci beckoned. Out came Geoffrey, white-faced but not protesting.

"How did it know?" he said drearily.

"Modern technology," said Chrestomanci.

This time the gold box went on without being told. It beeped, moved, and beeped again. Person after person got miserably up and trailed out to the front. Charles thought it was a dirty trick. Chrestomanci was just trying to break his nerve. The box was level with Lance Osgood now. Everyone waited for it to beep. And waited. The box stayed beside Lance, pointing until Lance's eyes were crossed with looking at it. But nothing happened.

"Go on," said Chrestomanci. "He's not a witch."

The box moved to Dan Smith. Here, it made

the longest, loudest noise yet. Dan blenched. "I covered up my tracks!" he said.

"Out here," said Chrestomanci.

Dan got up slowly. "It's not fair! My stomach aches."

"No doubt you deserve it," said Chrestomanci. "By the noise, you've used witchcraft quite recently. What did you do?"

"Only hid a pair of running shoes," Dan mumbled. He did not look at Charles as he slouched up the gangway. Charles did not look at Dan either. He was beginning to see that Chrestomanci was not pretending that people were witches.

By now, the front of the class was quite crowded. The box went to Nirupam next. Nirupam was waiting for it. It beeped even louder for him than it had for Dan. The moment it did, Nirupam got up and fled with long strides to the front of the room, in order not to be asked what witchcraft he had done. Then the box came to Charles. The noise was deafening.

"All right, all right!" Charles muttered. He too trudged to the front of the class. So Chrestomanci was playing fair, but he was still obviously trying to teach Charles a lesson by devaluing witchcraft. Charles looked around at the other people standing out in front. He knew his was the strongest magic of the lot. And he wanted to keep it. There were still a thousand things he could do with it. He did not want to blend with another world, even if they did not burn witches there. As to being burned— Charles looked down at his blister—he found he rather enjoyed being frightened, once he got used to it. It made life interesting.

Meanwhile, the gold box followed Charles down the gangway and pointed to Delia. There was silence. Delia did not try to hide her smirk. But the smirk came off her face when the box moved to Theresa. It gave one small clear beep.

Theresa stood up, scandalized. "Who? *Me*!"

"Only a very small, third-grade sort of witch," Chrestomanci told her comfortingly.

It did not comfort Theresa in the least. If she was to be a witch, she felt she should at least be a first-class one. It was a disgrace either way. She was really angry when the box moved to Karen and did not beep for Karen either. But she was equally annoyed when the box went on and beeped for Heather, Deborah, and all her other friends. She stood there with the most dreadful mixed feelings.

Then the box beeped for Estelle too. Theresa tossed her head angrily. But Estelle sprang up beaming. "Oh good! I'm a witch! I'm a witch!" She skipped out to the front, grinning all over her face.

"Some people!" Theresa said unconvincingly.

Estelle did not care. She laughed when the box beeped loudly for Nan and Nan came thoughtfully to join her. "I think most people in the world must be witches," Estelle whispered to her. Nan nodded. She was sure it was true. She was sure this fitted in with all the other things Chrestomanci had discovered, but she still could not think how to explain it.

This left four people scattered about the room.

They were all, even Simon, looking peevish and left out.

"It's not fair!" said Karen.

"At least *we* won't be burned," said Delia.

Chrestomanci beckoned to the box. It wandered up the gangway and put itself in his hand. Chrestomanci put it back in his pocket while he looked around the crowd of witches. He ignored Charles. He had given him up. He looked at Nan and then across at Mr. Wentworth, who had been crowded against the door in the crush. "Well, Wentworth," he said. "This looks quite promising, doesn't it? We've got a fair amount of witchcraft to draw on here. I suggest we make our push now. If Nan is ready to explain to everyone—"

Nan was nothing like ready. She was about to say so, when the classroom door flew open. Mr. Wentworth was barged aside. And Miss Cadwallader stood in his place, stiff and upright and stringy with anger.

"What are you all doing, 6B?" she said. "Back to your seats with the utmost rapidity."

Mr. Wentworth was behind the door, white and shaking. Everyone looked doubtfully at Chrestomanci. He had gone very vague. So everybody did the prudent thing and scuttled back to their desks. As they went, three more people came into the room behind Miss Cadwallader.

Miss Cadwallader faced Chrestomanci in angry triumph. "Mr. Chant," she said, "you are an imposter. Here is the real inquisitor. Inquisitor Littleton." She stood aside and shut the door, so that everyone could see the inquisitor.

Inquisitor Littleton was a small man in a blue pin-striped suit. He had a huge man on either side of him in the black uniform of the Inquisition. Each of these huge men had a gun holster, a truncheon, and a folded whip in his belt. At the sight of them, Charles's burned finger doubled itself up and hid inside his fist like a guilty secret.

"You move, and I'll order you shot!" Inquisitor Littleton snapped at Chrestomanci. His voice was harsh. His little watery eyes glared at Chrestomanci from a little blunt face covered with bright red veins. His blue suit did not fit him very well, as if Inquisitor Littleton had shrunk and hardened some time after the suit was bought, into a new shape, dense with power.

"Good afternoon, inquisitor," Chrestomanci said politely. "I'd been half expecting you." He looked across his shoulder, to Simon. "Nod, if I'm right," he said. "Did you say an inquisitor would be here before lunch?"

Simon nodded, looking shattered.

Inquisitor Littleton narrowed his watery eyes. "So it was witchcraft that made my car break down?" he said. "I knew it!" He unslung a black box he was carrying on a strap over his shoulder. He pointed it at Chrestomanci and turned a knob. Everyone saw the violent twitching of the dials on top. "Thought so," grated Inquisitor Littleton. "It's a witch." He jerked his blunt chin at Mr.

Wentworth. "Now get me that one."

One of the huge men reached out a huge hand and dragged Mr. Wentworth over from beside the door as easily as if Mr. Wentworth had been a guy stuffed with straw. Miss Cadwallader looked as if she would like to protest about this, but she gave it up as useless. Inquisitor Littleton trained his black box on Mr. Wentworth.

Before he could turn the knob, the black box was torn out of his hands. With its broken strap trailing, it hurried from the inquisitor to Chrestomanci.

"I think that was a mistake, Brian," said Chrestomanci.

Both huge men drew their guns. Inquisitor Littleton backed away and pointed at Chrestomanci. His face was purple, and full of a queer mixture of hate and horror and pleasure. "Look at that!" he shouted out. "It has a demon to wait on it! Oh, I've got you now!"

Chrestomanci looked almost irritated. "My good man," he said, "that really is a most ignorant assumption. Only a hedge wizard would stoop to using a demon."

"I'm not a demon!" shouted Brian's shrill voice. "I'm Brian Wentworth!"

Delia screamed. The huge man who was not holding Mr. Wentworth seemed to lose his nerve. Glaring with fear, he held his gun out in both hands, and aimed it at the black box.

"Throw it!" said Chrestomanci.

Brian obeyed. The black box sailed towards the

window. The huge man was muddled into follow-ing it around with his gun. He fired. There was a tremendous crash. Quite a few people screamed this time. The black box exploded into a muddle of wire and metal plates and half of the window blew out. A gust of rain blew in.

"You fool!" said Inquisitor Littleton. "That was my very latest model witch-finder!" He glared at Chrestomanci. "Right. I've had enough of this foul thing. Get it for me."

The huge man put his gun back in its holster and marched towards Chrestomanci. Nirupam quickly stuck up a long arm. "Please. Just a moment. I think Miss Cadwallader may be a witch too."

Everyone at once looked at Miss Cadwallader. She said, "How dare you, child!" but she was as white as Mr. Wentworth.

And this, Nan realized, was where she came in. She was not sure how, but she surged to her feet all the same, in such haste that she nearly knocked her desk over like Estelle. Everyone stared at her. Nan felt terrible. For a long, long instant, she went on standing there without a thought in her head and without one scrap of confidence to help her. But she knew she could not just sit down again. She began to talk.

"Just a moment," she said. "Before you do another thing, I've got to tell you about Guy Fawkes. He's the reason almost everybody in the world is a witch, you know. The main thing about Guy Fawkes is that he was the kind of man who can never do anything right. He meant well, but he was a failure—"

"Make that girl shut up!" Inquisitor Littleton said, in his harsh, bossy voice. Nan looked at him nervously, and then at the two huge men. None of them moved. In fact, now that she looked, everyone seemed to be stuck and frozen exactly where they were when she first stood up. She looked at Chrestomanci. He was staring vaguely into the distance and did not seem to be doing anything either, but Nan was suddenly sure that Chrestomanci was somehow holding everything in one place to give her a chance to explain. That made her feel much better.

She had gone on talking all the time she was looking around, explaining about the Gunpowder Plot, and what a mistake the conspirators made choosing Guy Fawkes to do the blowing up. Now she seemed to be going on to explain about other worlds.

"There were an awful lot of Guy Fawkeses in an awful lot of worlds," she heard herself saying. "And he was a failure in every one. Some people are like that. There are millions of other worlds, you know. The big differences get made at the big events in history, where a battle gets either won or lost. Both things can't happen in one world, so a new one splits off and goes different after that. But there are all sorts of smaller things that can go two ways as well, which *don't* make a world split off. You've probably all had those kinds of dreams that are like your usual life, except that a lot of things are not the same, and you seem to know the future in them. Well, this is because these other worlds where two things can happen spread out from our own world like rainbows, and sort of flow into one another—"

Nan found herself rather admiring this description. She was inspired now. She could have talked for hours. But there was not much point unless she could persuade the rest of 6B to *do* something. Everyone was just staring at her.

"Now our world should really just be a rainbow-stripe in another proper world," she said. "But it isn't. And I'm going to tell you why, so that we can all do something about it. I told you Guy Fawkes was a failure. Well, the trouble was, he knew he was. And that made him very nervous, because he wanted to do at least this one thing right and blow up Parliament properly. He kept going over in his mind all the things that could go wrong: He could be betrayed, or the gunpowder could be damp, or his candle could go out, or his fuse might not light— he thought of all the possibilities, all the things that make the rainbow-stripes of not-quite-different worlds. And in the middle of the night, he got so nervous that he went and lit the fuse, just to make sure it would light. He wasn't thinking that November 5, the day he was doing it, was the last day of Witch Week, when there is so much magic around in the world that all sorts of peculiar things happen—"

"Will somebody silence that girl!" said Inquisitor Littleton.

He made Charles jump. Charles had been sitting all this time trying to understand the way he was feeling. He seemed to have divided into two again, but inside himself, where it did not show. Half of him was plain terrified. It felt as if it had been buried alive, in screaming, shut-in despair. The other half was angry, angry with Chrestomanci, Miss Cadwallader, 6B, Inquisitor Littleton—everything. Now, when Inquisitor Littleton suddenly spoke in his loud grating voice, Charles looked at the inquisitor. He was a small man with a stupid face, in a blue suit which did not fit, who enjoyed arresting witches.

Charles found himself remembering his first witch again. The fat man who had been so astonished at being burned. And he suddenly understood the witch's amazement. It was because someone so ordinary, so plain stupid, as Inquisitor Littleton had the power to burn him. And that was all wrong.

"Oh come on, all of you!" said Nan. "Don't you see? When Guy Fawkes lit that fuse, that made a new spread of rainbow possibilities. In our proper world, the world we ought to belong to, the fuse should have gone straight out again, and the Houses of Parliament would have been perfectly safe. But once the fuse was alight, the night watchman could have smelled it, or Guy Fawkes could have put it out with water, or the thing could have happened which made us the way we are: Guy Fawkes could have stamped the fuse out, but left just one tiny spark alight, which went on burning and creeping towards the kegs of gunpowder—"

"I told you to shut that girl up!" said Inquisitor Littleton.

Charles was in one piece again now. He looked from the inquisitor to Chrestomanci. Chrestomanci did not look so elegant just then. His suit was crumpled as if he had fallen away inside it, and his face was pale and hollow. Charles could see sweat on his forehead. And he understood that Chrestomanci was putting out a huge effort and somehow holding the whole world still, to give Nan time to persuade 6B to use their combined witchcraft to change it. But 6B were still sitting there like dumb things. That was why Inquisitor Littleton had started talking again. He was obviously one of those people who were very hard to keep quiet, and Chrestomanci had had to let go of him in order to have strength to hold everything else.

"Will you be quiet, girl!" said Inquisitor Littleton.

"BOOM!" said Nan. "And up went Parliament, but with no people in it. It wasn't very important, because even Guy Fawkes wasn't killed. But remember it was Witch Week. That made it a much worse explosion than it should have been. In it, this whole stripe of the rainbow, where we are now, and all the magic anywhere near, got blown out of the rest of the world, like a sort of long colored splinter. But it wasn't blown quite free. It was still joined to the rest of the rainbow at both ends. And that's the way it still is. And we could put it back if only we could make it so that the explosion never happened. And because it's Halloween today, and there's even more magic about than usual—"

Charles saw that Chrestomanci was beginning to shake. He looked tired out. At this rate, Chrestomanci was not going to have any strength left to put their splinter of world back where it belonged. Charles jumped up. He wanted to apologize. It was obvious that someone with power like Chrestomanci's could easily have just gone away the moment Inquisitor Littleton arrived. Instead, he had chosen to stay and help them. But saying he was sorry would have to wait. Charles knew he had to do something. And thanks to Nan, he knew just what to do.

"Sit down, boy!" rasped Inquisitor Littleton.

Charles took no notice. He dived across the gangway and took hold of Simon Silverson by the front of his blazer. "Simon. Say what Guy Fawkes did. Quick!"

Simon gazed at Charles. He shook his head and pointed to his mouth.

"Go on! Say it, you fool!" said Charles, and he shook Simon.

Simon kept his mouth shut. He was afraid to say anything. It was like a bad dream. "Say what Guy Fawkes did!" Charles yelled at him. He gave up shaking Simon and poured witchcraft at him to make him say it. And Simon just shook his head.

Nirupam saw the point. "Say it, Simon!" he said. And that made all the rest of 6B understand what Charles was trying to do. Everyone stood up in their seats and shouted at Simon. "SAY IT, SIMON!" Mr. Wentworth shouted. Brian's voice joined in. Witchcraft was blasting at Simon from all sides, and even Karen and Delia were shouting at him. Nan joined in the shouting. She was bubbling with pride and delight. She had done this, just by describing what happened. It was as good as witchcraft any day. Everyone had understood that they could make this world part of the other one again— part of the world to which the witches' rescue service sent witches—by making Simon say what had *not* happened in that other world. "SAY IT, SIMON!" everyone screamed.

Simon opened his mouth. "I—oh, leave *off*!" He was terrified of what might happen, but once he had started to speak, all the witchcraft beating at him was too much for him. "He—he—Guy Fawkes blew up the Houses of Parliament."

Everything at once began to ripple.

It was as if the world had turned into a vast curtain, hanging in folds, with every fold in it rippling in and out. The ripples ran through desks, windows, walls, and people alike. Each person was rippled through. They were tugged, and rippled again, until everyone felt they were coming to pieces. By then, the ripples were so strong and steep that everyone could see right down into the folds. For just a moment, on the outside of each fold, was the classroom everyone knew, with the inquisitor and his huge men on the same fold as Miss Cadwallader, and Chrestomanci on another fold beside them. The inner parts of the folds were all different places.

Charles realized that if he were going to apologize to Chrestomanci, he had better do it at once. He turned around to say it. But the folds had already rippled flat and nothing was the same anymore.

16

❧·❦

"I'M VERY SORRY, SIR," said one of the boys. He sounded as if he meant it, for a wonder.

Mr. Crossley jumped, and wondered if he had been asleep. He seemed to have had that kind of shiver that makes you say, "Someone walked over my grave." He looked up from the books he was marking.

The janitor was in the classroom. What was his name? He had a raucous voice and a lot of stupid opinions. Littleton, that was it. Littleton seemed to be clearing up broken glass. Mr. Crossley was puzzled, because he did not remember a window being broken. But when he looked over at the windows, he saw one of them was newly mended, with a lot of putty and many thumbprints.

"There you are, Mr. Crossley. All tidy now," Mr. Littleton rasped.

"Thank you, Littleton," Mr. Crossley said coldly. If you let Littleton get talking, he stayed and tried to teach the class. He watched the janitor collect his things and back himself through the door. Thank goodness!

"Thank you, Charles," said someone.

Mr. Crossley jerked around and discovered a total stranger in the room. This man was tall and tired-looking and seemed, from his clothes, to be on his way to a wedding. Mr. Crossley thought he must be a school governor and started to stand up politely.

"Oh, please don't get up," Chrestomanci said. "I'm just on my way out." He walked to the door. Before he went out of it, he looked around 6B and said, "If any of you want me again, a message to the Old Gate House should find me."

The door closed behind him. Mr. Crossley sat down to his marking again. He stared. There was a note on top of the topmost exercise book. He knew it had not been there before. It was written in ordinary blue ballpoint, in capital letters, and it gave Mr. Crossley the oddest feeling of having been in the same situation before. Why was that? He must have dozed off and had a dream. Yes. Now Mr. Crossley thought about it, he *had* had the strangest dream. He had dreamed he taught in a dreadful boarding school called Larwood House. He looked thankfully up at the bent, busy heads of 6B. This was, as he well knew, Portway Oaks Comprehensive, and everyone went home every evening. Thank goodness! Mr. Crossley hated the idea of teaching in a boarding school. You were always on the job.

He wondered who had written the note. And here, as his eyes went over the class, he had a momentary feeling of shock. A lot of faces were missing from his dream. He remembered a batch of tiresome girls: Theresa Mullett, Delia Martin, Heather Something, Karen Something Else. None of them was there. Nor was Daniel Smith.

Ah but—Mr. Crossley remembered now. Dan Smith should have been there. He was in the hospital. Two days ago, the stupid boy had eaten a handful of tintacks for a bet. No one had believed he had, at first. But when Mr. Wentworth, the headmaster, had put Dan in his car and driven him to be X-rayed, there he was, full of tintacks. Idiots some boys were!

And here was another mad thing about Mr. Crossley's dream: He had dreamed that Miss Cadwallader was head in place of Mr. Wentworth! Quite mad. Mr. Crossley knew perfectly well that Miss Cadwallader was the lady who ran The Gate House School for Girls, where Eileen Hodge was a teacher. Come to think of it, that must have been why he dreamed of Theresa Mullett and her friends. He had seen their faces staring out at him from the prim line of girls walking behind Eileen Hodge.

And now Mr. Crossley remembered something else that almost made him forget his dream and the mysterious note. Eileen Hodge had at last agreed to go out with him. He was to call for her on Tuesday, because she was going away for half-term. He was getting somewhere there at last!

But even through his pleasure about Eileen, the dream and the note kept nagging at Mr. Crossley. Why should it bother him who had written the note? He looked at Brian Wentworth, sitting next to his great friend Simon Silverson. The two of them were giggling about something. The note was quite probably one of Brian's jokes. But it could equally well be some deep scheme masterminded by Charles Morgan and Nirupam Singh. Mr. Crossley looked at those two.

Charles looked back at Mr. Crossley over his glasses and across the piece of paper he was supposed to be writing on. How much did Mr. Crossley know? Charles's writing had gotten no further than the title: *Halloween Poem*. Neither had Nirupam's. On the floor between them was a pair of spiked running shoes and, filling them with wonder, was the name marked on the shoes: *Daniel Smith*. Both of them knew that Dan did not own any running shoes. Of course, Smith was not exactly an uncommon name, but—both of them were struggling with strange double memories.

Charles wondered particularly at the sense of relief and peace he had. He felt at ease inside. He also felt rather hungry. One part of his memory told him that this was because Brian Wentworth had invisibly eaten half his lunch. The other half suggested that it was because chess club had taken up most of the dinner hour. And here was an odd thing. Up till that moment, Charles had intended to be a chess grand master. Now those double memories caused him to change his mind. Someone—whose name he could not quite remember now—had suggested to him that he was going to have a very strong talent indeed for something, and it was not for chess, Charles was sure now. Perhaps he would be an inventor instead. Anyway, the chess club half of his memory, which seemed to be the important half, suggested that he hurry home early so he could eat the last of the cornflakes before his sister Bernadine hogged them.

"Guy Fawkes," Nirupam murmured.

Charles did not know if Nirupam was referring to witchcraft, or to Dan Smith's idea of half-term. They had been going to collect money for the guy, using Nirupam for a guy. Nirupam, in the Morgans' old stroller, made a beautiful long, thin, floppy guy. Now they were both wondering if they would have the nerve to do it on their own, without Dan to keep them up to it.

"Why did you have to bet Dan he couldn't eat tintacks?" Charles whispered to Nirupam.

"Because I didn't think he would!" Nirupam answered grumpily. He had been in a lot of trouble with Mr. Wentworth about that bet. "Could we get Estelle and Nan to help push me?"

"They're girls," Charles objected. But he considered the idea while he underlined *Halloween Poem* in red ink, with blood drops. Those two girls might just do it, at that. As he inked the last drop of blood, he noticed a blister on his finger. It had reached the flat, white, empty stage by now. Carefully, Charles inked it bright red. He was not sure he wanted to forget about things that soon.

Mr. Crossley was still considering the note. It could be another flight of fancy from Nan Pilgrim. Nan, as usual, since she had arrived at the school from Essex at the beginning of term, was sitting next to Estelle Green. They were thick as thieves, those two. A good thing, because Estelle had been rather lonely before Nan arrived.

Nan glanced up at Mr. Crossley, and down again at her pen rushing across her paper. Fascinated, she read: *And in this part of the rainbow, Guy Fawkes stamped the fuse out, but a little, tiny smoldering spark remained. The spark crept and ate its way to the kegs of gunpowder. BOOM!!!*

"Estelle! Look at this!"

Estelle leaned over, looked, and goggled. "Do you know what I think?" she whispered. "When you grow up to be an author and write books, you'll think you're making the books up, but they'll all really be true, somewhere." She sighed. "My poem's going to be about a great enchanter."

Mr. Crossley suddenly wondered why he was worrying about the note. It was only a joke, after all. He cleared his throat. Everyone looked up hopefully. "Somebody," said Mr. Crossley, "seems to have sent me a Halloween message." And he read out the note. *"SOMEONE IN THIS CLASS IS A WITCH."*

6B thought this was splendid news. Hands shot up all over the room like a bed of beansprouts.

"It's me, Mr. Crossley!"
"Mr. Crossley, I'm the witch!"
"Can I be the witch, Mr. Crossley?"
"Me, Mr. Crossley, me, me, me!"

DIANA WYNNE JONES has been writing outstanding fantasy novels for more than twenty-five years and is one of the most distinguished writers in this field. With unlimited imagination, she combines dazzling plots, an effervescent sense of humor, and emotional truths in stories that delight readers of all ages. Her books, published to international acclaim, have earned a wide array of honors, including two *Boston Globe-Horn Book* Award Honors and the British Fantasy Society's Karl Edward Wagner Award for having made a significant impact on fantasy. She lives in Bristol, England, with her husband, a professor emeritus of English literature at Bristol University. They have three sons.

Visit her online at www.dianawynnejones.com.

For exclusive information on your favorite authors and artists, visit www.authortracker.com.